GRACE

Susan Sherrell

Workwomans Press

Seattle

Harvest For The World
Words and Music by O'Kelly Isley, Ronald Isley, Rudolph Isley, Ernest Isley, Marvin Isley and Chris Jasper
© 1976 (Renewed 2004) EMI APRIL MUSIC INC. and BOVINA MUSIC INC.
All Rights Controlled and Administered by EMI APRIL MUSIC INC.
All Rights Reserved   International Copyright Secured   Used by Permission

ISBN 978-0-9820073-1-0

First Printing September 2009

Workwomans Press
Seattle
www.workwomanspress.com

Table of Contents

GRACE

Dress me up for battle
When all I want is peace
Those of us who pay the price,
come home with the least.

—The Isley Brothers
"Harvest for the World"

PROLOGUE

Two Asian teenagers found Grace's body around five am Monday morning. They had been fishing with their father near the makeshift pier down the hill from Golden Gate race track when they noticed something tangled among the wooden posts that support the pier. One boy lowered himself into the water. He saw a body, submerged, unearthly white from the cold waters of the bay, blonde hair tendrilled with seaweed. They ran to tell their father. A white woman, they kept repeating.

That's how Joey told me the story, later, when I found the courage to ask. A confused babble of voices, excitement and horror intermixed. Hands gesticulating. They had reminded him of kids he had seen in Vietnam.

Time has altered the details. She would appear to me that way in dreams through the years that followed. Sometimes I would awake in terror, seeing her body floating among the pilings. Later memory softened the image. She would have been rocked to the shore by the waves, passed beyond the violence of her murder. I was trying so hard in those years to take something from her death, something I could live by.

That day, August 7, 1972, cast its shadow over the rest of my life. I was twenty-three and had begun working at the race track that summer. I met Grace working there. Life at the track was exciting to me then, with an edge of seediness which I mistook for glamour. Grace too, despite her beauty, had a raw edge about her. I was intrigued by her combination of toughness and vulnerability.

That particular Monday comes back to me as I write: the cordon of police cars at the bottom of the hill, the cops and plainclothes detectives running back and forth, shouting instructions to each other and herding away the groups of onlookers that formed and reformed in clusters at the edge of their yellow marking tape. I felt an electrical tension in the air, a sense of fear masked by nervous chatter. I remember flashes of my emotions: a touch of nausea, a distracted sense that something awful was taking place, a grinding progression which I could not stop.

11

Police were everywhere: shouting out orders, talking on walkie talkies, pushing onlookers aside. They paid attention only to those of us who wore Golden Gate Fields uniforms, asking questions about what we might have seen or heard. A black security guard moved too close to the yellow tape and was shoved aside by a large white cop. The two began swearing at one another. Suddenly the black employee was handcuffed and pushed in the back of a police car. A light-skinned black cop ran over to the car. He was talking to the white cop through the window.

"Time to get outta here," a man next to me said. I realized it was Freddie Corster, a young, nervous guy who was a hot walker for the trainers. "Come on," he said, grabbing my arm. "The police are freaking out."

"Who was it?' I asked. I had gotten a glimpse of the body, a shape under a blanket closely guarded by the police. "Someone who works here?"

"They aren't saying," he answered. He kept hold of my forearm with his thin fingers and wrenched me away from the scene. "They keep asking about a tattoo on the left knee."

"Tattoo?" I repeated.

"Grace had a tattoo on her knee," Freddie muttered. "Let's get outta here." I let him pull me up the hill toward the low-slung buildings of the race track. He was sweating and his fingers dug into my arm.

"How do you know that, Freddie?" I asked.

"Oh boy. Shit's gonna hit the fan."

"Did Grace have a tattoo on her knee?" I asked. My voice sounded high-pitched, almost hysterical.

"Stop asking me!" he shouted. "Jesus Christ. Whoever thought it would go this far?"

We had reached the clubhouse and Freddie ran off toward the office where we signed in for work. I could still feel the imprint of his thin fingers, biting into my arm like steel wires. I rubbed my wrist.

I had known Grace little over a month. She was five years older than I was—a woman of experience in my eyes.

This story covers that period in my life. It began a month before the murder and wound to an inadequate resolution some months later.

Writing this story, so many years later, has forced me to relive a period I wanted to forget. Not all the discoveries I made that year were painful, although many were painful enough. But the memories of those blue-washed mornings, driving up a fog-strewn hill toward a view of a bay that stretched toward infinity, has stayed with me always.

I had known Grace Neville. She stood like a signpost in my life, a warning. She was the woman I wished to, then feared to become. Although this story tells more about me than I would like, the book is for her.

I

"Get up to the Turf Club and relieve Grace Neville," Beatrice Barlow, my supervisor, snapped. "She needs a break." Beatrice was a thin-lipped woman who seemed constantly on edge.

"I've never met Grace," I said. Beatrice looked at me like I was stupid.

George Mooney, her boss, interrupted from the back room, where he sat with a perpetual cigar. "Easy to spot Grace. Grace is a looker." George was a big, florid-faced Irishman. He rarely spoke except to mutter orders to Beatrice. None of us knew exactly what he did.

I took the elevator to the third floor of the clubhouse. The Turf Club occupied the whole top floor. As I stepped out of the elevator, a woman bounded up the staircase across from me. She reminded me of a lioness, full of energy and the joy of life, full-breasted, with the body of a dancer.

"I'm Grace," she said. Her voice was husky. Grace was a beauty. Her face was pale, with delicate, fine features, under a cap of blonde hair.

"Hi, I'm Leah. Beatrice sent me up to relieve you."

"Thank God," she said. "I could use some relief."

"She wants you to work Mainline." Mainline was the ground floor of the clubhouse.

"The bitch. She knows I hate Mainline. Come on with me to the little girls' room."

I followed her to the ladies' room. Grace had a strong back and a neat indentation to her waist. Her round butt filled out her slacks. "This woman loves to use her body," I thought. Behind us came sounds of laughter, glasses clinking. The loudspeaker announced four minutes left to post.

The women's bathroom was empty, smelling of disinfectant. Grace sank into a chair in front of the large mirror, examining her image. Certainly she liked what she saw—the delicate jaw line, long throat, the high cheekbones. Only her eyes conveyed a certain sadness, deep set, with slightly hooded lids. She pulled out a cigarette and lit it. Her hands shook slightly.

"I hate going to Mainline."

15

"Oh, I really like it," I said. Mainline was my favorite floor at the track, with its melting pot of African-Americans, Asians, Mexicans, and lower-class whites.

"I know some of the guys who hang around down there."

"Oh," I said.

"Know in the biblical way," she said. She laughed, a dry, barking sound. "You married?"

"No," I said.

"You've escaped then," she said. She took a long drag on her cigarette. "Although every now and then you do meet someone worth the trouble."

"Have you?"

"Not lately," she said. "Unlucky with men."

"That's hard to believe."

"My astrologer told me why. Too many planets in flux."

"You believe that stuff?" I asked.

"You gotta believe something," said Grace, thoughtfully. She inhaled. "Leo with my moon in Scorpio. But too many planets in flux. From the moment I was conceived," she said. "Which means forever, I guess."

She finished her cigarette, tossed it, and turned to the mirror as if to a lover. She pulled out a small cosmetic bag, full of brushes and vivid colors, and proceeded to outline her lips, filling them in a deep scarlet. She blotted her lips slowly. Grace Neville surveyed herself with obvious satisfaction.

"Think I can handle 'em now," she said. She lifted her head. "Come on. Let's get out of here and give 'em hell."

Grace Neville shone with a patina of glamour. She exuded a worldliness I knew I could never achieve. I could not imagine how a woman like Grace could have any trouble with men.

Grace and I were pari-mutuel clerks at the track. We stood behind the windows on Mainline and helped the patrons purchase their tickets, accepting their money and making change. After the race had started, we would total the number of tickets sold and cash received and forward this to our boss, Beatrice Barlow, for counting. When the race was declared official, those holding winning tickets could come see us and get cashed out.

My first two months at the track felt like a party held everyday. The clerks came onto the floor during their breaks, gossiping about each other's

16

marriages and affairs in places like Walnut Creek or Vallejo. People of different races and nationalities flowed around me, intent on wins and losses. I quickly learned the various forms of bets—the quiniela, the perfecta, the trifecta, the superfecta. Sometimes a security guard or another mutuel clerk would give me tips on the horses. Sometimes they hinted at the darker stuff—drug use, race-fixing. It was totally different from my life as a Cal student. My classmates at Berkeley could not understand my fascination with the race track. "Doesn't the noise drive you crazy?" "Don't you find it boring?"

I found it exciting. The track suited me. If I was a misfit, I was surrounded by other misfits. An obsession with gambling equalizes gamblers in the same way alcohol levels alcoholics. Surgeons, security guards, bankers, delivery truck drivers—all mingled in the rough camaraderie of the track. The tellers, the security guards, even the patrons reminded me of the people I had grown up with, working class people who had gone on to become TV repairmen or cops, like my cousin Joey.

My mother had died when I was ten. My father had remarried, started a new family. It had been a relief to leave upstate New York for the University of Michigan. After two years there, I took a Greyhound bus to Berkeley, California, drawn by all the myths and excitement coming out of the Bay Area. I found a room in a household of other students and worked the kinds of jobs available to young people with no specific skills, talents, or family connections—nurse's aide, waitress, and housecleaner. For a while I trained as an emergency medical technician, or EMT. I was pleased when I was accepted into UC Berkeley as a California resident after a year. Tuition was low enough that I could support myself in school by working part-time.

My closest friend was a Japanese student, Yoshi Ito. He was studying political science at Cal with an emphasis on international relations. I had been his English tutor when I first arrived in Berkeley. Yoshi and I shared a house on Russell Street with Paul Cohen and Carol Sweet. On June 13, 1971, my twenty-second birthday, the New York Times published the first installment of the Pentagon Papers. On June 17, 1972, a few days past my twenty-third birthday, five men were arrested for breaking into the Democratic National Committee headquarters in the Watergate Hotel.

Since arriving in Berkeley I felt more connected to national events. Carol bought a black-and-white television set at a garage sale, and the four of us followed national events on the evening news during our communal dinners. We sat up late talking about the Pentagon Papers and about the Watergate break -in. Paul said that Daniel Ellsberg's leak didn't tell us anything antiwar activists hadn't known for years, but he thought the Watergate break-in might have longer reaching implications. I was excited to be part of these political discussions, but I offered no opinions.

Besides these three roommates, I had few friends. I was ready for new, colorful people in my life, people who moved in the big universe outside the confines of my little world. That was how I saw Grace.

II

One Thursday after work I was waiting in line for my paycheck. I spotted Grace Neville ahead of me and called out to her. She turned around. "Leah!" She came back and joined me. "How's the Turf Club?"

"Everyone asks about you."

"I'll be back," she said, making a face, "just as soon as I can get away from Mainline."

"Is it rough down there?"

She hesitated. "My life feels kinda rough right now, in general. —But, hey, wanna go out for drinks after we get our paychecks?"

"Okay."

"I'll drive. I know a place." She did a dance step, wiggling her hips in a little shimmy. "Who knows who we might run into." I expected we would go to Charlie Brown's in Emeryville or Solomon Grundy's out on the Berkeley Marina. Instead Grace drove out the MacArthur Freeway in a beat-up little Renault, past Mills College, deep into East Oakland, an area as foreign to me then as East Berlin. She parked on a block with vacant lots and cyclone fencing, trash blown up against the metal grids; straw-like yellow grass. The July evening was grey and chilly.

Grace reached in the back seat for a leather jacket and wiggled into it. She pulled out a thick blue cashmere cardigan and offered it to me. As I slipped into it, Grace studied me with an appraising eye. "You're really pretty, Leah," she said. "That blue sweater suits you. Keep it."

"Oh no," I said instantly. The sweater was more expensive than anything I owned.

"Oh, go ahead," Grace said. "I can get more where that came from."

"I'll just borrow it for now," I said.

We hurried down the sidewalk to a brick building, its small windows made of glass cubes. A sign on the door stated that Vinnie's Inn offered live music four nights a week. Next door Akinyi's Boutique sold Fine Gents' and Ladies' fashions. This seemed to be a neighborhood of vacant lots, taverns and barbeque joints, but I could see a church on the corner.

19

We walked into the dimly lit bar. Vinnie's Inn. A center table was strung with electric blue lights illuminating a hand-painted sign, "Georgia." On the table were two large crock pots, one with red beans, one with rice. A man was pounding an old upright in one corner of the room, belting out blues in a powerful baritone. The place smelled of cigarette smoke. I felt uneasy. We were the only white people in the place. Grace however seemed at ease. She made her way to a small table.

"You nervous, Leah? Don't worry. I know the owners. Nobody's gonna bother us here—unless we want them to!' She laughed her knowing laugh and walked confidently over to the bar to give our order. Men stared at us. I had never been in an environment even remotely similar. The air had an electric feel to it. Grace ordered a shot of Jack Daniels with a beer chaser, and a draft beer for me. An enormous bartender with a bald skull brought the drinks to our table with elaborate courtesy.

"To two beautiful women," he beamed, setting the glasses on the bare wood. "This is on the house, ladies."

"Thanks, Vinnie," Grace said. Grace raised her glass theatrically. "To us, Leah—a new breed of woman!"

"To us!" I replied, enthusiastically. I was not sure what she meant.

I could feel Grace's eyes on me again, studying me. "Your hair, Leah— you ever think about letting your hair grow out?"

I pulled at my curly hair. "I don't like to mess with it."

"Got to mess with your hair, honey," she said. "That is, if you care about men at all." Grace's own short hair was expertly streaked; her makeup, impeccable. "Why don't you grow it out? I could help you with it. My mother says I have a knack."

"What is your mother like? Does she live around here?"

"Oh, Lord, no. She's up in Lake County. Close to Clear Lake. She shacks up with this guy in a trailer outside of Middletown. Yeah, got her a young one. She's fifty—he's at least ten years younger. He's not much, to tell the truth." I was impressed that a fifty-year-old woman could find a younger boyfriend and "shack up" with him. Grace and her mother both seemed to have mastered feminine powers.

"Well, good for her," I said.

"Yeah, good for her," Grace repeated. Her voice sounded bitter. "He's been saved—and Momma has converted."

"What religion did she convert to?"

"Beats me," Grace said. "All that born-again stuff sounds the same. Hard to believe she's a churchgoer now. Mom spent her life in bars up and down the coast. Called herself a singer. Opened those bars up and then closed them down again—with a few pints to spare." She added, in a shift of mood, "When I was little, I used to fall asleep summer nights, listening to her sing as she cleaned up after supper. I was three or four. It was before she gave me to aunt Millie. I used to feel so safe. She would sing, 'Summertime, and the livin' is easy.' I liked that because I knew my Momma was home. —There's no fool like an old fool," Grace said, in still another shift of mood. "Let's not talk about her. You go to Cal? I used to live in Berkeley."

"You don't live there any more?"

"No, I have a studio apartment near Lake Merritt now. So tell me what you're studying at school."

"I'm a journalism major. I like to write," I said.

"Oh, that's wonderful. I love poetry."

Journalism wasn't exactly poetry, but I didn't want to embarrass her.

"What're you going to do with your degree?"

"I don't know. I'd love to work for a newspaper. I worked on an ambulance last year but it was hard. I like the race track better."

"You like it now," she said. "It's a novelty for a person like you. Don't fool yourself that it's your future."

"Are you bored with it?" I asked.

"Not bored." She said. "Never bored. A place so full of men and money? Not good for a woman like me, though." She waved her hand with its pink-tipped nails in front of her. "Women like me," she repeated, "Women who like men too much. And money— I've never hated money, either."

It occurred to me money might be needed to achieve Grace's casual elegance. Yet her wages couldn't be much higher than my own. I lived in a shared house and paid $100 a month rent, shared the food bills, and still scraped by for books and tuition. Of course Grace wasn't paying tuition, but how did she manage her perfect makeup and beautifully cut hair?

"I don't know anyone who dislikes money," I answered. "You're not alone there."

"Yeah," she said. "But the dues come in."

"What do you mean?"

"You like to ask questions, Leah, and get people talking. Let's just say I got my own problems. Oh, look, there's some people here I know."

She pushed back her chair and walked to a group gathered at the back. There were four black people, two women with their backs to me, and two men. I caught glimpses of the women as they turned toward one another in animated conversation. One was slender and very young. The other was taller, with an Afro and dangling silver earrings. The men sat facing me. The smaller man wore a tight red shirt open to the breastbone, and a gold chain. His bloodshot eyes seemed fixed on Grace, as if he were sizing her up for predatory purposes. The second man was heavily built, powerful. He stood up as Grace approached. Grace said something to them, but I couldn't hear the conversation. I stared at the group. I hoped she would call me over.

Grace saw me watching. She hit the tall man on the arm. "Gotta go, Wilson," she said. "Catch you around."

"Let's get outta here, Leah," she said, as she returned to our table. Before this, she hadn't seemed to be in a hurry. "Our drinks are on the house, but I'll leave a little something."

She pulled a couple of dollars from a soft red leather wallet, with initials monogrammed in gold. Everything about Grace suggested expensive tastes. She pressed her fingers to her lips, extended her palm, and blew a kiss toward the back of the room. "Bye, Wilson!" she said, brightly.

He looked up. "See you around, Grace," he said. His voice was even.

"Are they friends of yours?" I had hoped she would introduce me.

"Not friends, " she said, "Comrades."

"Comrades?" Grace was walking out of the bar, and I followed close behind. I wondered why her mood had changed.

"Black Panthers," she answered. "Well, two of them, anyway. The other two are wannabes." Grace laughed, but it was not a good laugh.

In the spring of 1967 I had watched on television as two dozen young African-Americans, armed, wearing leather jackets and berets, marched into the

22

California General Assembly in Sacramento, and gave the black power salute with clenched fists. Tommie Smith and John Carlos, two black runners from San Jose, had raised their fists in the same salute at the 1968 Olympics awards ceremony, saying they believed the words of freedom in the US national anthem applied only to Americans with white skin. Only a year ago, I had read about George Jackson's death at Soledad prison, and the manhunt for Angela Davis. Yet this world had seemed light years away from my own. Now this world was sitting here in this bar in East Oakland.

"You have friends in the Black Panthers?" I was intrigued. We were getting into her car.

"Not friends. Comrades," she repeated. "Subject of another conversation."

"Aren't the Black Panthers dangerous?"

Grace shrugged. "They're hooking up with the Peace and Freedom Party. They're working with Berkeley leftists."

I was silent. I knew Berkeley leftists had formed something they called the Peace and Freedom Party, but I didn't know much about it.

We ran into each other a few times after that in the office where we signed in. Although one evening we drove up to Point Richmond for beers with Freddie Corster, we never were able to schedule a time to work on my hair.

Two weeks after this foray into East Oakland with Grace, a fellow worker from the track, Edna Banks, suggested that I join her to go "clubbing." It was the first Saturday night of August. I wasn't totally sure what "clubbing" meant, or where we might end up, but it sounded like a hip thing to do and I was eager to go. I put on a black sweater, jeans, and lipstick to mark my debut into a more sophisticated world.

Edna Banks was a lively black woman in her late thirties, with a cat face, and a full Afro. She cooked at The Hot Spoon, one of several small restaurants at Golden Gate Fields owned by the track management. She was a good cook, fast and efficient, and her little eatery was one of the most popular at Golden Gate Fields. Privately Edna disparaged white people, although she got along with them. But for some reason, she had taken a liking to me.

I had met Edna a year ago, when I waited tables in a Lebanese restaurant on Telegraph Avenue owned by Hassim Sayid. Edna was the cook. She had saved her money, lived frugally, bought a little house in El Cerrito and moved her mother out from Louisiana to live with her.

I was slow waiting table, and Hassim wanted to let me go. Edna, who had become good friends with him, insisted he keep me on until I could find something else. He tolerated me for a few more weeks thanks to her intervention. I found the job at the race track in June. The summer racing season was underway, but the cook at Hot Spoon had just quit. Beatrice and George were in a bind. I told Edna about the opening, and Edna applied for it.

Edna kept the job at Hassim's for the evenings and ran Hot Spoon at the track during the day. She had amazing energy. With her two jobs, Edna still found time to party, date, and outsmart her lovers. Edna viewed her lovers as adversaries. She would tell me stories about them when I came down to Mainline for a lunch break. In these stories she always emerged victorious in her struggles with them.

Given her animosity toward whites, I never completely understood her affection for me. I had helped her get a job, and Edna understood the value of money. I suspected there was more to it. Edna was a smart, independent woman, with a strong belief in herself. My lack of worldliness, or as she would term it, "street smarts," aroused her protectiveness. I reassured her that white superiority was truly a myth.

Edna had repeated the protocol to me several times. "We come together, we leave together," she had said. "No picking up some man and disappearing." She had stared at me with a fierce look. "Get this straight, Leah, or we ain't going nowhere together. It's you I'm worried about, girl, cause you don't know the streets. You have no idea how many women meet some loser and end up dead at the side of the highway."

Edna and her group picked me up. Hassim was driving. Freddie Corster from the track was in the back seat, chain-smoking Kools menthol cigarettes. Hassim drove us to a couple of places in Oakland that Edna knew about, but she complained the places were dead.

Around eleven pm we ended up at Eli's Mile High Club on Grove Street, near the Berkeley-Oakland city line. Hassim parked a block away, almost under the MacArthur freeway. The night streetscape was composed of strangely shaped rectangles of shadows, a study in blues and blacks, punctuated by long beams of the headlights passing on the freeway overhead. The neighborhood seemed ominous, but I had been to Eli's Mile High Club once before with Paul and Yoshi. The club was a favorite with left-leaning Berkeley students. On weekend nights whites sometimes outnumbered blacks on the dance floor. I would not be out of place here.

People milled around the doorway, smoking and talking. Then I saw Grace Neville emerge from the front door leaning against the most handsome man I had ever seen. The flat planes of his face were like those of a Cherokee. He was wearing a turtleneck and a long leather coat with wide lapels. His walk emanated balance, coordination, agility and strength. Against the shoulder of that dark, handsome man, Grace's hair was a bright blonde patch. Her dress was made of some shimmery, fine-spun material. Emerging from the front door, they looked like a glamor-ous couple out of a magazine. But as they drew closer to me in the half-light, I saw Grace was a bit unsteady. She may have needed that strong arm that encircled her. She did not see me as she passed.

"That's Grace," I said to Edna, after they had passed us in the dusk. "You know her. She works at the track."

"H'mm," Edna said sharply. "Your friend looks turned out."

"What's turned out?"

"Never mind." Edna said. She turned up the collar of her own fur coat and patted her Afro. "She ain't bad looking. Not that I have a whole lotta re-spect for white girls who run after the brothers."

"Do you know the man she was with?"

"I do," said Edna. "He's Big Jim. He runs security for the Black Panthers."

We entered the building. Although it was summer, the bar was adorned with strings of Christmas lights. Four pillars separated the bar from the lounge area on the left, with round tables facing the stage. A saxophonist called Cool Poppa had just taken over as we sat down, opening his gig with a blast of hard-blowing sax. The spotlight shone on his big straw hat and black glasses. Be-hind him a drummer in a thin T-shirt kept a beat on the snares, clanging the cymbals.

Edna ordered herself a cognac with a soda chaser. Trying to act as if I hung out at blues joints all the time, I ordered a beer. A man came over and asked me to dance. I felt self-conscious, but I did my best, taking a deep breath and trying to follow his moves on the crowded dance floor. Edna watched me from our table. When I returned, she smiled at me. "Just slow down, Leah," she said, "Ain't no need to try so hard. Nobody's in a hurry here."

During the band break someone put on a record by Bill Withers. It was Lean on Me, the summer's number one hit. Listening to it, people seemed to move closer to one another. Hassim's arm snaked around the back of Edna's chair. She relaxed sideways, leaning into his broad chest. The next time someone asked me to dance, I, too, felt relaxed and happy. I was able to match my partner's dance steps. "Right on, sister!" said my new partner. He was an older black man with a little goatee, wearing a green turtleneck. "Just keep it coming, smooth and simple, girl!"

I thought of Grace's aura of burnished glamour. Perhaps I was approaching her level of sophistication, dancing with strangers at Eli's Mile High Club. But by midnight I was dizzy from the beers I had drunk and tired of the attentions of a Berkeley law student who kept laying his damp hand over mine. Edna was laughing with Hassim and Freddie about getting high on some Thai sticks. I wasn't sure what they were talking about and I didn't want to know. My elation had worn off. As I made my way toward the ladies' room, I passed an open door leading to a backyard patio, festooned with more Christmas lights. I stepped outside to cool off. Small groups of people were talking at picnic tables dragged under some sort of tarpaulin. A couple was kissing. In the distance I heard the wail of a police siren. The crowd began to move back toward the door. A young black man sprinted toward me.

"What's going on?"

"Fight," he said. "Police. Get inside."

I started to follow him inside. Then I saw Grace. She was still in her shimmery dress, but she was limping and her face looked swollen. As she got closer I could see a necklace of dark bruises on her neck.

She grabbed my arm and pushed me ahead of her. "Let's get into the bathroom," she said.

I followed her. "What *happened* to you, Grace?" The club noise made it hard for me to hear her answer. She set a big purse down on the floor and splashed her face with water, wincing a little. I could not take my eyes off the ring of dark splotches which encircled her neck.

"Leah," she said, urgently, "Could you take me back to your place?"

26

"I didn't drive. I came with Edna Banks. Freddie Corster. You know Edna. She runs the Hot Spoon on Mainline. Her friend Hassim drove."

"Don't tell her," Grace said.

"I came with her, Grace. If I'm leaving, I have to tell her."

"Just don't say anything about me. Promise?"

At our table, Edna was flanked by Hassim and Freddie. "There you are. I was just about to send Freddie to look for you."

"I'd like to go home, if somebody can give me a ride. I ran into a friend, outside. She's in trouble. She wants to stay in my place tonight."

Edna looked at me sharply. "This friend ain't that blonde we saw earlier, is it?"

I was silent.

"What kind of trouble she in?" Edna persisted.

"I don't know."

"You want my advice, Leah, stay away from her. Grace Neville. Just stay away from her, girl."

"She needs my help, Edna. She's a kinda friend."

"Kinda is right, honey," Edna said. "Help her out tonight. I can see you're determined. But, Lord, Leah, stay away from her after this. Some people just pull trouble to them."

"Police just got here," Freddie said. "You see the fight? Some white boy," he said. "Liquored up and went for a brother. White boy better remember where he's at."

"Oh, it happens all the time when Eli's gets ready to close," said Edna.

"Even in Berkeley?" I asked.

They all laughed, throwing their heads back. "First of all," Edna said, as she struggled to stop laughing, "This is Oakland, honey. Second, it's closing time. Men who ain't getting any action are pissed. That's universal, Leah."

"You got us men all figured out, don't you Edna?" Freddie was wiping tears from his eyes. I didn't think what I had said was that funny.

"I got you guys figured out a long time ago!" Edna said.

"But you, sweetheart," Freddie turned to me. "Seems like you think Berkeley's the city of brotherly love!"

27

"Never mind Freddie. You ready to go? Hassim will give you a ride."

Grace was silent as Hassim drove us home. We sat in the back seat. Occasionally she touched her neck with a gesture of disbelief. I didn't ask her any questions either, because of Hassim's presence and for other reasons. My work on the ambulances of Berkeley had been my first initiation into the reality of a woman's vulnerability. There I had been protected by the distance my job gave me. This was different: more real and more ugly.

Hassim dropped us off in front of a pink stucco house on Russell Street, a block above Telegraph Avenue. "See ya," he said. "I'll head back, see what Edna and Freddie are up to."

I lived in a neighborhood of large homes and big gardens, more prosperous than the student ghetto bordering the university. It was close to bus lines and within walking distance of the campus, an ideal place for me.

We walked into the house. Grace sat on the couch with her big bag on the floor by her feet. I walked into the kitchen to make a pot of tea to take upstairs. Glancing into the living room, I could see her now and again putting her fingers to the bruises on her neck. Her gesture made me uncomfortable. "You want some ice for that?" I asked abruptly.

"Oh this," she said in an offhand way. "Is it noticeable?"

"Yes," I said, pouring the boiling water over the tea bags into the pot.

"Never mind," she said. "It'll go away soon enough. I'm sorry to bother you like this, Leah. My life isn't always this dramatic. I've had a mean streak of luck lately. I can't seem to pull myself out of the spiral."

I didn't say anything, placing the pot of tea and two cups on a metal tray. I did not want to know what had happened—perhaps it was the beers, or the late hour. I worried our voices might awaken my roommates. And I was frightened by something I couldn't name—Grace's vulnerability and my own. My need to be safe was threatened by that blue-black mark on Grace's neck.

"Let's go on up to my room," I said.

My bedroom lay at the front of the house, facing the street. It was large enough to accommodate a king-size bed in the right-hand corner of the room, and a sofa bed directly opposite. My desk looked out onto the street itself. I loved my room, which I had furnished from garage sales: pale white curtains at the windows, an orange and black Mexican rug on the floor, and bright prints with red and orange tones: Cezanne's apples, and Gauguin's big-breasted nudes covering the walls. It usually comforted me to come inside and to know it was my own. But tonight, as I set the tray down on my desk, turned on the lamps, and drew the curtains, I continued to feel uneasy.

I opened up the sofa bed and made it up while Grace disappeared into the bathroom. She came out ten minutes later in a gold silk robe with a red dragon patterned over the left breast. Her face looked stark white, absent now of makeup, and the bluish rings under her eyes looked so deep they could have been mistaken for black eyes. I was startled to realize that without makeup and the help of clothing and jewelry, Grace was not really a beautiful woman. Good bones and a full-breasted figure, but with pallid skin and eyes that looked exhausted and full of sorrow. I had pulled on a red checked flannel nightshirt and now went to climb under the blankets of my bed, my cup of tea in my hand. Grace got her cup, and lay down on top of the covers on the sofa bed.

"How'd you happen to have that robe with you?" I asked.

"I'm always prepared," Grace said, patting her enormous purse. "Came from traveling with Mom, I guess. We always carried a change of underwear and a toothbrush."

I didn't pursue the subject. I guessed that she needed to talk as much as she needed a couch to sleep on. Whenever I remember this night, as I have remembered it over and over again, striving to recall or read meaning into details which may have never existed, I regret my underlying resistance toward Grace and what she may have wanted to tell me. My resistance made me feel dead tired. The truth was also that I dreaded hearing what Grace needed to say.

"Who was the man you were with?" I finally asked, sipping my tea. "When you left Eli's?"

She looked up at me. "Oh, you saw me then? I didn't see you."

"A good-looking man," I said. "Black."

"James," she said finally. "Long ago lover."

"How long ago?"

"A few months. More or less. Now just a friend."

"A few months? That's not that long ago. He's very good-looking."

"Yes," she said, smiling a little. "Women always say that about James."

"How'd you meet him, Grace?"

29

"Where else?" she said, "At the track. That's where I meet all my men. He came in one day, bought a ticket. That was it, for me. I was crazy about him."

"And he was crazy about you too?"

She smiled. Her voice became more animated. "Yeah, he felt the pull. He had just come out here from the south. Who knows, if he hadn't been in the Black Panthers, we might still be together."

I remembered Edna's words when she had seen the two of them together. Hadn't Edna said that James headed up the Security for the Panthers? "He was in the Panthers?"

"Still is," she said. "He was not the boy next door, I'll say that."

"Like those friends of yours at Vinnie's Inn? They were Panthers, weren't they?"

"Them." Grace sighed. "Yeah, two of them are Panthers."

"Isn't it a problem?" I asked. "Your being white?"

"Oh, Leah," she laughed. "You sound like a social worker. Of course there were problems. But not the kind you have in mind."

"It couldn't have been easy," I insisted, "They're militant."

She shrugged. "That's what the television stations love to say. That isn't the whole story. The Panthers are trying hook up with the Berkeley Peace and Freedom Party, unite with the white students. But too much is always happening. It takes all their time and energy just to survive."

"You make them sound like a group of Berkeley intellectuals," I said. "If that's all they are, why is it so hard for them to just survive?"

"Because Americans hate niggers with guns, as my high school boyfriend, Ronnie, would say. Nothing changes that. I was never in it for politics, anyway. I was in it for James."

"But you broke up?"

"A lot happened," she said. "More than I could ever tell. He got busted. Caught in a house with weapons in the cellar. Sent to San Quentin. He got out early. But by the time he got out, things had changed between us."

"Did you find someone else?"

"Hell, Leah." She took out a cigarette. "I'm not the kind of woman who was meant to be lonely. Even before James went to prison, the Party took

30

up all his time."

"Despite that, you're still friends?"

"More than friends." She inhaled deeply. "James is loyal to those who are loyal to him."

"How could he consider you loyal?" I asked. She had just admitted that while he was in prison she had found someone new.

"I'm not talking about sex. It goes way beyond that."

"Was James the love of your life?"

"I suppose so—at least, he was one of them. There was a time I would have jumped off a cliff for James. Maybe, in a way, that's exactly what I did."

"One of the loves of your life. Who were the others?"

"Remember what I said about your curiosity? You really get me talking!" She sat for a while, smoking, inhaling, looking at the wall that lay somewhere to my left. "Two or three, I suppose. Ronnie, my high school lover. Ronald Xavier Jones." Grace sighed. "With some men you don't know until later that things will be hard. With Ronnie you could see trouble coming. He was crazy." She smiled again. "But sexy."

"Are you in love now?"

"Maybe that's the problem," she said, "I have to wonder if I'm capable of love at all."

At twenty-eight, Grace was five years older than me. Her sad, urbane air of disillusion in love was captivating; and of course, my admiration flattered her. Like an actress with an appreciative audience, she mesmerized me with her performance; yet I felt her inner detachment. She exhaled a circle of smoke, followed by a second. The circles floated up into the room. Grace Neville was the most fascinating woman I had ever met.

I fell asleep soon after that, but was awakened in the early hours of the morning. The light next to the couch was on, and Grace was moving around.

"Sorry, Leah," she said, "Did I wake you?"

"Yes," I said. "What's wrong?"

"I'm nervous," she said. "I just keep thinking about things."

"What kind of things?" I struggled up toward wakefulness, grudgingly. The clock next to my bed read three am.

"I thought I heard something outside. A car slowed down and stopped. I got up to look but I couldn't see anything. Then the tree branches were brushing against your window. It's nothing. Sometimes I wake up in the middle of the night scared, and my whole life seems to amount to nothing."

I was too young to have experienced those nights when, sleepless, you face the failures of a lifetime. I slept deeply every night, exhausted by my forays into the world of school and work. I could, however, remember the wretched dreams I had had for years after my mother died, and the early morning wakefulness.

"Your life hasn't been nothing, Grace," I said, "You could write some great stories about it."

"That's just like you, Leah," she said, "You can make me laugh, though, you sure can." Her laugh had a bitter sound that I didn't care for.

"What are you in over your head about?" I asked. It was the closest I came to referring to her bruises.

"Oh, you know," she said finally, "I've had a lot of lovers. A couple who meant a lot to me. But sometimes I think you can't go back."

"Who did you go back to?"

"I hoped I could go back to James."

It was obvious to me that, although she wanted to talk, she wasn't going to tell me anything. I was sleepy, impatient. "What's wrong with going back?" I said. Even at twenty-three, I had memories that were painful to revisit. I had come to Berkeley to get away from them. Nevertheless, I pushed on. "Seems to me people are always going back, to their home, their old lovers, whatever."

"It's not a good idea," she repeated. "It's just something I feel. I didn't even want to go home tonight. Didn't feel safe."

Soon after that I fell asleep for the second time.

I awoke at nine. The morning light filtered through the white curtains and revealed Grace sitting on the sofa bed. She wore blue jeans and the smoky blue cashmere sweater I had passed up. Her enormous shoulder bag seemed to hold a lot. Her makeup had been carefully applied. Foundation over the bruises on her neck made them almost indiscernible. Incredibly, she appeared rested and almost radiant, her face vivid. "You seem to have recovered," I said, sitting up.

"Born resilient," She said, with a husky sound that was a cross between a laugh and a sob. "Got to be, baby." She picked up her shoulder bag, large enough to be an overnight case, and slung it across her shoulder.

"You're leaving already?" I asked. I didn't need to ask; she was already moving toward the door. "You need a ride?"

"My car's not far. A few blocks."

"Want me to drive you?"

Grace shook her head. "Places to go; people to see."

I crawled out of bed to walk her to the door of my room. Now we were standing close, and I could see the purple scar beneath the foundation. It seemed to pulse there beneath the skin. She opened her arms to give me a hug. I could smell her sweet, warm floral fragrance.

"Leah, thanks a lot for taking me in."

"You're sure you're okay, Grace?" I asked. It was just a thing to say; I really wanted to go back to bed.

"Got to be," she said, smiling. " See you Monday."

I heard her go down the steps, heard her say something to my roommates. Open and close the front door. I'm not even sure I remember these details. Did I think I remembered them because Paul and Carol told me later they had said good-bye to her as she left? I do remember my feeling of relief, which would return later to haunt me. Her problems were her problems, not mine; her unusual life was no longer my concern. I was glad to go back to sleep.

Later, straightening up the room, I found a betting slip on the floor near the sofa bed where she had been sleeping. There were numbers written on it, and names next to the numbers. Mighty Luck/Bucky Timmons, Stella's Star, scribbled next to the numbers. I picked it up and put it on my desk, in case she asked me for it in the future.

This comprises the sum total of experiences I shared with her. Words she spoke to me; my impressions, however faulty, of a vital yet fragile human being.

I have searched my memory over and over again to come up with even this much.

I learned about other Graces in the year that followed. Graces who emerged from the testimony and remarks of family, friends, enemies, and old lovers, in depositions, journals, confidential files, and scraps of poetry.

Writing this, many years later, my view of Grace has shifted. Many things changed, and then changed again: my information, my experiences, even the social perspectives on the history we shared.

Eventually another Grace emerged from my search through her life and my own. I will try my best to describe our story, as it happened to me then.

III

I wish I could say that I had some presentiment that Sunday of what had happened to Grace. I did not. I slept late Sunday morning. When I awoke, I persuaded Yoshi to walk with me to the Med for a cup of coffee. "The Med" was the abbreviation we all used for the Mediterranean Café on Telegraph Avenue, with its black-and-white tiled floor like a gigantic chessboard, where the beat poets had famously hung out. Bearded professors and unemployed artists could still be found there at its small square tables, with berets and cappuccinos, discussing existentialism or Karl Marx.

We strolled up Telegraph Avenue in cold lingering morning fog. We talked a little about my outing with Edna and her friends at Eli's Mile High Club. I was more interested in Yoshi's description of the party he had been to the night before. My ex-boyfriend had been there.

I returned to work at the track the next morning, Monday, the day the body was found near the pier down from Golden Gate Fields. I heard rumors and speculation. Grace hadn't shown up for work. My boss, Beatrice, called us into her office. The body had been identified as Grace Neville. She apparently had drowned after being beaten and shot. Beatrice told us management would prefer the track to continue operating normally, but we could go home if we wanted. I stayed on at work. The routine was a distraction. As long as I was helping people place their bets, the events of the morning seemed less real.

I was home shortly after four. The evening Oakland Tribune had come out. Because Grace had been a resident of Oakland, the Oakland Police Department was handling the case. Forensic experts had determined the time of death to be around two am Sunday morning.

I read the article twice. This was not right. At two am Sunday morning Grace Neville had lain sleeping, quite alive, on the fold-out sofa in my bedroom. The article reported that she had last been seen leaving Eli's Mile High Club with James Ferguson, a high-ranking member of the Black Panther Party and Head of their Security. He was being sought in connection with the killing. Anyone with information regarding his whereabouts was requested to notify the Oakland Police.

I was on the telephone immediately.

"Joey!" I said," I have to talk to you."

I called him at home. Joey was my cousin, six years older than I was. In my childhood he was my older cousin Joey, crazy-acting and stupid at times, opinionated and brave at others. After my mother died, I rarely saw Joey or his family. Joey enlisted in the Army in 1961, getting out just as things were getting hot in Vietnam in 1965. After that he joined the Oakland police force. Joey was now Acting Lieutenant in charge of the Homicide Section of the Oakland Police Department, a big guy, with a hawk-like profile. He was keen to be named to the position permanently. I had watched the antiwar movement erupt on the evening news, along with live footage from the front lines, as the protestors battled with the OPD. I began to feel an aversion to Joey. In my mind I called him my "law and order cousin." While students were being tear-gassed on Sproul Plaza and knocked around at Santa Rita, Joey was making a career for himself in the OPD. It surprised me when Joey started referring to Vietnam as his "stint in hell."

Yet it was Joey who had come to my mother's funeral in 1959, sixteen years old in a badly fitting black suit. He looked ill at ease, but he had come and hugged me on the saddest day of my life. When we reconnected in California, it was hard to see in him the teenager who had been my idolized older cousin. We would each have preferred to have a different kind of cousin, one who was on the right side, but all we had was each other. "Hey cuz," he said now, "What's up?"

"Joey," I said. "You heard about the woman whose body was found off Golden Gate Fields today?"

"Sure," he said, "Today's news."

"She's a friend of mine," I said. "This stuff in the paper, and on the evening news, Joey, they got this stuff all wrong."

"What do you mean?"

"This business about the time of death being two am on Sunday morning—that's wrong," I repeated.

"Why do you say that?"

"Because she was with me," I said. "She was here with me, in this house, at that time."

He was silent so long I wondered if he had heard me. "Joey?"

36

"Are you sure?"

"Of course I'm sure."

"Anyone else there? At your house?"

"My roommates. They saw her in the morning when she left."

He swore softly, under his breath. "What time did she leave?"

"Sometime after nine in the morning."

He stayed silent again for along time. Finally he said, "Don't say a word to anyone about this."

"What do you mean?" I asked. "I've got to talk to someone. They're looking for that guy, that James Ferguson, and he's probably not even the right guy."

"They aren't looking," he said. "They've got him."

"Even more reason for me to report this."

"Just sit tight," he said, and then, to himself, "Shit! How'd they screw this up? I tell you what," he said finally. "Let me buy you some dinner. I'll come pick you up and we'll talk."

"Talk about what?" I said. "I need to get down there and give my statement. They can't hold someone for murder when the woman was still alive!"

"Goddamn," Joey said, "if this ain't a bitch. You said anything to anyone about this yet?"

"I can't remember," I said. Was it me or him who wasn't making sense? "Anyway, she liked that guy—that Ferguson."

"She wouldn't be the first babe liked a guy who offed her," Joey said, and then, with a note of suspicion, "how do you know that?"

"She told me," I said. "There were other men she was afraid of."

"I'm on my way, cuz," he said. "I'll be right over."

As I waited for Joey by the front door, Paul opened the sliding door from his room and stuck out his big head with its halo of soft blonde curls. "Hey, Leah, that wasn't your friend, was it, whose body turned up in the bay out at the race track?"

"It was, Paul. I'm really upset."

"Scary."

Paul was twenty-five, with the bull-like torso and physical strength of a boxer. He had grown up in San Jose. His conservative father owned a furniture store, but Paul had become a Marxist. He was doing graduate work in political science. He looked more like a teddy bear than the socialist and part-time labor organizer that he was. Paul was our house radical. "Who are you waiting for?" Paul asked now.

"My cousin," I said, "He works for the Oakland Police Department." I warned Paul because the sight of a police car in front of our house would make him nervous.

"Your cousin's a cop?" Paul asked, "A tool of the oppressors?"

Paul talked like that. He used expressions which sounded like something out of a Marxist textbook.

"There are good men who are cops, Paul."

"There must be," Paul answered. "Problem is, I've never met one. I keep telling myself to remember they're just the sons of the working class, pressed into the service of the state."

"I don't know about all that. I think my cousin just needed a job."

"There are other jobs around," Paul responded.

There were other jobs, but Joey had grown up fighting his father. His skills were honed in Vietnam. He had only the skills he had picked up during his Army enlistment. He liked violence.

Joey pulled up in a unmarked patrol car. I was glad he was not driving OPD's telltale black-and-white Ford. Paul would have been angry to see what he called the fuzz parked outside our communal home.

I ran out to the curb. Joey reached across the seat to open the door for me. "Hey, cuz," he leaned over to give me a hug. "Let's just go on up the street to Dave's, if you don't mind."

Joey despised the Telegraph Avenue coffee shops where I hung out with my friends. "Why would I want to pay a dollar for a thimbleful of bad coffee and drink it with a bunch of wimps?" He liked seedy diners and doughnut shops. He headed up Ashby, turned on College and again on Broadway. Just past Pleasant Valley Avenue with the big Safeway, Joey pulled into Dave's Coffee Shop. Joey ordered two cups of the house coffee and a piece of blackberry pie and lost no time in starting in on me. "What kind of friends you hangin' out with these days, anyway? This gal who got killed—? This Grace Neville kept some pretty heavy company."

"What are you getting at?"

"Like James Ferguson, this Panther SOB they just picked up. The guy heads up their Security operation. He's a trained killer."

"So are you!" I flashed back.

Joey's face reddened. "Back off," he said. "I just want to know one thing—" It seemed to burst out of him. "Were you banging this guy?"

For a second I had no idea what Joey was talking about. Then comprehension flooded through me, and incredulity, and a futile sense of anger. "Joey, I don't even know the guy." I stared at him. "He was my friend's lover."

"Wouldn't be the first time this guy was banging two broads," Joey said. "Friends or not. Black guys—"

I didn't want to hear what was coming. "Let's start again. My friend got killed. I feel terrible. The Tribune states she died around two am Saturday night. That can't be. The fact is, I have information. She was sleeping at my house that night. She didn't leave until after nine in the morning."

He let out a long sigh, and took out a cigarette. "Okay," he said. "My buddies thought they had Ferguson this time. He was responsible for this cop death in New York a while back. We thought we had him at last."

"So you pick him up now, and accuse him of killing Grace Neville?"

"I don't know all the details, but they found her blood in the trunk of his car. Point is, your information will blow their case to smithereens. I hate to have them look so bad. Them Panthers are slick when it comes to the media. They'll blow this up big time. Damn, I hate this happened. And you've got to be right in the middle of it."

"Doesn't it matter to you that the man might be innocent?"

"Hell, no," Joey said immediately. "It's like my daddy used to say. If you didn't do it this time, I know you did it some other. That goes double for this dude. If Ferguson didn't do this, he did something worse."

It was useless to argue with him. "It doesn't matter. I've got to go down there and tell what I know."

"Yeah, I guess you do," he said finally. "But I'm gonna go down with you, and wait around so they don't give you too hard a time. And maybe you should consider getting a lawyer."

"Why on earth would I get a lawyer?"

"You may have been one of the last people who saw this woman alive. This is what's called a politically sensitive case. There's a lot riding on it— from all directions."

I didn't get it. I knew what needed to be done. I was going down to the Oakland Police Department like a good citizen and give information which would help them find out who killed my friend.

IV

An hour later, I was sitting in a dingy green room at Oakland Police Department headquarters. Joey introduced me to two sergeants, Gary Bond and Chester Sims, the field investigators. Bond had a receding hair line and tired eyes. He opened up the interview. He asked me about the sequence of events which led to Grace's presence in my room Saturday night. "Who was she with when you saw her leaving Eli's?"

"James Ferguson," I answered.

His name hung in the air for a fraction of a second. Bond cleared his throat.

"How did you know that was Ferguson?"

"My friend Edna Banks recognized him."

"What exactly did she say?"

"She called him Big Jim—said he ran security for the Black Panthers."

Bond leaned forward. He smiled, but the look in his eyes had changed.

"Had you ever seen this man before?"

"Where would I have seen him?" I asked, confused.

"Anywhere. The track, for example."

A number of black men came and went at the track. Could Ferguson have been one of them?

"No," I said, finally, "I never saw him there."

"How can you be sure?"

"He's too good-looking," I said. "I would remember him."

The two cops exchanged a look.

"Did you know Ferguson before that Saturday?"

"I just told you—" I began.

"You said he was good-looking. Did you think about going out with him?"

"I just told you I never met the man—"

"Slow down, slow down, Gary," Sims interjected. He was younger than Bond, but homely, with acne scars pitting his face. "You're getting Leah all upset. Let me talk to her."

41

"Leah, you thirsty? Want a soda?" His tone was solicitous.

"Sure," I said. My mouth felt dry.

"Gary," Sims said, "Get Leah a coke. Stretch your legs a little." Bond left the room and Sims took a seat on the edge of his metal desk, smiling at me as if we were great friends. "Gary was trained in the old school, Leah," he said to me, swinging his leg. "*I* know you want to tell us the truth. You saw Grace Saturday night with James Ferguson. Your friend Edna Banks mentioned his name, right?"

"Yes," I said. "And Grace mentioned him too."

"How did Grace look when you first saw her at Eli's?"

I thought of Grace in her shimmery dress, leaning against James Ferguson's shoulder. Her face looked radiant, from a distance. Yet, closer, she had looked different. Unsteady, perhaps upset.

"She looked happy. Absorbed in him. She didn't see me."

"Any marks on her? Cuts, bruises, anything like that?"

The air in the room felt charged. Sims seemed to be pursuing a lead.

"It was dark. I wouldn't have seen anything." But I had seen something later, in the bathroom, I thought. The ugly ring of bruises on her throat. "Later, in the ladies' room, I noticed some bruises on her neck," I added.

Bond came in with a Coke and slid it across the table to me. He took the chair that Sims had vacated. "Did she say anything about these bruises?" Sims was asking.

"Nothing," I said.

"Nothing?" Sims's voice sharpened a fraction. "Didn't you ask her about them?"

"She didn't seem to want to talk about it."

Sims continued to stare at me. "You said she was a friend," Sims said.

"A kinda friend—"

"The kinda friend you'd open your home to. Give a bed to sleep in. That kinda friend?"

"I would have done that for anyone in that situation."

"A bad situation?"

"Yes."

42

"This woman, in this bad situation, you wanted to help her so much. She has bruises on her neck the size of dimes and you don't ask her how she got them?"

I didn't say what the bruises looked like, I thought to myself.

"Did you ask her about the bruises?" he persisted.

"No, I didn't know her that well. It seemed too personal, and—" I stopped because of the disbelief in Sims's eyes.

"Let's move on," he said. "You have three roommates?'

"Yes."

"Any of them political?'

I thought about Paul, our house radical and labor union-organizer.

"How do you mean?"

"You know—active in those causes you got out there in Berkeley. Vietnam—stuff like that."

"They marched in some rallies," I said.

"Anything else?"

"Like what?"

"Panther causes?"

"Not that I know of."

"Any of them give money to Panther causes?'

"My roommates are usually broke."

"Anyone in your house know James Ferguson?"

"I've already told you. I didn't know him. Nobody knew him."

"Except Grace," Bond intoned, standing up. "She knew him all right!" He slapped a page of photographs down on the table between me and Sims. Mug shots of a black man. Shots of James Ferguson, although in his wild, straight-ahead stare at the camera, he looked completely different. He looked like a hunted animal.

"Recognize him?" Bond said. His voice grew louder and more strident. "Want to know how he murdered a cop in New York two years ago—just shot him down cold in an alley in Brooklyn? Want to hear about the other women he's beaten up, like your friend Grace? Is this the guy you want to protect?" He slammed his fist down on the table, flat on James Ferguson's photograph, so

43

hard the table shook. I stared at him. Sims leaped up from his chair, put his hand on Bond's shoulder, and spoke in a low voice.

"Take a break, buddy," he said. "Get yourself some coffee."

Bond was perspiring. I stared at his flushed face. Memories flashed. Things I had heard from Paul, about a protester at Santa Rita whose head was banged against a pole so hard she still suffered from headaches. Rallies where Paul had been dragged to a police van by his hair. Bond took a deep breath. "Sorry I got so carried away."

Sims looked at me. "That cop that got killed in New York—," he said, "Gary worked back there. Gary knew him. He gets revved up on the subject."

"Look, none of this has anything to do with me," I protested. My voice sounded shaky, but I continued, "I never laid eyes on James Ferguson before Saturday night."

Sims's eyes rested on me. He did not seem to believe me. Joey had told me cops never believed anyone. "Just tell me again what Grace told you that night," he said.

"Look, do you really want to find out who killed Grace Neville?" I said. "I've told you everything I know. There's nothing more to tell."

"Okay," Sims said, with finality. He picked up the phone. "Joe, come pick up your cousin. She ain't a whole lotta use to us. You can take her home for now."

I walked back into the waiting room. Joey was talking to a cop with tan skin and a small mustache—the same cop I had seen in the parking lot the morning Grace's body was found. He was of medium height with a compact build. I heard Joey address him as "Mike." From what I could hear, Mike was describing his first impressions of Grace's body to Joey. Apparently he had been the first cop on the scene. Joey interrupted him when he saw me. "Catch you later, Mike," he said. "We'll get back to this."

"What did you say to Chester?" Joey asked me on the way home. "He sounded a little upset when he called me."

"I asked him if the OPD really wants to find out who killed Grace."

"Jeez, you musta set them back on their heels with that remark. You look so innocent, Leah, but you say the damndest things. So did Grace have any bruises on her when you saw her?"

44

"I explained all that to those two cops," I answered, "Why are you asking me?"

"Mike, the guy I was just talking to, he found her body. He noticed bruises on the throat. I wondered if they had been there before she was murdered. If she had said anything to you about it." I felt nervous and keyed up with a nagging fear. Why had Grace been murdered? And were the cops really interested in finding out?

Joey pulled up in front of my house and turned to me. "Leah," he said, "I'm gonna try and explain this to you once more. But only once. You're my cousin, and I worry about you."

"Joey, do you guys really want to find out who killed Grace?"

"Yeah, well, let me try to explain all that to you."

"Explain what?"

"This is one hell of a case." he said. "Try to forget that you knew this woman. Try looking at it from our point of view, okay? A woman turns up murdered. That's not unusual—hundreds of women get murdered in Oakland every year. Most of the cases are never solved—that's just between you and me. This babe is nothing special. There's no money behind her. She's not well-connected. Nobody's setting up any hue and cry. Nobody's gonna pay attention whether we find her killer or not. Murders? Two-thirds or more are committed by lovers, husbands, boyfriends. The rest are committed by creeps with a previous record. —But nothing's riding on this case, Leah. I know she mattered to you. Don't look like she mattered much to anyone else."

He lifted his shoulders in a gesture of helplessness. "Let's not argue about it," he said. "I'm trying to explain something to you. What this case is like for us. Nobody cares about this dead girl—not really. Except us. We've been watching Ferguson for years—we hate the bastard—we think he got that cop in New York City a while back."

"How do you know he did it?" Joey's cynicism always disturbed me.

"Never mind how we know it. We got our sources, you can be sure of that," Joey said. He pulled a cigarette out of his shirt pocket, pushed in the car lighter. "This case? We knew she left Eli's hanging on his arm. She was dead the next day. Some reporters got hold of the story and it broke that afternoon. It looked like we had the bastard at last. Then—holy shit—it turns out she was still alive Sunday morning. And my little cousin has to be the one who was

45

with her. So what did she tell you about her and Ferguson?" Joey continued, lighting his cigarette.

"She told me they were still friends," I answered. "Why does this ruin your case if you have all this other evidence against him?"

"Your testimony is enough to make us look bad. To get this sleaze ball out on bail. On top of everything else, you're my damned cousin. We can't even discredit you the way we'd like to."

"Discredit me? Thanks, Joey. I happen to have told the truth."

He kept right on talking. "Papers have the story already—how we screwed up. Panthers will milk it for all it's worth. They love to play up the bad cop routine, the OPD pigs. It makes me so angry I'd like to go out and blast away all them sons of bitches."

"So? Find the killer. Isn't that what OPD is supposed to do?"

"You don't understand, Leah," he said. "Mike found a gun in the bushes. It traced back to Ferguson. We just need a little more."

"Okay, but shouldn't you investigate everything? She told me about other guys in her life—maybe someone at the race track—"

"There's problems," he said. "More than I can possibly convey."

"Like what?"

"The way she was murdered. I don't really want to subject you to this." But Joey went on. "That cop, Mike. He was first on the scene. Called Alameda County Coroner's Office. He was there when they pulled the body out of the water. He told me about it. Tremendous force. Bones broken so bad they were in splinters. You only see that in crimes of passion."

"The papers said she had been shot."

"Shot too. Execution style. A different kind of murder. Something paid killers do. They don't have an investment. Nothing personal to get even about. They just want their money. No. An angry boyfriend—a paid killer— only one man fits both categories. James Ferguson. And we may never get him now."

"Joey," I said. "She had other boyfriends. What kind of backgrounds do they have? She left a betting slip behind in my room. It had all kinds of numbers on it, and the name of this jockey, Bucky Timmons."

"This matters to you, doesn't it?"

"I keep trying to tell you that."

"Tell you what," Joey said, "I have a little leeway here. I could hire you to do some undercover work. Nothing dangerous. Check out that betting slip, for example. Keep your ears open at the track. Ask around a little— nothing conspicuous. Write it up and report back to me. Make yourself a little extra, maybe enough to cover your tuition this fall."

I frowned. The idea was hardly my style.

"Think it over," Joey said. "It might help me out, and I know it would help you. Can't be easy—sharing a house with all those Berzerkelyites." He smiled at his own humor.

"Goodbye, Joey," I said, opening the door. "I'll call you tomorrow."

"Think it over," he said again, as I stepped out. "And while you're at it, get yourself a lawyer. Sensitive case, like I said."

V

I didn't get myself a lawyer, although a lawyer came into my life. When I woke up around nine on Tuesday morning, I left a message for Beatrice at the track, requesting a week's leave of absence. I was only half awake, when I got a call from Art Leopold. He was James Ferguson's attorney.

I had heard of Art Leopold, of course. He was famous on the left for taking and winning controversial and socially relevant cases. Paul had spoken glowingly of this man who worked with a small collective of lawyers defending white radicals and black activists. Leopold's deep, resonant voice conveyed a forceful urgency. He wanted to meet with me at noon. I did not even consider refusing. We made an appointment for one in the afternoon.

Without wasting time, I got dressed and took the bus to San Francisco's Embarcadero. When I was shown into his office, Art Leopold rose immediately from behind his cluttered desk. He was a large man with a shock of white hair and sharp hazel eyes, in his late fifties, a handsome and imposing man.

Sitting in a chair near the window that overlooked the plaza was James Ferguson. A black leather jacket was slung over the back of his chair. The room felt filled with his presence.

"Thank you for coming," Art Leopold said. James Ferguson did not stand up. His face remained impassive.

"We learned you spoke to the Oakland police last night," Leopold said, motioning for me to sit down. "Your testimony got James released. Temporarily, at least. Would you mind repeating for me what you told the police?"

Not looking at James, I summarized my conversation with Bond and Sims.

Art Leopold listened intently, jotted a few notes. When I had finished, he said, "She left your house shortly after nine Sunday morning?"

"Yes."

"You are sure about that time?"

"When I woke up, I glanced at my clock. It was nine am. She and I talked for a few minutes, but I was very tired. She left, and I went back to sleep."

"Your two roommates also saw her leave?"

48

"Yes. Paul Cohen and Carol Sweet saw her leave a little after nine."

Art Leopold looked at James for a moment before turning back to me. "This information is very important to us, Miss DeMartino. Thank you for coming forward with it."

"It's what happened. There's nothing to thank me for."

"I'd like to know a little more about the time you saw Grace leave Eli's with James. That was around eleven pm the previous evening?"

"I think so. We were just arriving."

"How did Grace appear to you at that time?"

"Happy. She was looking up at Mr. Ferguson. They were absorbed in each other."

"Did she seem to be in any distress? Any kind of trouble?"

"Not then."

James leaned forward and whispered something to Art. Art looked at me for a few seconds before speaking again. "Later, you saw her at what time?"

"Maybe twelve or twelve thirty."

"At that time, how did she appear to you?"

"She was limping. Her face looked swollen."

"Anything else?"

I hesitated. "She had some bruises at her throat," I said.

"Did you ask her about them?"

I shook my head. "I know it seems strange. I didn't ask about it, and she didn't say anything."

There was a long silence. Art Leopold looked at me. James sat still in his chair in the corner. "Later," I said, nervously, filling in the silence, "we talked in my room. I asked her if James had been the love of her life. She said he was one of them. She said she cared about him." I paused, not sure where I was going. James was staring at me with a startled look.

"Miss DeMartino, are you aware of the history of the Oakland Police Department and their actions against members of the Black Panther Party?"

"I gather they are not on the best of terms," I said.

"Did the police talk to you about Grace's physical condition? Did they ask you if she had talked to you about the events of the previous evening?"

49

"They kinda hammered away at it, in fact. I told them what I'm telling you. Grace and I didn't talk about the bruises."

"You realize how important your testimony is? You don't plan to alter it in any way?"

"I have no intention of changing anything I've said."

Art stood up, and grasped my hand again. James also stood up, coming forward to shake my hand with an unexpected force. The warmth of his brown hand sent an electrical current through me. "Thank you again," Art Leopold said. He looked at me with his sharp hazel eyes. I wondered what he was seeing. "I'd like to set a date to take down your story formally, and then I'll walk you downstairs."

I agreed to meet with him on the following Tuesday at five pm. Art Leopold ushered me out the door and walked with me to the stairs. I felt keyed up and excited. I was pleased the meeting had gone so well.

He descended the worn steps just behind me. "Miss DeMartino," he spoke in such a low voice that I stopped on the first floor landing until he was next to me. "I want to warn you that you must be very careful."

"Careful of what?" I asked.

"We have a source inside the Oakland Police Department who has proved reliable in the past," Leopold said. "He has indicated this case is complicated. If anyone has tried to set up my client, they will want to discredit your testimony. Which means they will want to discredit you."

"How could they do that?" I asked.

"I can't tell you that because I don't know. I can only repeat that this situation is serious, more serious, I suspect, than anything you have ever encountered. You shouldn't talk to anyone about this; you shouldn't go to places you don't usually go. You live with roommates, I take it?" I nodded.

"That's good," he said. "Keep people around you. Don't go places alone. Let your friends and family know where you are at all times. Only go places with people you know well and can trust."

"I don't get it," I said, stupidly. "I've already told my story." I didn't want to understand him. Everything he said sounded conspiratorial and insane.

"I'll feel better when we've made it public," he answered. "You'll have done your worst by then, and they'll have less reason to give you any trouble."

Why was he telling me all this outside James Ferguson's hearing? Standing on that darkened hall landing with one of the most celebrated trial lawyers on the left, I felt I had stepped into a plot I did not want to be part of.

"Are you worried about the Oakland Police Department?" I asked.

"We don't know who are the policemen nor who are the policemen's informants," he answered. "Remember that. An informant could be someone you know at the track, or a neighbor, or a member of the Black Panthers. Be careful. Call if you need help. Here's my home number, if you need it." He scribbled a number on the back of a business card and handed it to me.

He walked me down the remaining flight of stairs to the ground floor. I noticed he watched me for a while as I walked away from the building.

My father had worked with an engineer who had emigrated from the Soviet Union in the early sixties. He had told my father that in Russia he had lived, as everyone lived, surrounded by spies and informers. But, he said, there was this to be said for it. We always knew who the spies were. Not like your country, where the spies are invisible.

VI

I rode back to Berkeley on the F bus. My hand shook handing my bus ticket to the driver. I transferred to the wrong bus after I got off the F and landed in downtown Oakland. I had to transfer back to a Berkeley bus. I rationalized these moves would confuse anyone following me, but I was rattled. I scanned other bus riders. Were any of them following me? Everyone looked intent on their newspapers and their own lives. I had read about people who lived under conditions of constant fear: revolutionaries in South America, resistance fighters in World War II. I had assumed a worthy cause made fear manageable. My newfound cause, although worthy, did not mitigate this embarrassing anxiety. I could not live like this indefinitely. I hoped that it would all be over the following Tuesday, when I officially gave my story to Art Leopold.

When I got home, it was late afternoon. Yoshi was lying on the couch, smoking a Marlboro, listening to Simon and Garfunkel on the record player. Yoshi was two years younger than me and no taller. He was like a younger brother.

Simon and Garfunkel were singing. A time of innocence. A time of confidences. The song conveyed sorrow for a time now lost. The song made me think of Grace. Her beauty, her confidences, now obliterated. I could hear Paul in the kitchen. He emerged with a big bowl filled with popcorn and took a seat next to Yoshi, the bowl in his lap. Paul wanted details of my visit to Art Leopold's office. He threw a handful of popcorn into his mouth.

"What's your impression of Leopold?" he asked. "He's taken on several cases for the Panthers and managed to win some of them. That in itself is amazing. There are people who think he's their dupe. Not me. I respect what he's done."

"Why do they call him a dupe?" I asked.

"Maybe the Panthers did some of the things they were charged with," Paul answered. "I say, maybe they had to! You know what Chairman Mao said, you can't have an omelet without breaking eggs."

"Chairman Mao said nothing of the kind," Yoshi interrupted. "He said the revolution isn't a tea party." Yoshi exhaled a long leisurely smoke ring which drifted its way toward the ceiling.

"Dinner party," Paul corrected. "Maybe Stalin made the statement about breaking eggs." He tossed back another handful of popcorn. "But Leopold and Ferguson struck it rich with Leah. Hadn't been for Leah, Ferguson would still be staring at the inside of a jail cell." Paul wiped his mouth with the back of his hand. "What do you think, Leah, is he innocent?"

I didn't have the slightest idea. I had seen Grace leave Eli's Mile High Club with a handsome black man. I saw her an hour or so later; she was bruised and shaken. But alive, most definitely alive. And Grace Neville sat on the sofa bed in my room and described James Ferguson as a loyal friend. "I would walk off a cliff for that man." Possibly James Ferguson had hit Grace Neville that night. But why hadn't Grace spoken about it?

It was Joey who made me question Ferguson's guilt. When we were children, I could always tell when Joey was lying. He would start talking so fast I could barely understand him. Joey's rapid-fire way of talking about the case made me nervous. I knew he must be concealing something, but I wasn't ready to share that with Paul or Yoshi. I wasn't ready for them to know too much about my relationship with Joey. "I don't know what I think," I said. "All I know is the police had the time of her death wrong. It seems suspicious."

"It's a hell of a story. I bet Ramparts would just snap it up." Paul said.

I sat forward. "So what's the story?" I asked.

"What happened to Grace. What she told you. How OPD got it wrong—on purpose, seems like."

"You're the journalism major," Yoshi said. "Why don't you write it, Leah?"

I looked at Yoshi, then Paul, then back to Yoshi. I was excited. All my life I had confided my confusions in a diary. I hadn't had a moment to write in my diary since my trip to OPD the evening before. I had wanted to go upstairs to recount the events of the last twenty four hours. Now Yoshi and Paul had suggested another way to structure my outpourings. An article could help focus my fear.

My mind raced ahead. This would demand the attention of my journalism professors. I saw myself at twenty three, a published author, regarded as an up-and-coming writer. Of course there were the people who could be impacted by my story. James Ferguson. My cousin Joey. There was also Grace. Would I be exploiting her confidences, her death, for my own purposes? "I'd need help for some parts. Like the history of the Panthers. Paul, would you help me with that? Yoshi can help me research the parts about Grace."

Yoshi squashed out his cigarette and now he sat up on the couch. "What parts about Grace?"

"There's a lot I don't know about Grace's family and her background. Her other boyfriends. Maybe we could come up with some other suspects."

"Are you crazy?" Yoshi said, but I sensed a spark of interest. I was Yoshi's guide in the amazing adventure of America. He was usually ready to follow my lead. What had Joey told me? Murders were usually committed by boyfriends or hit men. We could check out boyfriends. Hit men might be harder. In fact Joey had even offered to pay me to listen for information at the track, although I wasn't about to tell that to Paul and Yoshi.

"I am going to Grace's funeral tomorrow," I said to Yoshi. "Come with me. Maybe we can talk to a few people who knew Grace. We might find out stuff that way."

"The things I follow you into," said Yoshi, dubiously. But he looked happy.

VII

"Those who sow the wind shall reap the whirlwind!" cried the slack-jowled man in the minister's pulpit.

The people in the pews murmured, "Amen!"

Yoshi and I had arrived late to the funeral service at this nondescript church in Concord and had been directed to a pew on the balcony. We sat there in the front seats, looking down at the group below us. Our plan was to introduce ourselves to Grace's family after the service and get ourselves invited to the wake, if there was to be one, afterwards. Our only company in the balcony was a young man in a fawn-colored suit, who sat a few rows behind us. I looked at Yoshi.

The red-faced man in the pulpit paused for breath. "Walk in the way of the world, and the world—will—destroy you!" he thundered. The audience murmured its submission. "All that the world offers will cost you your soul!"

"That makes me feel a lot better," Yoshi muttered. I was afraid he would be heard. But we were alone up there in the balcony, except for the young man who seemed preoccupied with his own thoughts.

"Only one can save us from the pitfalls of this world," the man continued, waving his fist in the air, then opening it to point a thick finger at the congregation. "And you, you, my brothers and sisters, must let Him in. Come to Him and be saved, as we pray that Grace was saved." With this admonition, he ended his service. People began standing up and filing out.

I sat in the balcony for a few minutes, watching people below me as they left their seats. I thought of the Grace I had known: joking, irreverent, flaunting all the qualities this minister warned against. Death was hard enough on a family, I thought. Murder must be impossible to accept. I supposed the minister was trying to give some meaning to terrifying events. Nevertheless, the service irritated me. As I followed Yoshi out of the pew, my eyes fell again on the young man behind us. He remained sitting, looking fixedly ahead with a small smile on his face, as if he too found the words of the minister ludicrous.

Downstairs in the vestibule of the church, a small line had formed. Grace's family was greeting the guests. I followed a tall young man with a shock of light brown hair. A stout woman grabbed his hand. "Ronnie!" she cried. "It's been too long!"

"It's been a long time, Millie." He spoke with a faint country twang.

The woman clung to his hand as if gripping a lifeline. "It takes me back. Just to see you, it takes me back, it does."

"I'm sorry this had to be the occasion," he said.

"I don't pretend Grace and I didn't have our differences," said the stout woman. "Still it's hard."

"I know Grace was grateful when you took her in," said the young man.

"You're coming over to my place?"

"You still over on Valley Street?"

"Same place," said the woman. "Helene and I put together a little spread."

"I'll be there," he promised, and moved on.

The woman turned to me. Her look was not friendly.

"I'm so sorry about your loss," I said.

"The Lord giveth, and the Lord taketh away," she answered.

"I knew Grace from the track, Mrs. Neville. I'm Leah DeMartino."

"I'm not Mrs. Neville. My sister, Helene, is Grace's mother." With these words she passed me on to a woman standing next to her.

The woman's hair was back-combed and teased into a blonde beehive; her eyes outlined in black eyeliner that was beginning to streak. Her eyebrows had been plucked to a fine line. Yet it was clear Grace had inherited her beauty from her mother.

"I was a friend of your daughter's, Mrs. Neville," I said. "I'm so sorry about this."

She stared at me. "How did you know Grace?" she asked.

"We had friends in common," I said. I didn't mention the track again. She passed me along quickly to the man beside her.

"My husband, Bud Kemp," she said. "Grace's step-dad."

Bud Kemp was wearing a Stetson hat and a black shirt, a kerchief tied rakishly around his neck. His belly hung out over his belt buckle; his pants rode low on his hips. He ignored the hand I extended. He barely looked at me, exuding an air of insolence.

56

Although I felt chagrined at the way I was being dismissed, I was not going to leave without getting more information about Grace. I struck out after the young man I had heard addressed as Ronnie. Grace had mentioned an old boyfriend by the same name. Ronald Xavier Jones. I reached him as he was descending the church steps.

"Excuse me," I said. "Are you Grace's high school friend, Ronnie?"

"Sure enough!" he said. "How'd you know that?"

"Grace talked about you."

"No kidding?" he said. He was tall, rangy, confident, with a runner's long-limbed frame. His face was bony in an attractive way, his green eyes spaced wide apart and twinkling with lively energy. I pegged Ronnie as one of the lucky ones, good-looking and easy-going, not given to agonizing introspection. "What did she say about me?"

"You were important to her," I said. "She still thought about you."

His smile was big and infectious. "Not bad for a high school romance. What else she say about me?"

"Oh, you know, girl talk," I said. "You seemed to mean a lot to her."

"You were close friends then?"

"We hung out together," I said. "I worked at the track."

"You coming over to the reception?"

"I wasn't invited. I'm not part of the family," I said.

"Don't worry about that," he said. "This is for Grace, not for them. You can come as my guest."

I gestured toward Yoshi, standing on the sidewalk. "I brought my friend with me."

His glance followed my hand. "Where is your friend from?"

"He's Japanese," I said.

"Japan." He smiled. "I spent some time there on my way back from Nam. Hey, just bring him along. The two of you can follow me in your car." He pointed to a Chevy pick-up up the block. "That's my truck. What are you driving?" This Ronnie had undeniable charm; earnest and unpretentious, like a farm boy down from the hills.

"Oh, I have a VW Beetle. I'll follow you," I said.

Yoshi and I followed Ronnie's pick-up out Monument Boulevard to Clayton Road. The distant hills were scorched and shrubby and treeless, backlit by a glassy sky. Millie's house sat on a cul-de-sac, a red brick ranch-style tract home built in the 1950s. An American flag flapped in the light wind, hung from a pole attached to the front porch. Someone had left a plastic cooler there on the front porch; three chairs with green-and-white plastic webbing; a rusted bar-beque sat under a palm tree whose dead fronds drooped miserably. As I looked around, I saw a ginger cat slink out from under the porch. It turned its face to me, staring at me with pure hostility.

I entered the house with Yoshi. The living room floor was covered with wall-to-wall carpeting. Hanging above the television was a picture of Je-sus with blue eyes and light brown hair. A series of concentric halos radiated out from his head like the rings of Saturn. Without anyone's realizing it, the television had become the de facto altar. Its rabbit ears formed a V, one of its wands just grazing Jesus's enigmatic smile. People stood around talking. In the dining room a small buffet had been laid out. It struck me again how out of place Grace would have been at her own funeral.

Ronnie found me eating tunafish salad on a paper plate. "Come with me," he said, putting his hand on my arm. "I want to show you something." He led me down a hall toward a tiny bedroom with a window opening onto a side yard. The bed was covered with a blue chenille bedspread. There was a book-case filled with Reader's Digest Condensed Books. A small wooden chair sat next to the bookcase. "Grace's bedroom," Ronnie said. "More than ten years ago."

"Where was Grace's mother?"

"Where wasn't Grace's mother?" Ronnie laughed. "Helene had no time for Grace. She dumped her off on Millie while she earned her keep."

"Singing?" I asked.

"That, too," Ronnie said, "She liked men, Helene did, and they liked her."

"She's pretty, "I said. "Something like Grace."

"Yeah, Helene isn't bad. Kinda blurry around the edges now." Ronnie was leaning over the bookcase, looking for something, but talking to me as he searched. "Millie raised Grace. She was strict, but Grace outsmarted her every time. I spent some blissful nights in that little bed, let me tell you." His long nervous fingers flicked through the volumes. "I pulled a lot of stunts in my day.

When I was seventeen, I dressed up in a priest's collar and robes. I told Grace I would take her confession." He laughed. "You can imagine what that was like." He grabbed a book and began leafing through it. "Okay, our old high school yearbook. Clayton Valley High School, class of 1962. Take a look."

Ronnie had opened a page with the banner, Senior Ball. He pushed the book toward me. "Here's Grace's best friend. Betsy Boyle. She's a Puckett now." He pointed to a photo of a stocky blonde whose ample bosom threatened to overflow her prom gown. Another snapshot showed a young Grace standing next to a tall boy with a lop-sided grin. The caption read: "Grace Neville and Ronald Xavier Jones exchange a joke at the Senior Ball."

"That's me," he said, taking the book back. "Me before Nam. Almost didn't know me, did you? Hey, your boyfriend won't mind?" He closed the yearbook. "You and me in here, talking and all?"

"He's a friend," I said.

"I acted odd when you pointed him out." Ronnie talked as if he were resuming a former discussion we had been having. "I was feeling competitive. When I see a woman I like, I want all her attention." Now he moved on to another thought. "I don't have any bad feeling about them, you know. At least, not all of them."

"Them?" I was baffled. He was jumping from topic to topic as if I could follow him.

"Orientals," said Ronnie. "If they look like Viet Cong, I get this weird sensation. I still can't eat in a Chinese restaurant."

I changed the subject. "Any more photos of you and Grace?"

"Nah," he said, "but I have some around somewhere. Some letters she wrote me in Nam." He took a card out of his pocket and scribbled a number on the back. "What's your number? I'll give you a call, we can talk about Grace." I gave him the telephone number at Russell Street. "Her family doesn't know her. Her aunt Millie especially. Millie always thought Grace was headed down the road her mother took. The road to perdition. Now this proves it," he said.

"Millie seems a bit—" I searched for a word which would not be too insulting. "—conventional."

"She looked at Grace and me as two bad apples who would ruin the bushel. We were rebels. We were always looking for ways to kick up dust."

"She seems to like you a lot now," I said, remembering the hand grip.

"I proved myself," he said. "Went to Nam. I didn't like what I saw over there. Joined Vietnam Vets against the War when I got back. According to Helene and Millie, I'm all mixed up. But the fact that I went, that's enough for them. I'm family to them now." He gave me a long look. Ronnie's green eyes were set deep in his face. Sometimes they sparkled, but at this moment I could not read them. He seemed to be a country boy, but his eyes hinted at other complexities.

"You're one of these liberated women, Leah," he said. "Bet you're one of those Berkeley antiwar types. I'm not sure you could understand. Way Helene and Millie see it, I came back to them. Grace never did." Ronnie stood up. He had broad shoulders, long legs, moved with an athletic grace. "Well, we better go join the others."

I followed him back into the living room. Yoshi came up to me and steered me toward the dining room. "I want you to meet Becky Puckett," he said, "Grace's pal from high school." Becky had become a sturdy woman in a tight-fitting sleeveless sheath with plump, freckled upper arms. Her small hands held a plate of potato salad, ham, biscuits, pie, and ice cream. She was busily moving the refreshments into her mouth.

"Leah, this is Becky Puckett," Yoshi said. "Leah knew Grace from the track." With this note of explanation, Yoshi had disappeared into the kitchen. Perhaps he had been trying to get away. Becky Puckett's eyes darted around the room as if searching for an escape herself, then looked back at me, resigning herself to my company.

"You know Grace long?" she asked.

"Just this summer, but I admired her," I answered. "So you were friends in high school. What was she like then?"

"We did some dumb things. Smoked up a storm. Got tattoos. We were wild." Becky and Grace must have been sweater girls in high school, girls whose bodies and breasts developed early. Now Becky was just a heavy young woman in a black dress that was too tight. There was a hard look on her sun-weathered face.

"Yeah," she said. "I got a tattoo above my knee. Got infected and hurt like hell. My husband finally made me get rid of it." Freddie Corster had said that Grace had a tattoo on her knee.

"Is your husband here?" I asked.

"Carl's a trucker. On the road a lot."

"Did he know Grace?"

"Jeez, you ask a lot of questions. We all hung out together at Clayton Valley High, but I didn't start going with Carl until after graduation. It seems like a lifetime ago. Speaking of which, I need me a cigarette." No one had mentioned smoking. Although I sensed she wanted to get away from me, I followed her outside onto the front porch. She fished inside her dress pocket for a cigarette. "Millie never did allow smoking in her house," she said, "Just one more thing Grace found to drive her aunt Millie crazy."

"What else?"

"Everything about Grace drove Millie nuts." Becky said. "Cigarettes, drinking. But mainly boys. Grace had boys coming around from the time she was fourteen."

"Yes," I said, "Grace had charm."

"Charm, shit," Becky said, "Grace was like her Mom. Millie was sure Grace would end up like Helene, and that's just what happened. But now Helene's got religion, Millie's forgiven Helene for her old life singing in bars. Those two are thick as thieves—and now they both see Grace as the slut."

"Well, you hung around with Grace. Were you two sluts?" I was pushing the envelope, but I had to get something from this woman.

She glared at me, and took a long drag on her cigarette. "Come off it. I grew up. Got married. Got two little boys. With kids the problems never stop. Grace never really grew up. It was *always* just good times for her," said Becky. Her small mouth sucked on the cigarette. "I guess she got her payback."

"You remind me of her." I was pushing again.

She turned her head. "I remind you of Grace?"

"Are you surprised?"

She threw down her cigarette and stamped it out on the cement steps. "I'm as different from Grace Neville as night is from day. She changed a lot from the girl I used to know. I know I'm not supposed to say it at her funeral, but I don't much care for the person she became."

"It's all crazy," she said. "All of it. I hardly seen her in the last ten years. Now it seems like yesterday we stole those cigarettes. We skipped English class to smoke them." Becky sighed. "It's sad, isn't it?"

In the darkening afternoon, her features looked softer. She brushed at the corners of her eyes.

Something had gotten to Becky. I felt sad, too. I wasn't happy that I had tried to hurt her. I saw Ronnie coming through the door, and I turned back inside the house. Behind me I could hear them talking. "How *you* been, Ronald Xavier?" she was saying. Her voice sounded considerably brighter.

I decided to pay my respects to Grace's mother. Maybe I could arrange to meet with her. "Mrs. Neville," I said, going over to her, "I wanted to tell you how many times Grace spoke of you." I was stretching the truth.

"She did?" She looked at me with a vacant expression.

"Yes," I said. "You meant a great deal to her."

"That's odd," Grace's mother said.

Well, she had that right. At Vinnie's Inn I had the impression Grace felt contempt for her mother. Helene's eyes roamed the room as if she, like Becky, wanted to escape from me, but after a minute she returned my gaze. "It's my sister, Millie, who raised Grace. I woulda thought she'd talk about her aunt Millie."

"She never mentioned Millie to me," I said. "Only you. She loved your singing."

Helene's lips moved in a faint smile. "Well, don't mention this to Millie. Of the two of us, Millie's sure she was the better influence."

"Grace told me you live up near Clear Lake," I said. "I go up there often to visit some friends. I was wondering if I might stop in and talk to you more about Grace." The bit about the friends was a lie, but I remembered Paul Cohen had friends up in Middletown.

"Talk to me? Whatever for?" Her eyes roamed the room.

I pressed on. "I'm driving up there this Saturday to have dinner with them. Could I stop by and see you? I'm upset by what happened, it would help me to talk to you. And maybe it would be good for you, too. Talk to someone who knew her."

"Oh, I have Bud to talk to," she said. Her eyes darted around the room again, as if seeking him out. "Though he does go off Saturday afternoons, fishing or card playing. No soaps on Saturday. I guess you could come by."

I was glad to accept her invitation, no matter how reluctantly offered. I took her phone number, got directions, and told her I would see her Saturday afternoon.

"It might be better than sitting around with my own thoughts," she said almost to herself, as I moved away.

VIII

Paul was driving me up to Clear Lake in his white Econoline van. I would drop in on Helene while Paul visited friends—*progressive workers*—who lived up in Middletown. The day before I had called Beatrice at the track and extended my leave of absence for a second week. She wasn't happy, but I had a good record, and, grudgingly, she said I could take the time off.

It was a clear August day. The sky opened up big and clean in front of us as the van chugged up Highway 29. We passed out of the low-lying stretches near the bay and began climbing the upslope to St. Helena. Long poplar-lined driveways resembled the driveways of French estates. After St. Helena, the road meandered thorough sun-drenched trees, shallow creeks, the hills curved yellow and green. I felt soothed by the beauty of the terrain.

"Funny how people respond to loss," I said to Paul. "Grace's mother seems almost indifferent."

"You remind me of my revisionist colleagues." Paul often used political terms like that. "Idealists who believe in the noble worker. People are motivated by more prosaic needs. The mother may have been so glad to have a man in her bed, she forgot all about Grace."

"You remind *me* of my cousin Joey. He always looks for the worst in people—and he always finds it."

"I'll say this for coppers. They've seen their share of human nature. It can make them even sicker than they started out, and some of them start out pretty sick. What does Joey think about Ferguson?"

"That he's dangerous. What do you think?"

"Cops are paranoid. Only people more paranoid are leftists."

"Why would I be in any danger from him? My evidence got Ferguson out on bail."

"Maybe you have other evidence that could lock him right back up."

I had not mentioned the bruises on Grace's throat to my roommates. "Like what?"

"How would I know? But Joey knows what you told those detectives, and Joey's not dumb. For a cop."

"So what do you know about the Black Panthers?" I asked him.

"I'm gonna lay it on you. They started in West Oakland, October 1966. Huey Newton and Bobby Seale. They wanted to resist the brutality of the Oakland Police Department. Huey coined the expression *pigs* to describe the OPD. He saw them as an occupying army in the black community. He and Bobby Seale formed neighborhood patrols which followed the police to see how they treated black people they arrested. Those patrols scared the hell out of the cops. They also caused quite a stir in the black community. And with the California State legislature," Paul added, grinning.

"I remember seeing some of that on the evening news—all these black guys with guns."

"May 1967," said Paul. "The California State Assembly was meeting to talk about the Mulford Act, which would ban public displays of loaded firearms. At that point it was still legal. A group of thirty Panthers, headed by Bobby Seale, went to Sacramento to protest. They entered the assembly carrying their weapons. Stood and gave the Black Power salute. Panthers gained world-wide press coverage with that move. It was in the papers next day."

Joey had said the Panthers knew how to work the media.

"It was a risk," Paul continued, "but it worked. Afterward Panther membership exploded. Then a few months later, Newton shot and killed an Oakland cop, name of Officer Frey. Newton accused Frey of shooting and brutalizing black people. Newton was convicted of voluntary manslaughter. The radical left got involved and started a Free Huey campaign. He was released in 1970. While Huey was in jail, the Party set up chapters in thirty-eight cities. There were more confrontations with police. In April 1968 a seventeen-year-old kid, Bobby Hutton—the first member to join the Party—was shot dead by the Oakland police. Bobby was unarmed, but the police shot him ten times. Eldridge Cleaver was shot, too, but Eldridge lived."

"I never heard about this," I said.

"Probably because Martin Luther King had been assassinated two days earlier. *That* dominated the news."

That period was coming back to me. In April 1968 I was living in Ann Arbor with a crush on a radical sociology student who lived next door. I had canvassed door to door for Eugene McCarthy. Then the incredible news of King's death.

"I was in Michigan then," I said to Paul. "I remember the riots."

"All connected," Paul said. "King had begun to say he could not continue to advise young black people to stay non-violent, while their own government condoned violence in Vietnam. J. Edgar Hoover was afraid that the Panthers would start riots all over the United States after King's assassination. The Panther membership exploded again and they forged an alliance with white leftists. Huey Newton had a plan to hook up with the Peace and Freedom Party. And that didn't sit so well with the Black Nationalists. So that was one potential division right there. Right now the Panthers see themselves as an international organization tied to the revolutionary struggle all over the world. The Party has members from all backgrounds. Some of them are educated, really sharp, and committed. But most of the rank-and-file are lumpens."

"What are the lumpens?" I asked.

"The lumpens are the unemployables. The proletariat is America's employed working class. Black people aren't usually in unions. They haven't benefited from the reforms the white working class has enjoyed. They're still last hired, first fired. The Panthers see the lumpens—the residents of the black ghettoes—as the vanguard of the revolution. These folks are motivated to want change. Whites on the left still believe the proletariat will lead the revolution. This leads to ideological rifts with the Panthers. Marx referred to the lumpen proletariat as the scum of the earth. A lot of white lefties see the black ghettoes that way, whether they admit it or not."

Paul loved discussions of inevitable class struggle. I found them academic, but I was interested in the Panthers.

"The Panthers point to the Chinese revolution. That's why Huey makes the new recruits read Karl Marx and Mao's Little Red Book. He believes America's urban ghettoes are part of the third world. In China the peasants were the backbone of the revolution, even though the working class led it. But the US is not China. We're rushing toward a future based on automation and it will eliminate American industry as we know it now. As workers become unemployed, they will become lumpens, and the ground will become more fertile for revolution. The lumpens will cast off their chains and move mountains, as Huey Newton once said."

"Can the Black Panthers do all that?" I was dubious. "Huey Newton doesn't sound like a gang leader. He sounds more like one of your professors."

"Maybe yes, maybe no," Paul answered. "Some people think Huey is brilliant. He gave a three-day seminar at Yale with Eric Erickson. Like Orson Welles said about Macbeth, a gangster with a conscience."

"But still a gangster?"

"I've heard of shake downs, extortion—gang-type stuff. Let's face it, some think the Panthers are criminals."

"That's how Joey sees them," I said.

"It's hard to know how much of the bad stuff you hear about is really criminal activity, and how much is government propaganda. They've started a breakfast program. A school, a health clinic, a program to visit prisoners. At one point the Panthers were feeding ten thousand people across the country every day. Those kinds of successes make them dangerous and the government is cracking down on them."

"How?"

"The government trains undercover agents to join groups on the left and provoke violence."

"There's certainly been violence."

"Maybe too much. The Panthers are soldiers. They follow orders. But I don't see them as bothering to waste a white girl," Paul added.

"I hope not," I said. I wasn't reassured.

"You know, Leah," Paul added, "it all connects to Vietnam. Even Martin Luther King explained it that way. Did you ever hear King's speech at Riverside Church? Spring 1967?"

"I don't think so."

"It was powerful. King said he used to counsel young black males to seek change through nonviolence. But they came back at him—What about Vietnam? Wasn't the United States using violence to effect the changes *it* wanted in southeast Asia? In that speech, King says before he can counsel the young blacks to seek a nonviolent path, first he has to speak out against the greatest purveyor of violence in the world—the United States government."

"Martin Luther King said that?" I said. "For a man who won the Nobel Peace Prize, he sounds almost radical. I thought he believed in working *with* the government. I thought he was different from Malcolm X. Revolution by

67

any means necessary. You're making King sound a lot more like Malcolm X. Closer to the Panthers."

"Martin Luther King, Malcolm X—they're both dead," Paul replied. "That's how much the government liked either one of them."

It was a lot to think about. We were high in the hills, the road twisty, with sheer drop-offs, then suddenly at the summit, winding our way down toward Lower Lake, with forest on either side of the road forming a green canopy overhead. When the road widened for a space, Paul pulled over to let six cars behind him pass. The country had turned to chaparral, grasslands with occasional oaks, more exposed rock, fields marked off with the long chalk-white rails of horse farms. A hot, dry wind blew through our rolled-down windows.

We passed Middletown, but Paul drove on. Helene lived out closer to Lower Lake, and Paul would head back to his friends after he dropped me off. Just before Lower Lake, Paul pulled in at the Lollipop Motor Home Resort. Fifteen trailers were lined in five rows of three trailers each. Paul turned down a row marked Peppermint Lane and stopped at number twelve. A plastic pinwheel clacked furiously in the breeze.

"I'll wait," Paul said, "If she's there, give a wave, and I'll come back around two."

Helene came to the door on my first knock. I turned and waved to Paul. The van made a scrunching sound on the gravel as Paul drove off.

"You're right on time, Leah," Helene said. She had pulled her blonde hair back, her blue eyes signposts of life in an otherwise deserted face. "This ain't much, but it's home." The stale haze of cigarette smoke hung in the air. She gestured toward a minuscule kitchen on the right. "Care for a beer?"

"A glass of water would be fine," I said. She handed me water from the tap and popped a Budweiser for herself. Next to the sink was a paper bag filled with empty beer cans. She motioned me to a seat at the tiny built-in table.

"I feel terrible about Grace," I began.

"Millie used to say that a wild start ends in dead stop. Guess she saw something I didn't."

I was struck by her bitter tone. "Grace was wild?"

"Born wild. I can see her now, face all dirty and full of tears." Helene's blue eyes looked unfocussed, as if remembering a distant past.

68

"Neighbor dragged her home. Found her in their garage. Little boys paid her a dime to touch her privates."

"How old was she?"

"Musta been six. I handed her over to Millie after that. I was on the road a lot. I let her come back and stay with me sometimes. Split her time between my place and Millie's—she was at Millie's for school, though. Millie was a lot stricter than me. She used to slap Grace silly. Spare the rod, spoil the child. Millie said I was too easy on her."

"Were you?"

"Couldn't raise a hand to her, myself," she said. Her eyes remained unfocussed, staring at her beer. "Millie always said Grace would end up bad. I can still see her, mouth all streaked with lipstick, giggling out there on the back porch. Boys gave her things. Rings, T-shirts, stuff like that. More fool me, I believed she was getting that stuff for free."

"So Millie raised Grace?"

"She helped me out. When I was on the road. Any time Grace got in trouble, Millie blamed it on me, so I musta been doing some of the raising. Late nights and singing in those clubs—Millie didn't like that. But I was just out looking for a Daddy to keep me and Grace together."

"Did you find one?"

"It took a while. Grace was twelve by the time I found Bud. "

Helene's stories disturbed me. I glanced around the kitchen. A television was placed on a rickety stand, and on it was a framed photograph of Bud, posed before an enormous American flag. A second photo showed a younger Helene, blonde hair tossed over her shoulder, lips in a pout. She saw me looking at it.

"I had a lot of admirers. But I had limits. I never went with Negros."

The word hung there in space. Students were using the word black.

"I was desperate enough, God knows, days when I didn't have enough money for a pair of stockings. Working in the clubs, like I did, I met all types. But I could never bring myself to mix."

"Mix?" I repeated, like a moron.

"It's against God's laws. One species of birds never mates with another." She lifted her head up, as if daring me to refute this bit of scientific

69

wisdom. I marveled at how rapidly she had become clear. This topic seemed to have rallied her diminished energies.

I tried a protest. "Maybe all humans come from the same species. We can have babies together, after all."

She looked at me in disbelief. "Those who try to mix—have mixed babies—those people reap what they sow." Those were the words of the pastor at Grace's funeral. Helene looked at me with defiance.

"You think Grace's murder was a punishment from God?"

Now her eyes faltered and she looked away. "Not exactly that, no," she said. "Just that God moves in mysterious ways." I could see her twisted logic. Grace chose the worldly life. She had chosen to *mix* with the wrong species. To Helene, her death at the hands of her black lover was a grisly kind of justice.

I needed to take a break from this. "Could I use the bathroom?" Helene motioned toward a tiny space between the kitchen and the living room. A shoe caddy hung on the bathroom door held dozens of women's shoes— stiletto heels, gold thong sandals, patent leather pumps. Perfume bottles and face creams were arrayed on a glass-and-metal rack above the toilet. It was evident Grace and Helene shared a fascination with the accoutrements of femininity. I splashed cold water on my face, drying it with a starched embroidered tea towel. Helene must have put that out, expecting me.

"Grace told me how she used to fall asleep summer nights, listening to you sing as you did the dinner dishes. She said she'd drift off to sleep, feeling safe because her mother was home," I said as I walked back into the kitchen.

Helene had been smoking, her head back, face to the ceiling, but now her face changed, making strange movements, as if she were crying, and she didn't know how. She dabbed at the corner of her eyes with a Kleenex. "Why couldn't she have accepted God and been saved? You see how it all turned out."

"Did you talk to her much this summer?"

"No. She sent me a birthday card, with some money in it." She blew her nose with the Kleenex. "She wrote me a little note, how I should be happy now. How her boyfriend was the right color, this time—just not the right age. I was nervous about the money. Police had come round to ask me about Grace in the past. When she was with that Black Panther. Now they say he's the one who did it."

"He didn't kill her, Helene."

"How do you know that?" She looked at me suspiciously.

"I'm working with the police." I wondered if I should have said that. I changed the subject. "When was the last time you saw her?"

"It musta been six months ago at least. She dropped off her teen-age diary for me to keep. She was always scribbling."

"Could I see it?"

"You can have it. I can't stand to look at it." She stood up slowly and walked to a built-in drawer, pulled out a brown notebook. "Don't know what good it'll do you," she said, "but since you're so damn interested, take it. You seem to be the only woman friend Grace had."

My instincts warned me not to act too interested. Paul wouldn't be back for a while. I had to keep her talking. "How did Grace and Bud get along?"

"They were okay with each other. Hardly spent any time together." Helene's face brightened as her memories took a different turn. "Bud lets me stay here rent free. I was lucky to get him." I looked around at the trailer with its imitation knotty pine wood paneling, the kitschy objects. Could Helene be grateful for so little?

"It's nice," I said insincerely. "You've fixed it up."

"Bud brought me home to God. You'll find when you get older, you'll want to go back."

I hoped not.

A car pulled up outside. Helene stood up. "It's Bud! He's back early. Musta wondered what we were up to." A car door slammed shut, and Bud Kemp stomped into the trailer, throwing his hat down on the little table. He was missing a molar on the left side of his face. He looked at me in an unfriendly way. For a man of medium height, he filled up the tiny space.

"What's she doin' here?"

"Leah's working with the police," Helene said. She was standing at the kitchen counter opening a can of tuna. "Helping them find out who murdered Grace."

"Police found their man," Bud said. He dropped heavily onto the bench of the built-in table and reached for a cigarette from a pack in his shirt pocket.

"They made a mistake." I tried to sound firm, but my voice wavered.

71

"Cops don't make mistakes," Bud said. He looked at me with hard, bright eyes. "Seems strange they would ask a girl like you to help them out."

I rushed ahead without thinking. "I was with Grace the Saturday evening they said she had been killed."

"That so?" he said, slowly. "What we knew, we told the police. They're the experts, far as we're concerned." His eyes bored into mine. I was holding Grace's notebook in my lap, forcing myself not to look down at it, lest it attract his attention.

"Don't mind Bud," Helene said. "He's a man's man. He and those cops get on like a house afire."

"Yeah, the cops and me—we understand each other," said Bud, speaking slowly. "But we sure don't understand anything about Grace. That girl lived a life like the devil's own."

Helene was setting food on the little table—tuna sandwiches, beer, a German chocolate cake in its aluminum foil container. "I have a *very even* temper," Bud Kemp said, to no one in particular. "I'm mad *all the time*."

"Bud's grouchy because he's hungry," Helene said. "To think that when I first met him, he said I couldn't cook!"

"You couldn't," he insisted. "I had to show you."

"Sure I could," she said. Her laugh was coquettish. "I just wanted to save some surprises for later!"

"Plenty of those," he said.

"Now he wants me to lose weight," she said to me. "I try to tell him, he can't have it both ways!"

The Helene-and-Bud show. No doubt they had been performing it for years, exaggerated now for my benefit, performing with renewed zest before a different audience. They were grotesque and touching. Bud ate two sandwiches, gulped down a beer, consumed half the tin of cake. Then he unfastened his belt. He did not address any further remarks to me.

A scrunching sound on the driveway announced a second car. "Oh, that must be Paul," I said. "Don't get up. I'll just go. Thank you for everything. Helene, I'm so sorry about Grace."

"I'll walk you to the door," said Helene. "It's not that far!" As I stepped out, she reached into her pocket of her house dress and handed me a folded paper. "Good bye, Leah!" she called in a bright, girlish voice. "We'll have to do this again!" It seemed forced. She was looking me in the eyes. She seemed to be giving me a message I couldn't read.

I hurried down the steps to Paul's waiting Econoline van. "Let's go," I said. I was holding Grace's notebook and the folded-over sheet of paper. I placed the paper inside the front cover and put both in my shoulder bag. Helene had given me at least this much of the Grace she had known.

"Not exactly compañeros?" Paul asked. He circled the van back onto the highway.

"They wouldn't understand that kind of language. "Not that I totally understand it either."

"Compañeros. Workers. United in the struggle. Allende in Chile uses it a lot. Now there's a government worth something. Though if Nixon gets re-elected, I don't know how long Allende will last."

We were sailing down the highway now, into Lake, then Napa Counties. Red and yellow leaves fluttered gently in the late afternoon sun. Paul had bought a bag of apples in Middletown and their fragrance filled the van. I picked up an apple and rubbed it on my jacket as Paul drove us back down into the lowlands of the Bay Area.

"So what do *you* think of Nixon?" Paul asked me.

"Would you buy a used car from this man? That's what my father always said. Joey's father got so angry when Dad said that. He loved Nixon. It's funny, Joey hates his father, but he's got the same politics. Probably Grace's parents do, too. I grew up with people like them. I may be more like them than they know."

"Yeah," Paul said, "but you escaped, and they sense it. They think you've got an out with your education."

I thought about the room I rented for a hundred dollars a month, the communal meals I shared with Paul, Yoshi, and Carol. Most students lived like that in Berkeley. It was a way to make the rent, and then there was the camaraderie. "I don't know how far I'll escape with a degree in journalism, even if we do publish this article."

"It's not just economics," Paul said. "You want to get away from the dreams of the American working class. It's the most reactionary working class in the world."

Paul's vocabulary warned me he was about to embark on one of his socialist lectures. But there was something else I was trying to explore. "Isn't it odd?" I asked. "Grace was Helene's daughter. And yet I get the feeling Helene doesn't seem to care."

"Maybe she does care," Paul said, "Maybe the only way she can deal with what happened is to pretend Grace deserved it. Grief does funny things to people. Guilt too."

"You think Helene feels guilty about the way she treated Grace when Bud came along?"

"Didn't she abandon Grace when the kid was six? All that religious talk you just mentioned. That kind of life is steeped in guilt. Maybe Helene thinks she somehow contributed to Grace's death. Anyway, you may be asked to testify. Don't you think you should get in touch with Art Leopold again?"

"I'm seeing him Tuesday at five," I said, "That's soon enough."

"Better not wait," Paul said. "You need to know more about what you've gotten into. Remember I said there were tensions between the Black Panther Party and the Black Nationalists? I talked about that on the way up here."

"How could I forget, Paul? When you get started on a topic, there's no stopping you."

"Two Black Panthers leaders headed up the Los Angeles chapter. Bunchy Carter and John Huggins. The LA Panthers members were rivals of a Black Nationalist group called US founded by Ron Karenga. In 1969 the Panthers and the US group supported different candidates to head the Afro-America Studies Center at UCLA. Carter and Huggins got into an argument with the US members—next thing you know, they were shot to death. Panthers insisted it was a planned assassination, but US always maintained it was a spontaneous event."

"Perhaps it was a shoot-out between rival organizations," I said quickly. I wanted to head off one of Paul's left-wing paranoid rants.

"John Huggins was shot in the back. That's murder, Leah. The Los Angeles police raided a Black Panther apartment and arrested seventy-five members and charged *them* with conspiracy to murder the 'US' members in retaliation. Sure sounds to me like US was being used."

74

"Used how?"

"Used by the FBI to target the Panthers. Not long after, some of the 'US' guys killed two Black Panthers and wounded another one."

"Paul, let's continue this discussion another time. I already have plenty to think about."

"I just want you to understand what you're dealing with," Paul answered. He reached over and gave me a reassuring pat on the hand.

I thought about Joey: his advice that I find myself a lawyer, his suggestion that I snoop around at the track. I had not told Paul nor Yoshi about this. Whose side was I on? It was clear to me that whichever side I chose, the decision could be deadly.

Back at Russell Street I went up to my room. Taking a deep breath, I sat down on the bed and opened the notebook. I felt excited. I thought I might find Grace's life laid out for me there.

The folded paper that Helene had slipped me turned out to be the autopsy report. I looked at it quickly. The wording was technical—words like lividity, contusions, stomach contents, rigor mortis. Grace had tested negative for drugs. She hadn't been sexually molested. There was no water in her lungs. She had two bullet holes in her head. I folded the paper and put it back in the notebook. Maybe Paul or Yoshi could find a medical student to help me understand the report.

The notebook was not what I expected. The entry dates meant Grace had begun this journal as a teenager. The first pages were haphazard notes in a childish scrawl, full of misspellings. Cartoons appeared from time to time; then the cartoons developed into caricatures of girls, cartoon beauties like Betty and Veronica from the Archie comics. I realized these were cartoon impressions of Grace and her friends. Grace had drawn clothes on her figures: a full skirt paired with a black leotard, or an identical skirt with a jacket, and notes, "red pin, blue earrings—be sure to check out the view from behind." I hadn't had that awareness of my appearance and its impact on men when I was fifteen. I didn't have it even now.

Most of the drawings were teen-age girls, although a few were grown women who looked like Grace's mother. Cartoons followed her developing figure with some exaggeration. Breasts enlarged, waists nipped in, and lips were outlined with Betty Bow precision. Awareness of boys was ever-present:

> I could die! Just DIE! He asked Karen out! But Greg told Bob
> the day he talked to me in the hall was the happiest day in his life.

Pages were dated sporadically, and cartoon figures intruded, along with homework assignments, short notes. The handwriting was smaller. The diary entries which began in February 1959 caught my attention:

> February 1959: Walking to study hall. I had washed my hair, rinsed it with lemon juice (Momma told me to do that, dimwit Millie says use vinegar—how would that SMELL??) I was wearing my yellow jumper (I used the money Bud gave me to get it.) "You're like a sunburst, Grace," Ronnie told me

> March 1959: Broken open into wonder that summer afternoon. I was fourteen. It was hot, miserably hot, and I felt restless. Always restless then, bored, and nothing much to do. Wearing a thin cotton dress, light green, Bud said it matched my eyes. My eyes are blue, not green, but it was a nice thing to say, I guess. The windows were all open, and outside a real loud sound of road equipment, or steam shovels or something, repairing the roads. Why was he up in my room? I didn't really know.

> We were just fooling around. Next thing I know my panties were off, he was pressing up against me. I didn't really know how it all worked. I didn't think anything could happen, I was too small. But he pushed and he pushed and he pushed and it hurt like hell and I started to yell and he put his hand over my mouth. I guess he was afraid someone would hear us but no one could with all that noise outside. He did one big strong push and I guess that was it, something had broken, and I bled and he stopped.

> And he had a stupid grin on his face, all satisfied with himself like he had really accomplished something and he kind of sneered, How do you feel now? I said "Not very good." He brought me a towel to wipe myself off with and then he left. I went upstairs and got hot and cold chills and was sick until Momma came home. Then I just pretended I was sleeping. Bud was Momma's friend and she might get mad. I never knew if Momma knew. I came downstairs next day, and I was wearing a summer dress

76

with little pink daisies, and I walked different. And I felt armed
with a new kind of power: I was a woman now.

I stopped, horrified. Was this why Grace had given her mother the diary? And had Helene read it? I flipped through months of entries, finally arriving at this one.

April 1960: Told Ronnie what had happened with Bud. He was real mad for me. "That scumbag!" Mad at Momma too. Becky said: "Those eyes of his are wild eyes, Grace!" Like the guy sings in West Side story, I feel like something's coming, it's on its way. My life is beginning. Ronnie is the beginning of my life.

May 1962: Ronnie steals cigarettes from the corner grocery and then steals kisses from me—hot smoky breath and I'm so turned on. We went out in the woods yesterday behind the barn. I was wearing one of Momma's old perfumes—Tabu. I put it on my wrists and neck and ankles and the scent is still over me. Every time I breathe it in I remember yesterday afternoon and Ronnie's smoky breath and the feel of the grass on my legs. "My first real sex," I told him, he said, "Real, how?" and I said, "Real, with love, you know." He got mad at Bud all over again and called him scum and I felt protected, even though it was years ago. I wish Ronnie had been there then.

June 1962: Millie got hold of this notebook, snooping in my drawers. She hit me again, says as long as I live under her roof, I'll do as she says. She's always shouting these crazy lines from the Bible, only she says them wrong. I have to stop myself from laughing, cause it would make her worse. Harlots—she calls them harlettes, like starlets. I can't wait to get away from her.

Graduation night, Ronnie almost didn't make it. Up all night until the sun rose, harsh and bright. But my head ached so bad. Remembered Ronnie in his white suit and red flower dancing with Becky. She likes him. She thinks I don't notice.

June 1962:   Always the girl who falls in love too quickly;
                Always the girl who falls out of love too fast.

That was the end of the journal. Had Grace's mother read this notebook? Why had Grace given the notebook to her mother? Did she want her mother to read about her first sexual experience with Bud, her mother's boyfriend? It sounded like a rape. But why had Helene given it to me? and the autopsy report.

Grace's mother had also given me that. Maybe Helene did want me to learn something more about Grace's murder.

Now I knew more about Ronnie. This information could help me get Ronnie talking.

IX

I was not surprised when I got a call at noon on Monday. A black woman's voice on the other end. Brusque, with a slight Brooklyn accent. "James Ferguson wants to meet with you," she said. "Vinnie's Inn. This afternoon at three."

"But I thought tomorrow, on Tuesday—" I would be seeing Art Leopold tomorrow for the deposition. It was odd that James Ferguson wanted to see me before that.

"This afternoon," she said. "Vinnie's Inn. Know where that is? East Oakland? Come by yourself; take a seat at a back table." She hung up.

Neither Paul nor Yoshi were home, and I did not know when they would be. She had said to come alone. And I wanted to speak to James Ferguson alone. I wanted to hear his side of the story without Art Leopold listening to every word. As a compromise, I would leave a note for Paul and Yoshi, telling them where I was going. I would ask them to come look for me if I hadn't returned by five.

At three pm I parked my VW in front of Akinji's Fine Gents and Ladies Fashions. Coming toward me was a black man, wearing a white silk suit and carrying a bouquet of red carnations. He did not meet my eyes.

I crossed the street and pushed open the door. The smell of beer and cigarette smoke hit me right away. A large, bald-headed man smiled at me from behind the counter. I remembered him from my previous visit in July, with Grace. Was this man Vinnie himself? A couple other men sat on stools at the bar, talking to each other. They looked at me. James was not among them.

I nodded at Vinnie, making my way over to a table in back, as I had been instructed. I tried to act nonchalant.

One of the men at the bar detached himself and came over to speak to me. He was mahogany colored, with big eyes, and an easy, rolling walk. A gold tooth flashed in his big smile.

"Hi, honey," he said, "You want a drink?"

"No," I said, "I'm waiting for someone."

79

"A male someone?"

"Yes," I answered. Was he connected to James, sent to my table to deliver a message? I didn't know what to make of him.

"What's his name?' he asked.

"His name is James."

"Boyfriend?"

"No."

"Then he won't mind me sitting here for a minute and talking to you," the man continued, "My name's Al. Al Brooks. What's yours?" He sat down in the booth across from me.

I was nervous. The woman on the phone had made a point of saying to come by myself. It might not be cool to be sitting with another man I might have brought along.

"Leah," I answered, "But I think—"

"Hey! Two beers over here!" The man called, snapping his fingers at the baldheaded man behind the counter. "Tell me about yourself, Leah. You a student?"

"Yes," I said, "In journalism."

"I worked for a newspaper once," Al continued, "Back in Louisiana. You like to write stories?" His smile was confiding, but underneath the smile, I sensed something else.

"Yes, I do," I said. "But please get up. I'm meeting a friend for a private discussion."

"Let's not worry about it, Leah. As soon as your boyfriend gets here, I'll make myself scarce. Now, tell me, what's a white girl like you doing down here at Vinnie's Inn?"

"Excuse me," I said. "I need to use the restroom." As I stood up, the front door opened. James Ferguson walked in, followed by two other men. The man on his right was young, with a high forehead and receding hair line. He looked Ethiopian. The other man was heavily muscled but light on his feet. His face was scarred. Something about him looked familiar.

The impact of James' physical presence jolted me. Everything else receded around him. He was undeniably good looking, powerfully built. James was the kind of man women noticed. Around him other men grew cautious. He carried himself with the alertness of a powerful animal. A black panther, in-

80

deed. Grace, I thought, you really knew how to pick them.

I waved. Al Brooks slid out of the booth, moving quickly toward the back of the room. "James!" I called. He lifted his head, then walked straight over to my corner.

"Leah?—What in hell are you doing here?" James stared at me coldly.

I stared back at him, confused. "I was called. I was told to come."

"Who in hell called you?"

This was not the reception I had expected. James jerked his head toward his two comrades. "Ollie? Wilson? What do you know about this?"

Wilson. The man Grace had been talking to at Vinnie's Inn. It felt so long ago.

The thin man, Ollie, shook his head. Wilson made a negative gesture. I realized that something had gone wrong, or perhaps had never been right.

"Sit back down," James said, sliding into the bench Al Brooks had just vacated. I could see Al watching us from the end of the bar. "Who called you? Tell me what happened."

"A woman called me. I thought she was from the Party. Your assistant, or something."

"I don't have a woman assistant," James said. "Was she white or black?"

"Black. I think."

"Young or old?"

"I couldn't tell."

"Anything else you can tell me about her?"

"She sounded like she was used to being obeyed."

"Ain't this a bitch?" He looked over at Ollie and Wilson. "We'd better leave. You too, Leah—you'd better get outta here."

Al was approaching our table again. "This your boyfriend?"

"No," I answered.

"Someone bothering you?" Al Brooks said.

"No," I answered, but he had put his hand on James' shoulder. James turned around and in one movement had grabbed him by the throat and pushed him up against the wall. It happened so quickly I was stunned. I tried say something, to tell James this was just a guy who had tried to pick me up, no one

81

to worry about, but I couldn't speak. Ollie and Wilson were moving closer to Al. Al reached toward his jacket, but Wilson grabbed his arm. He wrestled a small automatic from the man's grasp. Wilson looked back at James; James nodded. Wilson picked up the gun by the barrel so the handle became a hammer to strike Al Brook's head. I turned my head so I wouldn't see the blow.

I was never sure who slammed Al Brook's head with the pistol. I heard the sound of police sirens, shouts and curses. I turned my head to see James and his two assistants running out the back door. There were police everywhere, five, six of them, telling Vinnie to come out from behind the bar with his hands raised, slamming other black men to the floor, pointing guns at their heads. Where had all these police come from? The men shoved me aside, fanning out and running through the back. Al Brooks was slumped on the floor, with blood trickling down his face. His eyes looked dull. A thin cop knelt beside him, feeling for his pulse, shouting for an ambulance. A large cop approached me to say they were taking me down at headquarters to answer some questions.

He led me out to his car. Outside the afternoon sun was harsh. An ambulance pulled up. A small crowd had gathered. A newsman took photos as various black men were escorted into the squad cars. As I stepped out into the street, the newsman's flash went off. He had taken a photograph of me.

James Ferguson and his two friends had vanished. I did not understand what had just happened. I was frightened. But I was relieved I had worn my black turtleneck sweater. In my newfound notoriety, I would appear sophisticated. Would Paul and Yoshi see me on the evening news and come get me?

I was sitting on a hard bench at OPD headquarters, outside a tinted glass door. I was waiting to be questioned. I felt dazed, a little hungry, with a throbbing headache over my left eye. I was trying to remember what Paul had told me about my rights. Could I ask to make one call? Should that call be to Joey, or should I leave him out of this?

I looked up. A light-skinned black cop with a small mustache was walking toward me. He had kind brown eyes. I remembered him. That day they had discovered Grace's body at the track, he had tried to intervene in the scuffle between the white cop and the black employee. He was looking at me. He slowed his pace

82

imperceptibly, and asked in a low voice, "Aren't you DeMartino's cousin?"

I nodded.

"What in hell happened? They pull you in with that mess at Vinnie's Inn?"

I nodded again.

The glass door opened. A young officer with a narrow face, like a fish, called my name. His name badge read Officer Alvin Sykes. The light-skinned cop straightened and kept moving down the hall, as if we had not spoken. I walked into the brightly lit, dingy room. I was nervous.

A second cop took the lead. The name badge on his shirt read Officer Elroy Deane. He looked like a bad-tempered accountant. "When you going to give up protecting your boyfriend?" Elroy Deane asked.

"He's not my boyfriend," I said.

"Who's not your boyfriend?" Alvin Sykes asked.

"No one. I don't have a boyfriend."

"You run down to bars in an area I wouldn't send my dog to pee in? You go down there to hang out with black men you don't even know?" This came from Elroy Deane.

I did not have a chance of convincing them, but I made the attempt. "No, I don't go to bars very often," I said, "I got a call."

"From who?" Sykes' eyes became narrow, more alert.

This was impossible. I had gotten a call from a woman I didn't know. I had dropped everything to run down to Vinnie's Inn to meet James Ferguson. Even I couldn't understand it. These two young cops, with their contemptuous smiles, would not believe a word of it. "I don't know," I answered, flushing.

"You don't know?" Officer Sykes repeated, his voice rising with mock incredulity. "You don't know? Why don't you admit Ferguson called you?"

"He didn't."

"Come on," he said. "You like Ferguson, don't you? He invited you down there. You told two of our officers you thought the guy was a stud. You liked him, Leah, you couldn't keep yourself away. You went racing down to that bar to check him out!"

"No." I answered. I saw myself in his eyes—an inhibited young Berkeley student, overly studious, with a prurient curiosity about big black men. "I

83

don't even know the guy." They laughed. The sound filled the room, harsh and discordant. I noticed my palms were damp.

"You like black men, Leah?" Elroy Deane turned his face toward me. "Lots of Berkeley girls like that. More white girls running after Black Panthers than I knew existed. White men can't get no action anymore." The two of them laughed again. Deane's eyes were sizing me up as if I were a prostitute who worked a beat. "You think black men are better?"

I said nothing. I tried to concentrate on how they looked. I looked at the badge on Alvin Sykes's shirt. He saw me looking. "Leah, you think black men fuck better than white ones?"

I was trying to remember something Paul had told me. What to do when one was stopped by cops. What to tell them, what to demand. My mind was frozen. I couldn't remember any of what he had said.

"Why would she admit it?" Deane broke in, "The guy's a scum bag. Even Leah knows that. Why would she want to admit he turns her on?"

I found my voice. It came out feeble and cracked, to my embarrassment. "You two are crazy," I said.

There was a second of silence, before Elroy Deane leaped out of his chair. I saw his heavy holster belt, his night stick. I flinched back in my chair.

"Don't get wise with us, Leah!" He repeated my words. "Hear that, Alvin? We're crazy! This broad's been sleeping with a murdering piece of scum like Ferguson, and she tells us we're crazy? You like sleeping with killers, Leah? It's not enough that he killed your friend? You so dumb that you haven't figured out you're next?" He pointed his thick finger at me with a sharp, jabbing motion. "You're next, Leah DeMartino! Don't you know you're next?"

Perhaps he believed it. I also knew this man, pointing at me with his angry finger, would be glad if I *were* next.

"Let me read you Ferguson's rap sheet," Alvin Sykes interjected smoothly. "A rap sheet as long as his dick. He's got charges on him from ten years back."

My cheeks were hot. I looked into their faces, again tried to memorize their names, their features. "Aren't you supposed to let me call a lawyer?" My question stopped Alvin Sykes for a second. It made Elroy Deane angrier.

"Tell us the truth, you got nothing to worry about. No need for a lawyer."

84

Sykes moved in smoothly, playing into Deane's improvised scenario. "The sooner you answer our questions, the sooner we can let you outta here."

"We can keep you twenty four hours if we want to," Deane put in, smiling at me. His smile displayed his sharp rodent teeth. "We get breaks, but you don't. We don't even know if we can find a female cop to take you to the bathroom. Just tell us what happened, Leah."

"Tell you what?" I asked. What exactly did they want to know? The thought of twenty-four more hours in this harsh light with these two menacing idiots left me shaken. My head was throbbing. I did need to use the bathroom. Something told me it wouldn't be a good idea to admit it to these two.

"Leah," Deane said. His tone became friendlier; he inched forward in his chair. "That man in the bar—that Al Brooks—told us everything. How he saw you come in today; how he tried to pick you up. You told him you were waiting for your boyfriend."

"I did not."

In fact, I couldn't remember. Al had wanted to talk to me. I had made some excuse. I thought I had said I was meeting someone. Perhaps he assumed I meant a boyfriend; perhaps not.

"Come on, Leah," Deane's tone was soft and wheedling. I remembered how he had leapt up, five minutes ago, with such force I thought he might strike me. "Brooks told us how he sat and talked with you. You told him all about yourself."

I thought we'd talked about journalism. I felt panicky. I couldn't remember. What had I said?

"Ferguson came in, picked a fight with Brooks because you were talking to him. Next thing you know, the poor slob was on the floor with his face bashed in. They broke his nose, Leah. You saw it all."

I remembered Al Brooks on the floor with a trickle of blood down his face, his eyes blank and unfocussed. But Deane didn't have the story right, though I didn't know exactly what was wrong with it. The pain over my eyes was throbbing. I tried to hold on. Yoshi. Paul. The article. What had I said to Al? What had happened in that smoky bar?

"No," I said. Deane's face darkened. His body shot forward on the chair. I thought he might leap up again. I tried to steel myself. Whatever he did to me, I could put it in the article.

"Jesus Christ, Leah, admit it! You saw that fucking Ferguson smash Al Brooks in the face, didn't you?" In fact, I had not. I had averted my eyes as the two men had advanced on Brooks, after a nod of assent from Ferguson.

"No," I answered. Deane leapt to his feet. Sykes, far away, leaned over the desk, whether to restrain or to encourage Deane I didn't know. There was a knock at the door. Deane, already moving toward me, pivoted.

The tan-skinned policeman named Mike put his head in the door. "Lieutenant DeMartino asked me to check—"

"Close the door!" Deane shouted.

But I swiveled my head and called out, "Contact my cousin, Lieutenant DeMartino. Tell him I need a lawyer."

"Shut up!" Deane roared at me. I thought he had completely lost control, but he turned back to Mike, and said in a lower tone, "Fisher, don't you dare—"

"DeMartino's her cousin?" Mike asked, looking at me, although he already knew that. "I think he's already asking about her."

"They want me to talk about things that I never witnessed. They're threatening me. Tell Joe DeMartino. I asked for a lawyer, they won't let me have one." I sounded like a babbling child, but this might be my last chance to reach anyone. Was it wise to bring Joey into this? I felt desperate. Mike, at least, looked kinder and more intelligent than the fools I had been dealing with.

Sykes was looking from one to the other of them. He suddenly looked younger, more vulnerable. I could almost feel sorry for him. Joey's name, coupled with my own, seemed to unhinge him. "Everything's perfectly legal, Fisher." He said, with a trace of uncertainty in his voice. "She's only here for questioning. We haven't charged her with anything. The girl's hysterical."

"Get out of here, Fisher," Deane snapped, "We've got this situation under control." Mike Fisher gave me a careful look. I pleaded with him with my eyes to stay. He looked at me with concern. Then he closed the door, to my intense disappointment.

Sykes and Deane looked at each other. They were deflated; I had put a break in their momentum. "Let's go outside and talk," Sykes said to Deane. "Don't try to go anywhere, Leah." Where did they think I could go? I heard their voices outside the door, the name DeMartino mentioned once or twice. When they came back in, Deane looked even surlier than before.

86

"If you don't wake up, Leah," he said, "those Panthers are gonna get you. Ferguson ain't no one to play around with, believe you me. And if you don't stop covering up for him, we'll get you for that. Either way, it's crackers for you. Out of respect for your cousin, we're gonna let you go. We'd hate to see an officer like DeMartino brought down cause of your stupidity. Take my advice, and go back to your books. This shit is way too deep for you."

Sykes sat while Deane delivered this lecture. He wore a strained smile, fixed on his face like a grimace. I stood up, and my legs almost buckled underneath me from weakness and relief. I realized how urgently I needed to pee. I had to stop myself from thanking them. I was so relieved to be able to leave them behind that I could have blessed them by mistake. As I walked out the door, I thought of James Ferguson, and what he must endure at the hands of people like these two. How much less likely that he would walk away from them as easily as I could. And I had Joey to thank for my reprieve.

But the first thing I did was to find the ladies' room.

X

When I walked into the lobby, Paul and Yoshi were waiting for me.

"Am I glad to see you! How did you know I was here?"

"Us and half the city," Yoshi replied. "That scene at Vinnie's was on the evening news."

"I'm glad you're okay," Paul said. "Now let's get outta here. Reporters were calling the house but we refused to talk to anyone. We were worried shitless. I called Art Leopold right away." We walked out the front door and into the cold evening. Fog had come in from the bay, and the wide streets of downtown Oakland were bathed in a grey light.

"What did he say?" I asked.

"You expect him to be out celebrating? He was upset," Paul answered. "A brawl in an East Oakland bar, and you're right in the thick of it? It doesn't look good, Leah."

Paul's van was parked a block away on Franklin Street. Paul jumped in the driver's seat; Yoshi slid open the side door to climb in back. I sat next to Paul. "Can we drive out MacArthur and pick up my car?" I asked.

"We went out there first. Yoshi drove it back to Russell Street," Paul answered. "Cops—or someone—had gone through everything—glove compartment, seats, trunk, you name it."

"What were they were looking for?" I asked.

"Anything they could find to incriminate you, tie you to the Panthers, use as an excuse to hold you. It doesn't take much, Leah. Remember I told you about the FBI. J. Edgar Hoover has called the Black Panthers the major threat to the security of the United States." Paul started the ignition. "Art Leopold doesn't want you to go back to Russell Street tonight. He says the reporters will keep calling, and the cops could come back. Yoshi called Kanji. You can stay at Kanji's tonight. He's going to sleep over at his girlfriend's."

I had been looking forward to our communal dinner where I would be the center of attention, fascinating my roommates with stories of the day. "Leopold doesn't want you to talk to anyone about what happened at Vinnie's Inn," Paul continued, "at least not until you've talked to him. He'll see you as

88

planned at five pm tomorrow. He'll take your deposition and you can go over these new developments."

I spent the night at Kanji's one-bedroom apartment in a new building on Parker Street with the improbable name of the Sir Francis Drake Arms. Yoshi slept on the sofa to keep me company. We watched the eleven pm news on Channel 4. There was a brief report on a fight that had broken out at a bar in East Oakland involving three Black Panthers—James Ferguson and two others. A fourth man was now in serious condition at Highland Hospital. Leah DeMartino had been in the bar at the time of the fight and had been taken in for questioning. Police were looking for James Ferguson in connection with the incident.

Paul showed up around two pm the next day and tossed the early afternoon edition of the Oakland Tribune on the kitchen table. It was open to Section B Local News. Below the fold was the story—"Panther Girlfriend Instigates Brawl?" An altercation had broken out the day before at Vinnie's Inn in east Oakland. Police had been called to break up the scuffle. Leah DeMartino, who had provided an alibi for James Ferguson in the murder of Grace Neville, had been questioned by the police and let go. I read the following paragraph with mounting anger.

> Police found a man lying on the floor with a head concussion, later identified as Al Brooks. Brooks told police he had seen a white woman enter the bar. He approached her. DeMartino said she was waiting for her boyfriend, Panther security strongman, James Ferguson. When Ferguson appeared, he harassed Brooks and provoked a fight.

"Your cousin's been calling, wanting to know where you were," Paul said.

I didn't know how I would deal with Joey and I didn't want to discuss it with Paul or Yoshi. I stood up. "Well, look, I have an appointment with Art Leopold at five. It's late. I better get going if I'm going to catch the F-bus."

"I'll give you a lift to the bus stop. But we want you to make some agreements with us. For your own safety, and ours. We want you to clear it with us before you talk to reporters or cops. We're involved too, you know." Paul's face looked serious despite his blonde ringlets.

"I'm not used to monitoring everything I say."

"You're not used to tangling with the pigs in a murder case, either," Paul shot back. "I want you to clear it with us before you say anything to that pig cousin of yours. Or to any cop at all, as far as that goes. You have no idea how he might use any information he has."

"Fine," I said, "My lips are sealed."

"Good," said Paul. "Let's get going. We can talk again when you get back from Leopold's."

At five pm I was knocking on the heavy oak door to Art Leopold's office. He came to the door, circles under his eyes, looking weary. Nonetheless he was as immaculately turned out as ever.

He gestured to the chair in front of his desk. "So here we are. You remember, I told you to be careful."

"You didn't tell me what to be careful of."

"Didn't it seem odd that a woman who didn't identify herself would call and ask you to meet James? Don't you think James would have called you himself, or I would have called you on his behalf?"

"I thought she was his assistant," I said. "Who *was* she?"

"No one knows," Art replied. "Whoever she was, she accomplished a lot. She has helped discredit you with the public, or with a jury if you have to give testimony. And now James distrusts you."

"Why?"

"He was told, at the last minute, to drop by Vinnie's Inn," Art said. "You're there. A strange man approaches him in a hostile manner, and seconds later the cops are swarming the joint. It stinks of a set up." Art Leopold sighed. "I tried to explain to him that you are gullible. I don't believe you would knowingly set James up." His sharp hazel eyes searched my face.

It occurred to me that perhaps James had also been gullible. Who had told *him* to show up at Vinnie's Inn? Did he obey all orders so unquestioningly? Looking at Art Leopold, I felt this was not a subject he would be open to discussing with me. I had my own questions, of myself. Joey's name had gotten me out of that harshly-lit room in OPD headquarters. Joey had also offered me work with the police. What if Art Leopold or James found out? Telling the truth to Art Leopold could risk everything: Art's trust, the chance to speak to

90

James in person. Did I have to mention an offer I hadn't yet accepted? I needed to talk to James Ferguson. I was curious about his relationship with Grace. I wanted his side of the story for my article. And there was that sense of energy, of excitement, that his presence conveyed.

"Let's go ahead with the deposition," Art was saying. "Afterward, you can speak directly to James. The cops picked him up last night, but I got him out on bail this morning. I've persuaded him to come over and talk with you. Here in my office we shouldn't have to worry about anyone listening."

"Mr. Leopold, I would never set James up," I said. "My testimony got him off in the first place."

"But you were *used* to set him up," said Leopold. I heard the note of finality in his voice

"Could I ask a few questions?"

"If it's about this investigation, I may not be able to answer."

"The cops said they found Grace's blood in the trunk of James' car," I began. "They found a handgun, the murder weapon, in the bushes. The gun was registered to James. Doesn't it all really point to him?"

Art seemed angry. "Goddamn it! They're trying to sway you, Leah, can't you see it? Let me explain a few things to you. James Ferguson doesn't own anything but the clothes on his back. The car he drives, the guns he carries, may be registered to him, but many people—not just Panthers, but people simply connected to the Panthers—have access to the car and possibly to the weapons as well."

"That would indicate a Panther killed Grace," I said.

"Not necessarily. It only means that someone got access to the car and the murder weapon—if it *is* the murder weapon, which hasn't yet been proved."

Behind his desk were two framed photographs. In one photo Leopold stood with his arms around two large white men in Teamsters T-shirts. In the second, he was with three black men with large Afros. Art motioned toward the second photograph. "Let me give you a rundown on Black Panther origins," said Leopold. "The Panthers were formed in 1966 by Huey Newton and Bobby Seale. Initially it was a local organization—"

"—law books and guns," I said, interrupting. "Self-defense from police brutality." Paul had given me quite a bit of the background.

"More or less," Leopold said. "They were a militant development of the civil rights movement. They grew rapidly after the murder of Martin Luther King, as the black community responded to the brutality of their government. Seeing this, young blacks rejected King's message of nonviolence. And within a couple of years there were chapters all over the country."

"James Ferguson came here from Houston, Texas," Leopold continued. "He told me once that cops would fall asleep in their cars when they were taking black men to jail. They were that sure that a black man wouldn't react to their intimidation. That was before the Panthers. James headed up a chapter back in Houston. Then the Oakland leadership sent for him. They were sending for many of the local leaders to consolidate a national power base. James had a reputation for courage in dealing with the police, so they put him in charge of security out here. But in the past year, everything has changed."

"There's a war going on now between the East Coast and the West Coast chapters," Art said. His voice had taken on an edge. "Eldridge Cleaver wants to emphasize the militant stance—the armed revolutionary struggle. Huey Newton and David Hilliard want to emphasize service to the community. It's gotten bad over the last couple years. How much of it might be FBI infiltration, we have no idea. We've learned of this program, Cointelpro. Neutralizing the Black Panther leadership is its main focus. Totally covert. Uses informants, snitches, even black police officers, to infiltrate the Party and sow suspicion. *Neutralizing* is a euphemism, of course. Elimination by any means is what they have in mind. I know Panthers who travel the country with a .38 and a bottle of Maalox. This internal conflict is weakening them."

"Cointelpro," I repeated. It sounded ominous, heavy.

"Cointelpro is an acronym for a series of FBI counterintelligence programs designed to neutralize political dissidents. The program is set in motion through bribery, forgeries, the activities of informants and agents provocateurs. It employs any means to further its goals—character assassination, criminal frame-ups. In some cases, murder. This has been particularly true in its campaign against the Panthers."

"I've heard about J. Edgar Hoover's campaign to destroy the Party." I remembered the unsettling conversation with Paul on the trip to Clear Lake.

"Yes. As the Black Panther Party grew, Cointelpro began a nationwide crackdown on the Party. They recruited local police agencies for their campaign of misinformation and lies. Two years ago Eldridge Cleaver became a target. He was living in exile in Algiers. Cleaver received letters. One letter was signed by Connie Matthews, Newton's personal secretary; another was allegedly from the editor of the Black Panther newspaper, Elbert Howard. The letters criticized Huey Newton and begged Cleaver to take control. The big split came when Huey Newton did an interview on a television talk show. Cleaver was on the phone in Algiers. Cleaver expressed disgust for what was happening in the Party and demanded that David Hilliard, the Chief of Staff, be removed. As a result, Cleaver himself was expelled from the Central Committee. This was the beginning of the split in the Party between the East Coast and the West Coast branches."

Why was he telling me this? To justify how James had pushed Al Brooks against the wall, the nod I had seen him give to the two men with him? Or was Art Leopold warning me that James was capable of murderous violence? Perhaps even the violence that had killed Grace?

"Okay," said Art Leopold. "Enough of the history lecture. Let's get on with the deposition." Art took out a legal pad and we began reviewing the statement I had given him a week ago. For the next hour and a half we went over every detail of the Saturday night and Sunday morning I had last seen Grace Neville. Finally Art Leopold set aside his legal pad. "I think that's it," he said. "If I have any more questions, I'll give you a call. —And here's James."

James Ferguson walked through the door wearing his habitual black slacks and turtleneck. His brown eyes, flecked with gold, appraised me intently. Again I felt jolted by his presence.

"Hello," he said. He extended his hand. I sensed the handshake was a gesture made for Art's benefit. Art turned to me.

"I'll have my secretary type up your statement, Miss DeMartino. Give you two a chance to talk.—There's coffee over there on the credenza." He left the room, closing the door behind him.

James poured himself a cup from a stainless steel thermos and sat down easily behind Art Leopold's big desk. He had a faint smile on his face.

I plunged in. "Thanks for coming. I feel really bad about yesterday."

"Art asked me to come," James said, "I listen to Art." His voice was matter of fact, but I sensed a very slight amusement, perhaps at my expense.

"Look," I said. "It is the way I told you. I got a call. I went to Vinnie's. I never expected anything like what happened there."

"I know, Leah," he said. He leaned back in Art Leopold's swivel chair, his hands laced behind his head. "Art has explained it all to me. You don't have to apologize for nothing. It's your testimony first sprang me from the hole." His voice was husky, deep. The faint Texas drawl made his simplest sentences sound confidential. "Some folks might not have done that much." His eyes continued to study me. Then he leaned forward a little. "So you want to talk to me. How'd you know Grace?"

"We both worked at the race track. Isn't that where you met her?"

"Yeah. When I first got out here from Texas, we'd hang out sometimes. Then I got other responsibilities."

"Security?"

"Other responsibilities—let's leave it at that. We tried to keep our thing going. Then I got sent up to San Quentin—and that was that. I never promised anything to Grace, she didn't make any promises to me. Grace wasn't the kind of woman to wait. For me or for anyone. Things people do don't surprise me anymore."

Nothing he said exactly contradicted what she had told me, but I did not think Grace had been as casual about "their thing" as he implied. Grace had called him the love of her life.

"So it wasn't romantic?" I ventured.

"The Party comes first. The Black Panther Party," he said. "For people like me. If it didn't, I wouldn't be here today."

"You were important to Grace."

"When things started up, we were tight. Then it cooled off. We stayed friends. She worked for us. Before I joined the Party, I'd never known something like that, a white woman working for the good of a black political group. I grew up in the fifties, in the south. Do you know what that means? My mother made me pee before we went downtown. She was never sure we could find a colored bathroom. I remember seeing an old black woman with tears running down her face, humiliated because she couldn't hold out any longer. That's what it was like to grow up under segregation." James Ferguson had a slow, mesmerizing quality to his speech.

94

Now, as he picked up his coffee cup, I noticed that his hand shook slightly as he lifted it to his lips.

I remembered my article. This might be my only chance to get James Ferguson's side of the story. I had questions but I hesitated to ask them. Maybe I had to risk it. "That night at Eli's—you and Grace had a fight?"

James' gold-flecked eyes looked darker now, ominous. "What makes you ask?"

"Something about the way she looked," I hedged.

"Don't play with me," he said. "I've been played with by experts, baby. You know something, spit it out."

"I already told you and Art, the first time I was here. Grace had bruises on her neck. I saw them clearly at my house when she spent the night. That was after she was with you at Eli's."

"You said the cops asked you about them bruises, and you told them you didn't know anything."

"That's right. I didn't know where she got them, and I didn't ask her. They didn't believe me. They accused me of lying to protect you."

"Were you?"

"Why would I protect you? I didn't know how she got those bruises. Do you?"

He looked at me a few more seconds with an unreadable expression. "You ask better questions than the pigs. You sure you're not a cop yourself?"

I stared at him. Did he know about Joey?

James shrugged. "I might know how she got them bruises, and I might not. I would need to know a whole lot more about you, before I gave you any information."

"It's obvious the cops want to incriminate you any way they can. I don't understand why they're so determined to do it."

"Because they're pigs," he said, "Pigs and Panthers are natural enemies, like lions and hyenas. Those guys want me so bad they can taste it."

"So what *were* you and Grace doing at Eli's Saturday night?'

"That's on the record. Why don't you ask the pigs? She called me up at the last minute. Asked me to meet her at Eli's. Said she needed to talk to me. She had been drinking; she was messed up. I told her I'd meet her, but I wouldn't have much time."

"What was wrong?"

"She didn't tell me," he answered, "But I knew the signs. Booze. Pills. Looked to me like Grace was fooling around with the wrong man."

"Were you jealous?" I asked.

"I'm married to the Black Panther Party," he replied. "I'm trying to survive. If I let myself get caught up in jealousy over a woman?—a white woman at that—I wouldn't have lasted this long. I was angry at her—not jealous. I hate stupidity. Grace had been through way too much to let herself get used. Too much, come to that, to let herself get killed the way she did."

"Maybe she was hoping the two of you would get back together."

His eyes flicked over me again. "Maybe so. I keep telling you, I belong to the Panthers. That's been my life since I was sixteen. I told her to behave with more self-respect. She got angry, jumped out, slammed the car door. That's the last I ever saw her." James shook his head and laughed. I felt relieved. "You're something," he said, "One thing I do know about you, now—you're no cop."

"How do you know that?" I had never met a man like James Ferguson. His voice, his bearing, made other men seem like shadows.

"I can smell cops. Smell 'em a mile away. Just what you are, I don't know yet. But you ain't no cop." His white teeth flashed in his brown face. His smile was dazzling. James and I sat silent. I didn't want him to be too certain of my loyalty. I wondered how I had passed his test.

A light tap on the door, and Art Leopold re-entered the room. "James, there's some things we should go over. You two done talking?"

"Yeah, we're done," James said. "Art, she's okay."

His approval pleased me in a way I knew was dangerous. I could not let myself get pulled into his spell. "I hope we can talk again." I extended my hand. His hand lay over mine for a second.

"Yeah, well, I ain't exactly easy to get in touch with," he said. "That is, unless you're a member of the OPD." He laughed, with a bitter note. "You can always try going through Art. Then again, I just might ring you up sometime. I've got a few more questions for you."

It would be easy to get in this thing over my head. I was in over my head already.

XI

I caught the F bus home, keyed up; disturbed by James' impact. Images returned—James pinning Al Brooks against the wall with one swift movement, James' eyes on me when he asked what I had told the cops about the bruises. James' dazzling smile, showing his strong white teeth, when he declared I was no cop. Outside the dirty bus windows West Oakland flashed by, with its shabby houses and small back yards. Nothing made sense to me anymore. Too much had happened in too short a time.

All three roommates were waiting for me in the living room. Carol's long legs hung over the arm of the sofa. Paul was reading the newspaper. Yoshi, smoking a cigarette, squashed it out as I came in. Paul put down his newspaper. "Your cousin's been calling all afternoon," he said. "Last time he called, he said he was coming over."

"How long ago was that?"

"Oh, fifteen minutes ago," Paul said. "He'll be here any moment now."

"I don't want to see him," I said.

"Well, you're going to," said Paul. "He just drove up."

I glanced out the living room window. Joey's blue Chevrolet had just parked curbside. With a sigh, I picked up my shoulder bag. "Hello, goodbye," I said to the trio. "I better go talk to him."

As I stepped up to the car, Joey rolled down his window. "Leah! I knew you'd come home sooner or later. We need to talk. I'll take you to Dave's Coffee Shop."

"Dave's? Again? Why does it always have to be Dave's?" I said. "If you're going to grill me, how about Narsai's?" Narsai's restaurant was the most expensive restaurant in Berkeley.

"Ha, ha," said Joey. "Very funny. So why didn't you return any of my phone calls?"

"I've been busy."

"Busy, shit. Busy getting into all kinds of trouble."

97

I sighed and got in the car. Joey drove straight to Dave's Coffee Shop. We sat in a booth and he ordered coffee, a hamburger and fries. "I'll have scrambled eggs," I said to the waitress. She wore a perky starched hat on her sprayed hair.

"Anything to drink with that, sweetheart?"

"Tea. Lipton's is fine. Thanks."

Joey lost no time. "What in hell were you doing at Vinnie's Inn?"

"Read the police report. I told the truth, although those nasty buddies of yours didn't believe me. Where are you getting cops from these days— reform school?"

"Don't get wise with me, Leah."

Wise with him. Same cop talk I'd heard from Sykes and Deane. I wished I were wise, but I was not wise enough, it seemed.

"You're the one was down at Vinnie's Inn with some reform school types. Panther thugs. Why in hell did you go?" Joey continued.

"I was curious."

"Curious, she says. Curious." Joey made his voice high-pitched and squeaky on "curious," as if imitating me. Then he lowered his voice again. "Always sticking your nose in other people's shit."

"Hey," I said, "you asked me to check around for you."

"At the track, Leah! At the track, goddamn it! Not sniffing around some bar in the slums."

"Anyway," I added, hoping to distract him, "do you really have the authority to hire me?"

"I have the authority to do whatever I need to do to solve this case," Joey answered. "Including finding and paying informants."

I did not like the sound of the word *informant*.

"James Ferguson was arrested at eighteen for assault on two officers. Cop death in New York—probably Ferguson. Did time on weapons charges. Now he's suspected of killing your friend. And that's just the shit we know about. There's other stuff we can't prove yet."

"Like this murder," I said.

"Oh, he did it," Joey said. "One way or another, he did it."

98

I knew it was useless, but I had to try. "Grace had other lovers. So did he. Jealousy's not a motive."

"What planet you been living on, Leah? Jealousy's a motive for everyone. Half the murderers in San Quentin are there because of jealousy. I don't care what your little red book says. —Anyway jealousy isn't the only motive."

"What is?"

"Maybe he didn't trust her because she's white. Maybe she didn't go to enough political education classes. Maybe she dropped her little red book down the toilet. What the hell do I know? The question is, do you hear a goddamned word I'm saying?"

I was still hearing Ferguson's husky voice from this morning, that lingering drawl, making me feel trusted, part of his inner circle. As if I were a confidante. For a moment this morning I had understood Grace. "I'd walk off a cliff for that man." But there were other memories—Al Brooks, slumped unconscious against a wall on a single nod from James Ferguson. The menace in Ferguson's eyes when he warned me not to play with him. The look on Grace Neville's face the night before her murder—as if she knew she was going to die. The way her hands reverently touched the bruises at her throat. I pushed away that memory.

"So, look," Joey was saying. "Do we have a deal, or do we have a deal? You report back to me what you find out at the track—and only the track, mind you—and I'll find some cash, help you pay your fall quarter tuition at that nutty university."

"Okay," I said. How could information from the track be of value? If he wanted to pay me for track gossip, there was a lot of that. "I'll report to you from the track. Everything I hear and see, just like you suggested."

"Write down everything you hear out there," he said. "Mail me a report each week. Names, dates, details. Call me if it's something big. But I'm warning you, Leah; we're talking about the track. Don't even think about going near Ferguson again or any of those Panthers."

All I needed was a man—my father or uncle or Joey himself—to forbid me to do something, and I would be determined to do it. I thought to myself, Joey should take some courses in psychology. The waitress in the starched cap put a little tray on our table with the bill. "I'll take care of this," said Joey, covering the tray with his hammy fist.

99

When he pulled back up in front of Russell Street, I got out. "Thanks for the dinner, Joey," I said.

Joey started up the car, pulled a U-turn in the middle of Russell Street, then slowed and rolled down his window. "Don't forget, Leah. The track. And nothing but the track. I'm telling you, this is one hell of a case."

XII

I could hear Carol's voice in the kitchen, but no one noticed I had come in. I went upstairs into my room and lay down on my bed in relief. Little more than a week ago I had been just another Cal student with a part-time job at the race track. Now I was on a first name basis with local celebrities like Art Leopold and James Ferguson. I had been on television. I had been interviewed by policemen. My two male roommates were paying more attention to me than ever before.

It was intoxicating, in a strange way, to suddenly be at the center of something, even if that something was horrible, frightening, unresolved. I felt this addictive need to do more, know more, to make my mark, to prove myself, no matter what the cost.

Some information would not be revealed to anyone, not even Yoshi or Paul. For now I would keep Grace's notebook a secret. Anything I learned from reading it could be attributed to information Grace's mother had given me.

I would figure it all out in my notebook. I got up from my bed, cleared a space on my desk, and began to work. I sketched out an outline for the article. I realized the project was a hornet's nest. If my article indicted the police, Joey would be furious. If my article indicted the Panthers, Art Leopold would be upset. Worse, if the article helped establish that Ferguson was involved in the murder, would the Panthers take revenge on me?

And what exactly had I promised Joey I would do in exchange for some financial help with my fall quarter tuition? I had agreed to report information from the track—where I should be going anyway. For two weeks I had taken a leave of absence. The loss of two weeks of work would make a big dent in my paycheck. Tomorrow I would go back to the track. I would ask questions, jot down what I learned. To write an investigative article, a journalist needed as much information, from as many sources, as possible. How bad was that?

I placed my notebook and Grace's diary under my mattress. I got into bed and pulled the covers up around my neck. I would start by going in early tomorrow morning and talking to Freddie and Edna.

The next day, Wednesday, I left home at nine-thirty. My shift started at noon. I loved the drive out to Golden Gate Fields. I drove up the road to the

101

knoll from which it seemed I could see all of San Francisco Bay, shimmering like a vast watery mirror reflecting light and purity, from Point Richmond on the north, to the Bay Bridge behind me. The road was lined with bare clay patches. Only raggedy-leafed wild radish with its hopeful white flowers grew in this dried mud, but there were reedy grasses growing closer to the water, among the chunks of purple-black basalt retainer rocks, and a twisted tree with the snaky trunk of a cypress was silhouetted against the day's glow.

Directly ahead of me, at the far end of a muddy crescent of beach, a derelict pier pointed out into the water. That was the pier, that was the place, where Grace's body had been dumped, to bob in the incoming morning tide until the Asian teenagers spotted it. I gave a deep sigh. It was strange that I still experienced the shining light on the bay as peaceful.

I parked my car, checked myself in the rear view mirror, ran a comb through my hair. Was I pretty? Sometimes people told me I was. My hair was dark and very curly. I thought about Grace again. She had never made that date to fix my hair.

The Golden Gate Fields clubhouse was a low white building with wings spread out on the knoll southern California style. It looked very 1930s to me, like something I had seen in movies set in Los Angeles. Here was where the East Bay came to enjoy thoroughbred horse racing. The King of Sports, the Sport of Kings—a gentleman's game. But not totally.

The excitement of the track always energized me. I entered Mainline on the ground floor. Bleachers ran down toward the race track, with small gates which opened directly onto the parade ground between the clubhouse and the paddocks. On Mainline one could get close to the horses as they were walked and exercised before post time. Trainers and jockeys were making last minute adjustments to saddles, bridles and gear or walking their horses.

I found Freddie Corster in the exercise ring with a frisky bay colt. A younger man strode along side him. Freddie was wearing blue jeans; "Here Comes Trouble" was blazoned across the front of his T-shirt. When I waved, he handed the reins to the boy and came running toward me with his jerking gait.

"Hey, Leah!" he called. "Where you been? I haven't seen you in a while. Walk down to Jose's truck with me, I need a bite to eat."

Jose's old lunch wagon was parked at the bottom of the road, with its hand-lettered signs: TACOS. BURRITOS. TORTAS. In the distance came the hoarse honk of a train making its way up the Southern Pacific rail line to Point Richmond. Its haunted, insistent questioning sound seemed to be asking, "Whoooo?" and "Why?"

Freddie had grown up in New Jersey. He had nervous energy, a wire about to short-circuit. I ran to keep up with him. "Freddie, remember the day they found Grace's body? You kept saying—shit's gonna hit the fan for sure."

"Who could forget?" Freddie replied. "I was terrified."

"But it didn't involve you, Freddie. Why were you terrified?"

He turned to look at me. "Because it happened out here. Because of who Grace was. Because of who she knew."

We hurried down the road, Freddie with his gimpy gait slightly ahead of me. Small waves lapped against the retaining rocks. Across the bay the white landscape of San Francisco glowed, although fog was already billowing under the Golden Gate Bridge. "Who did she know, Freddie?" I asked, breathlessly. Although Freddie walked with a gimp, he could still out-walk me.

"Who didn't Grace know?" Freddie spoke in a rapid staccato. His eye twitched. "Jockey name of Bucky Timmons. Owner by the name of Hugh Landis. She used to come down in the mornings, helped run the horses. Wearing jeans and a T-shirt." He coughed into his hand, a raspy bronchial sound. "Can't you just see it? That girl riding a horse, galloping across the field, T-shirt plastered against those knockers? The men were falling out."

"Who is Hugh Landis?'

"Big guy. Close to fifty. Big muckety muck on the racing board. I would see him talking to her sometimes after a run. Pretty clear they had something going on. More than just exercising the horses." He turned to me suddenly, "Why all the questions?"

"She was over at my house the night before she died," I answered. "The police called me in for questioning."

"So I heard," Freddie said. He didn't look convinced that this explained my interest.

"Look," he said, lowering his voice, "I saw her out at the track, that Sunday. She was out there Sunday morning. I swear it was her. Around one pm I saw her go up to the IRS window. She was wearing a scarf and big dark glasses, but it was Grace, all right."

"Are you sure?"

"Yeah, I told you the girl had a pair of knockers on her," Freddie said. "I'd know that girl in the dark."

"Shouldn't you tell the police about something like that?" I asked. "Did they question you, Freddie?'

Freddie jerked his head away from me. "I don't want nothing to do with the police. I'm not talking to no police. Maybe I shouldn't even be talking to you. Jesus. Who woulda ever thought it would go that far?" He was repeating his words from that first awful day.

I glanced at my watch—in forty-five minutes I needed to clock in. There was time for another interview. I bought myself a Coke and said goodbye to Freddie.

"Yeah, catch ya later," he said, digging for coins in his pocket.

The Hot Spoon, Edna's open-air restaurant, was down on Mainline. Edna was at work, early, as usual, frying onions and sausages on her grill. She had on a long white apron; her hair spun out around her face. Edna knew everyone at the track. She heard stories from the security guards, the jockeys, the trainers, the owners, the race track bosses themselves. Edna could be invaluable to me, but I would need to give her some motivation.

"You been gone a while, girl," she said.

"Yeah, I took some time off. But I'm back now." I sat down on one of the tall stools along her counter. "Edna, you know a jockey named Bucky Timmons?"

"Oh yeah," she said. "Little banty thing. Comes strutting in here sometimes—full of himself, like most of them Pecks." She narrowed her eyes as if taking in things no one else could see, pursing out her lips. She was all doubt and disgust. Edna had been raised in upcountry Louisiana. All white people, as far as she was concerned, were Pecks, short, she told me, for Peckerwoods. Living in the Bay Area had relaxed her attitudes, but only so far. Although she worked with, and sometimes dated, Asians, Hispanics, and Arabs, she held out against the Pecks. Most races were okay, she had told me, at least potentially okay—all but them Pecks.

"Why are you asking about Timmons, Leah?"

"I heard Grace might have dated him."

104

"That girl was trouble when she was alive, and she's more trouble now she's dead. Why you care about any of this stuff?"

"I feel bad about what happened to her. I liked her. I feel the same way about you, Edna. If something happened to you, I'd look for your killer, too."

Edna threw her head back, her mouth open in a beautiful yelp of laughter. "Girl!" she gasped, "No man's ever gotten the best of me yet, and no man ever will! I'd have long since blown the motherfucker's head to kingdom come. Search out my killer, she says."

"Grace Neville worked with the Black Panthers."

"You mean she slept with a brother, honey," Edna said. "One of the baddest brothers around. It ain't the same thing."

"She helped out at the school. Doesns't that tell you the kind of person she was?"

"Tells me she did what her man told her to do, like most stupid women. Ain't nothing new about a white girl shacking up with some brother. It's been going on forever. What makes me mad is when they don't even have the guts to admit it."

"But you respect the Panthers, don't you, Edna?"

"I wouldn't mess with them, if that's what you mean."

"Don't you believe in their goals?"

"Goals! Goals! Girl, they're one of the biggest gangs in town! Course I respect them for the way they stood up to those cops a few years back. That took guts. The Oakland police force was full of southern crackers. They recruited specially to get those fools. Black folks were terrified of the OPD. To go up against those crackers, Leah, you gotta be halfway crazy. I wouldn't be messing with any of them."

"They do other stuff now," I said. "Schools, breakfast programs."

"They do all that. I got a niece gets fed in that program. But don't think for a minute the white boys give a damn. They'll never forget how those Panthers started out. White boys don't play, when black folks talk revolution."

"All I'm saying, Edna, is Grace didn't seem like no Peck to me."

Edna leaped up again, laughing loudly. "Leah, you're too much!" She was doubled over. "No Peck to you. What do *you* know about Pecks?"

"I'm just saying Grace was okay," I said.

105

I took a deep breath. "She may have had her problems, Edna, but she was no racist. Anyway, I need your help with this. I need you to tell me what you hear—anything that might have to do with Grace's murder."

Edna gave me a long look. She was holding her mouth in that special way she had, frowning, a look that said she had seen this before and she wasn't sure about any of it. "I'll help you out," she said, finally. "But understand— I'm doing this for you. I don't care nothing about that girl and never will. I've been knowing white trash all my life. The woman will sleep with a brother, turn around and treat a sister like shit. Don't try to tell me this Grace was down in East Oakland feeding the little black kids out of the goodness of her heart, because I won't believe it. Trying to get next to her main squeeze, more like it. But I can see you're serious about this. So I'll listen up. I'll tell you what I do know—that jockey Bucky Timmons's tight as thieves with one of the owners. And Ferguson wasn't the only brother Grace was hanging with."

"Who is Bucky Timmons tight with?'

"Everybody knows who he is, because Bucky rides for him. Considered a winning combination. It's a guy named Landis—yes, that's who it is."

I left work that day, excited. I had managed to win Edna over. And Edna had mentioned James Ferguson wasn't the only black man Grace had been dating. I hadn't had time to ask her more, and I hadn't wanted to press my luck. Next time we talked, I would definitely get back to the subject.

As I walked into the house, Yoshi was leaving the kitchen. I grabbed his arm and pulled him upstairs with me. "Yoshi, you said you'd help me. I need you to research this Hugh Landis guy."

"Who?" Yoshi asked.

"An owner. Out at the track. Maybe also a trainer," I said. "Maybe on the racing board. Find out everything you can about him. And a jockey named Bucky Timmons, too."

"The INS sent me a letter today. There's a problem with my student visa. I may not have much time."

"Oh, Yoshi. You took care of that ages ago."

106

"I have to go in for an interview. Gotta prove I'm actually in school."

"Well, go to the interview. It will all work out." I was not giving his INS letter much attention. I had my own preoccupations. "You said you'd help me, Yoshi. There's so much to check up on. Look at this. Grace left this betting slip in my room. Check these names, the numbers—see what they mean, who was running that day. What the odds were? See if there's a record of people who won amounts large enough to have to register with the IRS."

"How exactly am I going to do *that*?"

"Oh, Yoshi, you're smart. It's *research*. Just figure it out. Old racing forms? I don't know, but you're smart, you can figure it out."

"Okay, yeah, sure," he said, pocketing the slip. "I'll see what I can do."

After Yoshi left, I lay down for a quick nap. I had barely fallen asleep when Carol called me to the phone. I walked to the hallway and picked up the receiver.

"You're a hard person to catch up with," a male voice said, confidently.

The voice was familiar.

"To whom am I speaking?"

"I'd have never believed you'd forget about Ronnie," he said.

"Oh, of course. Ronnie. You're the old friend of Grace's."

"I thought you were going to call *me*," he said. His voice was confidential, flirtatious, as if we already had a relationship. It was odd. I felt trapped, as if he were my boyfriend and had caught me waiting for the call of another man.

"You beat me to the punch," I lied.

"Yes," he laughed. "I've been known to do that. How about meeting for a drink? I'd like to talk to you."

We agreed to meet the next night at Charlie Brown's, a new restaurant which had just opened up over in Emeryville.

I knew I was overstepping the limits Joey and I had established. The track, and nothing but the track, Joey had warned. I had also agreed to tell Paul and Yoshi whenever I went out to meet people connected with this case. But this opportunity was too good to pass up. Grace's journal had plenty of references to Ronnie. I could use them to get him talking.

107

XIII

Ronnie was sitting on the porch at Charlie Brown's, wearing a fringed suede jacket, when I arrived at eight the following evening. Charlie Brown's was one of the hip new watering holes which were springing up in the East Bay. It sat on a rock pile on the Emeryville shoreline, close to I-80 whose roar could be heard as I parked in the lot in front of the restaurant.

"Leah! You've come!" Ronnie jumped up. His light brown hair fell carelessly across his forehead. He had the lanky grace of a distance runner. His long legs were encased in a pair of dark corduroy bellbottoms. His smile was eager, like a child expecting a gift. He hugged me as if we were old friends. "I've been thinking a lot about you since the last time we talked." Ronnie seemed to view this meeting as a date.

I countered with formality. "It's good to see you again, Ronnie. Grace talked so much about you." Grace may not have said much, but her diary had.

"That was the whole point of coming together, wasn't it?" He was smiling, but I sensed a slight withdrawal. The hostess led us to a table with a view of the bay, misty and magical; Mount Tamalpais' dark pyramid silhouetted by the sun.

"What'll you have?" asked Ronnie.

"A shot of Jack Daniels with a water chaser," I said. I was trying to seem more sophisticated. Normally I ordered tomato juice or a Coke.

"Fine for you," he said." I'll have an Anchor Steam Beer myself. I had to give up the hard stuff. It was messing with my looks."

"It didn't mess with them too badly," I said. I surprised myself. I didn't flirt often, but it was easy to flirt with Ronnie.

He looked pleased. Our eyes met with that start of recognition that signals attraction. "You look like jail-bait, yourself."

"Come on," I said, "I'm twenty three." Something was off here. I was enjoying myself too much. The conversation lingered over me like a caress.

"I would have taken you for sixteen."

"The waitress didn't ask me for ID when I ordered the Jack Daniels," I said.

"Of course not. She wants to sell drinks. What all did Grace tell you about me, anyway?" Ronnie added.

"You were the first man she was serious about." This seemed safe.

"Maybe. She always had boys after her. I was never sure I was the first."

"What happened after high school?" I asked.

"She got pregnant. I figured we'd get married. Wrong. I didn't know how wrong I was. I was outta step with the times," he said, "and outta step with Grace. That's usually been my luck with women."

"Did Grace have an abortion?"

"The way you put it. Like it was a dental appointment. It wasn't even legal then. She drove down to Mexico with some so-called friend and got it cut outta her. She told me all about it, afterwards. Woke up in a pool of blood; coulda died. Didn't want anything to do with me after that."

"That's sad," I said. I had wondered what had happened between them. I remembered Grace's cryptic line: "Fall in love too easily, out of love too fast."

"Eventually she moved over to Berkeley; I was off to Nam." When I had first met Ronnie, he had struck me as one of the lucky ones. Now I wasn't so sure. He looked straight at me with his green eyes. "I divide my life into two parts. Before Nam, and after. I figured nothing after could faze me. The before part I don't think about too much."

"First loves," I said. "They're all tied up with our childhood, everything we wished for and couldn't have. They're like ghost lovers, people you never finish with. You remember them as bigger than they were. You always think—if only."

His eyes appraised me over the table. "Yeah," he said, "you're the sensitive type all right."

"I hate for it to be so obvious."

"So you're sensitive, so what?" He frowned slightly. "In the military, they train that out of you. That's one reason I joined the Vietnam Vets against the War when I got back. I wanted to hold on to whatever feelings I still had. I like being around guys who were over there. I don't get on so good with these antiwar types who've never walked shit-deep in mud in a rice paddy. With them, it's all theory. —You know anyone else who went to Nam?" Ronnie added.

"A few," I said. I didn't want to mention Joey's name.

"Hey, you want to hear one of my songs?" Ronnie asked, abruptly changing the subject. "I wrote this for Grace when I was over there."

"I didn't know you were a musician."

"Oh, yeah. Wrote a few things. Had me an electric guitar."

We were seated by windows that overlooked the bay. The sun, red and swollen, was dropping down into the water. "Here, I'll sing it for you." He sang in a low voice:

> I just want to see you, now and again.
> Whatever else happens, just now and again.
> Have a drink, walk the pier, take a look at the bay.
> Whatever else happens, just have things my way.
> Now and again.

Ronnie sang these lines in a husky hillbilly drawl. Why did I feel as if they were addressed to me? The song wasn't written for me; it was written for Grace, wasn't it? I watched the light dwindling over the bay.

"That's wonderful," I said. "Did you ever show it to Grace?"

"No," he said, "she wouldn't have been interested. It started out for her, but now it's just a song. It could be for anyone. It could be for you."

I had finished my Jack Daniels and his beer glass was empty.

"So how about another round?" he said.

I felt a weird pull of attraction toward him which troubled me. This was definitely not part of my plan. "Ronnie. I have a lot to do tomorrow. I better get going."

"So soon? I thought we'd have dinner here."

"No," I said. "You said meet for a drink. I've already eaten. I can't stay."

"This isn't fair," he said. There was some pleading hope in his eyes, hard to refuse. "You meet me for a drink, let me pour my guts out, then say you have to go? I haven't found out a damn thing about you."

"We can meet another time," I said.

"Well, then," he answered, "three questions first."

"If they're fast," I said, "go ahead."

"Was Grace seeing anyone that you know of?"

I was startled. "I don't know," I said. "I'm trying to find out."

110

"Why do *you* care?" I was uncomfortable with the reversal in our roles. I didn't plan to share what little information I had. I had to formulate a plausible answer in the vicinity of the truth.

"I liked Grace. I feel really bad about what happened. I'm trying to understand it."

"Do you understand better because of talking to me?"

"A little better," I said. "And that's question number three."

He leaned forward, smiling his lopsided smile. "No, one more. You got a boyfriend?"

"That's personal."

"And the questions you asked me weren't?"

"I was asking you about Grace," I said. "I didn't ask you about your romantic status."

"I'll give it to you anyway," Ronnie said. "Divorced. One kid. Still pay child support. I'm older than you and rough around the edges. Not a likely prospect, I suppose."

I was attracted to him, but wary. "I have to go. We can talk again."

"I hope you mean it," he said.

Later that night I watched the eleven pm news with my three roommates. The Watergate burglars had been indicted by a Federal grand jury. Nonetheless victory for Richard Nixon was predicted against George McGovern.

Paul was teasing Yoshi about Buddhism. "So what did the Buddhist say to the hot dog vendor?"

"Okay, sock it to me."

"Make me one with everything."

Carol and Yoshi laughed. I was distracted. My mind was crowded with thoughts of Grace, wondering about Ronnie Xavier Jones. Who was he, anyway?

The next morning, I got another call. I was half asleep. I grabbed a robe to take the call on the upstairs hallway phone. "Sorry," Carol said. "He said to wake you up."

It was Joey. He was upset. "We've got to talk. I'll come by and pick you up."

"Hold on," I said, "I'm not even awake yet."

"Well, wake up," he said, "in more ways than one. It's eight o'clock. You should be up now anyway. I'll buy you coffee."

"I'm not up yet. Anyway, I have to be at work at ten—"

"That's two hours away," he said. "We gotta talk, cuz. I'm coming over."

"Maybe I won't be here when you arrive," I said. I hated his tone.

"You'll be there. I'm just around the corner. Anyway, this is your life I'm concerned about." I took a quick shower, threw on my jeans and sweatshirt. As I opened the front door, I could see Joey's Chevy parked at the curb.

"Pancake House," he said. "Breakfast." The International House of Pancakes was three blocks down Telegraph. I jumped in the car, and Joey started right in. "Thought we had a deal," he said. "Your field of inquiry was the track."

"I've started asking around out there," I said.

"The track, Leah. The track. Not up near St. Helena, not out in Concord at a funeral, or anywhere else. What in hell were you doing up in Clear Lake last Saturday, anyway?"

"How did you know about that?"

"The husband called OPD yesterday to ask about you. Said you told them you were with the police."

"I *am* working for the police, remember?"

Joey pulled into the IHOP parking lot. "You weren't working for me then," he said. "You'd better remember that you're an informant. You can't go around saying you're working with the police. You'll blow your cover. Who's gonna talk to you then?"

I definitely didn't like the word *informant*. The way I looked at it, I was helping in an investigation. "It's really none of your business who I talk to, you know."

"Leah—this is a murder investigation. You give your information to me. I know a lot more than you do about what's involved here, even if you are studying for a BA from that crackpot university."

He infuriated me when he attacked UC Berkeley. We had had argu-

112

ments about this before. In fact, we had months of not speaking. Our family history was based on blow-ups and recriminations. Sometimes when Joey got angry, his eyeballs bulged out of his head. I knew he had high blood pressure and I was terrified he would lose control. He had killed in Vietnam. Now he worked the streets as a legal killer. But he was also family. One of the few I had.

I would smooth the troubled waters. "Nobody denies you're the expert. I went to visit her parents. Big deal."

"What did that bitch mother of hers tell you, anyway?"

"How she always thought Grace would turn out bad—stuff like that."

"She give you anything?"

"Like?" I asked.

"How do I know? Like something she should have given us? Photographs, letters, I don't know. Something. Anything."

"Anything important, I would have told you," I lied. "That's my job, remember?"

Joey sighed. He sounded relieved. "That's what I kept saying to myself," he said.

But then a second line of thought occurred to him. "What the hell were you doing at Charlie Brown's last night with Ronnie Jones?"

"How did you know, Joey?" I asked, startled. "You wiretapping my phone?"

"That's just like you, Leah. All you know about cops and robbers is what you've seen in the movies. Tap your phone—maybe not such a bad idea."

He pushed open his door and got out. I followed him across the parking lot. Inside the House of Pancakes, fluorescent lights shown on bright orange naugahyde seats. The hostess found us an empty booth, surrounded by other empty booths and tables. IHOP was not a popular Berkeley student hang-out. We waited while the waitress had poured us coffees. Joey ordered the special—pancakes, eggs, bacon, hash browns, and a baking powder biscuit with jelly.

"Great deal," he said, to me. "Want me to get you one?"

"I'd like tomato juice. So—how did you know I saw Ronnie Jones?"

"We talk to everyone connected to a victim," he said. "We talked to Ronnie later last night."

"He hadn't seen Grace in years. Why do you care about him?"

113

"You answer every question with one of your own. You sure you ain't studying up to be a lawyer? It should be enough for you that someone was desperate enough to kill your friend. You don't want to wind up next to her in the morgue, do you?"

"You have a great way with words, Joey," I said.

"Yeah, well, looking at bodies laid out in that freezer, I'd prefer your body not be one of them."

His warning evoked a chill of fear which I tried not to show. "You still haven't told me why you talked to Ronnie last night."

"I don't have to tell you nothing, Leah. Get that through your head. You stumbled onto a little something. You saw Grace Neville before she got popped. That don't mean you get access to the whole goddamned case."

"It does if you want me to stop sticking my nose in your shit, as you so elegantly put it."

"God, I hate educated women," Joey said. He drained his coffee cup, looked me in the eye. "Don't you get it, Leah? Every time you start sniffing around, finding out things you're not supposed to know, you put yourself in danger."

"You told me to ask around at the track."

"You work there; it looks natural. Speaking of which, some leads out there I want you to follow up on. A guy on the racing board name of Hugh Landis. Lots of bucks—lots of horses." The same name Freddie had mentioned. Yoshi was supposed to get me more information about him.

"He's having a party this afternoon," Joey continued. "Turf Club. It's reserved from three pm on. Get your fanny up there and find out what you can. Who comes to the party. How they know Landis. Who shows up—the girls they bring along. Dress yourself up. Look cute, get the men drinking and talking. None of those damn hippie skirts down to your ankles."

"How does Landis connect to Grace's murder?"

"I'm hoping you can tell me. I got a couple leads she was banging Landis. I sometimes wonder was there anybody she wasn't banging."

He stopped when he saw the look on my face.

"Aside from Grace, there's a few other matters we're checking out about Landis," he continued, after a moment.

"Like what?"

"Can't tell you now," Joey answered. "A man is innocent until proved guilty—isn't that what you Berkeley liberals believe? A man has money, a bunch of horses, a lot of good-looking women, there's talk. I'm gonna give you a few names to listen up for." He scribbled some names on a pad, tore off the sheet, and slid the paper across the table at me. In his scrawl were the names Jay Landis, Junior and Senior. Bucky Timmons. Freddie Corster.

So Joey had questions about Freddie. This was interesting. But Freddie was my race track buddy and he had told me he didn't want to talk to the police. I didn't want to tell Joey about my friendship with Freddie. I would hold back for a while, at least until I had something worth telling. "This is great, Joey," I said, putting the paper in my purse. "You've given me something to go on."

"So you can leave off Ronnie Jones—and all those other people," he answered.

"Why are you so worried about Ronnie?" I asked. "Date the boy next door, you used to tell me."

"Not the boy next door who's gone to Nam. Look at me, you want living proof. Only masochists need apply." Joey smiled at me with some tenderness. "Jeez, cuz, don't go looking for losers. What good is all your education if it can't help you find a good man?" He wiped his lips with a paper napkin. "Yeah," he continued. "I've got to get through to you, Leah. This is serious stuff. You've grown up in a dream, your nose stuck in a book and your old man reciting Shakespeare. I've been dealing with the Panthers for years now. Seen bodies buried in basements. There was this one guy. Just a few days ago, we found him shot to death in a rusted-out car on East 14th. Billie Thomas. I knew him."

Again a chill rippled over my skin. That name. Had I heard it before? "You don't know who killed him," I said.

"He wasn't killed by an informant," Joey said. "He *was* an informant. He was working undercover for me. The Panthers executed him when they found out. We think it was your guy, Mr. James Ferguson, behind it. There's things you should know about these Panthers, Leah. It ain't all this peace and freedom stuff you believe in. They have something they call 'The Greater Fear.' You heard of that? It means they terrorize their own members. If the brothers and sisters get out of line, they get punished. Severely. Or offed, like this Billie Thomas."

115

Back in the car, Joey cleared his throat. "I got a little present for you, cuz," he said. He reached under the seat and pulled out a brown package which he unwrapped carefully. It was a small revolver, with a wooden handle. Its short metal barrel gleamed blue-black. I had never looked at a handgun up close. It lay there on the seat between us like a bad omen.

"Pick it up," he said. "I got a snubbie for you. It's a Colt Cobra—nice little gun for a lady. Put it in your purse. It won't bite. It's not even loaded."

"I don't want it." The thing lay there, blue-black and mesmerizing.

"You need it," Joey said. "Pick it up and put it in your purse. I'll take you out next week and teach you how to use it. Go ahead, Leah."

I picked it up. It was heavier than it looked. Gingerly I dropped it in my shoulder bag. I felt hypnotized, doing things because Joey was telling me to do them.

"You must think I've got real guts."

"I think you're fucking stupid is what I think," Joey said. "The problem is you're too crazy to know it. I've gotta do what I can to try and take care of you."

"I don't know who betrayed my informant," Joey added. "But I have my suspicions. Some people in my own department I don't trust. I'm not telling anyone that you're working for me. And don't you be telling anyone either." He handed me an envelope. "Petty cash for expenses," he said. "Three hundred in twenties."

I put the envelope in my bag. Three hundred dollars was a lot of money. I had crossed over yet another line. I wondered if I would like that person I was becoming.

XIV

I ran upstairs to my room to get ready for work. It looked different. I had left my books stacked neatly by my desk. Now they were strewn around; some were on the floor. My chair had been pulled away from the desk. A dresser drawer was open.

Yoshi tapped on my door and then entered.

"Who's been in my room this morning?" I asked.

"Nobody that I know of. Why?"

"Look at my desk," I said. I picked up a textbook from the floor. "It's a mess. I don't leave my books on the floor like this."

Yoshi shrugged. His own room was stacked with newspapers and magazines, schoolbooks lost under piles of papers.

"I don't have time to straighten this mess out. I've got to get to work. But, Yoshi, don't let anyone come in when I'm not here. I don't like it."

Yoshi took a cigarette out of his shirt pocket. He didn't meet my eyes.

"Look, I've gotta run. What do you want?"

"My immigration hearing," Yoshi began, "those guys—"

"—I don't have time for that now, Yoshi. Can't we talk about it later?"

"Okay," Yoshi answered. "Want me to hang out in your room until you get home? I'll study in here and make sure no one comes in." Yoshi often took naps on my bed or listened to my records while I was gone. I liked it. It made me feel like we were family.

"Make yourself at home," I answered. "But wait a few minutes. Right now I've got to get dressed for work." I felt uneasy, disorganized. After making sure the door was closed, I tucked the envelope Joey had given me in my journal, and then placed the journal under my mattress, on top of Grace's notebook. Anyone snooping around would have a hard time finding these.

I had arranged with Beatrice to work a short shift, to be free to check out the Turf Club Party at three. In my shoulder bag, I had a black rayon dress, earrings, and pantyhose. At two forty-five I slipped into the rest room to change. The black rayon was slinky against my skin. I felt loose and free inside it, as if I were naked. I applied red lipstick at the mirror, brushed out my hair, dabbed Chanel No. 5 behind my ears. The woman who looked back from the mirror was a stranger—darker and more glamorous than the Leah whose daily reflection I knew by heart.

I stepped off the elevator and entered the Turf Club, its tables set with linen tablecloths and sparkling wine glasses. Along a wall the hot table displayed huge hams and beef roasts, platters of pink-orange salmon. The clients here were older, fashionable people, well-dressed. They stood to gain or lose significant wealth by the performance of a particular horse and by what happened on the race track, but, unlike the crowd swarming and shouting in Mainline, these people masked their eagerness or their desperation. Racing's motto, I thought—the king of sports, the sport of kings. Up here in the Turf Club the kings ruled.

A large man stood with a group waiting to be seated. He was wearing a light blue suit of some expensive material; a yellow shirt. A handkerchief was folded into an elaborate point in his breast pocket. With him was a woman in an enormous hat. She had a nervous, bored look. I was sure she was the wife. From the way the man was holding forth, I suspected he was Hugh Landis. "I've bought some of the best," he was saying. "But to get your money's worth, you have to breed. It takes you right into the heart of handicapping."

A small man offered his views. "Everyone talks about the last quarter-mile of the race, but it's the first quarter-mile where the race is won," he was saying. "I gotta be real relaxed outta the gate. I gotta feel where I'm gonna set my colt up at. Gotta feel the way he's running. Finesse, now, he likes to get to maximum cruising speed fast as he can, but if I ask him for too much on the run to the first turn, it ends right there." Apparently he was a jockey.

"Take my colt, Mighty Luck, now—his sire—" Hugh Landis was interrupted as George Mooney, Beatrice's boss, joined them. George was wearing white slacks and an orange-flowered shirt which hung out over his potbelly. Hugh Landis took George's pudgy hand, placing his own left hand warmly on top of their joined fists. "George! Glad you could make it. We're just waiting for a table. —I think you're gonna see some real pretty running this afternoon."

"I got a couple of wagers on this race myself."

"I'm sure you do, George, I'm sure you do." Hugh Landis winked at him, as the hostess moved the group off to a table by the window.

Mighty Luck. I remembered the name on the betting slip Grace had left in my room. The horse was running in the last race of the afternoon, a heavily wagered race with many contenders. My assignment was to break into that group and get them talking to me, but I saw no excuse. I glanced around the Turf Club. A young man sat alone at a table, staring down at the track where horses were parading before the fifth race. He was in his early twenties, with pale, almost colorless eyelashes and eyebrows. The same man, I realized, who had sat behind us in the balcony at Grace's funeral. I walked to his table.

"Excuse me," I said. "Didn't I see you at Grace Neville's funeral?"

His eyes slid over my close-fitting black dress, then up into my face.

"Do I know you?" he said. His voice was languid.

"No," I said. "I was a friend of Grace's. I was sitting in the balcony, at her funeral, and I saw you there. My name is Leah. Leah DeMartino." He gazed at me slowly. Then he took my offered hand. His handshake was damp.

"A friend of Grace's," he said.

"And you are—?"

"Jay Landis," he said. I felt a slight rush of adrenaline. Jay Landis was one of the names Joey had asked me to check out. "Do you want to sit down?" This at least sounded friendlier. "May I get you something to drink? Waitress!" he called. "We'll have another Chardonnay, please."

"How did you know Grace?" I asked, taking the seat across from him.

"She ran our horses for us in the morning. In fact Mighty Luck was one of her favorites." I had had no idea Grace ran horses, although Freddie Corster had said something about her coming out to the track early. There was a lot I hadn't known about Grace.

"Was she good with horses?" I said.

"Very good," he replied.

"So you knew her for a long time?" I asked. I made my voice sound bright and superficial.

He shrugged. "Not that long. She was—you might say, a friend of the family. My father asked me to go to the funeral to pay our family's respects."

The waitress set a glass of wine in front of me, and I took a sip. "Thanks for this," I said. "Jay Landis," I said slowly. I pretended to think further. "Yes, that was the name, Jay. Jay Landis. Grace mentioned you."

He raised his head, suddenly alert. "What did she say about me?"

I was nonchalant. "Oh, let me try to remember . . . ?"

Two pink patches flared on his otherwise colorless cheeks. "I'd really like to know what she said."

"Look, I can't talk now. I'm meeting friends at Top of the Stretch. I shouldn't have sat down." Actually I needed to come up with some ideas.

"Are you free later? I could meet you after the last race."

"I'll have time then. Look for me down by the Hot Spoon on Mainline." I stood up. Beatrice sat a few tables away with an large woman in a pink pants suit. I hoped she hadn't seen me. Although she had given me permission to leave my shift at three-thirty, she might wonder why I was in the Turf Club, all dressed up. I didn't want to raise suspicions.

I headed into the crowds at Mainline to watch the next few races. It was crowded with men of every background and nationality, hawking, spitting, arguing in small groups. Admission to this lowest level of the track was only three dollars. Most of the female tellers hated working this floor, although when I had started in June, I had loved Mainline. This level was closest to the actual track, open to the air down in the lower bleachers. Mainline offered the best view of the horses when the trainers paraded these magnificent animals, high-strung and fine-boned, before they were to race.

I had loved it all, before Grace was murdered. Now the men's excitement seemed volatile and out of control. Their intense desire to win was followed by black moods of rage when they lost. "God damn, I shoulda played number two! I just missed putting him in the race! Let me show you where I almost played him." That volatility in the air of Mainline now felt to me like a signal of violence.

Standing in my tight black dress, among a thousand frantic gamblers on Mainline, I felt as if I were Mata Hari. Men looked at me with interest. I was learning that, like Grace, I could use personal charm to get my way. I could dissemble, lie, possibly seduce. This could be dangerous, and I was starting to like it. I had crossed over so many lines in the last few days, tried on so many new identities, that reporting on people I worked with seemed almost normal. Perhaps I could exonerate James Ferguson by learning information that would point the spotlight on the real killer. I was using this thought like a mantra to help justify what I did.

It was four minutes before the last race. The handlers paraded the horses in a circle. I caught a glimpse of Bucky Timmons about to mount Mighty Luck. Bucky was a short man with bowed legs. His slightly protruding front teeth gave him his nickname. As he swung up into the saddle, something shiny disappeared into the pocket of his racing jacket. Some good luck token, I thought. Jockeys were superstitious. A stumble during the race could end a career. Bucky Timmons saw me, waved, and said something to Mighty Luck's handler who was holding the reins. The handler looked over at me and laughed.

Were they responding to a pretty girl in the stands? I waved back, self-conscious, sorry I had attracted their attention. I did not want to miss a second of this race. Mighty Luck was a relative newcomer, running against several well-known favorites. Although Bucky Timmons and Hugh Landis were considered a formidable team, the odds today were on the favorite, Stella's Star.

Freddie Corster turned from a betting window and walked across the cement floor toward me. "Hey, Leah." His voice cracked with excitement. "Want in on a little secret? It might net you a grand." The tic in his eye beat nervously.

"We aren't allowed to make bets while we're on the job."

"You're the only one who takes that rule seriously. Live on the chump change we get from these guys? You see how those muckety mucks up at the Turf Club are partying. I just put a hundred on that new horse, Mighty Luck. You want to put a little something on her? I'll place the bet for you."

"No thanks, Freddie," I said. "But I'm curious, what kind of tip do you have?"

"Up to now, Landis has told Timmons not to push her," Freddie answered. "Not many people realize how fast she is. I think today he's gonna let her go all out. If I win, will you go to the window for me? I'll pay you a twenty." Co-workers often asked me to go to the IRS window for them. The taxes on their winnings wouldn't amount to much on my part-time salary, but on their salaries, the taxes could add up. Twenty dollars paid my groceries for a week. However I was already jeopardizing my principles, my whole life, with this damn case. No need to add the IRS to my problems.

"Not this time," I answered. Then I remembered his earlier story about Grace at the IRS window. "So, Freddie, when Grace went to the IRS window that Sunday, maybe she wasn't collecting her own winnings. She could have been picking up the money for someone else."

"Yeah," Freddie answered, "but Bucky Timmons had a jones for Grace. He probably gave her a tip. He was riding a horse for Hugh Landis. Horse came in first. Named Finesse. I was so mad I hadn't bet on that horse I promised myself I wouldn't lose out a second time."

"What do you know about Jay Landis? That's the son, right? Was he seeing Grace, too?"

"Who wasn't seeing Grace?" Freddie answered. "I catch that Jay Landis around here every now and then. He's an odd bird, all right. Looks like he doesn't want to hurt his nostrils with the stink of the horses." He lowered his voice, "You didn't tell the police anything I told you, did you?"

"No," I said. "Why?"

Freddie ducked his head, his eye winking in that nervous tic.

"They called me in. Said they heard I had some information on Grace Neville—that I saw her leave the track Sunday morning, with a black guy. Wanted me to say it was Ferguson."

"Was it?"

"I saw a black guy in a car. I didn't get a good look at him. How much can you tell when some guy is sitting in a car? Tan Buick pulled up in the parking lot. Deuce and a quarter—black hardtop. Man, that baby was clean. Grace walked toward it. I don't even know if she got in the car with this dude. I couldn't identify the guy—his face was turned away."

Our conversation meant we had missed the start of the race. Now we turned to watch. On the far side of the track the horses were approaching the curve in a close clump, moving as smoothly as if they were on wheels, a gleam of cinnamon, chestnut, and black. As they rounded the curve, Stella's Star was in the lead. By the second quarter, she was several lengths ahead. As the filly rounded the final corner, coming into the home stretch, Mighty Luck and God's My Witness were gaining on her. Suddenly she stumbled. Stella Star's jockey went flying. Mighty Luck missed the small man by inches as Bucky Timmons whipped his horse past to victory.

The crowd went crazy. The announcer overhead was stuttering, calling for an ambulance, a doctor, over and over again. People were arguing, thrusting their racing forms in each other's faces, shouting, "It was a foul! I saw it!" Someone swore Bucky Timmons had brushed up against Stella's Star before she fell. Others said Stella had too much of a lead to be touched. The video

122

cameras did a slow motion replay; the judges declared there was no evidence of foul play. Mighty Luck was the winner. Freddie leaped in the air, whooping with laughter, grabbing strangers by the shoulders, shouting, "I did it!" He waved his ticket in my face. Hugh Landis entered the Winner's Circle and clapped Bucky Timmons on the back. Flashbulbs went off.

I saw Jay Landis approaching. He hunched his shoulders inward with a fastidious look, as if he feared someone brushing up against him. His tall, thin frame resembled a huge bird, coming through the crowd, awkward in flight.

"Congratulations on Mighty Luck," I said. "Isn't that your horse?"

"My father's horse," he corrected me. "How about it, are you free now?"

"We could meet at Denny's in Emeryville."

"I haven't the slightest idea how to find Denny's in Emeryville," he said. "Couldn't we do something a little more—civilized?"

"I meet my friends there all the time. Get on I-80, take the Emeryville exit. You'll see Denny's from the freeway."

"Denny's it will have to be," said Jay Landis, with a little shrug, "since you seem to have a penchant for dives."

I hung around long enough to catch the next race, then jumped in my VW and drove to Denny's in Emeryville. Why had I chosen such a blue-collar place to meet this scion of the upper class? I enjoyed the irony of forcing him to move outside his comfortable and snobbish world. He was there waiting for me, grinding a cigarette into the sidewalk with the sole of his expensive loafer.

A waitress led us to a booth upholstered in red plastic, then bustled back with a stainless steel pitcher of coffee. He looked amazed when the waitress set a cup down before him. He tasted it carefully, then shook his head. "This is coffee? I didn't expect espresso, but this is pure shit."

I ignored this response. "Tell me more about Grace," I said. "You said she ran the horses for your father. Were you out at the race track in the mornings, too?" I planned to ask Jay Landis so many questions he would have no chance to find out how little I knew.

"Grace had a way with animals. She had a soft spot for them. She couldn't stand to see them hurt. I suppose that's why she was always getting involved with losers. Like the Black Panthers." Jay's colorless eyes drilled into mine. "But I'm still waiting to hear," he said, "what she told you about me."

123

"She said she had found the right person, but maybe he was too young."

"We came from such different backgrounds. The difference was a turn-on. She was a liberated woman. Very Berkeley. She accepted me as I am. Grace didn't expect anything from me." He tapped a new cigarette out of a tooled leather cigarette case, offered me one. I shook my head.

"A liberated Berkeley woman, what do you mean by that?" Grace had not struck me as a Berkeley women's libber.

"Grace had done drugs. She knew her way around sexually. That kind of liberated woman." I thought of Grace, with her finely chiseled face, with her shadow of sadness. Jay Landis did not have the charm of a Ronnie Jones, the magnetism of a James Ferguson. Why had Grace even bothered with him?

"Have the police talked to you?"

"Why on earth would the police talk to me?" His pale eyes drilled into me again.

"Her case is still unsolved," I said. I quoted Joey, sipping my coffee. "The police want to talk to anyone who has known a murder victim."

"Except for some legal technicalities, they have the case solved right now," Jay Landis said, but he looked uneasy. "The police haven't spoken to me. I assume her case is wrapped up. Grace's and my—our liaison, you might call it—was private. I'd like it to stay that way." He smiled at me. There was something strange in his smile. "My lawyer said for the police to consider me any kind of suspect was absurd. What kind of game are you playing with me, anyway?" So he *had* talked to a lawyer. He leaned back in his chair, his shirt open at the neck, careless in his youth and wealth.

"No game," I said. "Grace wrote something rather—cryptic—about you, and I wondered what it meant."

"I doubt Grace even knew how to spell *cryptic*," Jay Landis said. "But *cryptic*?—well, I'm not your everyday kind of guy."

"I can see that," I said, in my most flattering tone. I hadn't met a man yet who thought he was your everyday kind of guy. Jay looked as ordinary as any of them.

"I'm creative. That excited her. I like props, costumes—stuff like that." He continued to smile at me in an odd way. "You might be interested, being from Berkeley and all. You seem like a liberated woman, Leah."

124

I played along. "What do you have in mind?"

"A love drug. Some role-playing. We'd dress up." He wiped his fingers across his eyebrow, as if brushing something away. "It's odd. I feel free around you, Leah. I can be myself with you—like I could with Grace."

"It's because we're not of your class." I meant it as a joke, but he gave a laugh of recognition.

"Well," he said, "you're right, but that's not so important. What's important is that I feel free around you. Want to give it a try?"

"Give what a try?"

"A date. We would book a room somewhere."

"Oh, yeah," I said. "A sex date." I tried to sound like I knew all about these. I was trying to size him up. He had had a relationship with Grace. Could this pale young man have murdered her? Joey said lovers are always suspects. Or Jay Landis might know about other men Grace had dated at the track. Could I get Jay talking?

"Where?" I asked.

"You choose."

"It would have to be a very nice place," I said. A very crowded and safe place, I added silently to myself.

"The St. Francis in San Francisco?"

"It's a deal," I said. The St. Francis Hotel on Union Square was one of San Francisco's oldest and most elegant establishments.

"I'll give you a call. Dress the way you're dressed right now."

"And you?" I asked, "Will you be dressed just the way you are right now?"

"You'll see. I'll be a surprise."

He paid the bill. I noticed that he didn't leave a tip.

XV

I was home by six pm. "Hey, Leah! You got a couple calls today," Carol called from the kitchen. She was stirring a big pot of spaghetti sauce.

"Who called?"

"Male called," Carol said. "Maybe Mr. Right."

"Did Mr. Right leave a name?"

"A guy named Ronnie. He said he was going out of town for a couple weeks, but he'd be in touch when he got back."

"Ronnie?" I had seen Ronnie just last night, but I had almost forgotten about him in today's excitement—the deal with Joey, the Turf Club, Mighty Luck's upset win, the conversation with Jay Landis.

"He's not that guy tied up with your murdered friend, is he?"

"Yeah. Sorta," I replied, evasively. "Who was the second call?"

"A reporter from the Tribune. They want to do a story on you. Ruby Bailey, she said her name was. Hell, she even wanted to do a story from my point of view, if she couldn't get you. Give her a call and get your fifteen minutes of fame."

"Anyone else?"

"Art Leopold called. Said to call him. Said you had the number."

Art Leopold might help me set up an interview with James. Then, if this Ruby Bailey agreed, I would publish a story showing the inconsistencies in the case against Ferguson. It all worked out easily. Ruby Bailey, on the phone, had the voice of a young black woman. She was eager to read anything I had written. She thought she could get my article printed. She wanted to meet with me the following week. This could be my first break into print, a preview of my longer article.

Art Leopold was still in his office when I called. The Panthers were having a party Saturday afternoon at their Lighthouse Bar on Telegraph Avenue to celebrate one of the member's release from prison. James Ferguson was planning to drop by. James would be free to meet me before that.

126

"James can meet you at the George Jackson Clinic at one. He'll go on to the Lighthouse after that. You might want to go, too. It's a benefit to raise money for the other Panthers who are still in prison."

I agreed to meet James at the clinic. I called Edna. She and Yoshi would catch up with me at the Lighthouse. Despite Edna's views about not messing with the Panthers, she had changed her mind when she learned my friend Yoshi would also be there. "That little brother is cute," she told me.

"He's not exactly a brother," I said.

"Hell, baby, they're all brothers to me," she said, "All except them Pecks. You get him to come along, and we'll make it a party."

At a quarter to one I knocked on the grilled door of a shabby storefront on the corner of Adeline and Alcatraz. Behind the grill of the doorway a staircase led steeply upstairs. A sign in the window read GEORGE JACKSON CLINIC. A photo of George Jackson over the caption, "Soledad Brother," had been placed next to the sign.

Next door a restaurant specialized in Cajun, Fries, BBQ, Burritos and Burgers. A small grocery store across the street advertised Liquor Beer Wine Groceries. I knocked for several minutes. Finally a tall black man with a soft face and beard came down the stairs. He was wearing a stethoscope.

"I'm Leah DeMartino. "I'm meeting James Ferguson here, at one."

He looked at me, then looked up and down the sidewalk, before he opened the door to let me in. "I'm Clyde Turner. They just called to say you were coming." I followed him up the stairs and into a small room on the second floor. Venetian blinds were drawn halfway down over a window which looked onto the street. This seemed to be the waiting room. School chairs with little desks attached were arranged along the walls; there was a scarred metal desk in the corner. At the back the room opened onto a long hallway.

"Have a seat," he said, gesturing toward the school chairs. "I'm doing some paper work. You by any chance a nurse?"

I sat down on one of the school chairs, placing my shoulder bag beside me. "I worked as an EMT on the ambulances for a while."

127

"Emergency medical technician," Clyde said. "That could be handy. I'm always looking for volunteers."

"What kind of patients do you see here?" I asked.

"We started out as a clinic for Panthers and their children, and for the kids in our school on East 18th. We've opened it up to the community now. We do basic stuff at the moment: blood pressure screening, school immunizations. We've got a gynecologist who sees patients on Thursday night. I want to start a sickle cell screening program."

I looked around the room. A small table was covered with old magazines, Newsweeks, Ebony magazines, Black Panther newspapers. Clyde picked up some papers from the desk. "I'm going in the back," he said. "James and his men will be here soon. I'm pre-med myself, gotta do some studying." I looked at my watch. One o'clock. The clinic was quiet.

I stood up to examine the posters on the walls. A poster of Che Guevara read, *The revolutionary is guided by feelings of great love.* Underneath someone had taped another piece of paper.

> Patience has its limits. Take it too far, and it's cowardice.
> —George Jackson

I had read about George Jackson's death. A year ago he had been killed by prison guards at San Quentin. Newspapers reported he had tried to escape by hiding a gun in his enormous Afro. Angela Davis had been implicated in the escape attempt. There had been a shoot-out in a Marin courtroom. Both the judge, and George Jackson's brother, Jonathan Jackson, died in the melee.

I glanced again at my watch. It was now one fifteen. If James had to be at the Lighthouse at two, he would not have much time for me. Did he understand I planned to interview him? I gathered from Clyde that other people were coming with him. I didn't like that. His companions might not trust me.

I walked back into the hallway. A bookcase stood opposite the clinic examining rooms. I kneeled on the floor to look at its contents—a few more magazines, a hardbound copy of Dr Spock, Dorland's Illustrated Medical Dictionary, a Physicians Desk Reference. Under the curtains of the second examining room, several shotguns and rifles were stacked on the floor. I stood up quickly. Why were there guns in a clinic? Had there been shoot-outs even here on Adeline? I didn't want Clyde to know I had seen them.

I walked back to the waiting room and looked out the storefront window. A Lincoln Town Car was pulling up in front of the clinic. Two black men got out. James Ferguson led the way. He was wearing a white shirt and sharply creased black pants. Following him was one of the men who had accompanied him at Vinnie's Inn. The large man, with the scarred face. He was huge, tall, thickly muscled, a man whose sport would be the hammer throw or the shot put. A younger black man with an intellectual-looking face and eyeglasses was sitting in the driver's seat. He had been James' second man at Vinnie's. I walked downstairs and opened the front door.

"You been waiting long?" James Ferguson asked me. "Wilson," he turned to the man behind him. "I'll be here thirty minutes. Swing by the Lighthouse and drop Ollie off, then come back to pick me up."

Wilson looked at James, an expression of doubt on his face. He spoke in a low tone, making it difficult for me to hear him. "All of us got to be there by two. Why don't we bring her with us?" He gestured at me.

James shook his head. "Go ahead, Wilson. It's okay. Drop Ollie off and shoot right back here. We'll be there in time." Wilson turned back to the car, looking as if he wanted to say more. James closed the door and followed me up the stairs to the waiting room. He pulled out one of the school chairs and sat down. "We've got twenty minutes," he said.

I couldn't waste any time. I started to reach into my shoulder bag for my notebook and the tape recorder Yoshi had lent me. Then there was another knock on the door downstairs.

"God damn it," James exclaimed, jumping up. "What in hell is it now?" He ran downstairs and jerked open the door. I followed James to the top of the staircase. I could see Wilson Tyler's scarred face.

"You can't talk to her without permission," Wilson was saying. "We're running late as it is. Come on."

"I've cleared it with Central," James answered. "Twenty fucking minutes, Tyler! See you at the Lighthouse." He shut the door in Wilson's face and came back up the stairs, breathing hard.

"Why is this such a big deal?" I asked.

"Because they're paranoid is why," James answered, sitting down. "Wilson hasn't slept at all in two days. He's jittery. He also can't get past the color of a person's skin. So where were we?"

129

"I want to write an article explaining your side of things. Your history in the Party. What made you join, what life is like for you now. I'll take notes, and I want to tape it if that's okay." I took the tape recorder out of my bag.

"You can take notes, as long as I can look at them. No tape recorder. And I want to see the article after you write it."

James took a deep breath. "Why I joined—there were a couple reasons. I got stopped and beaten up by the Houston police. Left like a dog by the side of the road. A friend of mine, Carl Hampton, had opened up a chapter in Houston. Two months after that beating, I joined up."

"How old were you?"

"Sixteen," Ferguson answered. "I could barely read or write. I was the product of lousy schools. And, truth be told, books weren't my thing, comin' up. Lots of things interested me more. But after I got into the Party, they laid it out for me. They told me I needed to be down with Mao and Karl Marx and Dubois. I got that together. Pretty soon I was giving speeches. The Party gave me an education. It gave me a life."

"Are the Panthers a paramilitary organization?" This would explain the guns in the clinic screening room.

"We are much more than that," he said, with a quiet intensity. "The Black Panther Party for Self Defense is a political Party. We are dedicated to meeting the basic needs of black and oppressed people. We're a political vehicle with the objective of transforming America into a more just and equitable society. We have a Central Committee—members who make decisions that concern us all. We have several levels of authority, people to report to. For myself, I'm just a soldier in the people's army."

"Art Leopold mentioned you were sent to New York?"

"I was there for six months. Art probably told you about the East Coast West Coast split. Then the Party sent for me to come here to California. You heard of the program called Cointelpro? The FBI program? It's why I wanted to talk to you. That's part of the paranoia you witnessed today, Leah."

He had wanted to talk to *me*?

"You want to write an article about me, right? About this case? There's things about this case I want put into print. There's things I seen in Houston, and I think I'm seeing them here."

"Like . . . ?"

"Two guys broke into an FBI office a couple years ago. Got hold of some files which exposed Cointelpro. I remember receiving those files—they were sent to Houston—and I wondered, what do they tell us that we don't already know? Hoover is targeting the Black Panthers, trying to fill the leadership with informants. Snitches. Sometimes looks like the entire East Coast West Coast split is more about Cointelpro than it is about Huey or Eldridge. Like that Sunday Grace was killed. In the morning I was at a meeting at Panther Headquarters. Four other people were there. Then I went to a rally at De-Fremery Park—hundreds of people saw me. Then I got a call to come here."

"Here—to the George Jackson Clinic?"

"That's right. Clyde called me. There had been a break-in and he needed Security to help him. I came right over—Ollie drove me."

"Ollie, he's the young guy—with the eyeglasses."

"Right," said James Ferguson.

So," I was scribbling furiously. "You have an alibi for the entire day."

"It's more complicated than that. I want you to ask Clyde about that day. He'll tell you I was here. I want you to hear him say it. You can put *that* on your tape."

The phone on the front desk rang. James picked it up.

"Goddamn it, what happened?" Then he said, "Right." He let the phone drop back into its cradle and looked at me. "Cops have surrounded the Lighthouse. There may be a shoot-out. They may come here looking for me. We should go out the back." I pushed my notebook into my shoulder bag, and followed James to the back of the clinic. Clyde looked up from his books. "Gotta get outta here," James said to Clyde. "Shoot-out at the Lighthouse. You have a car at your house?"

"Yeah." Clyde jumped up. A door at the back of the room opened onto a staircase. We ran down the stairs and into an alley full of garbage cans. I followed James and Clyde to a metal gate which opened into a nondescript back yard. Up the back steps, into the kitchen of the house. In the next room, a television was going. Someone called out, "That you, Clyde?"

"It's me, Mom," Clyde said. "Got friends with me." He looked at us and brought his finger to his lips, motioning us to follow him down the hallway.

131

At the front door, he reached into his pocket, pointed toward an old brown De-Soto parked at the curb, and threw the keys to James.

"I want you to come with me," James said to me. I followed him out to the DeSoto. James was compelling. I had no idea where we were going. I would return for my VW later. "Tell me if you see anyone following us," he said. "I'm heading for the freeway."

Two blocks away I saw the OPD's black-and-white car. "Back a couple of blocks," I said. "Police car." James gunned the DeSoto and we sped up the on-ramp to I-80. His jaw was fixed. But by the time we'd passed a couple exits with no sign of pursuit, his hands had relaxed their clenched grip on the wheel. We were on I-80 south, flying past the flat industrial rooftops of Oakland with their ventilating cylinders, pipes, billboards.

"I think we've lost them," he said. He took the Hegenberger Road exit and turned back to get onto I-80 north. "I'm gonna head to the lake." When we got to Lake Merritt, he pulled up at the duck pond. We sat there in silence for several minutes. A group of coots swam toward us, white dots on their black bills. They seemed calm, curious, interested. Further away an emerald-headed mallard paddled peacefully, his downy mate swimming a foot behind him.

"I've gotta make a call," James said, getting out of the car. I watched him walk over to the pay telephones near the pond, put in a coin, speak briefly. Then he came back, sliding into the driver's seat with a sigh. "It's okay," he said. "Cops backed down. Doesn't mean they won't come looking for me, though." He sat for a few more moments, looking out ahead of him at Lake Merritt. "You know, Leah, my life ain't worth a plug nickel," he said, "Open the glove compartment, would you?"

I opened it. Amidst a clutter of worn maps and used candy wrappers, a .38 lay next to a blue plastic bottle of antacid. James smiled. "Just the Maalox," he said. "We don't need the .38 right now." He took the bottle from me and gulped it down as if he was throwing back a shot of whiskey. "Ouch," he grimaced. "What a statement of my life—.38s and stomach pain."

"It must be hard to live like this," I said. My diaphragm was beginning to unclench. I felt an almost overwhelming desire to laugh and to eat.

"You know," he said, after a moment. "You're an odd one. Most women would be shaking. You're cool. You're something, Leah. You clam up on the police and you waltz through a shoot-out. What's with you?"

Was James was speaking out of admiration or suspicion? If I were connected to the police, wouldn't I act fairly cool? I'd have nothing to fear from the pigs. "Was that a shoot-out?"

"Shoot-out at the Lighthouse. Almost a shoot-out for us," James said. "I still don't know why not. Pigs almost always use an excuse like that to go at us."

Was he suspicious of me? "So what happened?"

"There was an argument, and the brother came back with some friends. Friends had heat on 'em. They were carryin' some heavy iron. Next thing you know, the pigs are there too. You can't guess how often shit like that goes down."

"Do you think it's a set up?'

"How would we know? We've got enemies—all kinds of enemies. There's folks in the streets don't like us—some for good reasons. That's what's hard—we almost never know."

"That guy, Al Brooks," I said, "Was he an enemy?"

"How come you know his name? You ever see that guy before?"

"No," I said, "He came over and introduced himself that day."

"Then I wouldn't be mentioning his name." His words were final. "I don't know nothing about anyone by that name. You don't either."

He sat in silence for a moment, then began speaking again. "You know, part of being in the Party is political education. We go to classes. In one class they showed us a movie. An interview with a Russian soldier during World War II. Stalin had issued a decree. Any soldier who ran away from the front lines would be executed immediately. This soldier was saying the decree wasn't necessary. The comrades were so appalled by the Nazis that they would make whatever sacrifice was necessary. Dying, if that's what it took. He said he feared the enemy, but the greater fear was having to face himself and his comrades if he let them down. That's how I feel. That's how the brothers in the Party feel."

The greater fear. I had heard this expression from Joey, but Joey had used it differently. Joey meant that Black Panthers were more afraid of their own party than they were of the police.

James was looking out at the water of Lake Merritt in a reverie. "When I was in Houston," he continued, "I got to know what that expression meant.

The greater fear. I was with eight other comrades, winter 1969. We were trapped inside Dowling Street headquarters, surrounded by three hundred Houston pigs armed with shot guns, M16 rifles, tear gas. Reconnaissance helicopters were buzzing above us, lighting up the sky, so we could see the light rain coming down in waves. The Houston pigs wanted to raid our office, drag us out of our sanctuary in front of the national news camera, handcuff us and take us to jail like wet whimpering dogs.

"Our attorney called. Said the pigs claimed they didn't need a warrant, because they were pursuing robbery suspects who had run inside our headquarters. For over an hour we watched them position themselves for the attack. Each of us was behind one of the second story windows, protected by a sand bag. We were heavily armed, but we were no match for that army lined up behind their patrol cars. The pigs were less than a hundred feet from our door. We could hear them load their weapons. The loudest sound was the shotguns— the deadly cracking and clicking of bullets as they slid into the chambers. When they finished loading, we stuck our M-1 carbines through the peep holes of the sandbags and took aim.

"An old guy began to talk to us through a bullhorn. He had a real cracker drawl. He said he was the police sergeant and that all the occupants of Dowling Street should come out now with their hands up.

"We all looked at each other. We knew it was about to go down. I asked the other eight comrades—one was only sixteen years old—what should we do? The pig came over the bullhorn again. He said we had ten seconds to come out and surrender. He began counting, the rain still drizzling down. We felt a silence around us. It was okay. We were all in this together. We agreed to stay and shoot it out. We were ready to die that night. For us, that night, the greater fear meant a humiliating surrender in the eyes of the people who respected us. So we stayed put. Three hours after this began, the pigs packed up their guns and drove away."

James was more than attractive. He was mesmerizing. And Ronnie, too. Did the thrill I felt around them come from their masculine confidence? The physical confidence of men who had faced death, men who may have killed other men? The idea was disturbing. My thoughts frightened me.

James hit me lightly on the arm. Telling his story seemed to have drained his tension away.

"Tell you what, "he said," It's been a hard day. How about you and me getting a bite to eat somewhere? I'm starving."

I was hungry, and I did not want this time together to end. I wanted to stay with James. Both of us seemed to be on an adrenalin high, the high of survival. The ducks on the lake seemed to swim in a special light, and everything suddenly seemed ridiculous and funny. Food sounded wonderful.

James drove to Biff's, a restaurant near the lake, and bought hamburgers and French fries. We ate them in the car. Then he suggested driving around the lake and up into the Oakland hills. He turned on the radio. Johnny Nash was singing I Can See Clearly Now, and James began singing along. He had a deep, surprisingly beautiful, voice.

"*Sunshiny day*," I harmonized.

"My father used to talk to me about that song," James said. "He thought it was about a guy who had kicked drugs. Full of his pain, but then his joy at kicking the drugs."

"I never thought of that," I said.

"If you'd heard my Pops go on about it, he would have had you convinced." James went on to tell me his father had been an oil rig worker in West Texas. After his father and mother split up, his father moved to Houston and drove a bus. "Them oil fields drained him. Wasn't much left of him after that. Him and my mother split up. For a while I went down to live with my grandmother in the Alabama countryside. She was a tough woman. Part Cherokee. Had her own farm, raised pigs and chickens, butchered them herself. She always believed I'd amount to something. That's how she used to put it to me, too, 'You James—you're gonna amount to somethin'!'"

That Cherokee ancestry explained the smooth planes of his face, his high cheekbones. I was touched that James would talk to me about his family.

"So you want to know why I joined the Panthers? I told you how the police beat me. I was barely a teenager. They beat me shitless for no reason, just so I'd be an example to the younger brothers who were watching. When I was sixteen, my best friend, Carl Hampton, recruited me into the People's Party II. We became the Houston Black Panthers. I just planted myself in the Houston office and said, join me up."

"It was rough," James continued. "The police back in Houston shot up our free health clinic so bad we had to close it down. Carl Hampton, the brother

135

who recruited me—he was assassinated. The pigs attacked our headquarters—I was crawling around on the floor, trying to avoid their bullets. Bits of shattered glass were just falling on my back. I can't even begin to tell you, Leah, how deep the hatred of the pigs is with me. What I seen them do."

I told James about growing up in upstate New York. "Even though I lost my mother, I had my father. He bought me books with the Caldecott gold star on them, cloth notebooks in which I wrote my first journals. I used to think that was enough. One person in your life to keep you from getting lost. But then he just stopped paying any attention to me. At least I had him before he married my stepmother. But afterward it seemed all he cared about was his new wife and their children."

"A person can sure get lost," he said. "Walkin' lost. Even with one person caring. When I first joined the Party I thought my grandmother would have been so proud of me. She was dead by then. These days I'm not so sure she'd be so proud."

"Why not?" I asked.

"Leah, there's things about me and the Party you'll never understand. Look at the differences between us. Your Dad buying you books with gold stars on them. I know when your mama died, you had some hard times—but you think anyone was buying me books? The Party has members from backgrounds like yours, educated brothers and sisters, college degrees and stuff. But I don't come out of anything like that."

Were we beginning to trust each other? Could I ask him for more information? Information about the night at Eli's? Information that might help me write my article? I had to be careful. It was possible he had murdered Grace, or had ordered her murdered, although suddenly it was hard for me to believe that this man, so open with me now, was anyone to fear.

"Know this song?" James was saying. The radio was playing B. B. King. James sang along.

Now we were up into the Oakland hills. James dropped his voice, imitating various black singers: Lou Rawls, Stevie Wonder, Marvin Gaye. He sang the *ooh oohs* in a high falsetto. I was astonished by this new, playful side of him. Now we were driving up along the roads of Redwood Park. After a while we started to make up our own words and tunes. Every time I tried to stop, he pushed me on. "Come on!" he said, "Let's do another one!" And we would sing another song brought back by the train of our memories, songs by Aretha Franklin, the Chambers Brothers, Wilson Pickett.

"Where'd you learn all those soul songs?" James asked me.

"My black woman friend from the track, Edna. She loaned me some records," I said. "I spent a lot of time listening to them in my room. You've got a real good voice, too. How did you learn to imitate those singers?"

"Used to sing with my buddies," he answered. "When we got together at parties, stuff like that." He looked almost shy. "Sometimes I forget I had a life before the Panthers."

We drove all over the East Bay that afternoon but for some reason ended up at the Albany estuary as if drawn there by a force we had forgotten about. We got out of the car and walked along the water. Grace's body had been found not far from this spot. Suddenly I felt disloyal to Grace. She would no longer sit in cars humming Motown tunes with this handsome man.

Then I wondered if I could ask James more about the case. Surely Art Leopold would have warned him not to say anything which would compromise his defense. A cold breeze came up off the water. I thought of Grace's body, floating there.

"James," I said. "Those bruises on Grace's neck—how did they get there?" This was the first time I had mentioned her name all day. I felt a chill come over me.

He twisted his head to give me a strange look. "I've told you I operate under orders. One of my orders is never to discuss that night. When an outsider comes around asking questions, it looks bad. Some people might think you want to know too much."

"Is that what you think?" I asked. I might as well meet him head on.

"You helped save me from the can," he answered. "What can I feel but grateful? But I can't afford to trust anyone, and there's things I've never understood about you. You liked Grace, and when she left me that Saturday night at Eli's, you saw the bruises on her throat. Why did you go down and give testimony that helped me get off?"

"I didn't think you killed her."

"Why did it matter? You didn't know me."

"Grace loved you," I said. "I was doing it for her."

But the adrenalized excitement, the light-hearted mood was gone. Grace's name had changed everything. My blunt questions, his suspicions. His face looked preoccupied, grim. "What *did* the cops tell you about me?"

"That you killed a cop in New York. Other things." I had to be careful how I answered him. What could I say? I knew Joey and the OPD were determined to pin Grace's murder on James. I did not want to discuss this with James, certainly not my connection to Joey. Or was this was my opportunity to tell James I was related to a member of the OPD, the men he hated fanatically, the men who hated him back? I realized I didn't know.

"I'm going back to the car," I said. "I'm cold." I thought of the .38 lying in the glove compartment. James followed me and we got inside. I was silent while he drove back to the freeway. Then I said, "Could you take me back to Adeline and Ashby? I need to pick up my car."

"You have a funny kind of loyalty." James spoke as if he were following his own stream of thought. "When I was younger, I slapped a few women around. Didn't think twice about it. I seen that all my life. The Party taught me discipline. It taught me respect—for myself, and for my people." When he talked about the Party, James' voice took on a tone of reverence.

"I've heard women in the Panthers complain about how they're treated."

"You heard this *where*?" We had come to a light on University, and he turned his head to look at me.

"People on the left."

"Past history," James said. "We've had to grow up. We've got women in top positions these days. Fact is, you cross the wrong woman, it's the men who get disciplined." He laughed a bitter laugh. "So, getting back to your main question, Leah, you wanna know who killed Grace, you better look elsewhere. Where'd she get the kind of money she had those last few months? She was running through money like it was water. Whoever was giving it to her—" He broke off suddenly, looking in his rear view mirror. "Damn it. Pigs."

A patrol car pulled up behind us, lights flashing. James braked to a stop. He sat dead still, staring in front of him, but his mouth was moving. I could hear him. "Do whatever they say. Move slowly. As soon as you get a chance, call Art Leopold. Remember, them cops are jacked up." Within seconds we were surrounded by five more patrol cars, coming from everywhere, sirens screaming, squealing around corners.

138

A large cop with a megaphone emerged from the patrol car behind us. "Out of the car," he said, "Slowly. You, on the driver's side. First."

I could see James from the corner of my eye. He was sweating, perspiration forming on his upper lip. In a flash the cop had opened the door and thrown James against the side of the car. Five other officers stood nearby, their guns pointed at him from various angles. It happened so fast it felt unreal. I sat there terrified, afraid to move, thinking about the .38 in the glove compartment.

A young cop came over to my side of the car. "Your ID?" he asked. He looked frightened, too, something I had never expected. We were all, I suddenly realized, afraid for our lives—myself, James, even the cops. I fished in my pocket for the change purse in which I kept my driver's license.

"He's just taking me home, officer. We haven't done anything." I stuttered, handing him my license. I wanted to sound cool, but I didn't come close. He glanced at it, asked me a few questions, about myself, my job, how I came to be with James that day.

I looked around and saw James being handcuffed and thrown into the back of the police car. "He hasn't done anything!" I shouted at them. "He's my friend. I've been with him all day."

"We've got a warrant out on him," the young cop replied. "Afraid we'll have to take him in. As for you, young lady, I'd be more careful in my choice of friends."

I tried to catch James' eye as they took him away. But he was staring straight ahead of him with a fixed, immobilized expression. The laughing man who could imitate Lou Rawls was gone and replaced by a Black Panther, a soldier of the people, grim, fierce, frozen.

James had left the keys in the ignition. After the cops left, I started Clyde's DeSoto and drove back to the George Jackson Clinic. No one answered my knock, so I parked the DeSoto on Alcatraz, threw the keys through the mail slot with a note, located my Beetle and headed back to Russell Street.

At home I called Art Leopold at the home number on his business card. Art was brief. "I'll take care of this," he said. James and I had driven around the East Bay for hours, singing songs, telling one another stories of our childhoods. James had not done anything while he was with me. Nothing had happened. He had not been at the so-called shoot-out at the Lighthouse. Cops couldn't just pick someone up on the street and take them away, could they? There were laws to protect us from this. I remembered what James had said. Cops always seemed to come when I was with him.

I called Joey at home. "They picked him up again, Joey."

"Who?"

"James Ferguson. Just now. The cops picked him up."

"How do you know?"

"I was with him. That's how I know."

"You were with him? You were *with* him? What in the name of sweet, loving Jesus were you doing with James Ferguson?"

"It's a long story, Joey," I said. "But I was. All afternoon. Call your buddies off. He hasn't done a thing."

"Jesus, Mary, and Joseph," Joey swore into the phone. "How in the *hell* do you manage to turn up in the middle of every goddamned action? You've got some explaining to do." Joey was still swearing as he hung up the phone.

XVI

A knock on my bedroom door the next morning. Yoshi stuck his head in. "Your cousin Joey is here," he said. "I've made him a cup of coffee while you get ready."

I cursed silently to myself and threw off the covers. My dreams had been full of images from yesterday. Light falling on the bay. How James' face had changed when I mentioned Grace. His baritone voice, singing Motown hits. Our laughter. Insights into a man who had lived through so much. Then later, speaking about Grace, his eyes looked cold; his voice had an edge. By the time the cops had come, the human being James Ferguson had been was a man whose features had been frozen into a mask. These images had kept me awake all night. That had been hard enough. Now Joey.

Downstairs I found Joey sitting with Yoshi at the big table in the dining room. They had mugs of coffee; there was a small plate of toast on the table. Yoshi was describing some INS harassment he was enduring. Well, at least they weren't discussing me or James Ferguson. As I entered, Joey looked up. He was in street clothes, khaki pants and a blue shirt, a plaid sports coat hanging over his chair.

"Hi, Leah," he said, pushing back his chair. "We need to go somewhere. You and me. It will only take an hour. I'll bring you home." I made a face at Yoshi and grabbed a piece of toast from their plate. Let's get this over with, I thought to myself. I couldn't see a way out.

"Don't I get a cup of coffee?" I asked. Joey shoved his cup at me.

"I haven't touched it," he said. "Drink up. But we gotta hurry."

I gulped it down, wiped my mouth with my fist. Okay, let's go," I said.

In the car Joey was uncharacteristically quiet. He headed west on Russell, turned left on Telegraph, heading toward Oakland. "Where are we going, Joey?" I asked him. The Co-op at Telegraph and Ashby flashed by on the right, then the new, smaller Co-op at Telegraph and 51st.

"I got a call, asking me to talk to someone. I think I know why. It could be something you should hear."

"Why do you think I should hear this someone?" I asked. It didn't sound good. At least he hadn't started in on his usual interrogation of me—*why* had I been with James Ferguson yesterday? What had we been doing? I was sure he would get to that soon enough. I wanted to stall him until I had some counterattacks.

"Because you're in over your head again," growled Joey. "Just like that time I had to rescue you at Lake Oneida. In over your head, Leah. In over your head."

Upstate New York, a lifetime ago, a shallow lake with a sandy bottom that stretched out forever. An amusement park, a public beach, a long twilight summer night. As kids we had spent summers there, before my mother died, when she and her brother and their families all spent vacations together in rented cabins on the lake. I had stumbled and fallen and gulped some water. Joey swam out and grabbed me by the back of my bathing suit, hauled me back to shallow water. He liked to remember the story as if he had saved me from drowning. Over the years, I had given up on correcting him. "Yeah, you saved me that time, Joey," I said, knowing I had not needed saving. His teenage heroics.

"I'm trying to save you now," he said, right on cue. He had turned onto the I-580 freeway and was exiting at Park Avenue in Oakland.

Highland Hospital was the Alameda County hospital, a huge white building sprawling across an entire hillside. It had been originally designed in the elegant Art Deco architectural style of the thirties, but several newer wings in fifties brutalist concrete had turned the building into an architectural monster. Joey drove down a hill and into a parking lot marked Psychiatric. "You're not committing me, are you, Joey?"

"You know, cousin, if I thought it would keep you out of trouble, I just might consider it," he said. His voice had that warning tone that I despised. Condescending. In the small visiting room, Joey signed us in as visitors of Karella Cousins.

An old black man sat with two women, perhaps his wife, or his daughters, staring vacantly into space. A few seats away a middle-aged white man shook uncontrollably. An attendant led Karella Cousins in. She looked barely twenty, with caramel-colored skin and enormous liquid eyes, lovely even in a shapeless hospital gown of a faded print. A soft tremor coursed through her, as if an electric current were sending quick jolts through her body.

She sat huddled in her chair, staring at us with beseeching eyes. Joey spoke in a low voice. "I'm detective DeMartino, Karella. You called me and asked to speak to me. This is my cousin, Leah. You can talk in front of her."

She looked fragile, but her voice, rough and streetwise, surprised me. "They keep giving me these medicines," she whispered, hoarsely. "Then they take me to the shrink. I can't help it—I spill out everything."

"Don't take those pills," Joey said. "Act like you're taking them—then spit em out soon as you can."

"I be needin' somethin'," the girl said. "Somethin' to help me sleep at night."

Joey kept his voice very low. "I want you to tell Leah what you told me over the phone, sweetheart."

Karella Cousins fastened her frightened brown eyes on me. "Can she help me?" she whispered.

"Maybe," Joey answered. "Go ahead. Tell her."

"I been working for the Party since I was sixteen," Karella said. "They got me off the street. Sell the newspaper, collect donations, different things. Sometimes the Security Cadre want me to do things for them."

"Get to the point, Karella," Joey said, gently. "She's been around some of the top Black Panthers. Including James Ferguson," Joey explained to me. He glanced around the room, but no one was paying attention to us.

"James picked me up that Sunday the white girl got killed," Karella whispered. "I was on my way to Central and he gave me a lift. We stopped for gas down on East 14th. James was buying gas and I opened up the glove box looking for some matches. I seen this red wallet in there."

"Go on, Karella," Joey urged. She kept glancing around the room as if she was afraid someone would hear us.

"I opened it up—there was a driver's license inside. Grace Neville. Name didn't mean anything. Didn't know who she was. I didn't say nothing to James, just put it my pocket. When I heard that girl was dead, I was scared."

"So what did you do with it?' I asked.

Karella Cousins looked toward us. Her eyes were enormous, as if permanently startled or frightened. Then she reached in her gown's pocket and withdrew a soft leather wallet, dark red, with gold initials on the flap. I recognized Grace's wallet from Vinnie's. Karella handed it to me and as she did so, a business card fell out and fluttered to the linoleum floor. Joey was glancing around the room nervously; he did not see it. I bent down quickly and dropped the small card in my pocket before Joey had returned his attention to me.

The wallet felt like a token from the dead. I stared at it. "Just give it to me, Leah," Joey said. He took it from me and slipped the wallet into the pocket of his plaid sports coat. Karella watched him with her enormous, beseeching eyes.

"So can you help me?" she whispered, urgently. Her frame was shaking. "I don't want nobody to know I turned this in."

"We'll need a statement from you. Did you sign yourself in voluntarily?"

She nodded. "You know I signed myself in last night."

"Good," said Joey, standing up. "Then you can sign yourself out again. Don't take any more medications. Don't talk to anyone. We should be able to get you outta here later today."

Karella looked up at him. "Get me in the Witness Protection program," she whispered. "Get me in something. I'm scared I'm gonna spill everything to them shrinks." She stood up in her thin hospital gown. "You're pretty, lady," she said to me, softly. "You want to help me? You look like a nice person."

"Go tell them you're checking out this afternoon," said Joey, pushing her a little on the shoulder. "Get packing. We'll take care of you."

We drove off in silence, leaving the grim fortress of Highland Hospital behind. "How did she ever happen to call you, Joey?" I finally asked.

"Beats me. She left a message at headquarters yesterday. I called her this morning, then came over to get you. She told me she had committed herself because she didn't know what she might do. OD? Slit her wrists? She looks strung out," he said, "but she's probably scared shitless, is more like it." He twisted in his seat to look at me.

"Like *you* should be," he added.

144

XVII

Tuesday morning I found Edna at the Hot Spoon. She had tied a bright red bandanna around her soft Afro, but she looked grim, furiously slicing on-ions on a wooden cutting board, slamming down the cleaver. Her gold loop ear-rings jingled with each bang of the cleaver.

"You see how much attention they give a black girl, don't you?" she said, looking up. "Two damn paragraphs on the third page. Drug-related. You think anybody's gonna bother to find her killer?"

"What are you talking about, Edna?"

"Black girl, Karella Cousins. Found at noon floating face down in the bay near Point Richmond. Blindfolded—gunshot wound to her temple."

"No!" I sunk on to a counter stool, staring at Edna in disbelief.

"Third page of the Tribune. Gave her two paragraphs. Said it was probably drug related." Edna came around the counter, took the stool next to me, lit a cigarette, and took a deep drag on it.

I tried to absorb this latest shock. Lovely, vulnerable Karella. Joey's promise of protection. What had happened? "She was so pretty," I said.

"Like I said, pretty don't get you anything but fucked," Edna replied. "Double fucked, in her case."

"Did you know her, Edna?"

"Not really. Met her at the Lighthouse Saturday afternoon. She was waitressing there. Ollie introduced us."

"Who's Ollie?"

"Girl, I thought you *knew* the brother. He hangs with Big Jim." *That* Ollie. The slim, intellectual-looking man who accompanied James Ferguson.

"*Karella* was at the Lighthouse Saturday afternoon?"

"Yeah. Said something about waiting for James. But James never came." Edna gave me a sharp look. "He was with you, wasn't he?"

"Yes," I said. "I was interviewing James at the clinic when he got a phone call. Said there was a shoot out, to stay away. I didn't know what happened."

"Some brothers acted up—Panthers threw them out—it's a Panther bar, and they run the show there. Brothers came back packing. Someone called the cops—all hell broke lose. I don't plan in being in a situation like that again. You shouldn't either." Now she turned to me, hands on her hips. "You hanging out with James?"

There it was again. Edna was sounding worse than Joey.

"No." I thought about Saturday afternoon. That afternoon would never happen again.

"Good thing. James is too tough for you."

"Underneath that toughness, there's a sensitive person."

"We're all sensitive people," Edna sang in a sarcastic voice. It was the same song James had sung as we drove around the East Bay. "Big Jim heads up Security for the Black Panther Party. He's had to do some hard things. Maybe he's had to kill someone, before that someone iced him. Know what I mean, Leah? That kind ain't no kind to play with."

"Why do you keep warning me away from James, Edna? He didn't kill Karella Cousins. He's been locked up."

Edna made a sound between a snort and a laugh. "Because I live in the real world, girl."

"James has real feelings, Edna," I began, but she cut me off, impatiently.

"You think killers don't have feelings? I know different, girl. I grew up with boys who were killers. Maybe they didn't start out as killers, but they blew some folks away. Warm and charming one minute, cold as death the next. Did what they had to do."

"Is that the kind of person Ollie is?"

"Ollie? "She laughed. "I've been knowing Ollie a long time. Used to date his big brother. He wears those little glasses, like Franz Fanon, or one of those smart brothers. Ollie's a lover, not a killer. He was with me Sunday night, doing what that boy does best."

"Isn't Ollie kinda young for you, Edna?" The person I had seen with James had not looked much older than twenty-two.

"He may be younger than me, but he ain't inexperienced—if you catch my meaning." Edna caressed her soft, frizzy hair, smoothing it with her hand. Another new development, and I wasn't sure it was a good one.

"Listen." She swiveled on the stool to face me. "I like Ollie, always did. But I hung with him for you too, Leah. To find out a few things."

146

"Like what?"

"Like that Sunday your friend was murdered. James was at a meeting at Black Panther headquarters. Ollie saw him there. Four other Panthers were there too."

"Why didn't Ollie tell that to the cops?"

"I don't know," Edna said. "Ollie couldn't say more than that. Shouldn't have told me that much, but you know, he and I go way back. He trusts me. Ollie said that whether or not Grace was killed Saturday night or Sunday, they knew James didn't do it. They had a tail on him. They sat outside headquarters all night, like they were waiting for him."

"Why are you warning me away from James? Ollie's telling you he's innocent."

Edna blew out her breath dismissively, making her characteristic nose sound. "Not *innocent,*" she said. "James Ferguson innocent? Maybe of killing the white girl. Not other things. Think about it, Leah. What if James thought you'd leak something to the cops? Something that could hurt him? Or had some connections to the cops? What then?"

Sunshiny Day. Talking to Edna was worse than talking to Joey. I had not yet told Edna my cousin was a cop. Now I never could.

"Hell, Leah, if James thought that—or someone above him thought that—you could end up as dead as your blonde friend, and a whole lot quicker too."

Late Wednesday afternoon Joey took me to a shooting range south of Oakland. He showed me how to shoot to kill and how to shoot to wound. We practiced on paper targets with Xs over men's hearts and vital organs. I hated the kick of the revolver, the loud noise it made when I fired it. The thought that the paper targets represented potential human beings was chilling. I hoped I would never have to use the gun. Yet by the end, I had a heady sensation. Shooting it gave me a new sense of power. I could almost feel what Joey must feel every day, walking around with an enormous handgun on his hip. And James—a weapon made him the equal of the police who had brutalized him.

On the way to the range, I had wondered if Joey would mention Karella. He had not. On the drive home I felt strangely capable of dealing with

Joey. I had shot a paper man in the chest. It could have been a real man. I felt an eerie clearness and coldness. I tried an indirect approach with Joey first, to test the waters.

We were driving down out of the hills. The city of Oakland was a sea of lights below us. "You hear anything more Sunday from Karella?"

"Cut the crap, Leah. I feel bad she got popped. Someone musta seen her talking to us. When I came back to Highland a few hours later, they told me she'd signed out with her brother. I knew that wasn't good. She didn't have a brother."

"So our visit got her killed?"

"She knew too much. Whether she called the cops or not. Whether anyone saw her with us or not. That's probably why she checked in, in the first place."

"She was killed Sunday night?"

"Looks like it."

"James was still in custody Sunday night."

"Did I say Ferguson did it?" Joey sounded angry. He pulled off the road onto a turn-off. We had a view of the glittering lights of Oakland, the brilliantly lit arcs of the Bay Bridge cables looping toward Treasure Island. Joey cut the engine, then turned toward me.

"Don't start with me, Leah," he warned. "We're not sure when she was murdered. We don't know yet who did it."

"Just like with Grace," I shot back.

Last night I had reviewed everything in my mind. I had remembered how Joey had grilled me at Dave's Coffee Shop. When he learned both Paul and Carol had seen Grace leaving Russell Street around nine am that Sunday morning, he had reluctantly agreed I should give my statement to the cops. But without the two of them as additional corroborating witnesses, would he not have tried to convince me to stay silent? Bond and Sims had interrogated me. Then, when Joey drove me home, he kept repeating questions they had already asked me. Had Grace mentioned an argument with James? Had I seen any marks on her? Last night I realized that conversation with Joey was a continuation of the grilling the two cops had begun. An attempt to shake my story.

"Okay," I said, sarcastically. "No similarities in the two murders. — But what about this—OPD had a tail on Ferguson Saturday night, August fifth. You knew he couldn't have done it."

148

"So?" Joey's face in the dark interior of the car looked pale and pasty. A faint five o'clock shadow stubbled his chin.

"Panthers were with him the next morning, at a meeting. After that he was at a rally at DeFremery. You knew all along he couldn't have killed Grace."

"Oh, calm down, Leah," Joey said. "There's a lot you don't understand. Ferguson heads up a gang—or same as. All he has to do is give an order. It's still murder. He was followed that night to Panther headquarters, yeah. So he went in and gave them the slip getting out. And the Panthers at that meeting? Not that it would mean that much if they did try to defend him. But not a single one has come forward to testify on his behalf."

I had no answer to that.

"Fact is," Joey continued, "the only person eager to defend the guy is you. I have to wonder why."

"Try this," I answered. "It's the truth."

He thought he was slick, putting me on the defensive. I knew what he was insinuating with his *I wonder why*. It was Joey who had first suggested I was sleeping with James. In his eyes that would explain why I was defending him. It was absurd, since I didn't even know James at that point. But Joey hadn't known the full extent of my social life—or lack thereof. "It's not that simple," Joey was saying. "We've got sources we can't disclose. The Panthers have big-time lawyers, Commie pinko protestors ready to riot on their behalf at the drop of a hat. Like your fucking Berkeley Peace and Freedom Party. They get away with a lot these days."

"Yeah, Joey, I guess it's not like the good old days when cops could put black people away anytime they felt like it. And how about Freddie Corster— you pressured him to say Grace left the track with Ferguson. You cops aren't victims, Joey. You're a bunch of bullies."

"Bullies? And you're trying to tell me the Panthers aren't? Just when I think you've got some street smarts, Leah, you talk stupid. Your Huey Newton believes the lumpen will rule the country. You know that word, lumpen. Your Panther friends have a singing group with that name. *Bobby must be set free!"* Joey sang a high-pitched imitation of this newly famous song. "You know who Huey Newton's lumpen are? Small time pimps and hustlers. They're the criminal element. Talk about pressure—the Black Panthers shake down black businesses, pimps, drug dealers. They pop the guys that won't cooperate. *That's* intimidation, Leah—that's the real bullying. The greater fear, remember?"

149

Paul had talked about the lumpen proletariat when we had driven to Clear Lake. As Paul described them in his more academic language, the lumpen were the oppressed lower class—unemployed and unemployable. A socialist PhD candidate, and an Oakland cop. Two different world views. Karella and Grace dead—that was the reality.

Now Joey made his voice ingratiating. "So, cuz, where you hearing all this information you have?"

"At the track," I said. "That's where you told me to listen."

"What else you hearing there?"

"Not much. Grace had other boyfriends," I said. Leave it at that, I said to myself. I didn't know who had killed Karella. Joey had certainly not protected her. I didn't trust Joey anymore.

Joey started up the car. He seemed to be reading my thoughts.

"Look. There was more to the Karella story than I could tell you on Sunday. We caught her late Saturday night when she was heading to the Oakland airport. Late at night. She was so nervous she shot through a red light. She was heading out of town."

"Wait a minute," I said. "This makes no sense to me. We just saw her Sunday in the hospital. What are you telling me?"

"She's not the first one to want to disappear. Lots of Panthers disappear. They want to make people think they were killed by the cops or the FBI. But that ain't it—some of them are in a *big* hurry to get outta Dodge, and they ain't telling anyone else in the Panthers why they gotta leave."

My head was spinning. "So she was on her way out of town?"

"She was driving that big tan-and-black Buick we'd been looking for ever since your friend Grace got popped. When we pulled her over, she was scared shitless. So *we* put her in Highland Hospital. Told her to sign herself in. To protect her."

"But it didn't work, did it," I said.

We headed down into the flatlands of Oakland. Both of us were silent. I was thinking about Joey. Toward me he had a muddle-headed kindness. Toward a black man like James Ferguson, he had nothing but hatred. In his eyes all black men were potential criminals. Cop killers. The enemy.

Joey had given me a sense of safety. That safety was an illusion. Karella had counted on him, and she was dead. Joey had never told me everything he knew about this case. He still wasn't telling me everything. Probably his next promotion depended on how he handled this. He wouldn't want me to derail it. That put me in danger, and Joey couldn't see it.

It was time to write him off.

XVIII

The weekend before Labor Day weekend I escaped to Lake County with Yoshi. It was Friday afternoon. Sea-gulls formed lazy Vs in a cloudless sky overhead as we headed north on I-80 toward Vallejo. Our destination was Clear Lake. Despite the gorgeous weather, I could not shake a mood of disquiet.

I had spent a couple of evenings in the Cal library reading up on the Black Panther Party for Self-Defense. I read about Huey Newton's ten-point program for renewal of black communities. An immediate end to police brutality and murder of black people, no more occupation by The Man of the black communities—the right of blacks to armed self-defense. Powerful. Moving. And scary.

Yoshi, in the passenger seat, was full of ideas, strategizing ways for me to set up a sex date with Jay Landis in a way that would ensure my safety but still give me an opportunity to learn everything Jay knew. Yoshi thought I should let Joey in on the plan. "We need back up," Yoshi told me. "An undercover cop is what we need here, to make sure you're safe."

I didn't tell Yoshi that Joey considered me an undercover agent of *his*. I had already written two reports about the track and been paid for them. Some of that money was financing this weekend getaway.

"Look at this case from Joey's point of view," Yoshi was saying, "As head of security, Ferguson doesn't have to murder someone outright. If he gives the order, he as good as killed someone. It's like taking out a contract on someone's life."

"It's after the actual murderer confesses that you get the guy who paid him," I said. "You can't do it the other way around. There are leaders in the Panthers higher up than James. James may not be innocent of everything. But I think he's innocent of this. I can't trust Joey or the cops. Just because they say he killed Grace, doesn't make it so."

"Just because you're paranoid, doesn't mean they aren't out to get you," Yoshi reminded me. "Just because cops are racist doesn't mean they don't know a few things." Yoshi liked to play devil's advocate. He seemed to be advocating strongly for Joey these days.

"I don't trust the cops," I said, "Even Joey. The way they keep turning up after I talk to witnesses makes me nervous. Helene and Bud, Ronnie, maybe even Karella. They may have followed me to Highland that day. Just like they trailed Ferguson the night before Grace was murdered."

Yoshi did an exaggerated head twist, looking to the left, to the right. "Don't see no one trailing us now." We both laughed. "But why would you be that important to them, Leah?"

I didn't answer. We were driving a lovely stretch of road, lined with close-set sycamores on either side, recalling French chateaux landscapes, but I was feeling like the odd fish in the sea. Too liberal for family like Joey, too conservative for radicals like Paul, too white for Edna and James, not white enough for Carol and her Midwestern friends. The heat of the day and the twisting road up Mount St. Helena were getting to Yoshi. He slumped down in his seat. "Let me know when we get there," he said.

What did I know, after all? I didn't know much. I had looked at Grace's teenage diary. I had picked up a business card which had fallen out of Grace's wallet. I had talked to a few people who had known her. Yet Art Leopold and Edna Banks had both warned me to be careful. And two women had died in similar ways.

The drive was slow up the winding road to the summit with deep redwood forests on either side. Yoshi was snoring lightly, his head pillowed against the door on his folded-up sweatshirt. After Mount St. Helena, as I remembered from the earlier drive with Paul, we would lope down the same steep, twisty road with its 10 MPH curves, and then into the chaparral around Middletown. Just before the town of Lower Lake, Yoshi opened his eyes. "Are we there yet?"

"Just go back to sleep. *Please!*" I was feeling carsick myself from the heat and I was tired from too many sleepless nights. As we passed the Lollipop Motor Home Park, I thought of Helene and Bud, in their trailer right now with the television on, knocking back Budweisers. I remembered the paper bag of empties next to the kitchen sink. Was that why he was called Bud?—because he drank so many of them?

At Lower Lake we turned onto Highway 53 for the final descent into Clear Lake. The land was hot and flat, with dry yellow-beige hills, but the town of Clear Lake was marshy, built on the lake drainage. I pulled up in front of the Linger Longer Resort with its little white cottages. Yoshi sat up and rubbed his eyes. "Tell me again why we've come here?"

"Yoshi. You know I'm working on the article. I'm writing a story. I needed to get away this weekend so I could pull it all together."

"So what are your sources?"

"Those interviews I did with James Ferguson. And common sense." I had not told Yoshi about Grace's diary, nor the autopsy report, but these were even more important sources in my mind. "I'm going to put something together, write an article for that woman from the Oakland Tribune."

That night Yoshi and I goofed off. We drank beer in the local bar, then sat up late watching television in our room. Saturday morning a breeze came off Clear Lake, rattling the yellow leaves of the alders and birches. The water shimmered, with golden and green trees reflected close to shore. We hiked Anderson Marsh trails and waded barefoot in Cache Creek. I started to relax. "I should have done this a long time ago," I told Yoshi.

Late Saturday afternoon I settled in to work on the article. Yoshi sat on one of the two twin beds, smoking a joint, with the television turned so low it was almost inaudible. He was working his way through a six-pack of Heinekens. At times I could feel his eyes on me.

I had work to do. First I read over the autopsy report. Grace had been severely beaten. A cause of death could have been the loss of blood from the beating. The absence of defensive wounds indicated that Grace had not fought back, or she may have been unconscious when she received the most deadly blows. The autopsy report was signed by a Dr. Stuart Miller. He concluded the time of death could have been anywhere from twelve to fourteen hours before the body was found.

On one sheet of paper I wrote: The Case Against Ferguson. Ferguson's relationship with Grace. His gun found near the murder scene. Bullets near the scene matched his gun. The bruises on Grace's throat after she was seen with him the night before she died. Grace's wallet discovered in the glove compartment of Ferguson's car. Grace's blood in the car. All this pointed toward James Ferguson.

But according to Art Leopold, no one in the Panthers actually owns a car. All vehicles were shared, even if registered to a specific individual. Other people had access to the car James drove. Could I find out who they were?

154

And why was the chamber of the gun missing? Art told me although the bullets on the ground matched the bullets from James' gun, the bullets lodged in Grace's head did *not* match the bullets for James' gun.

On a second sheet of paper I wrote: The Case Against the OPD. This case might exonerate Ferguson. The autopsy reported the body had been found around five am on Monday, August 7th. Grace Neville could have been killed any time between three to five pm Sunday afternoon. The Oakland Tribune initially reported Grace was killed early Sunday morning. Had the police or the reporters screwed up? Or had it been deliberate? The autopsy report specifically excluded early Sunday as a possible time of death. Was that because of my testimony that Grace Neville had been alive and well at nine am on Sunday morning? Freddie Corster said he had seen Grace at the winner's window before noon that Sunday. He had seen her walking toward the parking lot minutes later.

Ferguson had been in a meeting at Panther Headquarters Sunday morning. Four other Panthers had also attended. That Sunday afternoon he was at a rally at DeFremery Park. Hundreds of Black Panther supporters had come out. James had told me that he left DeFremery for an hour or two to help Clyde out at the clinic. Was this the three to five time period when he was supposed to have killed Grace?

On a third sheet of paper, I wrote my final heading: Other Suspects. Grace's note to her mother that she was seeing someone who was the right color, but not the right age. Who was that—Jay Landis? or his father, Hugh Landis? What about the jockey, Bucky Timmons? Then there was an unknown black man Grace was seeing, a rumor passed on to me by Edna. Everyone believed Grace had been involved with several men at the time of her death. But who? All I had to go on was the phone number on a card that had dropped out of Grace's wallet.

I wrote out a timeline of Grace's movements on the day of her death. She had left my house at nine, the race track opened at ten. It takes less than fifteen minutes to drive from Russell Street to Golden Gate Fields, especially on a Sunday morning when there is no traffic. If she had gone out to the track that day, what had she done for the forty-five minutes in between? The police had picked Freddie up, tried to force him to say Grace got into a car with Ferguson. So the police must have known Grace was at the track Sunday morning. Why had Grace gone to the winner's window? How much money had she won?

Why hadn't the police or the papers reported any winnings? If she had been carrying a lot of cash, this in itself was motivation for someone to rob and kill her.

I tried to puzzle it out. Was there anyone else who should be added to my suspect's list? What about Ronnie? He had known her ten years ago; he hadn't been in touch with her recently. The police had questioned him, and Joey had warned me away from him. Why? I crouched over the little desk, in the lamplight, my shoulders hunched up. I studied my notes. I was upset and uncomfortable. I had been reading Grace Neville's diary as a voyeur, invading her privacy. I had such unsettled feelings—what was I doing? Replaying Nancy Drew, girl detective, as if I were twelve years old? What drove me to want to pursue this?

Yoshi watched me from across the room. Now he was smoking a Marlboro. He was wearing a white shirt under a black pullover, and the black of the sweater echoed the black of his hair which fell in a straight bang across his forehead. Two pillows were piled up behind his shoulders. An open Heineken's sat on the nightstand between the two beds. He exhaled, a circle of smoke rising lazily toward the ceiling. Yoshi had a beautiful face, I thought to myself. His eyes were clear-seeing beneath thick black eyebrows. "You look uptight, Leah," he said, taking a slurp from the beer can.

"With reason, don't you think? So—what do you make of Ronnie?" I asked him.

Yoshi shrugged. "Not too much. I talked to him at Grace's funeral a little. He knows something about Japanese culture. Said he did R&R in Japan. Liked samurai films. He even went to a Kabuki play. He told me working with the Vietnam Veterans Against the War means a lot to him."

"Ronnie says people like Paul are too theoretical in their antiwar stance."

"It makes sense," Yoshi answered. "Ronnie's actually been in a war."

I switched back to an earlier train of thought, "You know, all along I thought Joey was trying to protect me. Turns out he doesn't give a damn about my safety."

"Joey didn't know you were seeing James Ferguson. Remember how shocked he was when James got picked up, and you were with him?"

"The cops had James under surveillance, remember? Joey would know everything they know."

156

"Paul says the Panthers check up on each other. Maybe the Panthers are reporting on James to the police. Maybe they don't trust him."

"They don't," I said. "Art told me about that. When James came to talk to me in the clinic, he had two guys with him, but he sent them on to the Lighthouse. I had the feeling he wanted to talk without them around. But I can't imagine them reporting James to the cops. Only an informant would do that." I closed my notebook and stood up, stretching. "Here we are up in Clear Lake. This was my chance to get away, get some perspective. I'm starting to feel scared even here," I said.

Yoshi stretched, wiggled, actually. He wasn't much taller than I but he had a good body—thin, with tight, fine muscles. He stretched again and then patted the bed. "Come on over here," he said. "You look tired." He himself looked very relaxed. "Let me give you a backrub."

"Oh, Yoshi, no. That's not where we're at."

"It's where we *could* be at," he said.

"No, Yoshi. Please."

He squashed out his cigarette, angrily, and sat up. "Damn it, you never give Asian guys a chance."

"It's not *about* Asian guys. I love having you in my life—but, romantically? We've *never* been boyfriend-girlfriend."

Yoshi was silent. Had I insulted him? His knuckles were pressed against his mouth, his eyes squinting as if they hurt. Then he took a long breath, nodded his head. "Leah," he said. "Haven't you ever heard of the *graceful* put-down? I know you're not attracted to me, although I'm not sure why. Everything about you is so screwed up, your love life included."

"If I'm so screwed up, why do you hang around?"

"I never know what you'll be involved in next," Yoshi said. "Something's always going on with you. But I can't help thinking it's because I'm Japanese—that's why you won't take me seriously."

"That's ridiculous. I'm attracted to men of all kinds of nationalities."

"I wonder if Asian is one of them," Yoshi said, pulling another cigarette from his pack.

"Are you going to start in now about all the Asian men sitting home alone Friday nights?"

157

"You may not be interested, but Carol is." Yoshi blew a rather determined puff of smoke into the air. The smoke ring fell apart; it was not one of his best.

"What are you talking about? She has a boyfriend!"

"That's right," said Yoshi.

On the way home the next day we stopped in Calistoga to fill up the gas tank. Yoshi called Paul from a phone booth. He stayed in the booth talking a long time. When he came out, he jumped in the car and slammed the door shut. He looked worried.

"Shit," he said, "The police were at the house with a search warrant. They made everyone get out. They searched the place from top to bottom. Paul got into a shouting match when they tried to go through his personal stuff, but he said they concentrated on your room. I hope to hell they didn't find the grass hidden in my closet," he added.

By the time we got back to Russell Street, the police were long gone. They hadn't taken much, just a few of my notebooks, but my room was a mess. I sorted through the papers and notebooks they had piled on the floor. The only things missing were notebooks from journalism classes I had taken in the spring. I knew why the police had taken my notebooks. Joey thought I had something I was holding back. And I did. I was glad Grace's diary had come with me up to Clear Lake. Eat your hearts out, cops, I thought, you'll find nothing in those. Who had tipped them off? It seemed more than coincidence I had been out of town when they hit.

Monday morning I returned to work. Edna was waiting for me in the locker room, her hands on her hips. Her little cat's face was swollen and her left eye black and blue. "Girl," she said, "This is the last time I get involved in this kind of shit."

"What happened to you?"

"I don't know why I let you drag me into this stuff," she said. Her lips were pushed out, and she was frowning, angrily. "I ain't down with this kinda shit, girl."

158

I looked around the locker room. It was empty, but I felt worried. "Let's go up in the bleachers. You've got to tell me what happened," I said. "But I don't want anyone to hear us." Edna grabbed her coat with its fuzzy collar. We walked up the tiers of seats to the highest row. It was damp and cloudy. Edna pulled her collar up around her ears. She looked ready to cry.

"Just a fanatic who needed to get laid," she got out.

"Ollie?" I asked.

"He looked me in the eye and asked me, did I believe in the revolution? And I made the mistake of laughing."

"So what happened?"

"He went crazy. Started to hit me. Fool didn't know who he was messing with." Something in Edna's eyes warned me she held me responsible. "Let me tell you, girl, they turn them into fanatics. Fool thought I was trying to insult him and his family, as he calls them."

"Ollie knows you respect the Panthers."

"Enough respect to stay away from them," Edna snorted. "I always gave them credit. Hell, I never saw no black men with rifles going up against cops before. They may be crazy—but they have guts."

"You don't look too good, Edna," I said.

"You should see him, girl. He's the one don't look so pretty anymore."

"You hit him back?"

"I fought like a terror," Edna said. "Brother hadn't had no sleep, and he wasn't expecting that. In the end he backed down. It's against Party rules to treat a sister with disrespect. This could get him expelled." Edna laughed. She sounded more like her old self. "I don't want him in no trouble with the Party. He was really sorry. But you know what coulda happened if he wasn't sorry, don't you? I mighta shot the guy," she said. "Or one of my cousins mighta done it for me. The Banks family coulda ended up with a whole mess of Panthers against us. There's people left the state for less than that."

"I thought you could handle anything, Edna."

"I handled that punk, didn't I? But I'm warning you, Leah—them Panthers don't play. I'm pulling outta their scene; and you had better pull out too, if you know what's good for you."

159

"Look, I'm not even in their scene," I said. I seemed to be taking a lot of the heat for Edna's decision to sleep with Ollie.

"Read this." She reached into her coat and extracted a folded newspaper clipping. "Then hand it back to me, and forget you ever saw it." It was a small clipping from the Tribune which read:

> An Oakland man was found dead today behind the steering wheel of his car. It was parked outside his apartment on East 14th Street. He had been shot in the left temple. His landlady identified him as Al Brooks. She said he had recently moved to Oakland from Louisiana. He has no relatives in the area. The shooting apparently occurred early Sunday AM and remains unsolved. Nothing was stolen from the victim and there were no signs of struggle. Police are searching for a motive.

I looked up at Edna. I had told her about Al Brooks. The man who had come on to me at Vinnie's Inn. Now he was dead—two weeks after I had met him in Vinnie's bar. "Do you think the Panthers—?"

"I don't think nothing," Edna said, with finality. "And neither do you. You've never heard of this person, wouldn't recognize his name if you ever heard it again. You got that straight, Leah?"

"Yeah. Right." It was useless to argue with her.

Edna stood up, tugging her fuzzy collar close against the cold wet wind. She gave me one of her searching looks. "This was all for that blonde girl, wasn't it, Leah?" With that, Edna made her way back down the rows of bleachers. I sat looking into the empty race track, and the hills rising above it to the east.

XIX

Tuesday morning I called Ruby Bailey at the Oakland Tribune.

"I have something for you," I said, "A rough cut of a story about the unsolved murder of Grace Neville, if you're interested."

I had drafted an article that satisfied me. I had written it as a cameo of Grace, to arouse interest and sympathy for her. Perhaps other people would come forward with information after they read it. I included a sketch of James Ferguson—his background, his involvement with the Panthers. I described the prejudices of the OPD; how twice he had been picked up after I had been with him. There was much I left out. I did not discuss any details of the murder or the case against James. I thought Art Leopold would appreciate this. I left out everything about Karella, Ollie, Edna, Al Brooks. Over all it was a sympathetic portrayal of Grace and a neutral presentation of James. Paul and Yoshi had read it over and approved it.

"Very interested," she said, "I could meet with you today, if you'd like." I was pleased by her enthusiasm. We agreed to meet at five pm at the Bateau Ivre, a coffee shop and wine bar on Telegraph Avenue. Late on a Tuesday afternoon in August, it was almost empty.

Ruby Bailey was sitting at a table in the bay window when I entered. She had a large, Angela Davis style Afro, and enormous silver ear-rings dangled from her ears. She wore ironed blue jeans, a white blouse. She looked hip, competent. "So *you're* Leah DeMartino," she said. "The woman who got James Ferguson off."

I slid into a chair and handed her my draft. She read it quickly. "This is good." Her voice was fast and clipped. "I think we could use it. I'll run it by my editor. There may be some minor changes—okay with you?"

"Sure," I said. I was thrilled that my story might be published. I wanted to appear flexible and gracious.

"I'm curious," Ruby said. She rested her hand in her chin, gazing at me. "Your story is so sympathetic to Ferguson. Why is that?"

"It's just more balanced than the other things you've heard," I said. "The Oakland police are out to get him—I know that for a fact."

161

"You do?" She raised an eyebrow.

"The OPD sees James Ferguson as a gangster. They're not going to give him any kind of break."

"There's a lot of evidence against him," she said. "He owned the gun that was used to murder her."

"Members of the Black Panther Party have few personal possessions," I said. I felt odd lecturing this young black woman on the Black Panthers. Nonetheless I continued, "Cars and guns could have been used by any one. Also, doesn't it seem strange that the barrel of the gun was discarded?" Joey said Ferguson had deliberately removed the barrel somewhere so the bullets couldn't be traced to his gun. Would a murderer tossing a gun away at a crime scene have taken the time to remove the barrel? Like many things Joey had told me about this case, this was one more element which didn't make sense.

"I can't give you all the details," I continued. "That's up to his lawyers. I do know that the OPD was following him the night before the murder. He went into Panther Headquarters and never came out. He was at a meeting there the next morning. He was at a rally that afternoon. He has alibis for the entire timeframe Grace was murdered."

"None of the other people at that meeting will come forward to testify," she said. "And he wasn't at DeFremery all afternoon."

I took a deep breath and plunged ahead. "There are arguments on both sides. James Ferguson may have done some of the things he's accused of. I don't know. I'm attempting to write a portrait of a human being. A person who chose his road for a reason. He's not the gangster the newspapers want to make him."

Ruby Bailey was studying me intently, her chin on her fist. "I was just curious why you'd go to such lengths to defend a man who may have murdered your friend. Have you considered going more public with your views? Giving speeches or writing more articles, for example?'

"No," I said, "I'm basically apolitical. The Panthers have their own spokespeople. If you're interested, you could read their newspaper." I wondered if I sounded patronizing. *She* was the young black who should be up on the Black Panthers.

"No chance," she said. "My boss keeps me hopping." She took a ten dollar bill out of her wallet to pay for our coffees. She stood up. "I'll be in touch. Keep writing, Leah. You have a gift. Perhaps we could publish more of your things."

I stood up too. I was flattered.

Our little commune on Russell Street celebrated Labor Day with a bar-beque in the backyard. Paul invited his political friends. Carol and her ex—or maybe not so ex—boyfriend were there. Kanji and his girlfriend came over. The two days following Labor Day the television and newspapers were full of horrific news. An Arab terrorist group, Black September, had made its way into the Olympic Village in Munich and taken eleven Israeli athletes hostage, then murdered them.

The news from Europe seemed far away. I concentrated on getting my-self out to the track and putting my time in. I kept my ears open, but I didn't hear much. I felt that Edna was avoiding me, and I didn't make my usual effort to seek her out.

On Wednesday morning, the sixth of September, Ronnie Jones called. "I was out of town on business," he said. "Did you miss me?"

"I've been too busy to miss anyone," I said. "What were you doing out of town, anyway?"

"Do a lot of consulting. Keeps me on the road," Ronnie said. "I'd get bored, stuck in one place every day. In fact, I've gotta drive up to Chico on Thursday. Want to come?"

"I'd have to see if someone could work my shift at the track. What time?"

"I could pick you up at eight. Only takes about three hours one way. A pretty ride. Give us a chance to get better acquainted."

I never knew what tone to take with Ronnie. Joey had warned me against him but this only made Ronnie more appealing. Who hadn't Joey warned me against? Yoshi, Paul, James Ferguson—Joey had no use for any of them. Ronnie wasn't foreign or black; he was white working class, a Vietnam vet. Personally I found Ronnie a conundrum. Paul had decided Ronnie was okay, a real life example of working class war resistance. Yoshi liked him. I had my reservations. Joey had admitted Ronnie was not a suspect. This was a chance to ask Ronnie more questions about Grace. I would take precautions. I would bring the snubbie Joey had taught me how to shoot.

"I would have to be back in Berkeley by five o'clock," I said. I wanted to set a clear end point for any adventures with Ronnie.

"No problem," he said.

In the end, I called in sick, hearing the skepticism in Beatrice's voice as I said I had bad cramps and wouldn't be in to work. Ronnie was at the door first thing Thursday morning. I was ready for him. The snubbie which Joey had given me lay on the bottom of my shoulder bag. Yoshi and Paul put in an appearance as we left. Paul asked Ronnie about his work with Vietnam Vets Against the War. Ronnie got on Yoshi's good side by smoking a joint with him. Even Carol put in a sleepy appearance. Everyone reminded me loudly of the important house meeting with the landlord at six pm. I needed a fixed return time. I would call them in the early afternoon for an update. Paul added that if they didn't hear from me, they would call my cousin.

Ronnie drove a two-tone Chevy pickup with a gun rack in the rear window. I could see a rifle mounted there. His dog, a big chocolate Lab, ran back and forth, and when Ronnie lowered the tail-gate, came bounding up to us. "Lady, this is Leah."

Didn't Ronnie have it wrong? It should be, "Leah, this is Lady." You introduce the less important person to the more important. At least I knew where I stood. Lady watched me, calm, but interested. I patted her head. Ronnie grabbed the dog by her collar, gave her a slap on the rump, and Lady bounded up into the truck bed and watched us, with a dog's smile. I noted the big cooler pushed up against the back of the cab.

"Why the cooler, Ronnie?"

"Beer," he laughed. "In case we want to picnic."

"I'm more into tomato juice, myself," I said.

"I was afraid of that," said Ronnie.

He headed up I-80, past El Cerrito with its shaggy bump of dark trees on its crest. After the Carquinez Bridge, yellow rolling hills opened out on either side of us. It was Indian summer in California. The radio was playing Willie Nelson. Ronnie was singing along to the music.

164

"You sound happy, Ronnie," I said. I also felt happy. Happy for no good reason, I thought to myself.

"On the road again," Ronnie sang, along with Willie Nelson. "I gotta pretty girl beside me, my dog's sittin' in the back." He made the sentence part of the song. I laughed.

Ronnie turned to me. "My Daddy used to haul us all over God's creation on his hunting trips. All the way over to Nevada and back."

"Were you close to your Dad?"

"Hell, I loved the guy. He could shoe a horse, ride bareback. Women were crazy about him."

"What about your Mom?"

"She liked him too. Least for a while."

We drove on in silence. Lady pressed her nose against the rear window, keeping an eye on us. As we turned onto 505, Ronnie jerked his thumb toward the gun rack behind us. "There are some pretty areas a little south of Chico—Little Dry Creek, Howard Slough. Thought I might stop there for a little bit. I like to do a little shooting when I get a chance."

"You do a lot of hunting?"

"When I can," said Ronnie. "Good deer hunting in the Trinity Alps. I like to go up there with the guys, camp out. Then we go after the hogs near the coast, around Leggett, in the coast mountains. Now that's good shooting. Even some bear over there. Birds are good, up where we're going. Little Dry Creek ain't bad for deer. If nothing else, I'll take me a jack rabbit."

"As long as we get back in time," I hedged. The thought of Ronnie grabbing his gun bothered me, so I changed the subject. "Remember that first night we went out to Charlie Brown's? The next day my cousin Joe came by. He knew all about it. He said they had interviewed you later that same night. What for?"

"Joe's your cousin?" he asked. "Joe DeMartino? That's the cousin your roommates were talking about?"

"Yes. Why did he interview you?"

"I figured it was something you told them," he said.

"I didn't tell him anything. Then the next day I learned he had already talked to you."

"Shit, that's strange," said Ronnie. His eyes were fixed hard on the road; he didn't look at me. Then he added, "Are you close to your cousin?"

"He's family. My father and his dad are brothers. He used to steal doughnuts out of my mother's kitchen. But he's bull-headed. He gets some information all mixed up, but once he figures out someone is the enemy, you just can't reason with him. He's convinced James Ferguson killed Grace."

"It makes sense, don't it?" Ronnie said. "That happens when you serve in Nam. You gonna quibble that some gook with an AK and a hand grenade might be sensitive?" Ronnie made his voice high and effeminate on the word *sensitive*. In his normal voice, he said, "What else he tell you about this case?"

"Not much," I answered.

"How did you get so involved? Joe using you to do field work for him?"

His questions made me feel he knew something already.

"Joey doesn't take me seriously," I replied. That, at least, was true enough. "Of course, he's interested if there's anything I pick up at the track."

"Have you picked up anything at the track?"

"No," I lied. "I'm leaving the police work up to Joey."

"I always wondered what Grace told you about me," Ronnie said now. His eyes were on the highway ahead of him. "Or what Helene said about me."

"Only that you were her high school boyfriend. You both felt like orphans. Grace mentioned that."

"Did Helene give you anything belonging to Grace?"

"Why on earth would Grace's mother give me anything?" Joey had asked me the same thing. It was as if they knew about the diary, the autopsy report.

"I don't know," Ronnie shrugged, "mementos of Grace, photographs maybe. Helene is odd. She handed Grace over to her crackpot, Bible-shouting sister so she could blow in and out of bars. The woman's an alcoholic and a pill popper. Anything she tells you is probably one of her Valium dreams."

I could attribute to Helene some of the information in the diary. "She told me about some wild things you and Grace did together. You guys started a fire? Grace felt bad about that later."

"I saw my Dad do it back in Clayton. Somebody had cheated him on his pay. They thought they were something. And thought we were scum. Dad and his buddies got even fast."

166

"Did you and Grace get caught?" I asked.

"Nah, and she didn't feel bad about setting that fire, either," said Ronnie. "She didn't like snobs."

"You and Grace sure knew how to raise hell," I said. I put an admiring note in my voice. "And you did all those other things, too."

"What other things?" he asked. "What are you talking about?" He looked over at me. "I'm kinda surprised Helene knew anything about that fire. I don't think Grace ever told her."

"She must have told her," I lied, smoothly. "Anyway, Helene mentioned some other pranks."

"Oh, yeah, like when we stole a stupid painting from an art gallery? Stupid flowers and shit. That was a blast. The painter was probably flattered anybody wanted it bad enough to steal it. Grace hung it in the bathroom, above the toilet. It always made us laugh when we saw it."

"So were there more pranks after that?"

"Wasn't time for much else. We graduated, she got my baby cut outta her, and we split." Ronnie spit out the window.

We were on I-5 now. The coast hills lay to the left of us, cinnamon and blue through the valley haze. An occasional irrigation pond reflected the sky, and to our right, a power line marched with its thin, looping wires through the rice paddies and golden fields. We were passing peach and almond orchards, clumps of valley oaks and willow oaks. Farmhouses set back from the freeway were protected by poplar windbreaks. Tall green and red signs announcing the Olive Pit were appearing in the fields. A road sign warned soft shoulders next 23 miles. "You providing them soft shoulders?" asked Ronnie.

"That would be the pits," I punned. Ronnie groaned.

"You started it," I said.

The air was dry and still. Ronnie turned the radio back up. I wondered to myself, where am I going with this guy? Who *is* he? I had mixed feelings, on the one hand oddly happy—or was it hysterically light-hearted?—mixed with unease. I was glad I had the snubbie with me.

North of Williams Ronnie turned off the freeway onto a county road. After a few miles, we crossed the Sacramento River, headed north to Butte City, then drove east another few miles on state highway 162. Ronnie pulled off onto the shoulder. "Them there's the Sutter Buttes," said Ronnie, pointing. Far off to the southeast, past the rice fields and hammocks of willow oaks, I could see sharp jagged peaks.

"This is it!" said Ronnie. "One of the sweetest little spots around. I'm going to stop for a bit. Lady's acting anxious, like she needs to pee. I'm gonna go check out Little Dry Creek." He jumped down from the cab and ran to the back to drop the tailgate down. Lady leaped out in one bound and made a bee line for the fields, looking eagerly back at Ronnie. She ran down the field toward a row of poplars on the far edge, then stiffened, and pointed.

Ronnie threw down his cigarette, stamped it out, and stuck his head back in the cab. "I'm just gonna check out Little Dry Creek. Looks like Lady smelled something worth going after." He reached in the driver's side window, pulled the rifle off the gun rack, checked that it was loaded. "Come on Lady!" he shouted. His voice sounded high and full of excitement. "Come on girl!"

I pushed open the passenger-side door and stepped down out of the truck to watch them. Now Lady was running down a row of poplars, with Ronnie catching up. It was pretty country. To the left of the road, fields were flooded for rice. On our side were grassy uplands. Nearer in, golden cotton-woods hung over a slough. It was quiet. For a few minutes, I lost sight of them; then Ronnie came into view just in front of the poplar trees. He raised his rifle and took aim. Then a shot cracked out against the silence. A second shot. I couldn't see anything.

I waited for the third shot. A deer reached the shelter of trees and disappeared from my view. Everything remained silent. Ronnie disappeared back into the shadow of the poplar row.

I waited, but nothing happened. After a while, bored, I climbed back into the cab. I should have brought a book. Without thinking, I opened the glove compartment in front of me. There were maps, gas receipts. Still no sign of Ronnie, nor of his chocolate Labrador. I pushed open the truck door and stepped down. My shoulder bag dangled on my shoulder, heavy with the weight of the snubbie. I followed the track they had taken through the field.

As I approached the trees, Ronnie came back into view. He was standing on the far side of the poplars, completely still, his rifle to his shoulder, aiming out into the next field. "Ronnie," I shouted.

168

Ronnie wheeled around one hundred eighty degrees. His rifle was pointed directly at me. He had a wild look in his eyes. It wasn't clear he knew who I was. I couldn't speak. I thought of my own gun, useless in my shoulder bag. If I made any movement to get it, Ronnie might fire. Slowly Ronnie lowered his rifle. His eyes seemed to come back into focus.

"Goddamn it, Leah," he said, "don't sneak up on me like that."

He put two fingers in his mouth, gave a whistle, and Lady came bounding back. I turned and headed back toward the truck, my hand reaching unobtrusively in my shoulder bag. I felt the revolver. With my hand around it, I walked more quickly, half running across the field. I was breathless as I climbed back into the cab.

I wasn't sure how much more time went by. Ronnie finally returned, holding a dead jack rabbit by the scruff of its neck. Lady ran beside him, sniffing eagerly at the rabbit. "Good girl, Lady," Ronnie said. He grinned at me. "Not a deer, but a little something. Ever had rabbit spaghetti?"

I made a face. I did not like to see the bloody thing.

"Hey, I'll put it in the cooler so you won't have to look at it." He pulled a big plastic bag from behind the front seat, stuffed the rabbit into it, and threw the bag in the cooler. As he closed the lid, he grabbed a can of beer. Now Ronnie leaned against the driver's side window, staring in at me. He popped his can and took a long draft. "Sorry I scared you like that. But when I hunt, I go into emergency mode. All my survival training comes back. For a second it was like you were the enemy sneaking up on me. A lot of vets sleep with guns under their pillows."

Ronnie patted Lady's rump. She jumped up into the back, Ronnie got in on the driver's side of the truck. His face was glistening with a light sweat. His light brown hair lay tousled over his forehead. He started up the truck. He looked happy. "They have a name for it—post traumatic stress disorder."

"Why go hunting if it gives you such horrible flashbacks?" I asked. I didn't want him to know I was rattled. "Isn't it dangerous to live with reactions like that?"

"They give you counseling," he answered, as he pulled back onto the highway. "Bah—worthless. I got out of Vietnam, but Vietnam won't ever get out of me. They made a killer of me, Leah." He sounded proud. He was totally unlike the men I had known until now, men who studied books and argued politics. Ronnie's physical mastery of his surroundings was frightening, but it was also, in some strange way, attractive. Like James, I thought.

"Hunting keeps me sharp," Ronnie answered. "When I was a kid, I hunted deer. In Nam, I hunted men. Ain't much difference. Men were hunting me too. They would do it again. They're on the streets, lying in wait, believe me. I gotta be ready for them."

Was this how men saw the world? The woman had to hope her man was on the winning side? Men like Ronnie or James appealed to women because on some elemental level they could protect us. Of course they had a way of dragging us into situations in which we needed protection. And they could also use their violence to dominate and abuse.

We drove further north. Ronnie talked between swallows of beer. "I'll tell you one goddamn thing—I don't mean to sound egotistical—women like me. I'm like my Daddy that way." Ronnie seemed pleased with himself. Then his tone changed. "—Not that any woman ever really came through for me."

"What happened with your wife?"

"Lim was a teenager. Young and tough. She called me Hey You. Brought her over here from Nam and she was gone within the year. Took the kid with her; still payin' for *that*. Thought I had gotten me a submissive type—like hell!" Ronnie laughed. "Lim was about as submissive as a hand grenade."

I wondered how I might cut this trip short. I needed to call Yoshi and Paul. "I guess you and Grace both needed to rebel," I said. "You rebelled even after you came back from Vietnam. When you joined the VVAW."

"What I hated about the war was the way they messed it up," said Ronnie. "What Grace hated about the war was the way it messed *me* up. Still can't sleep the whole night through. My last visit back home, my Daddy said don't bother coming back unless I stop shouting in my sleep. One thing you had to say for the guy," Ronnie continued, "he stayed consistent. Didn't like me a whole lot to begin with, and didn't like me any better at the end." He laughed his whooping, cowboy laugh. It was a laughter that covered up a range of feelings.

I rolled down the window and inhaled the fresh scent of earth and manure. A strong feeling of uneasiness had replaced the irrational joy I had felt when we set out. We were on highway 99, on the outskirts of Chico. "Look, I'm hungry. Could we stop and get some lunch?" This would be my opportu-

170

nity to call Paul and Yoshi. I was also wondering about something Ronnie had just said—how Grace had not liked what Vietnam had done to him. Had he continued to see her when he got back?

"Sure, I know a great place," said Ronnie. We drove another mile; then he turned off 99, pulling into the parking lot of a big family diner. I followed him into a large dining room with dark wooden booths and racks of antlers on the walls. I called Yoshi and Paul from the pay phone near the bathrooms. "I gotta end this thing," I said, low and urgent, to Paul who had picked up.

Paul got it right away. "Tell your friend we've heard from the land-lord—our meeting's been moved up to four. You gotta get back."

"Hey, Ronnie, bad news," I said, joining him at one of the dark booths. "Paul says the meeting got moved up to four. Can you get me back early?"

"Sure, no prob," said Ronnie. He didn't seem to notice my discomfort. The juke box was playing American Pie. "I like this song, reminds me of Nam," he said. "Good ole boys, doin' some of the harder stuff along with that whiskey and rye. And, Miss Leah, you *will* note that I drive a Chevy. Drove it to the levee, too. Yeah, not quite twenty. About to get drafted, so I enlisted instead. They gave me a bunch of tests. Then they said, boy, we've got something special for you. Train you for Special Forces."

"What did you do in Special Forces?"

"Interrogation specialist. Phoenix Program. We showed the South Vietnamese how to find the commies. Somehow making peace with those SOBs don't sit right with me." Ronnie's face darkened, as Don McLean's voice filled the room.

"Satan's spell," he said. He hit the table with his fist. "You know what that is? That's the USA today. That's what we got now, everybody wanting a piece of the American pie." He made his voice high and squeaky on *American pie,* dismissive.

"You work with the Vietnam Vets Against the War," I said. "Isn't making peace what they stand for?" His words made no sense to me.

"Sure they do. Anyone in combat wants peace. It's no fun being some-body's target practice. It's no fun wondering if you've stepped on a mine—and even that ain't half as bad as knowin' if you step *off* of one you're finished. I've got mixed feelings about it—it don't come from the head. It comes from the gut."

171

"I see those mixed feelings in my cousin Joey."

"Joey and I have a lot in common," Ronnie answered. "We joined the military out of high school. We did our time. No college deferments or slipping into Canada for us. I don't know much about him, but that's a background I can deal with." Ronnie seemed to know a surprising amount about Joey. Had I told him some of this the night we met at Charlie Brown's? It was confusing.

Ronnie was continuing his thoughts. "You're someone I can talk to Leah. I feel like you understand me. I know I scare you, but there's a connection between us. Maybe you'd give me a chance?"

I was confused by my reaction to Ronnie. He was exciting, but he made me uneasy. "We don't know one another very well."

"Are you worried about me being in Vietnam? You Berkeley girls are all alike, a bunch of peaceniks." He didn't look angry. "You don't know nothing about combat; nothing about war."

"That's one of the ways we're different."

"You'll catch on, eventually. It's a war out there; that's what everyone has to face."

"You sound like Joey again."

"Joe was in Nam," Ronnie said. "Joe knows the score."

"That was a war," I said. "Back here, you have to think different."

"Back here, it's still war," Ronnie said. "Me and Joe know that. You just haven't faced it yet."

Ronnie got me back to Berkeley by four pm. His business hadn't taken much time. In fact, the Chico consultation consisted of parking his truck with the motor running while he ran up the steps of a shabby bungalow, disappearing inside, and re-emerging in five minutes. I hadn't had the nerve to ask Ronnie what *that* was all about.

After dinner Carol and I walked the rain-dampened streets of Berkeley. Carol wanted to hear about my trip with Ronnie. A light shower had started, then stopped again. Flowers bloomed all around us, brilliant marigolds, multi-colored zinnias, drooping red and purple fuchsias.

"Everywhere I turn, I run into suspicious men," I said to Carol. One man hates the police. Another hates the government. Is it just the men I run into, or is it the way the world is?"

172

"You're so dramatic, Leah," said Carol. "It's the men you pick. The men I meet aren't so caught up in the dark side."

"Are you still seeing Zeke?'

"History. I've started dating other men. You know, Leah, you make good money at the track. It's a good job, but you should look elsewhere for your dates." Neither James nor Ronnie were *dates*, I thought. Leave it to Carol to look at it that way.

"What do *you* think of Ronnie?" I asked.

"I've got cousins like Ronnie back in Michigan. They like to hunt, shoot a squirrel or a rabbit. They get mad as hell if you give them a hard time about it. Are you interested in him?"

I thought of the wild look on Ronnie's face as he had whirled toward me, aiming his rifle straight at my chest. "Joey warned me away from Vietnam Vets."

"You shouldn't get involved with a man who dated your friend. It doesn't make sense. Even if it was a long time ago. So you're not interested in Yoshi?"

"Not romantically," I said. I wondered why she wanted to know. Oh, right, Yoshi had mentioned Carol was interested in him. Why should I care? I wanted to keep Yoshi as my friend and partial, if inadequate, protector. I did not want him as a lover.

We parted on College Avenue. I gave a breezy wave as we separated. I hoped I was behaving with sufficient nonchalance.

XX

For days I had tried calling the number on the business card that had fallen out of Grace's wallet. The name on the card was Maura Sayid. The phone had rung and rung and rung. Friday after work I tried again. This time a woman answered. "Hello?" The voice was low and musical, with a pronounced foreign accent.

"Am I speaking with Maura Sayid?" I asked.

"You are."

"This is Leah DeMartino. I'm calling on behalf of Grace Neville," I said.

"Oh, yes." Her voice seemed guarded. "How is Grace?"

After a brief silence she said, "Has something happened?"

"I'm sorry," I said, "I thought you knew. Grace died a month ago."

"An illness?"

"Murdered," I said, "Her body was found near the race track."

"My God," she said, "My husband and I were out of the country. I hadn't heard. What happened?"

"The police haven't found the killer," I answered. "Your card was in some papers Grace left with me. I would like to come talk to you about her."

"Certainly," she said. She sounded dazed. "I would like to talk to you also. This is such a shock. What date was she killed?"

"August seventh," I said.

"We left for Europe that evening," she said, "This is so sad. I am free tomorrow afternoon. Could you come at one?" She gave me her address on Quail Road in the Berkeley hills.

Quail Road was a winding street in the upper hills. Her house, a small Tudor cottage, was set back on a steeply sloping lot. A large mullioned picture window faced the front yard. Fall-blooming chrysanthemums and marigolds competed with autumn saffron crocuses, and a red Japanese maple. I remembered Grace's funeral reception at aunt Millie's nondescript tract home in Concord. What did it take to create a place of beauty like this, a world in which all other worlds fell away?

174

The tall woman who answered the door had black hair streaked with grey, pulled back in an elegant chignon. She wore black slacks and a black V-neck sweater, a scarf of gold and black at her neck. Her ear-rings were heavy gold loops. She had large, dark eyes, close-set and a slightly hooked nose. Her face reminded me of one of Modigliani's portraits.

"I am Maura Sayid," she said, offering me her hand.

"Leah DeMartino. Thanks for being willing to see me." A hall led past a small kitchen and into a sunken living room. The far wall was a sliding glass door overlooking a deck, filled with urns of flowering plants. A tall man, with Maura's olive skin tones, was watering plants with a hose. Maura motioned me toward a white leather couch facing the fireplace. I sat down. "Are you any relation to Hassim Sayid?" I asked, remembering the proprietor of the Lebanese restaurant on Telegraph where I had briefly waited table.

"You know Hassim? He's my cousin," she said.

"I waited table there, when I first moved to Berkeley," I said.

"That's nice," Maura said. She seemed distracted. "I've made tea," she added. "May I get you a cup? Do you take cream?"

"Yes, to both" I said. I examined the large stone fireplace opposite me, the framed prints on the walls. I wondered again what resources a person needed to have to create a retreat for oneself so full of beauty.

Maura re-entered carrying a Chinese teapot, two cups, and a plate of Walker's shortbread biscuits, on a tray. Setting these down on the coffee table, she slid open the glass door and called to the man outside. "That is my husband, David," she said, coming back. "He may join us later. Despite my ambivalence about the British, I love the custom of afternoon tea." She had an air of reserve and kindness. I felt rested around her.

I knew I should start speaking, but I couldn't begin. The beauty and warmth of her house, the profusion of color in her garden, her quiet, unquestioning acceptance, created an oasis of safety in which speech seemed unnecessary. I thought about the houses I had entered in the last month—aunt Millie's in Concord; Helene's trailer in the Lollipop Motor Home Resort; even Clyde Turner's mother's house off Adeline. I had been pushed into so many lives and houses which depressed me.

"So, Leah," Maura said. She was pouring the tea. "Why did you come?"

175

I gathered my thoughts. "I'm trying to find out more about Grace," I said. "I hoped you could help me. How did you know her?"

"I teach comparative literature at UC Berkeley. I offer a creative writing class through the extension. Grace was a student in my poetry workshop. I was struck by a raw vitality to her words."

"Did you know her very well?"

"In the way one knows another when one reads the other's work. Details, specifics, very little." She was quiet again.

"I felt Grace was drawn to trouble," she said, after a while. "She had a compulsion to please. Men in particular." Maura lifted her cup. "And a certain type of man. A man whose wounds conceal tremendous anger."

"That could be a lot of people," I said, thinking of James—brutalized by the Houston cops. Ronnie—burned by Vietnam. Joey—abused by his own father, long before the army did its work on him.

"We may all be capable of violence," she said, "but we are not usually drawn to violent people. I felt Grace needed to provoke that level of anger."

"Why do you say that?"

"Directly she told me little," Maura replied. "Underneath her charisma, I sensed an emptiness. There was a sense of desolation in her poems."

"So you saw her charm," I said.

"A woman that determined to please rarely fails."

"I envied her that," I said.

"When I was younger, I envied it, too. By now I have seen that kind of flattery too often. Women use it as a defense. Such women often appear irresistible."

"It's a kind of power," I said.

"Grace used that charm to protect herself and to get things she wanted. She had nothing for you to envy. Grace was a person whose real self never had a chance to develop. Something essential was lacking." Her words hung in the room with a quality of finality.

I struggled to reply. "You learned all this from reading her poems?"

She was silent a moment. "Not just the poems," Maura said, finally, looking up. "I liked Grace, and I tried to help her. I believe she liked me. Looked up to me, in fact. Even so, her need to attract men led her to behave inappropriately with my husband." Now it was my turn to be silent.

176

Maura continued, "I had invited the class here for our last meeting. A goodbye party. We had lunch out on the deck, read each other's poems. That was the end of June. Grace spent a long time talking to David. She asked him for a tour of the house. Later he told me she had come on to him. I was angry. She had betrayed my trust. My husband and I are happy together, but other men might not resist such offers. I remember thinking something very bad could happen to a person who was so reckless with her loyalties. Igniting fires so recklessly, one can get burned. When you told me she had been killed, I felt my words had come back to haunt me."

"Did you see her after the goodbye party?"

"No. I thought I would. She had left some poems, her writing journal. Fragments of her writings. I glanced at the poems because she asked me to. I didn't read the journal; I thought she may not have meant to leave it. I assumed one day she would call me to come to pick it up and we would talk then." After another pause, Maura added, "I would like to give these things to you."

"Okay," I said, "yes, please."

She walked to a cabinet and withdrew a packet. "There are two note-books. This one seems to be a journal from the past. The other notebook, with the poems, is more recent. It's in my office in Dwinelle. I was planning to use one or two of her poems in a student anthology. I'll find them next week, and mail them to you."

"Don't mail it," I said. "Call me, say you have the list of recommended books we talked about. I'll know what you mean, and I'll come and pick it up."

She gave me a penetrating look. "Why is this so important to you?" She sat down on the sofa across from me. "What happened in your life to make you need to pursue this?"

Maybe it was the steaming cups of tea, or the beauty of these surroundings, but I found myself talking about my mother's death, my father's alienation from me after he remarried, my need to belong somewhere. "If I can discover the truth behind Grace's murder, it will give meaning to my life."

"My husband and I have lived through many wars," Maura said. "Scenes I want only to forget. I'm not sure, Leah, that you can find meaning in a murder."

The glass door opened and her husband stepped into the room. He was a tall man, with a slight limp, and deep black eyes. "David, this is Leah,"

Maura said. "She was a friend of Grace's."

He looked at Maura. It seemed to be a look of warning.

"We were shocked to learn of Grace's death," he said, after a pause.

I left shortly after that. Maura had told me to come back any time I wanted. I doubted that I would.

Sitting in her lovely house had given me a brief sense of peace. It was a peace that showed me how conflicted my own life was becoming. I did not want to face that. I feared that examining my motivations too closely would break the momentum, that if I stopped to look closely at what I was doing, I would realize how very foolhardy it was.

XXI

It was six o'clock on a Friday night at the St. Francis Hotel in San Francisco. I had taken the F bus and walked up to Union Square, passing the black doorman with his cap and brass-buttoned uniform, standing under a green canopy. The hotel lobby, with its black marble pillars streaked with white and green, the ceiling decorated with golden florets, radiated an aura of wealth. A granite staircase led to an ornate balcony ; three loges had a view down onto the floor below. A bar opened off to the right. The reception desk was to the left.

I took a seat in a leather chair at a low round table and waited. At another table, a heavyset man leaned close to a woman in a tight pink sweater. They clinked glasses. They were framed by palm fronds emerging from an enormous brass planter in the center of the seating area. Standing before a row of three elevators stood a black man in a white silk suit. He was carrying a bouquet of red carnations. He turned his head and his glance grazed me, but he did not meet my eyes.

Where was Jay? I was perched on a chair with a stiff brocade cushion, trying to fit in, and it wasn't easy. I was wearing a bright red leotard top and black pants, with ballet flats, but it seemed to take more than clothes to fit into this crowd. I straightened my spine, sat tall, and did my best to cultivate a look of polite amusement.

A tall blonde sat at a table opposite me, smoking. She wore a body-hugging black dress, dark black stockings. Her long, glossy hair fell over her face. I felt her staring at me. I glanced at her again. Perhaps she noticed how out of place I looked. She was staring at me intently. Something about the woman looked odd and yet familiar. Perhaps she was a prostitute, waiting for her John to come along. And then I looked again. It couldn't be.

The woman stood up. She was not a woman. It was Jay. He walked toward me in his tight, black sheath, smiling under a layer of artfully placed rouge and lipstick. "May I sit down?" he asked me. He took the chair across from me. We were separated by a little oval table.

"For God's sake, Jay," I said.

"I told you," he said. He seemed delighted by my shock. "I like props and play acting. I like to dress up. "

179

"Are you homosexual?" I blurted.

His voice, at least, sounded the same—cultivated, bored, with the hint of privilege and private schools. "Not at all," he said. "This is just a game. I like this kind of clothing—it's very sensual. My therapist explained it all to me. My love for this kind of clothing shows I like to be close to women."

A waiter in a starched white shirt appeared. "Make it two Scotch rocks." His tenor voice could have been a woman's voice roughened by years of smoking. "After all," Jay Landis said, "women like makeup. Why shouldn't men? Actors and musicians wear stage makeup under the lights when they perform." I could not take my eyes off his lipsticked mouth, his eyes with the dark eyeliner. "You're surprised, aren't you? I used to watch my Mom put on her makeup. When she left to go out with my Dad, I'd stand in her closet for hours. I loved feeling her dresses, the way her scent lingered there among her clothes." I was touched by the thought of the little boy standing alone in his mother's closet.

"Then when I was twelve, they sent me off to boarding school. Military boarding school. Dad insisted. He thought it would make a man out of me. Little did he know it would make matters worse."

"How did it make matters worse?"

"Even you, Leah, can imagine. Puberty, and the hormones are exploding. There aren't any girls around. Everybody's horny, everybody's lonely— things happen. Between boys and older boys. But it doesn't change anything. When the time comes, you're supposed to go out and score with women too. Only problem is, if you've fooled around with guys too much, you're at a disadvantage. I was messed up. I thought I was queer. I was terrified around women—tongue-tied and shy." He sounded petulant and resentful. "I met some guys outside of school who had this idea they were rock stars. They started to wear makeup when they performed. I was hanging around with them. I started wearing it too. I felt different after that. Bolder. It helped me find out I'm not queer at all. It was always women I picked up. "

"Always?"

"Always," he said, "But I found I was turned on by certain types. Permissive, like you. Rebellious—like Grace. Makeup was just a way to enhance the experience. There are other ways, too."

"What other ways?"

180

"Props, costumes, alcohol," he said. "And, of course, drugs."

Paul and Yoshi and I had discussed this encounter the entire week. If Jay Landis offered me alcohol, I would only pretend to drink. But drugs? I looked at the drinks the waiter had placed in front of us.

Jay leaned forward and whispered, "You first." He smiled as if he could read my thoughts. I didn't want to break this intimacy we were establishing. I wanted him to go on revealing himself to me. "Drink up," he said, "You'll never regret it. This is one experience I embrace with all my heart."

Drink up? An experience I would never forget? A Scotch on the rocks? Something didn't make sense here. I needed time to sort things out. "I'm going to use the women's room," I said. I hurried past a bank of phones to the right of the restroom. The woman's restroom was ornate, with Art Deco lighting fixtures, enormous bouquets of fresh flowers, low benches upholstered in pinstripe silk. I took a place on a bench, facing an oval gilt mirror. I looked flushed and excited, like a girl on a date. This investigation had improved my social life in some odd ways. I checked for the revolver I had hidden at the bottom of my purse. It was still there.

Paul, Yoshi and I had decided on a code. "No news is good news" inserted into a sentence meant trouble. I would call them from the room to let them know the room number. If necessary, they would come over. Perhaps I was taking too much time. My absence might make Jay suspicious. I went back and sat down. Jay clinked glasses with me.

"You seem to be terrified of alcohol. You're a prude, Leah, despite your Berkeley style. —To trying new things," he said, as our glasses touched. I swallowed. Even mixed with ice, the Scotch was harsh. I definitely preferred tomato juice.

I took second taste of my drink. I wanted to get Jay talking again. Jay Landis's face, its bone structure even more startling in makeup, was that of a classically beautiful person. He looked radiant. After the first round, Jay ordered a second. My dislike for Scotch abated as I drank more of it. A small orchestra was playing in another room, and we lingered, chatting about Berkeley. Jay had been an architecture major. He had deep admiration for the architecture of Gaudí. I must go to Barcelona to see La Sagrada Familia. I had not realized how fascinating a conversationalist Jay was. We must have spent thirty minutes in the atrium, drinking, our eyes lingering on one another.

I felt a rush of joy course through me, the blood beating up into my cheeks. I felt tremendously excited, as if I were on the brink of a great discovery. I looked at Jay. He was smiling, as if in anticipation. His lips, under flakes of pink lipstick, arched upward like a membrane of joy. I wanted to touch his lips, brush my fingers over his cheeks, as pink as the cheeks of an English schoolboy. I felt if I touched his face, I would understand Jay. Everything about him. Who he was. How he had been hurt.

Jay's pink lips were smiling at me, stretched away from his dazzling white teeth in a jester's bold laugh. Beneath the fog of my powerful emotions these impressions fast forwarded like a slide show. I struggled for words. "Am I having a contact high?" I asked. "I feel funny already, almost drunk."

"That's no contact high," Jay answered, "I put some MDA in your drink when you went to the bathroom. You're getting the rush now. "

I felt a thrill of panic and anger. Kaleidoscope colors and impressions assaulted my eyes. The room looked opulent, the carpet beneath us thick and multi-layered. A little voice in my head, far away, wondered if I hadn't better call Yoshi and Paul right now.

"MDA?" I asked, "What's that?" It was hard to talk, to make my mouth shape the vowels and words that matched my meanings.

"A love drug," he said. The pink lips stretched wide, the large white teeth menaced me. It didn't seem to matter. "I didn't want to be out here all alone. It's a hell of a feeling, isn't it?"

Tingling bubbles made their way up and down my body. The room was resplendent with colored lights swirling, tapestries coming to life behind me, unicorns moving through the brocaded trees, and the joy of sitting here, watching people eating and drinking in all their variety.

And Jay, too, was a marvel. An incredible piece of human workmanship, expertly crafted. Every detail of his person was a miracle. I could see the lost child in his face, the face pressed among his mother's dresses, inhaling her scent, the lost little boy waiting in a darkened closet in Kensington for his mother to come home. Our hands groped toward each other's on the table; our fingers laced and intertwined. That, too, seemed amazing: the strength and heat of contact, the wonder of palm on palm. Jay ran his hand down my forearm in a tender, caressing motion.

"Let's go upstairs," he whispered.

Fleetingly I thought of Paul and Yoshi. Was I supposed to remember to do something that involved them? It didn't seem to matter at all now. Whatever it was, was far away, unimportant, compared with the discoveries I was making now. What was essential was to make my way across this thick, rich carpet, whose sinuous floral patterns rose up to embrace me, hand in hand with this wondrous creature, a Shakespearean sprite out of The Tempest, who had opened up to his own androgyny. Together we would ride the magic elevator to a room of more wonders.

Room 935 overlooked Union Square. I stood at the window. The light had faded out of the sky; street lights were coming on in the square below. The glittering facades of the department stores ringing the park twinkled in the dusk. Then Jay was behind me, his hands on my upper arms, warm and insistent. I turned to face him and lifted off his blonde wig, seeing the boy's face underneath the vivid makeup. He nestled his head into my shoulder like a large bird coming home to nest.

"You smell so good," he murmured.

"Like what?" I asked, giggling. I traced the cord of muscles that connected his ear to the side of his neck.

"Like Leah," he said.

I laughed again. Somehow my jacket was off now. Jay was leading me toward the big bed.

"I thought you didn't like me," I said.

"Everybody thinks I don't like them," he said. "Even me, until I take MDA. Then I realize that I love everyone."

"Why didn't you like me?" I persisted. I had forgotten that I hadn't liked him either. That all was so long ago. He had stopped to pull off his tight dress. Under the dress, he was wearing black tights like a dancer. I could see the bulge of his penis. It did not excite me, but, like everything else that night, it exerted its own fascination.

"Because you come on as a liberated Berkeley woman, but I see the real you. You're a prude, Leah," he giggled. "You're so—Victorian! But we'll change all that." The next thing I knew he was touching me with long, tender strokes along every inch of my body. I wanted to laugh with pleasure, but my mind remained curious and apart.

"Did you do this with Grace?" I got out. After a long time, when I thought he had forgotten my question, and I could barely remember it, he mumbled something incomprehensible into my hair.

"What?"

"You're asking me to do something difficult," he said. "To remember what it was like before. When I take the MDA, that life seems so unreal."

It seemed that way to me too. My frenetic, crazed search for the person who had murdered Grace, my need to write that article and be recognized. A form of madness. Why hadn't I simply enjoyed the beauty of life around me? It suddenly was clear to me, the mistakes I was making in that other life, the error and silliness of it. I felt words rushing to my lips to explain.

"It seems to me you want to know too much," Jay said. "And I'm afraid of cops." He gave a soft, giggly laugh.

"Why?" Some part of my mind was still wary. Hadn't there been something I had been supposed to do once we got up here in this room? Did it matter what it had been?

"Cops hate guys like me," he said. "They're rotten." We were entwined on the bed, our feet touching with a current that felt like electricity. Our caresses and kisses had worn away his makeup. His face looked white and lost.

"They're rotten and corrupt," Jay repeated. "And my father—he's corrupt too. He thinks the worst thing in life is to have a son like me." His fingers clutched my arms and he buried his head in my shoulder. He was crying.

"My father," he said, "My father and Grace—"

I was high. For a second I recognized this fact, before I dropped back into the timelessness of the moment. Jay wanted to tell me something. The drug had opened floodgates of his memory, so that he could no longer hold it back. But I was in no condition to make sense of it. I should have brought a tape. Jay moved his knee closer to mine and I shuddered with the shock waves of the movement. What did it matter? The moment, the sensation, was all.

"Why am I talking about all this? You could betray me too."

"Who betrayed you, Jay?"

"Grace," he said. "In so many ways. Grace was an actress. She knew how to give people what they wanted. You give people what they want, sexually, when they're high—it's incredible."

184

"I imagine it is," I said.

"It gives a person an extraordinary power. You don't have that."

"I know," I said.

"Because you don't need it. You're stronger than Grace."

"So Grace was sleeping with your father?"

"With him, too. I was always scared she would tell him—about *this*."

"*Did* she tell him?"

"I don't know." He was moving now in an anxious, restless way. "I don't know what she told him. She turned up dead soon after." The words jarred, a discordant knocking on the door of memory. Grace. Grace's murder. Wasn't that what this was all about? Wasn't I supposed to find out something? I struggled, wanting only to bask in this warm sensuality. Yet some persistent voice urged me to continue.

"So Grace was sleeping with you and with your father?"

"There weren't many men Grace didn't fuck. My Dad helped her out financially. So did I. She sure knew how to play both ends against the middle."

"I heard Grace won a lot of money the day she died," I said. I didn't know this as a fact, but I hoped by saying it, Jay would give me information.

"Oh, yeah. She cleaned up. Ten thousand clams."

So that was it. Ten thousand dollars.

"That's a lot of money. Was your father involved in that?"

"He, Bucky Timmons, Grace—the three of them had some agreement."

Jay was looking into my face carefully. I had the uncanny feeling his high gave him some of the same insights into me that I had into him. "You're preoccupied with Grace, aren't you, Leah?"

"I liked her," I said. "But it's strange. How did your father—"

"Stop talking about my father!" he shouted suddenly. The words shattered the air. He smashed his hand down over my mouth. "Get rid of that smile—goddamn you."

I pulled myself away. Jay fell back on the bed. I struggled, but a dark tide of weariness engulfed me. Jay seemed to have fallen asleep and was snoring slightly. I would rest for a minute, then call Yoshi and Paul from the lobby, have them come get me. I lay down on the other bed and passed out.

When I awoke, pale morning light filled the room. The door to the bathroom was open. Jay was urinating loudly into the toilet. Jay had told me something last night, something which might prove important. What was it? I wanted to use the bathroom and shower. I couldn't do either. I had to get out of there. Jay came to the door of the bathroom. He looked young in white cotton underpants with his long white legs and faintly stubbled face.

"Post coitus, animal esta triste," he said.

"Excuse me?"

"After sex, the animal is sad," he explained. He looked at me with his old, disdainful smile.

"We didn't have sex."

"Oh, yes we did, baby," he laughed. "Don't get technical on me." His nose and eyes were red. All vestiges of his makeup and female clothing had disappeared. Had everything else been an illusion, some trick of the drug?

"It was sex all right," he said. "Don't kid yourself about that. I get high, I fuck who I please. Hippies like you, cunts like Grace. I can do it just like any other guy." He walked back into the bathroom with the barest intimation of a swagger.

I opened my purse for my comb and lipstick and was startled to face the revolver. I could hear Jay in the bathroom, water running in the sink. He was lathering his face with soap. I could catch a glimpse of him in the bathroom mirror, his left arm angled over his head pulling up his cheek while his right hand pulled a straight razor just below the cheek bone.

There was something he had told me about his father. Something I was supposed to remember. "Isn't your father a member of the racing board?" I called out. Jay reappeared at the bathroom door, his eyes glittering, and his face ludicrous with a beard of white soap.

"Leave my father out of this," he said. He held the straight blade in his hand, whipping it in the air in front of him with a slashing motion. Then he started walking toward me, slashing the razor through the air as he approached. "You say it wasn't real sex last night," he said. "Let's see if I can make it real for you this morning."

As he approached, I felt a click go off inside my head. In that second I entered the zone of perfect clarity that prefigures insanity. I understood everything in that white light. Jay and his hatred of women, his disdain toward me and Grace, his need to humiliate us. I picked the heavy little snubbie out of my purse and pointed it at him.

"Drop that goddamned razor," I said

His face lightened a shade. "What are you doing?"

"I said, drop that goddamned razor."

"Jesus Christ, Leah," he said, speaking rapidly, "Don't you understand a joke? I was joking, Leah."

"Drop the goddamned razor," I repeated. My hand was starting to shake, I heard Joey's admonishments in my ears. Squeeze the trigger, don't pull it. I kept the gun pointed straight at his knee, the point where Joey had told me I could cripple someone.

Jay dropped the razor. He was backing away from me, toward the bathroom, talking faster and faster.

"It's okay, it's okay, it's really okay, Leah," he said. "No harm done, just calm down, just stay calm." He backed all the way into the bathroom and closed the door quickly. I could still hear him behind the door talking, "Calm down, Leah, it's gonna be all right, just calm down."

"Don't come out of that room for thirty minutes!" I shouted, "or I'll blast your skinny knees off!"

Part of me stood outside myself and observed this scene with astonishment. I was no longer afraid. I felt powerful. The gun had equalized things between us in a way which thrilled me. My mind registered just how dangerous this feeling of power could be.

The room phone rang. I picked up, keeping the snubbie pointed toward the bathroom door. It was Yoshi. "Oh, my God," I said. "I don't know how you found me, but I'm coming down right now."

Yoshi was sitting at one of the round tables near the potted palms. Seeing me, he squashed out his cigarette and stood up. "Are you okay, Leah? What happened?" I was walking fast out the lobby doors, Yoshi running to catch up. "I parked your VW a couple of blocks away," he added.

"He put MDA in my drink," I said. "I'm just now coming down."

How had Jay described the MDA last night? His love drug? "A mild form of speed," he had told me. A mild hallucinogenic. Not dangerous in small amounts. I doubted this was true. "He threatened me with a razor this morning. I pulled my snubbie on him, that shut him up. But we need to get out of here."

"Your *snubbie*?" Yoshi repeated. "What are you talking about?"

I kept moving, too jacked up by adrenalin to slow down. I threw words back at Yoshi as we rushed toward my car. "Joey gave it to me," I said, "It's a little revolver. Colt Cobra .38 Special. He showed me how to use it. I'm glad he did."

"Joey gave you a gun?" Yoshi repeated. "How come you never told us? You were with a guy, high on drugs, and you had a gun on you? You could have been killed." My VW was parked at Montgomery and Third Street. Yoshi opened the driver's seat door and reached over to open the passenger side. It was occurring to me that there were quite a few things I had kept from my roommates. The Colt Cobra. Grace's diaries. My undercover work for the OPD, my status as a paid informant.

"How did you know where I was?"

Yoshi started up the car. It stalled. Yoshi's hands were shaking. "We were worried, Leah. You didn't call like you were supposed to. Jay Landis hadn't checked in under either of your names."

"How'd you find me then?"

"When you hadn't called by midnight, I called Joey. It took him until this morning, but he found out what room you were in. He told me to call you there and to call him back right away. That's what I did." Jesus, I thought, Joey again. Joey knew about all this.

I walked into Russell Street thirty minutes later. Paul and Carol were waiting for me at the dining room table, like stern and worried parent figures. "At least you're alive," Paul said gruffly. He hugged me, but the grim look didn't leave his face.

"The jerk put MDA in my drink. I drank it without realizing it. I'm fine now."

"So what was this?" Yoshi asked. "Some kind of thrill for you? An acid trip with a rich white guy?" I stared at him in surprise.

"For God's sake, Yosh," I said. "We went over all this before. It wasn't acid; it was MDA. The point was to get him talking. I don't even like the guy."

"So did you need a whole night to get the guy to reveal a few secrets?" He did not sound like the Yoshi I knew. He turned to Paul and Carol. "Leah had a gun with her. She was ready to use it on this guy."

"You have a gun?" Paul said. "Leah, have you lost your mind? How come you never told us about this?"

I thought again about all the things I had never told them.

"It's dangerous," Yoshi said. "It's crazy."

"And it's so cop-like," Paul said. "Are you getting your directions from Joey these days?"

I sat down, fighting sleep. Images crowded into my head. The perfection of Jay's makeup, as impeccable in its own way as Grace's. The stale smell in the hotel room this morning. And there was something else . . . something about Jay's father . . . and about Grace . . . I don't know how I ended up in bed. I didn't awake until five that afternoon when there was a knock on the door. Carol came in.

"Up yet?" she asked. There was an edge to her voice. "I have to talk to you about all this," she said, "You're affecting me, and everyone in the house. It's too much, Leah."

"This doesn't concern you."

"It concerns all of us," Carol said. "We were all waiting for your call last night. Turns out you didn't call because you were taking drugs with some nut case. You want us to worry about you? You don't even worry about yourself."

"It's not your thing, Carol," I said. "I really don't want to talk about it."

"I saw one of those Panthers on television last night. Smiling with his mouth, making circles in the air with his fists. His mouth was saying one thing, his hands were saying something else."

"You don't know anything about the Panthers." I thought of James, of Edna, of Al Brooks found dead in his car on 66th Avenue.

"You're in too deep," Carol said. "You don't know what danger you may be in. Or from whom." I hated it when she spoke with that air of authority.

"You don't have to be part of this," I said. "Yoshi and Paul understand."

"Yoshi and Paul are scared shitless," Carol said. "Paul's star-struck about this article he thinks you two may publish. Yoshi just follows along because he's in love with you."

189

"In love with me? Don't be silly!"

"You're just so naïve. Here's something that's right in front of you. Seems to me you could be more considerate of his feelings, if nothing else."

"You're wrong, Carol," I said, shaking my head.

XXII

The next day was Sunday. I drove up to Clear Lake to sort things out. I needed time alone. I couldn't seem to remember what Jay had said that had seemed so important. I wanted to read Grace's second notebook—the one Maura had given me—without being disturbed. Somewhere things had gone awry. I'd felt unfamiliar to myself since Friday night at the St. Francis. My eyes burned dark in my white face. My hair was growing out—I had my own frizzy halo. I looked too intense. I had nightmares of Jay Landis's sweat-drenched face, his mad jester's smile, his pale eyes looking into mine. Yoshi wasn't helpful with his constant references to my "night with the rich white guy." I no longer had anyone to talk to.

Edna was cooler to me now, angry about Karella and about what had happened to her with Ollie. I had stopped in at the Hot Spoon Saturday, to say hello, but she was reserved. I had told her a little about my night at the St. Francis, but I tried to make it sound amusing. "Do I seem different to you? Cheap, or something?" I asked her. "Men are acting funny."

"Girl," she answered, "you put on a little lipstick, like the rest of the human race, and you think you're tarted up!"

"I was getting on the bus last week," I said, "just handing the driver my money for change. He grabbed my hand and held it and asked me to lunch."

"He just dug you, Leah, "she said. "That ain't nothing. Where've you been living?"

"Things like that never used to happen to me, "I said. "Now here's another thing that happened. I was walking across campus this morning and a guy walked up to me and hit me on the shoulder. He wanted me to smoke a joint with him. I'd never seen him before in my life."

Edna laughed again. This time it almost sounded like her old laugh, deep and full. "Sometimes I wonder did you grow up in a convent. You've gotten sexier is all. About time, I'd say. You were on your way to becoming an old maid, nothing but those books for company. I'm glad you're stepping out."

I had left her feeling better, but there was still so much I could not tell her. Not the whole story, the way I would have in the past. I parked the VW near the lake and walked to the beach. Two men were fishing off the pier. I settled myself at a picnic table and thought about Grace, myself, my scattered life. Jay and his father. That was it. Jay had said Grace had slept, not only with him, but with his father. When I asked him about it in the morning, he had come at me with a razor.

Would Jay have killed Grace because she had slept with his father? Or would Hugh Landis kill her—or have her killed—because of his son? Jay had mentioned an agreement among his father, Grace, and Bucky Timmons. "I think my father helped her out financially," he had said. Oh, yes, and he said that Grace won ten thousand dollars. No mention of that in the police report. Where had that money gone after she died?

Perhaps the notebook Maura had given me would provide some answers. The last journal had been a teenager's diary, filled with experiments in sex and clothing. Grace had written in a large hand, ending her sentences with little round circles. It ended with Grace's graduation from high school. I opened the notebook Maura had given me. Grace had dated only a few of the entries. Skimming through, I found lists, scraps of poetry and conversations, then more personal reflections. The handwriting became smaller and difficult to decipher, and then, abruptly, larger. Words were jammed together, or crossed out; sentences meandered across the page haphazardly. Later pages had grease stains or coffee spills. The notebook began with lists:

> Things I Should Do to Find Work: Go to JV Liquors, talk to
> Bonnie re art class modeling, cocktail waitressing at Charlie
> Brown's. The manager made you bend over to show him your legs.

She had added—no problem there. Grocery lists, shopping lists (find patchouli). Cosmetic lists. What I Need in My Next Boyfriend. Things I Want to Do in Berkeley. The Mediterranean on Telegraph was her favorite place in Berkeley.

> Summer of 1969 Berkeley—Newsweek called 1967 the Summer
> of Love. This is my summer of love. Little girls in San Francisco
> with spray-painted faces, flowers and peace signs and hearts on
> their foreheads, and Indian beads. "It's in the air—like a proph-
> ecy," a guy said to me in Golden Gate Park. We were listening to
> Jefferson Airplane. I sure love Grace Slick. But the Haight has a
> harder edge now. More drugs in the Haight. Guys are shooting
> meth. Speed freaks. And more than speed. But it's as if I don't
> see it.

"More bookstores on Telegraph than in the entire town of Boise," a guy said to me, as I walked into Moe's on Monday. He offered to turn me on. Rock bands in Sproul Plaza. People talking about the war, and free speech, and free universities. I'm on fire. I'm where I want to be. Think about Ronnie in Vietnam. Goodbye Ronnie. Goodbye Millie goodbye stupid shouting about my boy-crazy ways. Yeah, I want to have a lot of lovers. So what!

Apparently she had a lot of lovers that summer of 1969.

Billie is from Oklahoma, just a skinny kid, really, studying Psych. Wants me to try mescaline. Met Jeremy on the bus. I gave him the wrong number on purpose but he found my address and caught a cab up the hill to see me.

High on weed, dancing like mad in the Steppenwolf. My hair down, everything a blur, people clapping. A girl shouting, "Who are we now? Will we ever be the people we once were?" Head all shaky, things fuzzy next day. Feel unsure. I don't want to be the person I used to be. Then who????

Reagan sent in the National Guard. Tanks driving up University Avenue, while I stood on the corner and watched. Days later I read how one man was killed, one blinded, at People's Park. Those same National Guards who had smiled at me days before.

A page later Grace wrote that a friend told her to apply for a job at Golden Gate Fields. "All those players—you'll love it, babes." Grace must have gotten the job; lists of horses and jockeys followed. Next to the names of Bucky Timmons and Hugh Landis, Grace had scribbled, "Big bucks!" Then came a passage in June of 1969, three years ago, when Grace first met James Ferguson.

I said to Fran: "Where'd June find HIM?" June talking to J. A big, black man, white teeth. Overwhelmingly MALE. SLOW Texas drawl. 'Glaaad to meet you, Gra-ace.' (I had never heard anyone say my name as if it were two syllables!) Despite his looks, all man, and his eyes, so serious, there's a shyness about him. Instant heat and shock of recognition. This man! This is it!

6/30/1969: Unlike me, to feel shy too. Usually I don't give a damn, feel confident cause I don't care. With him, want to be someone special. Tuesday at the track, he was with his friends, out here from Oklahoma, all he wanted to talk about was the Civil Rights movement. How it developed into the Black Panther Party when people got tired of being beaten up. Doesn't sound like me, but all I wanted to do was listen.

6/21/1969: He comes out once or twice a week. We can't stop talking. Talks to me at the betting window and the customers line up and get mad at the wait. Amy told me, "Look out for Beatrice! You'll be in trouble if the customers complain." I said, "Let the old stick just try and stop me!"

6/30/1969:   He's young but his eyes are old,
             shy but his mouth is bold

but he hasn't come out in a week. What if he went back to Alabama or Georgia or where ever it was he came from? What if he thinks I'm prejudiced and won't date him cause he's black? Mom would have a fit but I don't care anymore. Momma says I'm lowering myself to date a black man. She says, "You always like those foreign types, Grace- someday you'll realize that ANY man is foreign enough—no need to go out and look for problems."

2/2/69: He walked in today. My shift was almost over. He was laughing and smiling like he had never been away. I ran over to him and said it right out, "Where have you been? I've been so worried." He asked, "Worried about what? I'm here now, aren't I?" Our hands reached out and grabbed each other—it was crazy, right in the middle of Mainline, people all around me asking about horses and when to place their bets. I couldn't answer them, we were just smiling into each other's eyes. Black James, white Grace—it didn't matter. I held onto his hand and we walked right out of Mainline (people staring and customers calling "Grace!" and they all seemed so far away I could hardly hear them.) His friend drove us to my place and we made love for hours.

After this, Grace's writing exploded. Pages were filled with songs. poetry, drawings, cartoons. Newspaper articles, torn and tucked inside: one described the Haight Ashbury; another the creation of the Black Panther Party.

I stood up, stretched, walked to the pier and took off my shoes. I finished reading her notebook with my legs dangling above the blue water.

7/7/1969: Aretha sings it all in Natural Woman. I feel—so GOOD INSIDE! He makes me feel—SO ALIVE! My God, what that man has done to me!

194

Making love all afternoon. Skins and bodies intertwined: his skin, so burnished black; mine, so much lighter and paler. I said, "We're so beautiful." "Are we so beautiful?' he asked. "You know you are," I answered. I know I am, I thought to myself. I said, "We're each other's forbidden fruit." But then he replied, "There's quite a few people wouldn't think we're so beautiful together." "Like who?" I asked. "Lots of people—both sides of the fence."

8/15/1969: Scars near his temple. Scars down his back. His skin is blue-black. These marks are different, colored different, like stretch marks. I didn't want to know how he got them. He told me how the cops caught him. Left him for dead on a side street. The next month he joined the Panthers. He said, I been told all the time that I ain't worth shit. After a while, you know, you start to believe it.

Grace's summer of love came to an end. In early September 1969 a splash of coffee on the entry almost obliterated her words. She had written:

9/7/1969: Reading poetry by ee cummings to make myself feel better. I will close my life to you if that's what you wish—his poem makes it seem so easy to do. Makes it seem possible.

James said. "It's been good, hasn't it?" "It's been wonderful, "I said. "It can't be this way much longer." "Why?" "I'm going to be very busy. Things may get dangerous."

I felt panicked—fear of being torn away. How often have I been torn away from people? Even Helene—back when Millie took me over. Fear of being thrown back to the others—to Ronnie, to anyone. I said, "I want to go on seeing you." "You won't be able to. I'll have more responsibilities." "So?" "I'll be moving around a lot. I won't have much time for you, or for anyone." He seemed shaken up, but he had to leave. After he left, I wrote a bluesy poem for us:

> I just want to see you, now and again.
> Whatever else happens, just now and again.
> Have a drink, walk the pier, take a look at the bay.
> Whatever else happens, just have things my way.
> Now and again.

It could be a song. Someone could put it to music.

195

I was startled. That was the poem Ronnie had recited to me at Charlie Brown's—saying it was his. I thought about the Grace who emerged from this diary. Eager to try everything Berkeley offered—sexual liberation, drugs, adventures. Yet at the same time lost—promiscuous, wild, and lonely. A girl who was brought up by a bar-fly of a mother, Helene, then by aunt Millie, with her self-righteous evangelicism—had her share of confusions about men and sex.

I was struck by the discrepancy between Grace's polished exterior and this written record of chaotic and distressed emotions. It was as if Grace pulled herself together by an act of will, creating an image of herself based on women she admired in magazines or television, and then managed to sell this image to the many men she attracted. Yet this wasn't the real Grace. It was clear she had been in love with James. She was devastated when he told her they would have to break up. But why would she then get involved with Jay Landis, or Hugh Landis, or Bucky Timmons? Had she wanted the money these men could supply? Or had she been trying to forget James, or get back at him?

I had a list now of additional suspects—Grace's former lovers. In addition to James, there was Jay Landis. Hugh Landis. Bucky Timmons. I should also add Freddie Corster to the list. How often had I heard him say he would know what Grace looked like in the dark? And David Sayid? He had shot Maura a look of warning when she mentioned Grace's name. Maura's story reminded me there may have been women, too, who hated Grace, women furious with jealousy or betrayal.

Maura had described Grace as an actress. "A woman that determined to please others rarely fails," she had said. She had also said of Grace, "Something essential was missing." What was it that was missing? Loyalty? Honesty? I thought about Grace's descriptions of her love affair with James. She had implied they had a love so strong that it had transcended sex, jealousy, and prison. James had described their relationship differently—with deep feeling, but with a touch of cynicism. "Once you know what to expect of people, you aren't surprised," he had said. "Grace wasn't a woman meant to be lonely."

I was cold and put on my sweatshirt and then stood up. I skipped a stone across the water, watched it jump twice. I had known other women who romanticized a love affair or fantasized one with an indifferent man. I had done it myself, thinking about my high school boyfriend long after we had separated.

196

It had taken a murder and an investigation to make me forget him. What about Grace and Ronnie? What continued to haunt him? Was it the memory of the baby she had aborted? My mind lingered on Ronnie for a second. Ronnie's twangy voice, his green eyes full of mischief—Grace had said the night she stayed with me—"With Ronnie I could see trouble coming." The kind of man that some women take back time and time again. Had Grace?

Just three weeks ago Yoshi and I had driven up here to the Linger Longer Motel. Today I had not told anyone where I was going. No one appeared to have followed me. Was someone I knew talking to the cops? I didn't trust Joey, Yoshi, Paul or Carol completely anymore. It was hard to live like this. I would have to find someone I could talk to. Someone to confide in to help me figure this damn thing out. Or else I'd just have to solve this case. Whichever it was, it had to happen fast.

On the way back from Clear Lake, I switched on the radio. Simon and Garfunkel were singing Old Friends. They harmonized in their sweet tenor voices. I had loved to sing along with them, but now my stomach was constricted. A time of innocence. A time of confidences. I shook my head. The times no longer seemed so innocent. And confidences? Just who did I have to confide in?

On impulse, I decided to pay another call on Helene Neville. I drove over back roads, then took a left, traveled over more back roads, and arrived at Lollipop Motor Home Resort around three. Bud's truck was gone.

Helene answered the door, a cigarette in one hand and a can of Coors in the other. Her blue cotton dress emphasized the faded beauty of her blue eyes. In the background I could hear the television. Did she spend most of her afternoons like this?—empty hours until her Bud came home to keep her company?

"Leah," she said. She seemed a bit wary, but not surprised, as if she had almost expected me to turn up on her doorstep on a Sunday afternoon.

"I need to talk to you, Helene," I said.

I was surprised by my forcefulness. Helene let me in.

"Helene, I'm trying to find out who killed Grace," I said. "Every place I go, someone knows I'm coming. Why is that?"

"I wouldn't know, Leah," she said, carefully. "Want a seat?"

I took a chair. Helene took a seat on the couch with a view of the black -and-white TV screen. She didn't turn it off, and I could see her eyes darting to it from time to time with longing.

"One night I had a drink with Ronnie," I said. "The next day, the cops knew all about it. Why was that?" Joey had already told me Bud Kemp had called to complain about my visit. I wondered what Helene knew.

"Thought you said you were working with the cops," Helene said. She was sharper than she looked. "Why wouldn't they know what you were up to?"

"I don't tell them everything," I said. "I didn't tell them I came up here to talk to you. Yet they knew all about that too."

"After that time you came up, some men showed up here. Asked a lot of questions about you. What you knew—what you wanted to know."

"What about Grace? Did they ask you about Grace?"

"Didn't ask much about Grace," Helene said. "They were real interested in you, though. Were you a Panther sympathizer. How long you'd known Grace. Stuff like that." Her eyes drifted back to the television.

"Helene, do me a favor, please turn off the television. We're talking about trying to find out who killed your daughter, for God's sake." Helene squashed out her cigarette in a speckled plastic ashtray, already overflowing with butts, stood up slowly and switched it off.

"Who were these men?" I took out my wallet, and took out a snapshot of Joey. "Was he one of them?"

She glanced at the photo and shook her head. "No. That's Lieutenant DeMartino—he was with the detectives who came here the first time. These other men called themselves Federal investigators. They showed me their badges. They wore suits and ties."

"FBI?"

"They said they did domestic surveillance. Didn't say FBI. They did remind me of those FBI men who came to see me a couple years back, though."

"What was that all about?"

"They asked me a whole bunch of questions about Grace. Showed me photos of that Negro she was going with. They said he was dangerous. Said I could save Grace from jail or worse if I gave them information."

"Did you give them information?"

"Some." She looked down into her lap. "That was a hard time for me. I was getting a little old for my regular gigs. Sometimes a person wants to be able to go out, eat a decent meal, in a decent place."

"They offered you money?"

She looked up as if daring me to judge her. "I was having a hard time."

"You took money from them to give them information about Grace?"

"They told me they could help her," she said.

"And you believed them?" I was stunned. "And these men who just showed up recently—you think they're helping Grace, too?" I couldn't disguise the anger and bitterness in my voice.

"It's too late to help Grace now," she said, wearily. "Maybe it was too late all along."

"What did you tell these men about me?" I asked.

"We hardly know you, Leah," she answered, plaintively. "What could we tell them? They told us some stuff about you, though. Said you had lost your mother when you were little. Your Dad wants nothing to do with you. Says you're unbalanced." I was surprised at how hard that hit me. I felt tears start to my eyes.

"Actually," she said, looking straight at me, "Bud believed all that, but I didn't. Maybe it's losing Grace, I've started to see things differently. All this time sitting here thinking about my daughter. It makes me sorry for you and what you've been through." She reached over and patted my hand. "And then from you, they moved on. To Becky Boyle, of all people—a girl Grace hadn't seen since high school. She's Becky Puckett, now. She pretended to be Grace's friend, but she was always after Ronnie. He wouldn't give her the time of day. They wanted to know all about her, and her husband, too. As if I knew anything about that girl."

"So why did you give *me* that diary of Grace's?"

"Grace never got over Ronnie. She was crazy about him. They would break up just to make up, like the song said. They could never make a break-up stick. I thought you'd realize that from reading her diary."

"Did you read it?" I asked.

"I didn't sit down and read it page for page. Grace was a liar—I didn't need to see all the blasphemy she wrote. Drew me looking like a tart and

199

herself like a fashion model—Grace was always vain. I figured if you had the diary, you would understand about Ronnie and Grace. They never let go of each other. Not really. Ronnie used to call here every now and then. Trying to find her. They stayed in touch. Everyone thinks my daughter was going with that Negro—but it was Ronnie Xavier Jones was her true love, believe you me."

"Those Federal investigators had a lot of questions about Ronnie?"

"No," she answered, slowly. "It seemed like they had no interest in him whatsoever." As if coming out of a reverie, she stood up and looked at the clock on the wall. It showed a quarter to four. "Bud will be back soon, "she said. "It would be best if he didn't know you stopped by. He's crazy about Ronnie," Helene added. "He blames Grace for how Ronnie turned out. I don't see how that's fair, myself. Ronnie was always wild. Didn't take my girl to tip him over. But you better get going. It's best he don't find you here."

The next day, after my shift at the track, I drove out to Concord. Becky Puckett lived on Heavenly Drive, only a few blocks from aunt Millie's where Grace had grown up. The door was answered by a ten-year-old boy with a buzz cut. He stared at me with hostile eyes. "Is your mother home?" I asked.

"Mom!" he called out. "Mom!" he shouted again. "She's in the back," he said to me. He turned away, leaving the door ajar. When he disappeared down the hall, I pushed open the door and stepped inside. Becky came down the hall toward me, drying her hands on a towel. She was wearing green pedal pushers and pink slides which revealed her thick white calves and meaty toes. Her toenails were covered with dark red polish.

"What are you doing in here?" She brushed her sandy hair away from her face with an irritated gesture. She looked tired.

"The kid let me in," I lied. "But it's important. We need to talk."

She walked past me to the front door, closed it firmly, and gestured me toward a chair. She sank onto the sofa wearily. "Okay, what is this all about?" she asked.

"It's about Ronnie Jones," I said. "He was seeing Grace, wasn't he?"

200

"I wouldn't know anything about that," she said.

"You and Ronnie kept in touch," I said. "He would have told you." I was going on hunches. I had noticed the way Becky had looked at him at Grace's wake, the shorthand in which they had spoken, a language of people who are intimate. My conversation with Maura Sayid had made me aware there may have been women who hated Grace. She sat up on the couch a little straighter. Her eyes looked defiant.

"They weren't seeing each other. Do you have proof?"

"Call Lieutenant DeMartino," I said. "I'm working for him. I shouldn't be telling you this, but I want you to understand this is serious."

"Ronnie didn't tell me you were working for Lieutenant DeMartino."

So they *were* in touch. I tried not to show surprise at her admission. "He doesn't know," I said. "So did he tell you he was seeing Grace?"

"He never mentioned Grace."

"Helene told me Ronnie kept trying to reach her. Quite recently."

"So what if he did? The two of them were always hung up on each other. In a sick kind of way. He knocked her up, she killed his baby. After that there wasn't anything on two legs that Grace wouldn't screw." She tightened her face in a gesture of disgust. "Ronnie couldn't handle it. All that bad boy stuff? It was just an act. He was weak underneath. He enlisted and got sent to Nam."

"You've always had a crush on Ronnie, haven't you?"

She reached into her pocket and drew out a pack of cigarettes, lit one. Her hand trembled. "Hell," she said, inhaling, "who didn't? Me and half the senior class. I wrote him a couple times. He wrote me back. Maybe something coulda come of it—if Grace hadn't written him, too. Maybe she was having a downer on one of her acid trips, or one of her bearded protester boyfriends rejected her. Then she remembered ole Ronnie. That was all it took."

"For him to go back to her?"

"He'd go back to her. But by the time he got back from Nam, she was fucking a nigger. That's what he got for all his trouble."

"What about you and Ronnie?"

"He was interested, once he saw what Grace was. But by then I'd met Carl." She tried to say this indifferently, but I heard a lifetime of regret in her words.

"Ronnie must hate Grace for jerking him around like that."

201

"Oh yeah," she answered, "except he's weak. He's too weak for hate. He's just drifted around. Never known who he was."

"Carl is different?"

"Very different," she said. "Carl has an opinion, he sticks with it." She took another drag on the cigarette, reflecting back. "Ronnie went off to war, proud as you please. From what I hear, he had to do some tough things over there. Falcon program—something like that. Some sort of bird thing. Came back, joined Vietnam Vets Against the War. Total about-face. Seemed like he got guilty, all of a sudden. For what? Commie gooks were everywhere— kids—teenagers—still gooks. Didn't matter. Had to be killed. Those Vets Against the War are a bunch of losers. All they do is complain. I always wondered if Grace had something to do with that." She let out a stream of smoke. "But let anyone say anything against the vets, Ronnie still goes off. You never know where he stands."

"I guess you never knew where you stood with him either."

"What kind of guy lets a girl treat him the way Grace treated Ronnie. I like a man with guts." She squashed the cigarette in an ashtray overflowing with butts, stood up and opened the door for me to leave. "I don't care who you're working for," she said. "Just don't come around here with any more questions. I don't want to talk anymore about this."

I drove back to Berkeley, thinking about the woman who had been Becky Boyle. Stocky and strong, in her yearbook photo, proud and determined. Now she seemed defeated. And Ronnie—had Ronnie been in love with Grace ever since high school?

Joey had talked to Ronnie, to Helene Neville and Bud Kemp. But Helene had not given Grace's old diary to Joey. She had given it to me. Joey had warned me Ronnie was a loser but he denied that Ronnie was a suspect. There was so much that Joey had not told me. Maybe Joey knew less than I thought. It might be time, I thought, to talk to Joey again.

202

XXIII

I called Joey Tuesday morning and left a message with his secretary.

I also called Ruby Bailey, the Tribune reporter. I had already tried her several times to learn if my article would be published. I always ended up leaving a message. Twice Ruby had called back when I wasn't home. Paul reported, "She says just hold on, Leah. A fact checker is going over it." The second time Paul reported, "She says her editor's waiting for an opportune time to run it. In my experience there are often a lot of delays," he had added.

"Should I let Art Leopold know I talked to this woman? That the Tribune is going to publish my article?"

"What's to tell?" Paul shrugged. "They haven't even printed it yet."

"James was under orders not to talk about the case with anyone outside the Party," I said.

"Call Leopold then if you're worried," Paul answered. "You could look kinda silly if nothing ever makes it into print." The fall quarter started in less than two weeks. I was busy making up time I had missed at the track. I let it go.

I did corner Paul Wednesday afternoon on a different subject. "You know anything about the Phoenix Program?" I asked him.

"Of course," he said. "But why are you asking?"

"Ronnie said he worked for the Phoenix Program. Said he trained South Vietnamese to find Communists."

"That's one way of putting it. They trained South Vietnamese to torture and turn in anyone they had a beef with, is more like it. Ronnie was involved with *that*?"

"Yeah, well, maybe that's what turned him against the war." This was one more disturbing piece of information to be examined at some later time.

On Thursday Paul pointed out an article beneath the fold on the front page of the Oakland Tribune. Portrait of a Witness by Ruby Bailey. "Portrait of a witness?" I asked. "That's not my article." I scanned the sentences quickly.

> Leah DeMartino is a 23 year old UC Berkeley student who works
> part-time at Golden Gate Race track. She was friends with co-
> worker, Grace Neville. DeMartino spent an evening with Grace
> Neville. It turned out to be the last night of Grace's life. This
> event brought DeMartino into close proximity to the investigation
> into the unsolved murder of Grace Neville, and the prime suspect
> in the case, Black Panther James Ferguson.

Why would she write this without asking my permission? The article listed all the specific times I had been in Ferguson's company and described the unusual nature of those events. A brawl in Vinnie's Inn, possibly with me at the center. A shoot-out at the Lighthouse Bar involving some undisclosed triangle of which I may have been a part. Several sightings of Ferguson and me to-gether. Ruby Bailey went on to speculate I could be Ferguson's lover, and thus a dupe to an unscrupulous and violent, although charismatic, man, setting him up with an alibi.

I felt the blood beat up into my face. Ruby Bailey continued:

> Close friends report she has behaved erratically since the murder
> of her friend. DeMartino spent the night of September 15th with
> Jay Landis, a race track aficionado with a police record, at the St.
> Francis Hotel in San Francisco. Reports indicate the evening
> involved heavy drug use and sexual experimentation.

Anyone could read about me now—my journalism professors, other students in the program. I was humiliated. Who had given Ruby this information—someone in the house, someone close to me?

In her final paragraph, Ruby observed that I had a close relationship to Acting Lieutenant Joe DeMartino, the head of the Homicide Section and the lead detective in the murder case. There were some indications that, among my other roles, I was also a paid informant for the OPD. She concluded her piece by asking just who I really was? An unstable UC Berkeley student, caught up in a reckless fantasy of revolution? The girlfriend and dupe of James Ferguson, involved in a manipulative relationship with a dangerous man? Or was Leah DeMartino a shrewd paid informant and friend of the OPD, sent to gather infor-mation from Ferguson, and to sow distrust about him within the Party?

"This isn't what I told her! This isn't what I wrote!" I was trembling with rage and disbelief. I pushed the newspaper across the table at Paul for him to read. Paul scanned the article rapidly, his lips moving as he read half aloud.

"This is lethal," he said. "Call Art Leopold right now."

"And tell him what?"

"Tell him the truth," Paul said. "You are not a paid informant of the OPD!"

But I was. The OPD had paid me for information. I had thought no one but Joey and I knew about our agreement. I had pretended our agreement was innocuous. Yet someone knew, and that person had leaked the information to Ruby Bailey. "Paul, you know my cousin Joey is a detective with the OPD."

"So what?" Paul shouted. "That doesn't make you an informant! Do you understand how dangerous this could be? You have got to get your story to Art Leopold so he can talk to the Panthers! Jesus Christ, Leah—move!"

I walked into the dining room. My life was crashing in pieces around me. I had been wrong, wrong, wrong. I had been stupid and naïve, and now I had been exposed. The last thing in the world I wanted to do was to call Art Leopold and admit what I had done. The telephone sat on a small stand. I dialed his number with unsteady fingers. "Art?" I said, my voice cracking. "This is Leah DeMartino. Have you read this afternoon's Oakland Tribune?"

"Got a call about it," he said. "Haven't had time to pick it up yet."

"There's an article in it about me."

"Leah, I'm very busy—"

"I have to explain what happened."

"Okay," he sighed. "I'll meet you in my office in the next hour."

It was the worst fifteen minutes of my life. I told Art Leopold the whole story. When I described working for Joey, Leopold burst out, "Why didn't you tell me your cousin was in the OPD?"

"I thought you wouldn't trust me." I said. How stupid that sounded.

"Maybe we wouldn't have trusted you. Which would have left us all a lot better off than we are now. Why on earth did you agree to gather information for them?"

"I thought I could find out who really murdered Grace."

"Instead you gave them information they have used to ruin you and frame James," Art said. "For God's sake, I warned you to be careful! Did you think this was a game?"

"I thought I could outwit them," I said, miserably. "Can you talk to James and explain that to him?"

205

His phone rang and he picked it up. "What?" he asked irritably. "Oh yeah, but not now. Call me back." He hung up and leaned forward in his chair. "You've been naive," he said. "But you've also been set up, by the police, by this newspaper woman, by your cousin, by who knows who. Now you're of little use to us, if they charge James. Which it looks like they are gearing up to do. Worse than that, the Panthers may believe you're an informant. There's plenty of reason to think so, even without this article. He's been picked up each time you've met with him."

"Can you explain things to him?"

The phone rang again. He let it ring twice and then again picked it up, quickly. "Yes? Oh, hello. Yes, I heard. I'm talking with her now. What? Yes, I'll call you back." He hung up again, took a deep breath. I knew he was trying to drive something home to me. "Leah," he said. "Your cousin works for the OPD. You took money from him. It doesn't look good, even to me. And I have little influence on the Panthers when it comes to matters like these."

"I believed my article could help James."

"Do you remember the first day we met? I talked to you on the stairwell?" Art asked. I did remember the first time I had talked to Art Leopold, outside of James' hearing. Art had warned me to be cautious. Had he suspected James was capable of harming me?

"You were already in a dangerous situation. This Ruby Bailey has just made it much worse."

"Does the danger come from the Panthers?" I asked. "Or from the police and the FBI?"

"All of the above. It doesn't matter. Some people sell out; some people go crazy. Some Panthers could take you out and think they're being loyal to the cause. Never underestimate the strength of the oppression. They are masters at turning people against one another—unfortunately, it's not that hard to do. You just got sideswiped. You must get out of town."

My heart was pounding, but I talked calmly about my options, as if they were plausible. I could see Art was tired. He needed to get back to his work, and I had just managed to make that work harder. I thanked him for his time and walked out. I felt completely alone.

As I walked along Market Street toward the East Bay Bus Terminal, a Lincoln Town Car slowed down along side me. James Ferguson was in the driver's seat. He looked haggard, as if he hadn't slept in days. "Get inside," he ordered me, reaching to open the passenger door.

I felt a flash of fear, but my mind couldn't function. I got in. "How did you find me?" I asked.

"I called Art," he said. "He said you were in his office. I waited until you came out, then I followed you." Why hadn't he let Art know he was waiting for me? Why had Art given me his warning out of James' earshot that first day? Did the two of them trust each other? He was headed down First Street toward the on ramp to the Bay Bridge.

"Did you read the article?" I asked.

"Hell, yes, I read it," James Ferguson said.

"That woman tricked me. I have the real article right here." I pulled my draft out of my shoulder bag.

"You promised me you would show me what you wrote before it got published. That was our deal. Remember?" We were on the lower deck of the Bay Bridge now, driving toward Oakland.

"I was planning to show it to you. I never could get her to tell me when it was going to come out. This Ruby Bailey's story has nothing to do with mine. Where are we going?" My words came out disjointed, anxious.

"Give me a place. A friend's apartment—some place you don't usually go."

"Yoshi's friend, Kanji," I answered. "He's let me stay in his place before. I'd have to call him. But why are you doing this?" Kanji's apartment had been my refuge the night of the incident at Vinnie's Inn.

"You can call him from Emeryville," James answered. "You knew I was under orders not to talk about the case. Didn't you realize I could be expelled or worse if the Party believed I gave you information?"

"I thought the article would exonerate you."

"It didn't. It blew up in your face and mine. That's happened to us more times than we can count. It's another reason we don't talk to newspapers."

James took the Emeryville exit. I called Kanji. He would stay at his girlfriend's and leave the apartment key under the doormat. I asked Kanji to drive by Russell Street to let Yoshi know where I was. We walked up the shallow concrete steps to the second floor of the Sir Francis Drake Arms and found the key under the mat. The living room was littered with books on economics and business management. James threw himself down on the brown plaid sofa. I sat across from him on an easy chair.

"Did the cops pay you?"

"I was trying to get information out at the track."

"Information at the track?" James said. "Why in hell did you care about that?"

"I thought if I found out about Grace's other boyfriends, I would get information which would clear you."

James gave a bitter laugh. "I almost believe you," he said. "No one would make up a story as stupid as that."

"I know a guy out there named Freddie," I said. I heard my words rushing along; I was not sure what I was saying or why. "He said the cops took him in for questioning. Pushed him to state you had picked Grace up the morning she was murdered. He saw a black man waiting, in a Buick hard-top, but he never saw the man's face. He wasn't even sure Grace got in the car. But I knew from this story how hard the OPD was trying to set you up."

"You tell the pigs anything about me?"

"No. What could I tell them? Sometimes I felt someone was telling them about *me* and where *I* was." Words rushed to my lips. I had to keep talking, although I had no idea of what to say. I was holding the draft of my article in my damp hands. I thrust it over at him. "Read this. This is what I expected to have published."

James read it rapidly. Then he leaned back against the sofa. "You're right. They're using you to get to me, just like they did with Grace."

I had possibly won a reprieve. "I never thought they would use a white girl to get information on the Black Panthers," I said. "Why would a black woman like Ruby Bailey do what she did? It's like she's selling out her own people."

"Selling out ain't about color," James replied. "They'll use anyone they can. I've been set up so many times I can smell it coming. I was sleeping with a sister in New York—turned out she was an agent. She almost got me busted for that cop death. That newspaper article today was a giveaway—they're getting ready to indict me for Grace's murder."

"Because of the way the article portrayed you?"

208

"Because of the way it portrayed *you*. You're the one person who's come forward in my defense. Every time I get busted, you're out there, denying their stories. Then this article comes out, making you sound unbalanced, doing drugs, fooling around with Grace's lovers."

"So I'm no longer credible as a witness—Art said that, this afternoon."

"It's worse than that. The way that story ran, if anything happens to you, people will say you brought it on yourself. That's one reason I didn't believe all that shit they wrote about you."

"If anything happens to me?" I didn't like the way that sounded.

"Yeah, if you end up like Grace," James said, "they'll blame it on the Party. Blame it on me if they can. They'll say the Party thought you were an informant. And the Party does think that—thanks to this article. That's why I wanted to take you somewhere no one knows where you are."

"Why are you looking out for me?"

"You went down to that police station and told the pigs Grace was alive Sunday morning, when members of my own Party wouldn't step forward to say I was at a meeting. Maybe someone's using you. Maybe there's a leak you're not aware of. But I think you're for real. That Sunday morning Grace was killed, I sat in a meeting with four other Panthers. I think that's why the cops wanted so bad to make it seem like she had been murdered the night before. You ruined that, and I had an airtight alibi for Sunday morning—I thought. The meeting lasted from ten until two. Of those four people who sat with me in that meeting, one disappeared. One left the country. And the other two refuse to come forward."

"Why?"

"You've heard about the East Coast/West Coast split? The East Coast sided with Eldridge Cleaver, the West with Huey Newton. People on one side are out to gun the other side down. Cause I was in New York City, some comrades believe I'm part of the Cleaver faction. They've been ordered not to defend me. This shit has gotten so crazy, I've been demoted. I'm not in charge of Security anymore. I've been kicked off the Central Committee. They're either setting me up or they're pulling away so that if I go down, I won't take everyone with me."

James Ferguson had no one behind him now.

"Clyde knew you were in the clinic that day."

"Clyde Turner's gone. Don't nobody know where he went. It happens all the time—comrades split. It gets too crazy, or someone threatens them."

"Shouldn't you do the same thing? Go back home, to Texas?"

"I told you how those cops beat me up when I was sixteen. I was unconscious for hours. I might have died except my family kept calling. I joined the Party the moment I could walk again. I promised myself that day that I would never run away from a cop." James took a long breath. "The Panthers taught me everything I know. They gave me an education. They sent me to New York, other cities. There's nothing I wouldn't do for them. Nothing. I can't see myself running away, Leah. I don't think I ever could get far enough away from a murder rap. At least out here people know me. I've got Art behind me. For you, though, it's different. You have a chance to go somewhere where it's safe."

"Am I in danger from the Party?"

"You're in danger. I don't know where it's coming from. The Party has this policy toward informants. They call it instilling the greater fear. I wouldn't want you to come up against them. There may be other things threatening you. The point is, you're in danger, and you need to take steps to protect yourself. You can't trust anybody."

My mind jumped from one thought to another. "Who's after you, James?" I asked, "the same people who are after me?"

"It's the pigs who'll get me," James said. "At least I've made it harder for them. Who's cooperating with them, that's anyone's guess." He lifted his head, with a complete shift of mood. "I'm hungry. You think this Chinese guy has anything to eat? I haven't had a bite to eat today."

"He's Japanese," I said. "But I'll see if there's anything in his kitchen." James sank back on the couch and fell instantly asleep. He had told me he could survive on less than four hours sleep a night. That was what was expected of a soldier in the people's army I wondered how so little sleep might influence the soldier's judgment. How much of what James told me was sleep-deprived paranoia?

I walked into the kitchenette. Someone could be watching me right now. I pulled the kitchen window curtains closed, then tiptoed back into the living room to drop the Venetian blinds.

I struggled to put the pieces together. Members of James' own party were refusing to come forward for him. The police took their refusal to mean James hadn't been at the meeting and did not have an alibi. Ollie had told Edna the police had tailed James to headquarters the night of Grace's murder. If I believed James, then I had to believe the Party was willing to turn him over to the same kind of men they were fighting against.

Then there was Karella Cousins. Had there been any proof to connect James to her murder, the police would surely have produced it. Karella's death had gone unnoticed. I had thought James Ferguson had been Karella's lover. Why hadn't Ruby Bailey publicized *that* relationship? Instead the Tribune speculated on my possible romantic involvement with James. Joey had not shown much interest in Karella's death. Nor in the information I had uncovered about Jay Landis, nor about Jay's father, Hugh Landis, another lover of Grace's. Nor about Bucky Timmons, although the jockey seemed to be involved in illegal race fixing with Hugh Landis.

I opened the refrigerator door and stared at a six-pack of beer, two quarts of Coke, a few slices of prepackaged cheese. What could I prepare for James to eat from these offerings? I tried the kitchen cupboard. Three packages of Top Ramen noodles. Two cans of tuna. Okay, I thought—tuna sandwiches—if there's any bread. I spotted the bread, sitting on top of the refrigerator and took it down.

My mind traveled back to Ruby Bailey's article, with all those details from my past. I flashed on stories I had read the previous year—how George Jackson had been killed. People said he had been set up. I thought of Art Leopold's weary eyes this morning, advising me to leave town. I had nowhere to go. Who was I running from? Joey? The police? The Panthers? Yoshi and Paul knew some of my past, but I could not imagine them talking to the police. Jay Landis could have told the cops about our drug trip, although Jay had told me he feared the police. He also knew little else about me. Joey, of course, knew a great deal. He knew about Jay Landis. He had helped Yoshi track me down that night I had met Jay, even though Jay had used a fictitious name to register at the St. Francis. And Joey knew my family history.

I found a can opener and opened the tuna fish. Then I looked back into the refrigerator for mayonnaise. I searched in the cooler for celery and onions, in the cupboard for olives. This was all taking too long. I was slowing down, when I needed to be speeding up. My self-image had been shattered with the publication of the Oakland Tribune article. I was not cool; I was not courageous. James was lying disheveled and asleep on the couch. James was not as cool as I had imagined, either. He was a frightened, hunted, desperate man. My image of him had been glamorous—a tough man, immune to the terrors of the life he led. Perhaps courage was different from what I had imagined—perhaps courage meant being terrified, and muddling along in spite of it.

James still frightened me. He hadn't wanted Art Leopold to know he was waiting outside to pick me up. Had James missed my evasion of his question about my getting money from the cops? I could walk out the door right now while he was sleeping, but if I did, that would prove to him I was a snitch. He had almost no support right now. Yet he was trying to help me decide where to go. And, as crazy as this was, I still wanted to find out everything I could from him. I wanted to publish that article—*my* article, not the fake that Ruby Bailey had produced.

I walked into the living room carrying tuna sandwiches, vanilla cookies, a glass of Coke for me, a beer for James. He jumped awake with a start, his hand reaching automatically inside his black leather jacket. I could see a shoulder holster with a black revolver sticking out of it, much larger than the little snubbie which sat, completely useless to me, in my room on Russell Street.

"James," I said, "it's Leah. We're here at Kanji's place, remember?" I set the plate on the coffee table in front of him.

"What?" he asked. He gave me a disconnected look. "Oh, yeah, yeah. I was dreaming. Food? Great. Great!"

"Turn on the radio," James said, with another of his unpredictable mood shifts. "Let's lighten things up. I can't go anywhere until we've figured out what we're gonna do with you. Some music might help us relax."

I turned Kanji's desk radio to KDIA, a local black music station. I doubted the newly exposed OPD informant, formerly known as a Berkeley co-ed, would lighten up listening to KDIA. But James was used to giving orders. "This revolutionary life isn't what it's cracked up to be," I said, "It's hard on the nerves."

"That's what a lot of the sisters say. No orgasms until after the revolution."

KDIA was playing an Isley Brothers tune, and James sang along with the radio in a high male soprano: "Some people are up to *no good.*" But he sang *no good* in a deep bass, making me laugh.

212

James' mood had improved. He took off his shoes, lay back on the sofa, propping pillows behind his head. I was struck again by the broad strong planes of his dark face. How handsome a man he was. I thought about the good time we had had driving around the Oakland hills and singing to the radio. Just before James had been picked up by the police—again. And the very next day, Joey had taken me to meet Karella Cousins.

I decided to risk asking about another detail which bothered me. "James," I said. "You remember that woman, Karella Cousins?"

"Yeah. That young pretty sister that got killed. What about her?"

I wasn't about to describe my visit to Highland Hospital to see Karella with Joey. I altered the way I had gotten the information. "My friend, Edna, met her that day at the Lighthouse. She was waitressing. Said she was waiting for you."

"What are you talking about?" he asked, immediately sitting up. "Why would she tell Edna that?'

"She implied she was your girlfriend."

"What? That's a goddamned lie—I hardly knew that girl. Why on *earth* would she say she was tight with me?"

"She said she had Grace's wallet. She told Edna she found it in the glove compartment of your car that Sunday afternoon, same day Grace was murdered. Now she's turned up dead. You were in custody when they found her body. Otherwise the OPD would have tried to put that one on you, too."

"Grace's wallet in my car? You think I would have been stupid enough to leave her wallet there?" James looked agitated. Maybe it had been a mistake to bring up Karella's name.

"You were in custody the day she was murdered, but I always wondered why the police didn't tell the newspapers about your relationship."

"That's cause there *was* no relationship," said James, grimly. "That girl joined the Party when she was sixteen. Lot of young people like her—some of them runaways. The Party kept them off the streets. She slept with some of the brothers. I wasn't one of them. I don't like it," James said. "I hate distrusting another brother."

"Did you feel that way about Al Brooks?'

"I told you not to mention that name, Leah. I don't lose sleep over fools like that. But comrades are different. I wonder if you're telling me the truth."

He was silent a moment. I did not know how to read James tonight. I had never known how to read him. His moods veered dramatically, from warmth to suspicion. I had made a mistake, bringing up Karella's name.

James asked, "Why did you tell me about this?"

"It's another piece of the puzzle," I said. "Another reason I came to believe the police are setting you up."

Another song came on the station and James' mood changed again. He started singing along with Lou Rawls, an old Billie Holliday song, Don't Explain.

"That was our song," James Ferguson said, in a softer voice. "That's what Grace would say. How I was her joy, and I was her pain. She would sing that to me. She had a pretty good voice, you know. Her Momma was a night club singer. I guess it was a warning we were giving each other. A warning not to want too much." It was as if he had forgotten we were talking about Karella.

He pushed the pillow back under his head, stretched out. "I'd just come up from Houston, didn't have much responsibility yet. I had time. I'd never gone with a white woman before. A woman like Grace?—she was *fine*. A man's dream of a woman. She called us each other's forbidden fruit." James shook his head. "But I had a reason for coming out here. The Party. After a couple months, when they saw what I could do, I was promoted. I had a purpose for my life. And no woman, no white woman, could interfere with that. I had to stop seeing her."

"You chose the Party over her."

"She didn't have a family, she didn't have a political purpose, she didn't have anything really. When we broke up, she lost it." James was staring at the ceiling, his hands clasped behind his head. "She helped with the school and stuff. Helped with the breakfast program. She could help raise money. But where was this coming from? At first I thought she had a real commitment to the Party. To what we stood for. Then it dawned on me, she was only doing this stuff to get back with me. And that wasn't gonna happen. Not like she thought it would. She didn't like that."

"Do you think the Party had anything to do with her death?"

"I made sure she didn't know much. We're always careful with outsiders. Except for personal stuff—still, I shouldn't have talked to her. Every time the cops picked me up—they knew all about me. They knew how I thought, how I felt, how to get to me." James shook his head from side to side, slowly.

"When I was a kid, my grandfather got bit by a rattler. I can still see him running through the back yard, that thing hanging from his leg. He was shouting for my uncle. They cut the damn thing off of him. He was scared to death, gurgling and struggling for breath. He lived through it. But I've been scared of snakes ever since. When the cops used to pick me up, they would joke, like pigs do, 'You ain't afraid of us, Jimmie, you killed one of us already. Wonder how you'd do if you found a snake in your cell? That couldn't bother you, could it? a big bad cop killer like you?' I acted like it was nothing, but I'd get to wondering. Who would have known that stuff about me?"

"You had a lot of girlfriends," I said.

"I had a few," James replied. "You think I told them much about myself? When I first came out here, I had time to do what people do when their life is normal. Make love, lie awake all night talking. How many women listen like she did? Naw—it was Grace. It was Grace."

"You believe she informed on you?" I asked.

"All I know is, when I got busted, they knew a hell of a lot about me. It had to have come from Grace. After I got out of prison, she tried to make up to me. I still saw her—but I couldn't trust her. If anyone in the Party had known, they might have had her killed. And expelled me, for dealing with her."

I was confused. Helene had given the police information about her own daughter. Could Grace have done the same thing?—for money or revenge? James, moving in a world of constant intrigue and exhaustion, could make mistakes about people. I didn't want to believe Grace had betrayed him.

"Yeah, I told her my childhood memories. Party plans. Things I should never have told her in the first place. I was as mad at myself for telling her as I was at her for spilling it. That's why I hit her that time."

"That time at Eli's?" I saw Grace's swollen face, the mark on her throat.

"That time too," he said. "I still can't believe she would do that to me."

We sat for a while in silence. Outside the light was fading behind the partially closed Venetian blinds. We were aware of sounds, cars on the street, footsteps on the squeaky metal stairs. I was exhausted, yet jacked up with excitement and fear. Grace had died. I was still alive, sitting in this living room while the autumn dusk gathered outside.

When James patted the sofa cushion beside him, I crossed the room to sit on the far end of the couch, facing him. I was aware of his scent, an animal warmth mixed with the sharper tang of fear. Stronger than sexual attraction was the intensity of our predicament. James leaned forward and touched my hair for a moment. Then he relaxed back into the sofa.

James and I had lived through a lot together. His gratitude for my help was stronger than his anger at my stupidities. Even now, when his own life was falling apart, he was concerned for my safety. Now he lay stretched out on the couch. He did not look like anyone I should fear.

I was aware of his body, the smell of his skin, and his strong animal smell. James leaned forward and lifted his hand to touch my hair, lightly.

"Where'd you get this springy hair?" he asked. "And a heart you keep open in a hellish world? You're sure you're white?" James covered my hand with his. Our bodies were so fragile, next to all the death that lay waiting for us, outside, in the gathering night. His gesture was tender. I let his hand rest on top of mine. The moment stretched. I tried to divert its momentum. Into my mind like a warning came the memory of the night with Jay. That closeness had been triggered by a drug. This closeness might be fueled by another high—adrenalin and fear.

"When Edna and I are getting along, she says I'm Italian. Spanish. Anything but white. My father would be furious. Italians *are* white."

James laughed and dropped his hand. The moment had passed.

I realize as I write this all these years later, that the person I now am began that night. *"Nothing human is foreign to me"*—a line I read years later in The Family of Man. Before Grace's death, I had believed that people who killed were totally different from the people I knew. After Grace's death, I came to understand the lines that divide us are very fine. The morning with Jay at the St. Francis Hotel, I came close to losing control. I could have killed him, driven by anger I barely understood. Tonight danger and desperation had moved me into a sphere of intimacy with a volatile man. Consciously and without pleasure, I had resisted. At the time it felt like a negative choice, pulling back from life. Only later did I realize that this decision may have been one reason I survived, when Grace did not. James had fallen asleep again. I made my way to Kanji's bedroom and fell asleep with my clothes on.

The next morning I was awakened by a loud knock on the door. I stumbled to my feet and walked out of the bedroom. James pushed past me, with an abrupt movement. "Look out and see who it is!" he said. He strode into the bedroom and closed the door.

I looked out. It was Yoshi, in sunglasses, shorts, and flip-flops. I felt relieved—Yoshi was an old, familiar part of my life. The day and night I had just spent with James had been a journey to a foreign country, to a part of myself I hadn't known. "James," I said, over my shoulder, "it's okay, it's Yoshi."

I opened the door and Yoshi entered. "Leah, I got your message. Art Leopold called. It's not good for you to be here. We've gotta split."

James sat on the couch, putting on his shoes, then stood up. "Better comb your hair, girl," he said. He passed his hand lightly over my head. "It's gotten pretty wild. If you're not careful, you won't be passing for white."

Yoshi looked at James. "You leaving?"

"Pretty soon. I'll get my things, and lock the door behind me."

Yoshi and I descended the shallow concrete steps to Parker Street. "Did you drive over?" I asked him.

"I drove your Beetle. It's parked over on Ashby. Kanji said you were in danger. I wanted to make sure no one was following. Hey, strange item in the Tribune yesterday. Your friend, Jay Landis—he's turned up dead now. Another body. In the bay."

"Oh, my God!" I felt a cold chill. "Do they know who did it?"

"Do they ever know who did it?" said Yoshi. We were walking along Shattuck, the seven blocks to my VW bug. "They think it was a suicide. I think it's suspicious as hell."

"You drive," I said to Yoshi. "I'm wiped out by all this." Yoshi opened the driver's side door, settled in and opened the passenger door for me.

"When I got to Kanji's just now," he said, "two black guys were ahead of me on the stairs. When they saw me coming up behind them, they turned around and came down. Pushed right past me."

"Any black people live in Kanji's apartment?"

"No. Anyway, I've seen these guys before. At the Lighthouse."

"What would they be doing at Kanji's ?" I asked.

"Looking for you," Yoshi said, starting up the car.

217

"Or looking for James. You should have told James about them."

"Why did they turn around if they were looking for James? And how did they know that James was there? He might have told them where you were."

"James didn't know we were going to Kanji's until I called from Emeryville. He had never been there before. He didn't make any calls from Kanji's place." Yoshi drove up Ashby toward Telegraph Avenue.

"Stop at the Co-op," I said. "I want to call Kanji's place. If James picks up, I'll warn him."

Even as I spoke, I heard the wail of police sirens further down Ashby. I had the sensation that I had been expecting them all along.

"Wait, Yoshi, "I said "Let's go back there."

"Are you stone crazy?" Yoshi said. "Go back there why?"

"We have to go back. If you don't drive me back there, I'll get out and walk." We could hear the police sirens, baying like hounds of disaster. Had I ever once been with James Ferguson and not heard those sirens?

Angrily Yoshi twisted the wheel, turned around. I prayed this had nothing to do with me or James. A heart attack somewhere else, a hold-up in a liquor store down Shattuck, anything, but please, *nothing* to do with James or myself.

Parker Street was cordoned off. We parked near a Jaguar dealership on Shattuck and walked down Parker. Eight police cars were parked at crazy angles around the building. My heart was squeezed into a fist. Would James think I had set him up? If I had stayed, would it have worked out differently?

A man stood on the sidewalk, watching the building. Yoshi asked him what was going on. "I live downstairs. They blocked off one of the apartments on the second floor. Cops were investigating an anonymous telephone call. Woman shot. Maybe murdered. They haven't brought out a body, though."

A woman murdered? In Kanji's apartment? We were registering this information, as three police appeared on the second floor balcony. "False alarm," one announced. "No one in the apartment. You can go back to your apartments."

James must have left before they got there. I let out a deep breath. "Take me to a pay phone, "I said, "Right now, Yoshi." Yoshi drove me to the pay phone in the parking lot of Telegraph and Ashby Co-op.

An anonymous telephone call. A woman shot in the apartment where James and I had taken refuge. Except that she hadn't been shot. There had been no one there. An unsettling feeling came over me, and I couldn't shake it off. I had the feeling I had been meant to be the murdered woman.

XXIV

"Leah, you have to get out of here," Art said. "I'll call you right back." I was calling Art Leopold from the Co-op pay phone. Two minutes later the phone rang. "Look, we know a black cop in the OPD. Name of Mike Fisher. He's been helpful to us in the past," Art said. "He's one of the few black officers on the force. He knows your situation. Go over to Lakeshore Avenue at noon. There's a doughnut shop on the corner of Lakeshore and Trestle Glen. Order yourself a cup of coffee. If Mike sits down next to you, have a casual conversation. Like he's someone you just met. If he doesn't make it, I'll be in touch with you. Whatever happens, don't tell your cousin about this," he added. "Mike is about thirty, light brown skin, moustache. Just under six feet. He says you two have already talked."

I hung up the phone. I remembered the light-skinned cop—Mike?—vaguely. How could he possibly help me?

The sense was still with me, so strongly, that I was the intended murder victim over at Kanji's place. As Art advised, I should get the hell out of town; yet something in me resisted. What was holding me back? Scary things were happening every day, and yet they created in me an addictive need for more. Was it that I was writing an article about a murder investigation which could make my name as a promising young writer? I was keyed up, confused, overwhelmed.

And anyway, where would I go? Outside my very small circle of friends, who was there to take me in?

Yoshi was waiting in the parking lot. "I'm gonna drive. I'll drop you off at Russell Street, Yoshi," I said. "I have something I've got to do."

"Should you be going off alone right now Leah? I don't have a good feeling about what just happened at Kanji's apartment. What was that police stuff all about?"

"I'm worried, too," I replied. "Did they know James was there? How did it happen we were out of there just minutes before the cops came?"

"You don't think I called the cops?" Yoshi burst out.

"No. But who did you talk to about where I was?"

"Carol was there when Kanji came by. Right in front of her, he told me

220

you had asked to spend the night at his place. She could tell something was wrong, so she asked Kanji about it. He didn't tell her anything. Just said you called him, seemed a little upset. But Carol wouldn't call the cops. No way."

"Maybe she mentioned what was going on to someone else."

"But who?" Yoshi asked. "Who would Carol know who would even care? "

I knew my next request was a risk.

"Yoshi. Hang out in Carol's room when she's not there. Check her address book, her notes, letters. See if there's something that will explain this."

"You're asking me to spy on my lover! Leah, that's rotten. You sure you're not hostile toward Carol for having a life?"

"I didn't know you were lovers!" I replied, stung. It's true they had both been hinting at it, but things had moved quickly. "Look, Yoshi, someone knows almost everything I do. How are they finding out? James Ferguson's life is at stake, mine too. Can't you just do it?"

I felt bad. It wasn't right to snoop. Yet where was this advance information about my whereabouts coming from? How did the cops know so much?

"I'll take a look around," Yoshi said. "But that's all I'll do, Leah. God, I wish this investigation would come to an end." I was pulling up in front of Russell Street as he spoke.

"So do I, Yoshi."

I drove to Lakeshore Avenue in Oakland, parked in Lucky's lot, and entered Colonial Donuts through the back. A counter ran the length of the shop with high tables placed at right angles to it. A light-skinned black cop with a little moustache sat on a stool at one of the tables, the same cop who had been telling Joey how he had found Grace's body. The cop who had intervened when his colleagues grilled me after the debacle at Vinnie's Inn. The cop named Mike.

"The proverbial bad penny," Mike Fisher said. His arms were crossed on his chest, making him look judgmental, but there was a twinkle in his eye. "The girl who shows up at all the wrong places. Go get yourself a cup of coffee, then come join me." I bought a cup of black coffee and took a seat on a stool opposite him.

Mike spoke in a low, confidential voice. "If anyone I know comes in here, I'll cut this short. There's some things you and I have to discuss. Did you know they pulled me off that case right after I found your friend's body?"

221

"No. Why?"

"I can only assume I was in the way. Like you are. You have a relationship with Ferguson?"

"Is that all anyone can think about?" I said. I looked him squarely in the eyes. "I do not have, nor have I ever had, a *relationship* with James Ferguson. Despite what the Tribune article said."

"Ruby Bailey gets most of her information from the OPD. They took me off the case, and they're ruining your credibility." Mike looked warily around the room, then turned back to me. "Let me tell you how I got involved in this," he said. "I was driving home that Monday morning. I'd been up most of the night doing overtime on a couple other cases. Early morning I'm headed home with my radio on. I'm driving down Frontage Road, I overhear a call, woman's body found in the bay out near the race track. I'm right there, so I figured I should swing by."

"You were the first one there?"

"Yeah. There's these two kids, running back and forth, jabbering away, Chinese maybe, I don't know. I try to get them to calm down, speak English, tell me what they saw. They take me to the body. She was in the water, like the news reports said. Down by the pier. But she hadn't been washed ashore, that shit the newspapers said later. Her body had been placed there, and not that long ago."

"How had she been killed?"

"There were two bullet holes in her head. Her hair was matted with blood. I didn't want this going over the police scanner. I walked back up the hill to the race track, made the call from one of the outdoor pay phones there."

"Why worry about the scanner? That's how you got your information."

"Yes, but no need to publicize it further. All kinds of people try to listen in to our reports. A murder like that, near a well known place of business, employees arriving in a few hours—it was going to cause trouble. And I had a bad feeling about this murder—right from Jump Street it seemed unusual. So I made the call, then I went back to the body. Checked it for rigor mortis. It was what we call fixed—meaning she had been dead a long time, at least twelve hours. And yet the body hadn't been in the water long at all."

Mike had stared into his coffee cup as he spoke, but now he looked directly at me. He glanced around the room again, then continued speaking. "The body doesn't lie," he said. "It's your best witness in a case like this. There's something else we're taught to check for—it's called lividity, the way the blood pools in the body after the heart stops beating. She had this purple discoloration on her chest and thighs, but she was lying in the water on her back. That was another sign she had been killed first, then moved and placed in that position in the water."

Mike looked around again, then shook his head. "Look, I can't talk about this anymore, not in here," he said. "Meet me out in Alameda, Crown Beach, at the picnic area. Tomorrow at four. I'll see you there." Mike Fisher, like James Ferguson, gave orders easily. He expected to be obeyed. But I wanted to know what he had seen. I could get off work early, hurry down there.

But shouldn't I just leave town? Why would I drive down to Alameda to meet a cop, even if he had been recommended by Art Leopold, when my very life was in danger? My actions made no sense, even to me. It seemed almost as if something else was driving me. The cautious Berkeley student I had been was becoming a reckless, heedless investigator, determined to unravel the mystery of Grace's murder—even if it cost me my life. At the rate I was going, I could end up face down in the San Francisco Bay myself.

"Not a cop!" Carol exclaimed, the next morning. She was doing dishes at the kitchen sink, a white dishtowel tied around her waist like an apron.

"He's just a friend," I said. I had been trying to do the right thing, let my roommates know where I would be, not much more than that.

"I know this is connected with that murder," Carol continued. Paul came padding into the kitchen, wearing big white socks, no shoes, in time to hear her last words.

"I'm going to meet someone who might have some more information on this case. I just wanted you guys to know where I'd be."

"If this cop can help refute that newspaper article, that's one thing," Paul said, "But I'm pretty skeptical. The cops are a bunch of racist pigs. You shouldn't get involved, Leah." They no longer trusted my assessments of people. I didn't trust them either. I suspected one of them somehow had given information to Ruby Bailey for her article, not to mention to the police.

"This cop is black," I said.

"That makes it worse. He has more to prove," said Paul.

"This is no big deal, guys. I just want you to know that I'm going to Crown Beach after work. To meet with an OPD cop, Mike Fisher. If I'm not home by seven, I'll call. See you."

XXV

Crown Beach, on the western edge of Alameda, faced southwest. The sandy dunes with their low twisted cypress stretched for over two miles. The water was warm and shallow. I rolled down my window and caught a whiff of the salt breeze. The bay was an expanse of grey-blue ending in a band of turquoise, then a band of white, rising as mist at the horizon. Close to me was a stand of pampas grass with its froth of creamy white blossoms.

I pulled into the parking lot a few minutes past four. Mike Fisher was sitting in his car. He got out. He was wearing jeans, a windbreaker, dark glasses. "I like this place," he waved toward one of the rough-hewn picnic tables near the one-story bathhouse. A speckled brown-and-white gull flew in and landed on our table, looking as if he wanted to join the conversation. There was a brown dot at the tip of his white bill.

"So how do you know Art Leopold?" I asked, sliding onto a bench.

"Being a cop is how I'm supporting myself through law school. Art Leopold gave a guest lecture on criminal law. We got talking afterwards. He's a good man. Takes a lot of risks for the black community."

"Are you going to practice criminal law?"

"I'm not that altruistic. Art's brilliant, and he's done some great stuff. He also gets it wrong, especially when it comes to the Panthers."

"What part does he get wrong?"

"He thinks the Panthers are the oppressed. I don't think he understands how much the Black Panthers prey on others, just like the cops prey on them." Paul had said some people felt Art Leopold was the dupe of the Black Panthers.

"Art's much too sharp to be anyone's dupe," Mike said, as if picking up my thought. "I think he ignores the realities. His clients may have been set up. That doesn't mean they didn't commit the crime in the first place."

I thought of Joey's words, *There's a lot of other stuff he did that we can't prove. Yet.* To Mike I said, "So what's going on? Does the OPD want to solve this case?"

"I've got a lot of questions about that," Mike answered. "Some of them I think you can answer. That's why I wanted us to talk." Mike hoisted himself up onto the picnic table. I jumped up and sat beside him. Our gull had flown away. For a minute we were silent, looking out at the choppy waters of the bay. "Just how close are you to Joe?" Mike asked. "Are you going to tell him about meeting me?"

"Joey hired me to report back to him what I hear there out at the track. I don't owe him more than that." I added, "He doesn't follow up on anything I tell him, anyway."

"We've got a couple men undercover there already," he said. "And a shitload of snitches. I hear a guy on the racing board has a son who's a snitch. There's always something going on out there. More crooked deals at the race track than sand on that beach. What I'm wondering is what possible use can you be to them out there?"

"The guy on the racing board—what's his name?"

"Hugh Landis. The snitch is his son Jay. Or was. Jay turned up dead two days ago. Body found floating in the bay. A cross-dresser. Cops caught him having sex with another fairy at the track. They took him in for indecent exposure and soliciting sex. Then they learned he was one of the muckety-muck Landises. A family like that don't want stories getting out. So they got the son to snitch from there on out." Mike turned to look at me.

"Yeah, I heard they found him floating in the bay," I said.

Mike Fisher and I stared at the water again, in silence. The brown gull had returned, hopping toward the table. It stopped, gazing at us calmly, as if it had something to tell us. "Do you remember the first time we spoke?" I finally asked him.

"Yes," he answered. "That first night Joe brought you to the station. To tell your story. You've been nothing but trouble for them ever since."

"You had started to say something; then I walked in, and you stopped. I've always wondered what you were about to say."

He seemed guarded. I expected Mike Fisher to tell me he couldn't remember. A conversation from over a month ago, and I might have gotten the details wrong. But to my surprise, he answered.

"When we got her out of the water, I saw she'd been badly beaten. Excessive force—explosive hatred. I've seen that kind of force in some jealousy triangles. And in racial hate crimes."

"Hate crimes? Here in the Bay Area?"

Mike gave a mirthless laugh. "You thought we're exempt? The beautiful Bay Area? Concord, Richmond—we've had our share."

"Aren't racial hate crimes whites killing blacks?"

"Anything with a racial motive qualifies. For example, if a white man killed Grace for sleeping with a black man, that would be a hate crime. You hear of Emmett Till?" Mike continued. "A black kid who supposedly flirted with a white woman back in the south. They whipped that boy with a chain so hard they broke him in half. Hate crimes express a violence unlike any other. I've taken courses to try to understand it, it scares me so bad. Grace's body looked like what I'd read about Emmett Till's."

I sat staring out at the water, huddled in my sweater, hugging myself against the chill. I could hear the short hoarse blasts of a train horn in the distance. The same line that ran past the race track, past the Albany estuary.

"I did what I was trained to do," Mike continued. "I had certain responsibilities—secure the scene, make sure no evidence got lost. When it was all over, I filed my report. Then I waited. I had done research on hate crimes. This looked like one to me. No one ever checked it out. They ignored my report. They got all kinds of details wrong, and they gave the newspapers incorrect information. They even changed the time I found the body."

"When they tried to pin it on James Ferguson, you became suspicious?"

"The word was out Ferguson did it. A lot of times we know who did a crime. I heard we had evidence, maybe even some we got from the Feds. Maybe some of it was inadmissible—wiretaps, informers, stuff we can't use in court. Doesn't mean it's not good stuff. I went to talk to Joey about my take on it. Then I got pulled off the case. Even so I might have believed Ferguson was the guy. But you kept popping up. You showed they had the time of her death wrong. That opened the whole case up again. I started to wonder." Mike zipped up his windbreaker against the cold breeze. "When the case re-opened, I expected Joey to get back to me. Then I got transferred off the case. They implied I was stressed out. *Overworked*, they said. I figured they were giving me some kind of warning."

"It's a pattern, isn't it?" I said. "Joey ignores your report, gets rid of you when you ask too many questions. He gets me looking for information at the track—where he already has plenty of contacts—maybe to keep me too busy to look elsewhere. He ignores my reports, too. He knows the people I've talked to, and what we've talked about. No matter what I'm up to, the cops seem to get there just before me, or right after I leave—but they always seem to get there."

"What people have *you* talked to?'

"Grace's parents. Helene Neville and a guy she lives with by the name of Bud Kemp. They were upset Grace was dating a black man. Ronnie Xavier Jones, Grace's boyfriend from high school. Becky Puckett, Grace's best friend from high school. Bud Kemp called the cops to tell them I'd been up in Clear Lake, talking to them. Then Helene told me some Federal investigators, she called them, came back and talked to them again."

"Did she describe them?"

"Helene said men in suits, some special division of the FBI."

Mike looked at me sharply. "They show her ID?"

"She said they did. Flashed some badges. She drinks a lot, takes tranquilizers. I think she could be gullible. Let herself get conned."

"Jesus Christ," Mike said. He glanced around.

"Leah," he said, looking back at me. "No one should see us together. And don't talk to anyone else about this."

"What do you think is going on?" I asked.

"If the OPD is following you," Mike answered, "that could cost me my job. If the FBI is involved? That could be very bad. For both of us. Write down the names of everyone you've interviewed, everyone you've talked to about this case. I don't care who they are, how unimportant. Write them down." He pushed a small notepad and pen over at me. "If you know their middle names, addresses, dates of birth—anything at all—write that down too." I scribbled down every name I could think of: Becky Boyle Puckett, Ronald Xavier Jones, Bud Kemp, Helene Neville, Jay Landis, Hugh Landis. Paul Cohen. Yoshi Ito. Carol Sweet. Edna Banks. Freddie Corster.

"What are you looking for?" I asked.

"Previous records. Skeletons in the closet. Indications the police have followed up on them. Someone's tailing you. Seems like it must be someone who knows you. Who's giving them that information—where you're going, when, so they can get there first, or right afterwards? You seeing anyone?"

228

"How do you mean?'

"Romantically," Mike answered. "A boyfriend."

"No," I said. "I don't have a boyfriend."

"New boyfriends are the most common sources of information. If you'd started seeing anyone recently, I'd want to know."

I passed the pad back to him. "That's it," I said, "It's all there. Everyone I can think of."

"I'll call you in a few days," he said. "I'm assuming your phone is tapped, so I won't identify myself or leave any messages. If you call me, use a pay phone." Mike tore a deposit slip from his checkbook and handed it to me. "My phone number's on that. Don't mention any of this to Joe. I'm taking a risk." He leaped down from the picnic table. His shoes made squeaking noises on the sand as we walked back to the parking lot. When we got to my car, Mike put his hand on my arm. "Remember, if I call, I won't leave a name. If you call me, be careful. If we run into each other, we don't know one another."

I unlocked the driver's side door and started up the car. Our meeting had been secretive, crazy. A truly promising start.

Saturday night at Russell Street. I made myself a toasted cheese sandwich and took it to my room. Fall quarter would start in a week—would I be ready for it? I was settling in when there was a knock on the door. Paul came in. He had just emerged from the shower, wearing a faded terry bathrobe which barely concealed his muscular physique. Paul looked like a boxer on his day off. His blonde curls lay in angelic ringlets around his big head.

"Leah," he began, closing the door. He pulled up a chair. "We made a decision this afternoon. While you were gone. We feel you have to leave. For your own safety, and, to be honest, for ours." He handed me an envelope. "Here. We've put together some money so you can get out of here." When I didn't take it from him, he set the envelope on the bed. He was frowning. "There was a phone call this afternoon from some guy, asking for you. When I offered to take a message, he hung up. Thirty minutes later two black men drove by our house. Very slowly. Twice. We couldn't get the license plate."

229

"Did you recognize the voice on the phone?"

"You're getting a lot of calls these days. I can't keep up with all the guys calling you."

I let that pass. "Did anyone get a good look at the guys who drove by?"

"I watched the car drive by. It was an old Pontiac. The guys looked tough. It's not good, Leah. After that Tribune article, the Panthers probably think you're an informer. I don't like it. You've got to leave." Paul's face had a tender, strange look on it. "Things may blow over. But, Leah, things don't look good. We thought the Ruby Bailey article was crazy. Then we find out that you *did* accept a firearm from your cousin. You *did* take money from the cops. It makes even me think you don't have your head screwed on right—and I'm one of your defenders."

"Thanks," I said. "I'll figure out something by morning, okay? Now I'd appreciate it if you could just leave me in peace." I had no idea where to go.

"I never thought it would get so bad we'd have to ask you to leave. I'm sorry, Leah." Paul looked helpless.

"I'm sure you are," I said. I tried to sound nonchalant. Indifferent. The truth was I had no idea what to do. I leafed through my address book. Surely there was someone who might let me stay at their place for a few nights while my house mates got over their latest anxiety fit. I stopped at Freddie Corster's number. Freddie led a bachelor's existence. In addition to the track, he worked part-time as a bartender at night, and he had an occasional tap-dancing gig on the side. Maybe he could help me.

Freddie had been nervous about this case from the beginning. I had promised not to tell his story to the cops. I had honored that promise—but the cops had found out about him anyway. They put pressure on Freddie to say that James Ferguson picked Grace up from the race track that Sunday morning. Now I had just given Freddie's name to Mike Fisher. I should also call Freddie to warn him. It was seven o'clock—he might be home. I called his number.

"What is it, hon?"

"I need to ask a favor."

"Look, you at home? I've been wanting to talk to you, Leah, but not on the phone. I'll stop by on my way into work." He sounded restless, out of breath. Freddie's part-time bartending gig was at the Ruby Room in downtown

Oakland. When he rang the doorbell fifteen minutes later, Freddie was wearing his usual outfit, black jeans, red cowboy boots, a tight T-shirt. He sat down on our front steps and lit a cigarette. "So what's the favor?"

"I've got this new friend, a cop on the OPD. He's a good guy. He's trying find out who murdered Grace, thinks maybe OPD has some hidden agenda. He asked me for the names of everyone I've talked to about this case. I gave him your name along with everyone else's."

Freddie blew the smoke out in one exasperated breath. "Why in hell did you do that? I told you not to be giving information to no cops." He threw his cigarette down on the steps and squashed it with his boot. "Oh, shit! Shit and damn!—Leah, those cops have been on me from the git-go. Now it will start up all over again."

"Freddie, I'm in danger, too. I need some help."

Freddie lowered his voice. "Those cops kept pushing me to say James Ferguson picked Grace up that Sunday. Finally I gave in, I said it coulda been Ferguson. It *coulda* been him. That much was true. I hated myself for giving in to their pressure." He tapped another cigarette out of his pack, and twisted his face to look up at me. "Leah, that ain't no Alice in Wonderland out there at the track. I've made money off a few crooked races. Those Feds knew it too. They coulda made it hot for me if I didn't cooperate." He lit the cigarette, took a long drag. "I'm sorry for that motherfucker Ferguson. But I tell you, ever get your hands dirty, and they've got you."

"What difference does it make if Mike Fisher has your name? The cops are already on to you."

Freddie blew out a long stream of smoke. "This Fisher cat's gonna tell you, so you might as well get the story straight from the source. Grace dated Bucky Timmons. From time to time. You know what I mean—maybe not dated, exactly. He liked her. He gave her a few tips, and she passed them on to me. That's how she made the ten thou that day she was killed. It wasn't chump change, either. She told me she was going to give it all to James Ferguson. *For the Party.*" Freddie shook his head. "For a smart broad, she could be pretty dumb, sometimes."

Freddie took another drag. "I don't know if the payola ever got to Ferguson. I don't know who was sitting in that car when she got into it. *If* she got into it," he added. "It was a black guy driving, I'm pretty sure. Was it Ferguson?

Couldn't tell. But I've always known something was wrong here, way wrong, because the cops have never once mentioned that money. They keep threatening they'll make it hot for me for acting off all the other tips—but they never talk about that race."

"Strange," I said.

"They must know about it. Ten grand. Jesus Christ, ten grand isn't worth a life." Freddie looked at me. "Gambling, it gets into your blood like alcohol. Playing those tips, knowing the races are fixed." He sucked on the cigarette. "I run into those guys every time I turn around. Bucky Timmons. Hugh Landis. Jay Landis—the little fairy. All those fools. Something bad is going down, and I won't want to be around when it busts wide open."

"Bucky Timmons, Hugh Landis, Jay Landis. What part did they play?"

"Come on, Leah—Bucky and Hugh, they're the fixers. More than that, I don't want to know. They're cold characters. Laugh with you, drink with you, then, if they had to, they'd ice you in a stone cold second." Freddie shook his head. "I need to cool out. I've been running too hard. I've got family in Philly. I'm getting out."

"This thing is big mess for me, too," I said.

"Yeah, babe, but you've kept your nose clean. You'll be okay. It's when they know your weakness, that's when they've got you." Freddie darted his head around in a quick, nervous gesture, gave another bark of a cough. He stepped on his cigarette and stood up. Then he leaned over and gave me a kiss. "You'll be okay, kid," he said. "I'll send you a postcard of the Liberty Bell." I hadn't kept my nose so clean, I thought, watching Freddie pull away in his dented 1967 Catalina. I just hadn't broken any laws outright, like Freddie had. That could come next.

Mike called the next morning, Sunday. He wanted to meet me again, same time, same place. As I hung up the phone, it seemed everyone I talked to now always spoke in low tones. No one wanted to be specific about places or times to meet. My hand was shaking as I applied my lipstick. Was I trying to help James by finding Grace's murderer and get back at Ruby Bailey who had ruined my reputation with that article? Or was this mess all connected with a need to create drama and intrigue? I was on a course I couldn't explain.

I blotted my lipstick and drew a comb through my thick, unruly hair. It had started to grow out, as Grace had suggested to me back in July. "Got to mess with your hair, honey," she had said. "That is, if you care about men at all." Well, girl, I answered her back, looks like maybe I care about men after all. I hope it doesn't get me where it got you. At three-thirty I was on the freeway heading toward Alameda. A brown-yellow haze lay over the East Bay, the color of a migraine headache.

I pulled up at Crown Beach a few minutes before four. Mike was already there. He jumped out of his car and ran over, motioning me to roll down the window. "We gotta get outta here," he said, "Drive out to the Oakland airport. Meet you in the airport bar, up where you can see the planes take off." Spitting gravel as he made a fast U-turn in the parking lot, Mike sped off.

Oakland International was a few miles south of Crown Beach. I drove down Otis and Doolittle toward Hegenberger Road and the airport. To the east the Oakland hills were parched. Maybe I should change direction, and drive to Vancouver, Canada. Maybe leaving the country was the only solution. James was on the run. There was no telling if he would get away. I would be abandoning James, but how much more could I do for him? Wasn't it past time for me to take care of myself?

In the Oakland Airport lounge, Mike was waiting for me. A carafe of wine sat on the table with two empty glasses. Next to my glass was a little vase with one red rose. I slid into the empty chair across from him. "I thought it would be better," Mike explained, "if it looked like a date. A black-and-white drove by while I was waiting for you at the Crown Beach. Coulda been routine. But I can't take chances."

"Paranoia seems to be one of the fringe benefits of this case," I said. But I was pleased by the rose. So what if it was make-believe.

"I checked out all the names you gave me," Mike said. "Your roommate, Paul Cohen. He's got a record."

Paul had been arrested in antiwar demonstrations and beaten up by the cops. "He's active in the antiwar movement," I said.

"He was taken in for assaulting an officer."

"The cops moved in on the students first."

"When Gary Bond and Chester Sims interrogated you," he said, "they asked you about your roommates. You didn't go into all that detail with them."

"I'm sure you checked me out too. Find anything you want to ask me about?" I began to feel trapped. Rose or no rose.

"Look, I have to check out everyone. I don't know how far this damn thing goes. I've gotta know who I can trust."

"I don't know everything about my roommates. And it's not OPD's business what I do know."

"If you weren't honest then," Mike said, "how do I know you're not holding back now?'

"For God's sake, Mike!"

"I have to know that everything between us stays confidential."

"It couldn't get any more confidential," I said. "I'm the one who should be testing you. Cops haven't been my friends in all this, you know."

"You've had Joey."

So much for the rose, I thought. This was more like a married couple's squabble. "I have my doubts," I said. "Even about Joey."

"So do I," said Mike Fisher. "We'll talk about that later." He lifted his wine glass, and motioned toward mine. "Cheers," he said, clinking glasses. "Let me tell you what I found out. Hugh Landis—you were right—they never followed a single lead involving that guy. And I know why. He's too important. He's on the racing board, and Golden Gate Fields brings a hell of a lot of money into the area. Anyway Albany and the track are outside OPD's jurisdiction."

"You said OPD has undercover people out there."

"Yeah, to check out Oakland criminals. Only reason OPD got involved in this murder is because Grace lived in Oakland. And she may have been killed in Oakland before her body was dumped in the bay. Of course, you never heard that from me. It's not the official version, just the scuttlebutt."

"So they never followed up on Hugh Landis. What about the son?"

"Jay Landis? Minor record—deviant behavior, they call it. Picked up in a public bathroom for soliciting other men. Cops didn't know who he was— brought him in. Found out who he was, let him go. That's about it on little Jay."

"Anything else?"

"This is what Joey called a *special case*, remember? A lot is riding on it. The jockey Timmons—he's a real mess. Been investigated for years for

234

race fixing, illegal drug use. Wild, flamboyant guy—gets into scrapes, buys his way out. But there's not much to link him with Grace."

"So we're nowhere," I said.

"Not entirely," Mike said. "In the course of looking up all this stuff, I found some other interesting leads. Also never followed up on. There was an ex-con, name of Carl Puckett. Did a few years for manslaughter in San Quentin. Brought in for breaking his parole. He had heard about a contract out on Grace's life—contract offered by the Aryan Nation."

"Where did you find that?"

"When I got to Becky Boyle Puckett. She had been picked up for shoplifting in Berkeley. Second time Hink's pressed charges. As I was checking into that, I found out her husband's the interesting one. Carl Puckett. He's hooked up with the Aryan Nation." Mike looked at me. "Didn't believe me about those hate crimes, did you? I told you that kind of shit is all over."

"Becky seemed so ordinary," I said. "I never dreamed her husband was an ex-con. Not to mention the Aryan Nation."

"Doing time is no big deal where I grew up. I mighta done time myself, if I hadn't become a cop. One of the very *few* brothers in the OPD, I might add." Mike sounded bitter.

"They looked like everyday people. Kind of people I grew up with."

"Everyday working people," Mike said. Then he corrected himself, "—everyday working *white* people—are racists often as not. One thing you learn as a cop. You learn fast everyone's got their share of dirty laundry. It may make you paranoid, but it keeps you from being dumb."

Just because you're paranoid doesn't mean they aren't out to get you. Paul's favorite line. "So, Becky's husband is an ex-con. Involved in a racist organization. What else?"

"Starting about 1969, it's hard to find out anything about him."

"What does that mean?'

"I'm not sure. He may have turned informer. Maybe he's reporting on the Aryan Nation. We should find out."

"How are we going to do that?"

"I need you to talk to Becky Puckett. You talked to her before. Imply that you know something about Carl. Get her to confide in you."

"Becky Puckett doesn't want to confide in me. She made that clear last time I saw her. Anyway, why would she know what her husband is up to?"

"Most women have a pretty good idea of what their man is up to," Mike said. "I'll be your back-up. I'll be waiting for you out in the car. In case the old man is home and there's trouble." Mike had been looking at me intently. Now he smiled, and it caught me off guard. I smiled back. The plan might work the way he described it. But things rarely turned out as planned in this case.

"I'd like for us to go out there tomorrow," Mike said.

"Mmmmm," I said. I wasn't sure about the plan.

Mike swirled his wine in the glass. "There's even more mystery here. Take Ronald Xavier Jones. Born 1944. I looked up that man. It's as if he doesn't exist. There's no file. Nothing. No one by that name, with that birth date, anywhere, officially living in the U. S. No social security number, no address, no driver's license, no record of military service, nothing."

"He's in the Clayton Valley High School yearbook. Ronald Xavier Jones. Becky Puckett knows him. They were in the same class at Clayton Valley High with Grace."

"Becky Puckett knows Ronald Jones?"

"Absolutely. Ronnie introduced her to me at Grace's funeral."

Mike frowned. "Let me think about this. I was assuming Carl might be informing on the Nation. Ronnie Jones's records are gone. Here's my hunch— Carl and Ronnie know each other and they're both involved with the Aryan Nation. Let's see what more we can find out, going on that."

"Look, to change the subject," I said, "Art Leopold has advised me to leave the area. My roommates all want me out, too. They're scared for me, and for themselves. I have to leave town. If I can figure out where to go."

Mike looked startled. "What about our plan?" he said. Then he added, more sympathetically, "Where will you go?"

"To be honest, I don't know."

"Okay," Mike said. His voice conveyed authority. Another man, used to giving orders. "Here's what we'll do. I've got a studio over on Lake Merritt. I'm hardly ever there. My mother's been alone since Dad died. I stay out in East Oakland with her a couple times a week. The rest of the time I'm at my girlfriend Lily's."

"You're offering me your apartment?"

"I need you. We have work to do. Work we can't do if you leave town. You can use my apartment. I'll stop by sometimes—pick up clothes and things, but I won't bother you."

"That's kind of you," I said, dubiously. "But I'm not sure. I think maybe I should just drive up to Seattle. Or Vancouver, BC."

"You and I are going to crack this case," Mike said, firmly. "When we do, you'll go back to life as normal in Berkeley. But I need you to stick around while we work this."

"Thanks." At least *someone* wanted me to stick around.

"So you'll do it? Stay, and help crack this case?"

I was not sure this offer was the solution for my housing needs. But if I drove to Seattle or to Canada, I would be turning my back on all the work I had done so far. Could I accept his offer at face value? Finish the task I had taken on without quitting mid-way? I drew a deep breath, then let out the air in a long sigh. "Okay." The uncertainty in my voice did not faze Mike.

"Don't think two times on it, Leah. If I crack this case, I'll run for District Attorney." Mike laughed. "When I finish law school, that is. But go home, pack your suitcase, and bring it along tomorrow. After we're done with Becky Puckett, we'll swing by the apartment. I'll get a key made for you." Mike pushed back his chair and drained his glass. "Who knows," he said, "maybe I'll even get a good home-cooked meal out of this."

"If your idea of a good home-cooked meal is a toasted cheese sandwich," I answered.

I drove back to Russell Street. My doubts about the arrangement were dissipating. As I entered my room, I saw Yoshi leaving Carol's room. Had he been checking things out? I pulled him into my room and closed the door.

"Were you looking through her things?"

"She was gone for a couple hours this afternoon. So I looked through her calendar, some stuff on her desk. I get the impression she's seeing someone besides me." Yoshi sat down on my bed and pulled a cigarette out of his pocket, struck a match. Then he leaned back on an elbow. "I feel bad about this, Leah. It's not like Carol and I have claims on each other. But there are dates marked on her calendar. Little red stars, exclamation points, these days are something special. Always days when I'm not with her, or days when she knows I have exams and stuff. Some phone numbers. A note or two—she's excited about meeting someone. I would have thought she would tell me."

"Ask where you stand with her," I advised. "Carol doesn't beat around the bush. She'll be up front with you. But do me a favor and copy down those phone numbers for me." While we talked, I had located my overnight bag and was pulling some clothes out of drawers.

"What I don't do for you, Leah," Yoshi sighed. "Anyway, looks like you're packing up. You have a place to go?"

"I can't tell you, Yoshi. But I'll keep paying the rent. I'll be back."

"I feel bad about this, Leah," he said.

"I'll call you every day."

"If you don't, I'll call the cops." We laughed. How much help would the cops be if I disappeared? It would probably be the cops who disappeared me. Or the Black Panthers.

"By the way, would you keep this for me in a safe place?" I had placed Grace's teen-age diary in a manila envelope. It wouldn't be needed at Mike's.

"What's this?"

"My notes on the case. Background material. Stuff like that. Grace's teen-age diary." Background material—well, that was true enough.

"How the *hell* did you get her diary? You never told me about a diary."

"Look, Yoshi, there's a whole lot I haven't told you. A whole lot I *couldn't* tell you. Just hide this, okay. We'll talk about it later."

"I'll hide it in my closet. You know where." But he looked unhappy.

Yes, I thought, I knew exactly where. He would store the diary under his grass stash. When I retrieved it, the notebook would reek of pot. I continued to pack, putting my address book, my own notebook, the draft of my article, in my shoulder bag. Into a small suitcase went a red leotard, black slacks, a sweater, black ballet flats. Underwear, toiletries. The snubbie. I was wearing my standard uniform of blue jeans and a black turtleneck, white socks, Keds.

The phone rang in the hallway. I picked it up.

"Leah?" The low, musical voice of Maura Sayid. "I found the reading list we talked about. Do you want to pick it up? I'll be in my office tomorrow late afternoon."

238

"I could drop by at four-thirty," I said.

"Fine. I'll tell you more when I see you."

I finished packing, already nostalgic for the old times, when the Black Panthers were a group I read about in the newspaper or saw on television. That girl I had been was already a stranger to the person I had become.

XXVI

Mike followed me to Concord the next afternoon. I drove my Beetle; Mike followed in an unmarked patrol car. It was a hot day the last week of September. Coming out the east side of the Caldecott Tunnel, the dry gold hills of Contra Costa County were hotter yet. It had been days since I'd shown up at the track. I'd called Beatrice, told her I was seeing a doctor for some nasty migraines, but I was just blowing the job off, to pursue this crazy mystery.

Becky Boyle. Becky Puckett now. She disliked everything about me—my looks, my education, my questions, my friendship with Grace. How could I possibly get this woman to open up to me? Mike had given me instructions before we left. Go soft, get confidential at first. If she starts withdrawing, don't be afraid to get hard. Scare her. Use anything that works. Scare her how? I remembered how her face had softened when Ronnie spoke to her at Grace's funeral. How she had opened up to me about Ronnie the last time I saw her. She might still be vulnerable where Ronnie Jones was concerned.

A little after one pm I rang the doorbell on Heavenly Drive. I had to ring twice before she came to the screen door. I had caught her by surprise. Becky's bleached hair was pulled back with a rubber band. She was wearing sweat pants and a T-shirt. Behind her, ominous strains of organ music indicated some crisis in "As the World Turns." As she recognized me, a mask slipped into place hardening her features. "What do you want?" She pushed a strand of hair off her forehead. "I told you not to come back here."

"It's about Ronnie," I said, "It's urgent. I need to talk to you."

"What about him?" she said.

"Ronnie's in trouble," I said. "I've learned things—things you probably already knew."

"What things?" Her arms were crossed under her ample bosom. "This better be good." I folded my arms across my chest also. Mike had told me that mimicking body language often improved communication. We were like two boxers squaring off.

"Ronnie's life is in danger," I said, as forcefully as I could. "If you want to help him, you're going to have to tell me the truth." Reluctantly she unlatched the screen door. I stepped inside before she could change her mind.

240

"Truth about what?" she said, sullen, but with fear in her eyes.

"Truth about why Carl goes to those meetings of the Aryan Nation."

"You think I know about that shit?" Becky asked

"I think you know about *that* shit, and about a lot of other shit." I made my voice sound tough. Mimicking an opponent's language was a useful communicative device. Mike's instructions.

"Nothing to tell," Becky said. "Carl joined up while he was doing time. It doesn't mean anything. He just likes the guys, drinking the beer, talking."

"Ronnie went with him." I stated this flatly, although it was a big question mark in my mind.

"Yeah, sometimes," Becky admitted.

"And the Nation had a contract on Grace's life."

"Ronnie didn't know a damn thing about any contract. He loved that bitch—God knows why, she never gave two cents for him."

It was working. Becky was getting emotionally involved in her story, forgetting who I was. A door slammed in the back of the house. Heavy footsteps along the hallway. Then Carl Puckett was standing in the living room. Five foot ten, short legs, broad shoulders. His pants hung low. "Who the hell are you?" He was in a bad mood.

"This is Leah, Carl," Becky said. "Remember? Grace's friend from the race track?"

"What the *hell* is she doing here?"

"Ronnie Jones is in trouble," I said. I made my own expression as unpleasant as I could. "Along with you."

"What the *hell* you know about trouble, lady? You snooping in my business?" Carl shoved Becky aside in order to face me. "You want to see trouble? I'll show you trouble."

I saw myself as he saw me—a frizzy-haired Berkeley intellectual, a young woman with ridiculous pretensions to authority, invading his house. With a cop out on the street providing back-up, I reminded myself. Something stopped Carl Puckett from throwing me out then and there. Had he seen the unmarked patrol car parked on Heavenly Drive? I watched staccato pulses of emotion surge through his body, making a vein in his neck beat. He had an odd, fixed smile.

"Your wife lied about your whereabouts the night Grace was murdered." I made my voice flat and factual.

Carl continued to look at me. His lips were fixed in an awful smile. I took a breath. "Becky said you were on the road that night," I said, "But you weren't on the road. You were with Ronnie Jones."

"You dumb bitch!" The words exploded from him. "All this snooping—you're gonna end up like your friend Grace."

Becky interrupted, "It's not how it sounds, Leah. Carl wasn't—"

"I said shut up!" Carl Puckett shouted. He grabbed his wife, flinging her backward so hard her head hit the credenza. I could hear Becky's collection of bone china cups jingling in their saucers. "You've said too goddamned much already!" he said, raising his fist.

I moved toward the screen door, and the protection of Mike Fisher and the OPD. Carl jumped forward, blocking my way. He grabbed my wrist, jerking it downward with a sharp motion.

"Mike!" I screamed. How easily Carl, or any man, could break a woman's arm. Wrists, knees, ankles, all so fragile, so easily smashed by men who lost control. I hoped Mike could hear me. I backed away, but the stocky, sweating man was advancing toward me. Carl lunged forward. I felt him lift me. Then I was thrown to the floor. I rolled, dodging his muddy boots, his fists. What had Joey taught me? To protect my head. I cradled it in my arms as his foot hit one rib, and then another. I was silent now, saving my breath, saving my strength.

I could hear Becky screaming, "Stop it, Carl! Stop!"

Then Carl Puckett lifted me again and threw me out the front door. As I half-rolled, half-stumbled down the front steps, picking myself up, I saw Mike running toward me across the lawn. His revolver was raised. He was shouting, "Hold!" The whole scene was unbelievable, a badly done scene from a cops-and-robbers movie. I watched in paralyzed horror. Mike was shouting. "Come on out, Puckett." I could see Carl Puckett's indistinct bulk shadowed behind the screen door. "Come on out, Puckett. I can arrest you. Or we can have a talk. Out here in the patrol car. Which will it be?"

The screen door creaked open. Carl's head emerged. "Officer, this woman broke into my house—"

242

"Walk out nice and slow. Hands up, over your head, and no weapons." Mike jerked his head in the direction of the police car. Carl walked forward slowly. "Hands forward," said Mike, snapping handcuffs on his wrists. Mike shoved him into the front passenger seat and handcuffed Carl's wrists to the dashboard. "I sent Miss DeMartino in to ask you and your wife some questions," Mike said. "I'm still waiting for the answers."

"I swear to God—" Carl began, but Mike interrupted.

"I'd hate to take you in a third time," Mike was saying. "You've got a job. Wife. Kids to consider." I limped to the car, rubbing my ribs.

"Yeah," Carl muttered.

"So," Mike said, "Tell me about the Aryan Nation contract." He tapped his shirt pocket lightly. I wondered if he were activating a tape.

Carl's voice had a pleading tone. "I hang out at the Daisy Tavern—"

"That shit bar in Concord? I know the place. A lot of your buddies from the Nation go there, don't they?"

"Sometimes, yeah. This guy comes over while I was having a drink."

"What guy?"

"Ex-con from the garage. You don't know him. He'd heard about some money—a contract—heard about it through the Nation. Said it was good money. Only hard part it was whacking some broad."

"Who was paying?"

"I don't know. It was just talk. Shit like guys talk about in a bar. He said there was good money to pay."

"So this guy knew you'd be interested." Mike was a lot better at flat and factual than I had been.

"Naw. I wasn't interested. It was just shit talk. The guys in the Nation were talking, you know, about kinds of people they wouldn't mind wasting."

"What kinds of people would they be, Carl?'

"You know. Traitors. Informers. Race-mixers. Plastics."

"Plastics?"

"Means colored people."

"Black cops?"

"No cops. You think we're crazy? You guys have all the power."

"So you didn't take the contract. Who took the contract?"

"I don't know," Carl said, "Maybe no one. It was just floating around. Those guys are crazy, but not that crazy."

"Carl, I'd hate to see you do more time. Judge might just throw away the key this time."

"Some guy named Billie—he was strapped for cash—took it. But I don't think he did it."

"How about Ronnie Jones?"

"Ronnie Jones? What's Ronnie Jones got to do with this?'

"You tell me."

"That's crazy," Carl said. He seemed to regain some confidence. "You don't know who you're dealing with, do you?' I heard a new note in his voice. It was almost contemptuous.

"You know where Ronnie Jones is right now?"

"Sure I do," said Carl. I heard the sneer in his voice. Now he seemed to feel he had the upper hand. "San Francisco. Special Forces convention."

"Look, motherfucker," Mike said. "I'm gonna let you go for now. One wrong move and you'll be back inside." Mike unlocked his handcuffs. Carl swiveled his head around to look at me, a long, hard look of hatred. "Get out of the car," Mike said, pushing him out the door.

Carl stumbled out, turning to look at me again. "Bitch!" he muttered under his breath. I opened the back door and took a place in front. The seat was still warm from the weight of Carl's rear end.

"Okay, we're heading over to that Special Forces convention in San Francisco," Mike said. "I want you to get Ronnie Jones talking. Get him on tape."

"Get him talking? After what just happened? You've got to be kidding." I touched my ribs gingerly. If I laughed, it was painful. Then again, there wasn't too much to laugh about.

"You did good enough for an amateur. You got him to break." Now Mike turned his head. He looked at me sharply. "Hey, are you okay?"

"No," I said. "He kicked me in the ribs."

"Oh, shit," said Mike. Was this an expression of concern? Hard to tell. Probably he was disappointed that we might not go straight to the Special Forces convention. "I'll see how long this Special Forces Convention is booked

244

for. If Ronnie's gonna be there a few more days, we can postpone this. Head over there tomorrow. Better?" It was not all that much better. I would not have objected to giving the Special Forces convention a miss.

"I made you a key." He handed it to me.

I pushed open the car door. My Beetle was parked on Heavenly Way, across from Mike's car. "Okay, I'll be over around six," I said.

I returned to Russell Street, I threw my shoulder bag on the bed and headed to the bathroom for a shower. The hot water felt good. Then I lay down, trying to make sense of what I had seen out on Heavenly Drive. Becky Puckett's head snapping against the credenza, the jingling of the little cups. Becky was a victim, and, to my surprise and shame, this did not make me like her any better. Carl Puckett. The power of a violent man. He was a bully, but scared of cops, of being sent back to jail. Yet when Mike mentioned Ronnie's name, Carl changed. He no longer seemed frightened. Why?

I had to meet Maura at Dwinelle Hall at four-thirty. It was already past three. I brushed my hair, took a last look around the room I would not be seeing again for I didn't know how long, and drove to campus.

Her office was on the third floor of Dwinelle. The door was open; she was sitting at her desk. On the bookcase behind her desk was a framed photograph of a city with onion-dome spires—Beirut? Istanbul? A red-flowered begonia with heart-shaped leaves sat on the windowsill. Maura was dressed in a black suit, her dark hair swept back into a smooth bun. She had heavy gold loops in her ears. She looked elegant and professional.

She smiled when she saw me at the door. "Come in, Leah," she said. "You're right on time. Sit down." Despite the smile, there were dark circles under her eyes. Reaching into her desk, she withdrew a spiral notebook. She lay it on her desk, with her hands resting on top of it. "I wish to God I had never seen this thing," she said. "I knew nothing good could come of it from the moment I first saw it hanging on my door. I felt uneasy. I feared Grace was giving me a message about my husband." Had even Maura, with her cool beauty, felt alarm about Grace's sensuality and its possible effect on her husband?

"When you told me she had been killed, that sense of dread come over me again—the same feeling I had when I found this notebook hanging on our door knob. It was a Sunday morning in August. August sixth, to be exact. She must have dropped it off the day she died."

"You didn't tell me that."

"I didn't know the date she had died until you came to our house. I was afraid this could open a door—police, questions—maybe even create a chasm between my husband and me."

"You thought your husband may have been involved in her death?"

"David and I were together most of that Sunday, preparing for our yearly trip to London. But we are foreigners here. We have our own fears."

"Grace was killed Sunday between noon and four in the afternoon."

"David and I shopped for groceries Sunday morning. We got home around eleven. The bag was hanging from our door knob. The notebook was in that. We were together all afternoon."

Grace had left my house at nine Sunday morning. After she had picked up her Renault, she may have driven to Quail Road, and from there, to the race track. Freddie had seen Grace leave around noon, walking toward a tan Buick with a black hardtop in the parking lot. Mike thought she had been killed between noon and four. It all fit.

"You mustn't think I ever suspected David. I did not. But I was afraid. Then when you visited me two weeks ago, I worried again. I wondered if we would get drawn into this. After your visit, I forced myself to read this notebook. At least there's nothing about us in here."

"Why did Grace leave this diary with you?"

"I thought it contained a message for me," Maura said. "It did—but it was not the message I feared. It was not a message about David. It was a message about who she was. I think that Grace knew she was going to die."

"Will you just give it to me?" I asked abruptly. The words erupted out of me. I needed that notebook, and I needed to get out of there and get to Mike's apartment.

Maura seemed not to hear me. "I didn't read it very carefully. I'm not sure I understood what I did read. She had asked me to look at her poems, but it seemed to be a personal journal. I thought she might have left it by mistake." Maura looked up and fixed her dark eyes on me, penetratingly. "I'm afraid I may be putting you in danger by giving it to you. I want you to pause for a moment. Is this really what you want to do?"

"I'd like to have it," I said.

"Perhaps I should give it to the police."

"The police don't want to find out who murdered Grace," I said.

"They may not. There's such a dreadful feeling around all this, Leah. I'm concerned about you, too. You're young and intelligent. You have a life of your own to explore. If the police don't want to know, there may be good reasons to leave this alone."

Somewhere out there was a life of my own. Lovers, friends, a career, my own apartment, even my own house. She was right. I needed to move on. But I was so caught up in the drama of Grace's life and death that my own life had retreated into insignificance. There was one last question. "Maura," I said, "after I met you at your house, did anyone come by later to ask you about my visit?"

"No one," she said. "Why?"

"I had to ask," I answered. "I'll take this." I picked up the notebook. I stood up as she did, also, from behind her desk. She gave me a quick hug. Her perfume was one my Italian grandmother had used. Violetta di Parma.

"Be careful, Leah," Maura said.

I left, wondering why the people following me had not yet found out about Maura. What was different about her?

XXVII

I wanted to sit down on a bench in Sproul Plaza and open that note-book, but I forced myself to keep walking. Someone could be following me. Fall quarter would start in another week. Students walked through the plaza, carrying books, talking, laughing, holding hands. No one was interested in me. My VW bug was parked on Bancroft. I got in, locked the doors, settled my things. In my rearview mirror I saw someone in a grey Ford Galaxie two places behind mine put down his newspaper. I started up the car. His lights came on. His engine turned over. I turned the ignition off. His lights went out. He continued to sit there.

I started the car up quickly and pulled out into the traffic on Bancroft. He did the same. I drove down Bancroft toward Shattuck. He was two cars behind me. I put on my left turn signal as if I were turning left on Fulton, but when I reached Fulton, I kept on going, making a green light at Shattuck. I was heading down toward Grove. He had put his left turn signal on before Fulton, but didn't make the turn. He was still two cars behind me as I approached Grove Street.

I made a sharp left on Grove, another sharp left on Dwight Way, a left on Shattuck, a left down Channing Way. I was driving in circles, trying to lose him. Once I lost him, I could call Yoshi. Maybe Yoshi could meet me in Paul's car, and he and I could switch cars. That would put them off my trail. The Russell Street phone was certainly tapped. Could I even get my message across to Yoshi?

I was back at Grove Street. I had run a couple of stop signs in the process. I didn't see the tail behind me anymore. I pulled into a parking place and waited. Cars flashed by, but no one hovered behind me; no one pulled back and stopped; no one seemed to be waiting. I waited five minutes before I pulled back out and drove to Blake, down two blocks, over to Dwight, down to Sacramento, and then followed Sacramento south into Oakland. I stopped at a pay phone near a liquor store, deposited my money, listened to the ringing phone. To my relief, Yoshi answered. "Hello?"

"Hello. Remember where we met last time?"

"Yeah. Meet there again?"

"Yes. Now."

"Okay," he answered. Thank God for Yoshi, I thought, as I hung up. I headed to the place we had designated for situations like this—Aquatic Park, at the foot of Bancroft. Yoshi showed up in five minutes, driving Paul's van. He jumped out and ran toward me, as I opened my door. "What's going on, Leah?"

"I'm being followed. I've lost him for now—a guy in a grey Ford. I need to switch cars. You drive my Beetle back to Russell Street, park it in the driveway. Go in the house by the back door. They may think I've gone home. I'll drive Paul's van."

"Where are you going?"

"I can't tell you now. I'll call you tomorrow to let you know I'm okay. I'll return the van tomorrow. Paul can use my car."

"*Are* you going to be okay?"

"Yes," I said. "Just take my car home for now. And, Yoshi—?"

"Yeah?—"

"—Those journals of Grace's are somewhere safe, right?"

"I told you before. They're in my closet. Under my stash of grass. Nobody goes in there."

"Oh, great," I said, sighing. Still, it was better than nothing. I watched Yoshi drive away in my Bug, his black hair visible over the back of the driver's seat. I had a forlorn feeling, as if I were losing the last friend I had. It was seven pm and the sun was setting.

Mike's place was a 1920s Mediterranean-style building on Lakeshore at the upper end of Lake Merritt. A green canopy overhung the enormous front entrance, with evergreen topiary and bonsai framing the sides. A fire escape to the right climbed up the building's stuccoed exterior. Behind me on the lake path, an Asian woman in athletic pants clasped her hands together, then extended her arms ahead of her with straight elbows, in a yoga pose. A skinny black boy wobbled past on a big-fendered bike, his loose T-shirt blown back by the wind. Normal people, doing normal things, of an early Oakland evening.

I stood in front of the heavy door with its iron grillwork of heart-shaped scrolls. I could see into the lobby with its red tile floor and electric candles placed in sconces along the walls. Mike rang me in, and I climbed the red tile stairs with my suitcase, stopping on the second floor landing to catch my breath and to admire the view of Lake Merritt and downtown Oakland, magical in the twilight. One more flight up to the third floor. I knocked; Mike let me in.

His studio was huge and high-ceilinged. The living room looked over the lake. It was furnished with bachelor chic—a leather reclining chair and hassock faced the windows overlooking the lake. Framed photographs of Miles Davis and Billie Holliday hung on the walls. There was a small little breakfast nook, also overlooking the lake. I would be as safe here as anywhere these days.

"I'm not here all that much, but I like to be comfortable," Mike explained. He showed me light switches and fuse boxes, telephone numbers for the managers. He showed me how to unhook the Murphy bed from the wall. He handed me the keys.

"The Special Forces convention goes on for the next three days. Ronnie is booked into the St. Francis. I'll come by tomorrow around nine. We'll drive over to San Francisco and check him out. I left my Mom's number next to the phone," Mike added. "Call me if you need me."

"What about Lily?" I asked, "Shouldn't I have that number just in case?"

Mike looked embarrassed. "Me and Lily had a falling out," he said. "She called today, said she needed a break. She's never liked the idea of my being a cop—she's got grander dreams. A lot of ambition. And I've been so busy, what with night school, and this case . . ." he let his thoughts trail. "I'll just stay at Mom's for a while," he added. "No problem, Mom likes it."

"Why are you and Lily suddenly having problems," I said. "Does the fact you're letting me stay here have something to do with it?" Did I really want him to tell me more?

"Her parents are middle class. They look down on cops. They want more for their Lily. But they won't look down on a lawyer. And they won't look down on a cop who's cracked a case like this one. I have a hunch we're gonna crack this baby, and damn soon too."

Mike walked to the door, gave me a jaunty wave, and was gone. Using his keys, I locked myself in. Then I drew the heavy living room drapes, leaving a narrow opening between them so I could catch glimpses of Lake Merritt outside, the lights of Oakland starting to reflect in its waters. A car pulled up on Lakeshore and parked. No one got out. Okay, I said to myself, plenty of reasons for that, a person who wants to stay in the car a few minutes, a couple

250

having a talk by the lake. It looked like the Ford Galaxie but I couldn't be sure. It was getting too dark to see much.

I hadn't told Mike about this most recent journal. I wanted to read it first. Everything would have to be in order before I began. I made myself a cup of Earl Grey tea, folded a dishtowel neatly and placed it on the armrest of the black leather reclining chair. Then I set the teacup on that. As I settled into his comfortable chair, I wondered why was I using up time going through these rituals? What was I afraid to find out? I opened the brown spiral notebook with a sense of apprehension. It was a continuation of the notebook Maura had given me after Labor Day. The entries this time were dated.

> 8/25/1969: Ronnie walked into Mainline today—back from Vietnam. Learned from Becky where I worked. I was flattered he would look me up. "How's things?" he said, as if two years hadn't passed. He's different, though. Somewhere around the eyes.
>
>> with their hint of troubled flight,
>> a damaged bird on fire with night.
>
> That's how I see him. Those eyes with that crazy, funny, burning light. He told me my letter had meant a lot, he read it over and over; it kept him going. I'd forgotten that letter, forgotten about Ronnie, really. So long ago. I'd gone to that rally and they talked about writing to the men over there. So I'd written to him, remembering all we'd done and been to each other.
>
> Ronnie said he was gonna join the Vietnam Vets Against the War Asked me about the different groups I'd gone to. I told him a little about me and James. "Niggers with guns," he said. "You didn't used to be interested in stuff like that, Grace."
>
> 9/1/1969: Ronnie dropped by. Brought roses—upset and tearful—had he been drinking? I could barely understand him—he had never thought...he had always hoped ... Can't talk about Vietnam. Just wants to drink and go on about the old days. Then he talks about the gook girls in Vietnam, and how they double crossed him. I ended up sleeping with him again. Don't know why. To shut him up? To make him feel better? I told him it was for "old times sake." He seemed to like that.

"A wild boy," Grace had written. That was how I had seen Ronnie Jones. But why was Ronnie turning up in this diary? I had expected to read about James.

A sound outside startled me.

251

I looked out the window. The car was still parked on Lakeshore. So it was nothing, I said to myself. Nonetheless I checked the kitchenette. The window opened directly onto a fire escape. Someone could climb it and break into the apartment. Lakeshore was a busy street with traffic even at night. On the other hand, as it grew later, there would be less and less traffic. Someone climbing a fire escape might or might not be noticed. Someone might risk it.

I felt edgy but returned to the notebook. I could always call Mike if I got really nervous. I would wait another thirty minutes, check on the dark car again. Then I would decide.

> 9/9/1969: Ronnie called while I was in the middle of a crying jag. I was scared I'd never stop crying. "What's wrong, babes?" I told him all about James and the BPP. He got quiet for a long time. I expected another remark about "niggers with guns." Instead he said, "I've got an idea for you, kid. Leave all this to your old pal Ronnie."

> 10/10/1969: We slept together a second time. It was bitter-sweet—the old and the new. The memories came back. I used to tell him everything, about Helene and what her boyfriend did to me. He always got mad for me. He made me feel protected and special. First loves, first lovers. Do you ever forget?

> 10/11/1969: Ronnie's been gathering information for the government. He wants me to stay involved with James. Do everything I can for James and for the Panthers. Prove my loyalty. Find out what I can and pass it on to him. He makes it sound like it's no big deal. He cracked that Ronnie smile. "The money ain't bad, Grace. You always liked money. Who knows, you may help bust the Panthers, and get your Big Jim back." I told him, "I haven't even seen James in a while." "Don't worry," he said, "you will." I felt better when he said that. I don't know if the Panthers will ever bust up, and I don't know if I'll ever get James back. But Ronnie's plan gives me something to do.

I reread those pages. I remembered that night in my room, the way she had described her relationship with James. Grace had seemed mature and loyal. "What we had went beyond being lovers. We were more than friends," she had said. Was this what it amounted to—she had agreed to betray James? To Ronnie? For money?

No doubt Ronnie knew how to play on her vulnerabilities, her vanity. Her need for security. Still I was shocked. Helene had sold Grace out to the cops for a chance to "eat out, now and then." She had ignored Grace long before that, when her boyfriend forced Grace to have sex with him, and Helene chose not to know. ("Mom shouldn't know—she'll blame me"). She had abandoned Grace, sent her to live with the religious fanatic, aunt Millie. Helene allowed Bud to come between her and her daughter even now. Perhaps Grace betrayed James because betrayal was all she'd ever known.

James had suspected Grace, but he had not been willing to believe she had busted him. Had someone else in the Panthers found out? Whoever had would consider me a traitor as well. I reassured myself. No one knew I was here but Mike. No one else could know. The door was double bolted. The apartment was three floors up from the street. The windows were latched. I checked the window. The car was still there. Now a second car had pulled up behind it. It was one am. What was going on? Should I call the police, ask them to check it out? But Mike's phone might be tapped, and, anyway, would the police protect me? Maybe I was imagining everything. Uneasily I went back to Grace's journal.

Ronnie. What I had just read about him gave me the strange feeling I had known this all along. Ronnie had never totally disguised his sympathies. Working as a government agent made perfect sense. He had managed to convince me that he was a maverick, rebelling against authority. Why had I let myself be fooled? Grace's notebook continued, scattered entries after this. Her writing got smaller and more haphazard. Here and there a page was torn out.

> 3/03/1970: James still comes by. He says he can't get me out of his mind, but I feel him slipping away. I said, "What if I work for the Party?' He laughed, "You?" I got angry again, "Why not?" "Okay," he said, "You can help out in the clinic." My reasons weren't good, but I didn't care. I hate the Panthers, cause they took James from me. And of course, there's Ronnie's plan.

> Peach trees in bloom and the magnolia outside the house starting to open. Then James came back. We had a couple of hot afternoons. The long afternoons, twilight of the evenings. I'm full of love and trouble. Maybe because we were lying there, James told me more stuff. About his parents, how his mother left his father.

253

James told me things he had done for the Party before he got out here. The cop who got killed in New York. This is what R wants me to find out, things like this. James mentioned safe houses he called them. I filed the addresses away. I wanted him to stay, but he had to go. I wish he hadn't told me so much. I went to Ronnie. We sat around and listened to records. Then he took me out to eat on Shattuck, and I told him about the safe houses—that was what I supposed to do, right? To earn my salary? I didn't tell him everything. I felt awful afterwards. Torn up. I don't know if I can do this.

4/20/1970: Crazy month. I did more stuff for them, I met people, I learned things—mainly from J, who still sees me. Seems it's okay to see him as long as I'm doing things for the Party. R says—get them so they'll trust you—they'll let you know more stuff, details. Always offers from men—Jay Landis at the track, young, weird, wants to do kinky things. I like the father better—he's sorta old, but more of a man. It's not like my heart is in any of this. It's just a thing to do, a distraction from James. Bucky the jockey—he likes me too. Ronnie says go out with all of them, they can be useful. Ronnie is crazy. Everything is part of this conspiracy against the government. He says he's enlisting people to help fight the conspiracy. Says the fate of the country is at stake. Why do I keep going back to him? Ronnie's not right—was he ever right?—Vietnam messed with his head. But he's my past. He's my father confessor—that time he dressed up as a priest and had us all in stitches. God, the stuff he did in Vietnam. We hang out, I tell him stuff; he gives me money. I guess it's a kind of a thrill—espionage, I guess you'd call it.

9/1/1970: James got caught—weapons in the cellar. Newspaper says he may get sent up—not Santa Rita, but San Quentin. Sweet Jesus. I keep remembering those scars. And the knowledge that I had everything to do with this.

10/12/1970: Ronnie says keep on helping at the school, run errands. Says it will look good to J when he gets out, keep him from being suspicious. Says I might still get info worth having. Ronnie may have other "assignments" for me.

1/13/1971: My head is spinning—I don't know where I am. Ronnie thinks I hung with James for the thrill of sleeping with a black man. The ultimate rebellion. It was never just that. There's a poetry writing class at UC extension. Maybe I'll try it.

2/11/1971: James is out. I didn't even know. I heard it at the school, and Ronnie confirmed it. I'm breathless, excited, waiting, hoping, calling, calling, can't seem to get in touch.

3/15/1971: I found James at Vinnie's with Wilson and Ollie. He told them to leave. I told him I had to talk to him. I admitted everything. He kept saying, "Do you know what you've done? Do you know what you've done?" He hit me. He kept saying if the Party knew, they would expel him for being with me. "For miscalculating," was how he kept putting it. That burned me. The Party. The Party. Always the Party. What about me? I had a cut on my cheek. My eye started to swell. James didn't even notice. When he calmed down, he told me to keep working for R. Feed R information James would give me, and let R give me information and I would pass it on to James. James said it was the only way I could redeem myself. Otherwise the Party would expel him, he wouldn't be able to see me anymore. It's crazy, crazy, crazy. It's a mess. It's Mata Hari for real. Whatever I have to do, that's what I'll do.

4/9/1971: I was drinking beer and crying, just like a country western song. "Don't drink so much," James said. "Get a grip." I just couldn't pull it together. Everything is changed, everything's an act, be this way with Ronnie, be this way with J. Sometimes I can't remember the lines, but mostly I'm good at this—I'm too good. It scares me how good I am. R. thinks I'm the love of his life. He even said that. Despite the others, even the wife, it's still me he loves. But they've both changed. R with Vietnam, J with prison. Or is it something else. Something about me? They're both crazy. Ronnie thinks everyone is plotting against the government. James thinks everyone is plotting against the Panthers. Ronnie told me he has a contact in the OPD. Someone I should give information to. A big, burly guy. I met him once out at the track, name is Joey. James tried to talk to me. Do what I have to. Try not to get caught. Angry with me, but still a friend. Cares about me—but not enough. Hardly ever makes love anymore. It will never be the same.

After that, a few pages were ripped out. Then more scribbles, lists of books, notes she had taken at Maura's lectures. Nothing more. I read those last pages over again. Joey was a contact for Ronnie? Joey had known Grace? How much of this was a fantasy she created, how much was real?

255

A sound at the kitchen window, and I sat bolt upright. I reached in my shoulder bag and pulled out my revolver. The little gun was heavy, flat, cold in my hand. I heard the elevator door open down the hallway. Footsteps approached the door to Mike's apartment.

Mike's mother's number was scribbled on a pad by the telephone. I dialed it. After eight rings, someone picked up. "Who is this?" A sleepy voice. An older black woman.

"This is an emergency," I said. "I need to talk to Mike." The footsteps in the hallway creaked closer. Someone was breathing on the other side of the door. I prayed that Mike could get to the phone in a hurry.

"Hello?" Mike was barely awake.

"It's me. There's someone's standing at the door, I think they're trying to break in. I'm scared."

"Don't let anyone in. I'll be right there." He sounded completely awake now.

Someone was standing just outside the door. At the same time, it sounded as if the kitchenette window were being jiggled. My fingers tightened on the snubbie. I didn't dare check the peephole in the front door for fear someone else would enter through the kitchenette window. I pointed the gun, first at the door, then at the kitchen window, then at the door again. How unreal my first shooting practice with Joey had seemed, firing at images of men on a white paper target, firing toward the heart, the head, the knee. It had become real too quickly. At this moment I was fully able to kill another person. I would fire toward the heart, the head. Forget about the knee.

A car pulled up on the street below. I prayed that it was Mike. After a minute, the elevator doors in the hall opened a second time. Different footsteps in the hall. I swung my arm slowly from the kitchenette window to the front door. The double dead-bolts clinked as a key turned in the lock. The door opened and Mike walked in. I lowered the gun.

"Good Lord, Leah, what in hell is going on?" he asked.

I set the gun down and walked straight toward him. He put his arms out and I walked into them. I rested my head on his chest. I wanted to stay there forever. "What was it, Leah?" Mike asked, finally releasing me. "What happened? What was it you didn't tell me?"

"Grace had another diary," I said. "It shows Grace spied on the Black Panthers, for the government. Ronnie was involved. Someone must know I have this diary and they've followed me here."

"Jesus Christ, where did *this* diary come from?"

"I visited Maura Sayid earlier tonight. She was Grace's poetry instructor at UC Extension. She gave it to me."

"Why didn't you tell me about it before I left?"

"I didn't know what was in it. I wanted to read it first."

Mike switched off the lamp next to the armchair. In the darkness, a square of street light fell on the floor. He stood for a moment behind the living room draperies, surveying the street. Dropping down, he crouched his way to the window in the kitchen, looked down the fire escape. "I think we're okay. Anyone who was there probably decided to leave when I drove up. You should go to sleep. I'll stay up and keep an eye out." He walked from the window back to the Murphy bed on the wall.

"I won't be able to fall asleep," I said. I walked over to him, put my arms around him. That first hug at the door had been so comforting. "Come lie down with me." He unbuttoned his shoulder holster and lay down next to me. We turned to face each other. It was strange, seeing Mike up close, the texture of his brown skin, the short black hairs of his mustache, his even features.

He placed his fingers on my lips. "Don't talk. Don't talk about it now." He put his hands on my back, moving them down the knobs of my spine, with unexpected gentleness. I felt like a precious offering, something he would handle with the greatest care. Making love with Mike was slow and tender and passionate. We both knew it was temporary. We weren't thinking about where this would lead.

When I awoke at seven, early morning light filled the room. Mike lay next to me with his arms crossed under his head, Grace's journal folded open on his chest. "Did you read it?" I asked him, sleepily.

"Yes. It says a lot. But it doesn't prove anything. Grace was spying on the Panthers. That could be a motive for Ferguson to kill her."

"It implicates Ronnie. It shows that the US government is involved. I should give this journal to Art Leopold."

"Yes," said Mike. "We'll get it to Art. But we have to keep going with our plan. We'll go over to this Special Forces convention. Ronnie's the key. You'll get him to admit everything. The guy likes you. He's not expecting you to trap him. Get him drinking. Get him to tell you who murdered Grace. You'll get it all on a tape you'll carry in your pocket."

"It's dangerous. Maybe Ronnie's the one who's following me. You want me to be alone with that guy?" I touched my bruised ribs protectively.

"He might know about the notebook, but here's the beauty of the thing—he doesn't know what the notebook says. He'll think it says more than it does. That's how you'll trap him. Whoever's been following you," Mike added, "it's not the Black Panthers. Their means of obtaining information isn't that sophisticated."

"*How* will I trap him?"

"Act like you know he was involved in Grace's murder. If he wants the diary—use it as bait. Ronnie has always told you a lot. He told you he hated Grace—for having that abortion and dumping him afterwards. He told you about Vietnam and how the radicals don't have a clue what we were doing over there. Grace double-crosses him. When she's supposed to be spying on the Panthers for him, she's spying on him for the Panthers. He needs to tell his story. He'll talk to you. He knows you—he doesn't think you could hurt him." Mike patted my hand. "And you won't go anywhere without my knowing where you are. I'll be right behind you."

"He likes me," I admitted. But if Ronnie *had* killed Grace, why would he have any compunctions about getting rid of me? And Mike had been back up before. I remembered Carl Puckett's big muddy boot in my ribs. They were still sore.

Mike's voice was louder, more forceful. He was in command mode. "Don't mention the diary until he does," he coached. "But if he knows you have it, use it as blackmail. Tell him you'll give it to him—if he tells you who killed Grace. Pretend you already know who killed Grace, you just need to hear him confirm it. Act like you're attracted to him."

"Well, I *am* attracted to him." Now I had Mike's attention.

He unfolded his arms, turned his head sharply. "You're joking."

"No, I really was—" I started.

258

"Not that racist!" said Mike, sharply. "He's a white supremacist and a jerk," he added.

"We don't know for sure he's a white supremacist," I said.

"We sure as hell know he's a jerk," said Mike. He pushed himself up with an abrupt gesture. I watched his tight, muscled buttocks disappear into the bathroom. "Damn! I thought you had some sense," he said over his shoulder.

Was this a trace of male jealousy? First Mike described Ronnie as a guy who just wanted to tell his story, get a few things off his chest. So fond of me he'd spill all the information we needed—now, suddenly, he's a white supremacist and a jerk. I heard the shower running. When Mike re-emerged, dressed, he sat down on the side of the bed to put on his shoes. He seemed a bit more subdued. "Don't think two times on it, Leah. I guess I wasn't being fair to you."

We sat in the kitchenette, drinking coffee and eating toast, while Mike figured out the details of our trip to San Francisco. "I'll lock Grace's notebook in the trunk of my car," said Mike. "Anyone tries to break in here to get it, they won't find a thing. After you talk to Ronnie, we'll drop the diary off at Art Leopold's office."

"Shouldn't we drop it off at Art Leopold's first?"

"No time," said Mike. "We've got to get going. I'll call Art from the St. Francis while you're with Ronnie." Mike took a sip of coffee, then looked at me for several seconds before speaking. I waited. "You know, Leah, I've never been *involved* with a white woman before."

"Are you *involved* this time?" I said.

"Something is happening, but it shouldn't be happening. Not to us. Not now. I told you about Lily. We had words. But I'm still in love with her."

"Oh, right," I said. Our night together had erased Lily from *my* thoughts.

"My plan is to solve this case, get a promotion, finish law school. It would hurt Lily if she found out about last night. We take a break, and the very next night I'm in bed with a white woman."

"The very next night you're in bed with another woman, period," I corrected him. Just as with Edna, sometimes I was a real human being to Mike; other times I was just "white." A white woman, and none too welcome, either. It seemed that race always matters. "So what was last night all about?"

"This is all about finding out who murdered Grace," Mike answered. "Or did you forget?"

"Oh, right." Why was he talking about this Lily, and *his* hopes and dreams and ambitions—none of which included me? I stopped listening to what Mike was saying. Irreverently I thought of the gesture teen-age girls make, twirling their finger by their ear to indicate an interminable and boring phone call. I walked away. Unobtrusively I twirled my right finger toward the stream of words behind me, words like career, the future, his career, his future, the importance of this case to that future and that career, how we were very different people, how the important thing was the investigation, we had joined forces for the sake of the investigation. Nothing about the two of us so close an hour or two earlier. Nothing about the fact that soon I would face a psychopath who might be a killer. Mike was holding his coffee cup, staring at it as if it were his personal oracle. I would feel the pain of his words soon enough, and, remembering Helene Neville, I forestalled it.

"You have a good point, Mike," I said. "Like the birds, we should stick to our own species."

XXVIII

Mike and I hadn't spoken for the last ten minutes. We were on the free-way, heading toward the Bay Bridge. I was sorting through the roller coaster of emotions of the past twenty-four hours, how Mike had stroked my hair as we made love, how he had turned into a stranger in the morning.

Then I would flash on the violence with which Carl Puckett had flung Becky back against the credenza. The look of pure hatred he had given me. I remembered James Ferguson in Kanji's apartment, talking about Grace, with dusk falling; the intensity of our loneliness. And Grace's diary. Everything was violence and distrust, exacerbated by race and politics. Grace paid with her life, because she had ignored the barriers of race. And because she had crossed back and forth between political loyalties. I was replicating those conflicts, crossing lines I should not.

"Mike. Why are we doing this? Ronnie works with the government. Why are we going to mess around with him?" I was really asking myself.

"Because I'm crazy." More minutes passed, before Mike resumed. "OPD took me off the case. They ignored my notes, suppressed my evidence, had the balls to imply I was the problem. And all to jack up a brother to satisfy a bunch of racists. I'm mad as hell and I don't give a damn."

"You said you didn't like Ferguson."

"I'm a cop. I don't like cop killers. If Ferguson murdered Grace, that was one thing. If he didn't, that's something else. I don't want a brother going to prison for a crime some white cracker committed."

"Is that reason enough to risk our lives?"

"Your cousin Joey treated me like I was shit. Now we learn he was one of Ronnie's contacts on the police force." Mike drove with a ferocious focus.

"I had an uncle on the force," he continued. "One of the very first black officers. Got passed over and passed over and passed over. He was a heavy drinker. The white cops used that as the reason. That guy would take me fish-ing when I was coming up, talk to me like I was his buddy. Even back then, I knew there was more to it. He was drinking to be able to tell himself they had a reason not to let him get ahead. You know how many black men there are on

261

the force?" Without waiting for me to reply, he continued, "Fifteen. Out of seven hundred cops in the Oakland Police Department, fifteen are black. Two percent. The population of Oakland is almost half black. Yet fifteen crummy spots are all we get. I promised myself if the white man ever passed me over, I'd find a way to make him pay." He looked over at me again, "It's been five years. Seeing crap and taking crap. This is my way of dealing with it."

The suspension cables of the Bay Bridge flashed past us. An enormous oil tanker was moored in the shining waters of the bay. I didn't like this new Mike—his relentless drive, his personal vendetta. Yet I felt bonded to him, now more than before. The protection of his body, his rough tenderness, lingered as a visceral memory, despite his brutal words of the morning. Maybe I hoped to prove that I could come through for him even if I were white? And I thought of Grace. *I would have walked off a cliff for that man.* Were women always walking off a cliff for men out of sexual loyalty? As I was thinking this, Mike glanced over at me. "Hey, Leah. Maybe I was too harsh this morning. I like you. Hell, I like you a lot. It's just that—well—there's Lily, and . . . " His voice trailed off.

"You've already told me this," I said. "Lily would be so upset if she learned we were together last night."

"I want to make sure you don't get hurt." Why was it whenever men talked about not wanting to hurt you, that was exactly what they were about to do?

Mike laid his hand on my knee. "I was talking stupid this morning. I wasn't ready for all this to happen. Not so soon. We're heading into a situation right now that could be volatile. We have to be able to trust each other. Is there anything else you haven't told me?" His hand felt warm and possessive.

Whatever else happens, we've had this, I thought. Maybe it would all work out. "I think you've gotten everything important out of me now," I said.

Ronnie walked into the lobby of the St. Francis Hotel with a group of men in grey pants, white shirts, sports coats, and ties. Ronnie, too. Gone was the fringed leather jacket, the corduroy bell bottoms he'd worn when we met at Charlie Brown's. Even his hair was cut shorter. He was clearly a member of the establishment.

Mike and I were waiting for them. Mike sat in a corner with a newspaper in front of his face, half hidden by one of the enormous potted palms. I was wearing black pants, a red leotard top, a black jacket, red lipstick. I had slicked my dark, too curly hair back from my face. The plan was that I would bump into Ronnie as if by surprise, go for drinks with him, go up to his room. If I could make all this happen. Then I'd get him talking and record it all on the wire in the pocket of my pants.

The last time I had seen Ronnie he had been singing along to Don McLean's Bye Bye Miss American Pie on the jukebox at a restaurant in Chico. Then we'd driven back to Berkeley. Ronnie's chocolate lab, Lady, had pressed her nose against the rear window of the truck as if to check up on us. I had not been immune to his charm, but after he had pointed his rifle at me, I had promised myself never to be alone with him again. Looking up from his group of buddies, he spied me sitting on the satin-striped bench. His eyes went immediately to my legs.

"Leah! If we don't meet in the damndest places!"

"What are *you* doing here, Ronnie?"

"Friends from Nam," He said. "You?"

"I came over for lunch with a girlfriend. Then we did a little shopping at Joseph Magnin's." I smiled up at him, then crossed my legs, and straightened my spine, twisting my hips at the same time. "You know, Berkeley's starting to bore me, Ronnie. The city is *much* more sophisticated."

"*You're* looking pretty sophisticated," said Ronnie. "Whatever you've been up to, it's been a change for the better. So where's the friend?"

"Oh, she wandered off. I'll be heading home. I'm just waiting a little to see if she shows up."

"So you've got some time to kill?" said Ronnie. "Forget about your friend, let me buy you a drink. —Catch you guys later!" Things were moving faster than I had expected.

Ronnie steered me toward the restaurant off the lobby. We sat down at the bar. Bottles were stacked in front of a long plate glass mirror in which we could see our faces reflected back at us.

"What'll you have?" Ronnie was asking me.

"I'll have a Mimosa," I said.

"Orange juice and champagne? Well, that's a nice little breakfast drink," said Ronnie. "I'll make mine a Bloody Mary. Nothing like tomato juice to kick off the day. Now what can ole Ronnie do for you?"

I sighed dramatically. "I've got love problems, Ronnie."

"And I thought you didn't have a boyfriend," Ronnie drawled. "Although I guess that could be a problem in itself."

He smiled at my image in the mirror. Yet beneath the lazy drawl and the smile, I sensed his watchfulness.

"Things change."

"Nothing changes faster than a woman," Ronnie said.

"Like Grace changed?" I asked.

Ronnie's moved his elbow away from mine. Now his smile in the mirror looked guarded. "What is it with you, Leah? You're so hung up on Grace."

"Because she got to you first, I suppose." To be believable to others, you have to believe yourself. The strange part was at that moment I did believe what I'd said. My words were part of a truth I had not faced. I met Ronnie's eyes in the mirror. He laughed his raucous, country yelp.

"She got to me first, sure enough! But I always say, I don't care who came first, long as I'm last."

I laughed with relief. "You and Grace seemed so perfect," I said.

"First loves always seem that way," Ronnie said. He was still holding my eyes in his in our mirrored reflections. Under the table our knees brushed each other. My white face, bright red lips, wild dark hair, were reflected back at me. I looked glamorous, sexy. And Ronnie with his brown tousled mop of hair, his boyish grin, long arms and wide shoulders, was a cowboy paying court to the local beauty. Far down the bar I spotted a young black woman with short hair and enormous silver ear-rings. She was idly tapping a glass with a long, beautifully lacquered red nail. She looked familiar.

There was no time to think further on this. Ronnie was whispering in my ear, his lips tickling, sensuously. "Remember that poem I told you at Charlie Brown's that night?" he was whispering. "That was for you, you know."

I didn't know who had written that poem—Grace or Ronnie—but it had shown up in Grace's diary years before Ronnie said it out loud to me at Charlie Brown's. "I loved it," I said, going along with his lie. "When did you write it?"

264

"I made it up on the spot." Ronnie lies so carelessly, I thought. Does he think he won't get caught? This lie indicates he may make other mistakes.

"I wonder if I could help you to forget Grace." The brazen flirtation in my tone astonished me.

"Maybe," Ronnie said. He gave me a long, questioning look. "You're sure different from Grace." I raised my eyebrows. In the mirror I appeared flirtatious. "You're not slipping in and out of beds for one thing. I shoulda known what she was when she got with those bearded Berkeley fools."

"Joey mentioned a contract out on Grace's life." I segued into this, holding my breath.

"You mean that contract put out by those Aryan Nation fools? Those assholes are always ranting about something. Ninety nine percent of their talk don't amount to shit."

"You knew about it?"

"Yeah, I heard someone put out a contract, went to the Aryan Nation to see if there'd be any takers." Ronnie was loosening up. "Those guys wanted someone wasted. I never thought much more about it. If you're serious about killing someone, that's not how you do it. Aryan Nation guys aren't like Special Forces. Our guys know what the fuck they're doing."

"Were Special Forces involved?"

"Hell, no!" Ronnie drained his Bloody Mary and called for another. He was talking so loosely I wondered if he remembered who I was. "You think a trained professional would mess up like that? Whoever was involved, it was some local thug who did it. They botched the job."

They botched the job. The words rang in my head. Grace, his first love. "Didn't you warn Grace about that contract?"

"I was always warning Grace," Ronnie said angrily. "I can't count the times I told her to stay away from those black pimps."

"But it wasn't the Panthers who killed Grace," I said. "You just said— some local thug did it." The tape in my pants pocket was running. It occurred to me Ronnie knew all about tiny tapes that fit in a fountain pen or a pocket.

"I never believed it would happen."

"And when it did happen you knew it wasn't James Ferguson."

Ronnie moved the red-and-white plastic stick around his drink.

265

"Officers I knew in Nam were killed by motherfuckers like him. That was another war, Leah. Not just the one between us and the gooks. Niggers were killing white officers. It was a horror show."

"So back here—anything went?"

"War is war, no matter where you play it out."

"That's why you hung out with guys in the Aryan Nation?"

"You don't understand, Leah. I never really joined the Nation. I just informed on them." He watched my reaction.

"You informed on the Aryan Nation?"

"I was trained in Nam to get information out of people. It was my job." Ronnie watched me in the mirror. "I found out everything I could from Grace, too. She was a mess by the end, Leah. Uppers all day, downers at night. She would talk in her sleep, tell me her dreams in the morning. Just spill out her dreams to her ole buddy Ronnie." His green eyes sparkled, as if this were a wonderful joke.

"Didn't you care about her, Ronnie?"

"I had a job to do," he said. "Grace ignored my warnings." Ronnie drained his second Bloody Mary, stood up from the table. "There are more things I could show you. Let's go to my room."

A man was reading a newspaper a few tables over, but the paper hid his face. I hoped it was Mike. I was reminded of another evening, in this hotel, not that long ago, when I followed a man to his room. There was this difference. This time Mike Fisher was looking out for my physical safety.

Ronnie pulled me close to him in the elevator, seemingly oblivious of an older couple and a woman who got on at the same time. I could smell his scent, a mixture of citrus after-shave lotion and animal heat. "What I've always liked," he whispered into my ear, "is that I could never get anything out of you." The people in the elevator smiled and looked away. "Nothing!" Ronnie's breath tickled my cheek. He laughed a low laugh and kissed me under the ear. The doors opened and the other people in the elevator got out. He kissed me again on the mouth, a kiss of tenderness. Did Ronnie actually feel something for me? Did he like me enough that he wouldn't kill me, or allow someone else to?

The elevator doors opened up and Ronnie pushed me forward. He kept

266

his hand on my arm. At the door to the room, he slid the key into the lock, pulled me in, kissed me again. Full on the lips. "What are you all about, Leah?" he asked. His fingers touched my face, my neck, my hair. "I've never been able to get anything out of you. Of course," he murmured, "I never tried any of my professional techniques on you." He released me and flung himself on the couch, unbuttoning the top buttons of his shirt. "Want something to drink? Check that little mini-bar."

"I'll get us something." I poured myself a glass of ice water. For Ronnie, a glass of water and the contents of a micro-bottle of Jack Daniels. I handed him his drink. He pulled me close to him and put his hand around the nape of my neck. A sensation of heat and cold flashed over me.

"Yeah, Leah," Ronnie was saying, "I haven't been able to crack you. That's the thrill of my job, getting into a person's mind. It's a bigger thrill than getting into a woman's pants." I felt his fingers tighten again on my neck.

"Are you trying to scare me, Ronnie?' I asked, in what I hoped was a light, flirtatious tone. Mike had advised me to act the part of a girlfriend, a woman who was interested in Ronnie sexually. My stomach was knotted in fear. I didn't want Ronnie to sense that fear.

"If I wanted, I could put you out right now. Just this much pressure," he tightened his finger on a spot below my ear, "would do it."

"Is that how you killed Grace?"

He laughed, dropping his hand from my neck. "Hell, no!" he said, "You think I would mess up like that poor son of a bitch?" His eyes darkened. "Those men in the Nation, though, they were different. They were guys like me. Displaced. Fighting back. I could have been one of them."

"But you loved Grace. She wrote to you while you were in Vietnam."

"Yeah, she tore my baby outta her body, too, didn't she? Fucked that black bastard Ferguson. Kill a white baby, make a black one. Figure that one out."

He inserted his fingers into the pockets of my slacks, and took out the microscopic tape recorder. "You're cute, Leah," he said. "Pretty good for an amateur, but that's all you are. You think I wouldn't know about something like this?" He put the tiny device in his front shirt pocket. "You're just one lucky girl, Leah. I could do anything I wanted to with you. But your cousin on the force is a vet like me. So I hold back for Joey's sake."

His expression kept changing. One moment he was boyish, teasing Ronnie, the next moment menacing. I struggled to recall what a woman friend had once told me about an encounter with a rapist. *Treat the guy like a boyfriend. Treat the whole encounter as a romantic moment.* She kept telling the rapist how good it was. Asked him when could they see one another again. She had said, *you have to remember, no matter how sick and violent they are, underneath they're little boys looking for love.* She believed she had survived, because of this play-acting. So this was just me and good ole Ronnie—on a kinda weird date.

"Don't look so upset. You want to find Grace's killer? Sniff around at the track, find out who she left with." Ronnie lunged forward and turned a knob on a silver box the size of a small suitcase resting on the credenza in front of us. "Here, let me show you something." The portable television's small beam of light turned into an image of Ronnie and me, sitting there on the sofa.

"We're being taped?" I gasped.

Ronnie laughed. "Maybe. But that's not what I'm trying to show you." He turned the knob again. The screen went fuzzy for a moment, then flashed into black and white. A girl sat in a room. She looked nervous. She stood up, fumbling with her purse. Why was Ronnie showing this to me? I spoke as my mind registered the images. "My God," I said. "That's me."

"Yep, that's you. I can run the tape back a ways and show you making out on the bed with Jay Landis."

On the television screen the girl pointed a black handgun, shouting, *Don't come out of that room for thirty minutes, or I'll blow your skinny legs off.* I watched myself, awkward and out of control, the gun shaking in my hand. How had Ronnie gotten hold of this?

"We taped the whole damn thing," said Ronnie, watching me.

"But why?"

"Come on, Leah, get with it. You've been a problem from the start. You're always in places you shouldn't be. We had to find out what you knew. Along the way, you did a few stupid things." Ronnie ranged his long body into a more comfortable position on the sofa. "Which proved helpful. This was part of a side-project we had going in San Francisco. Project Mind Control. We wanted to see how that drug would affect you. We had no idea you had a gun in your purse, but there you were. Annie Fucking Oakley. Threatening one of our

268

snitches with that goddamn thing. The agent taping you was shitting in his pants, he was so scared you'd hurt his snitch. But then he got you on tape—he figured that would be worth something."

"You were going to blackmail me?"

"If necessary," said Ronnie. "By now we have enough on you to make you look unstable. And that fairy, Jay, was willing to say anything we wanted him to. We'd been blackmailing him ever since Grace got on to him. But he was supposed to get information *from* you, not be giving it *to* you. He told you too much. We realized the little fairy was unreliable. He lost value for us after that."

Ronnie had successfully trumped me. I heard Freddie Corster's words. *If you ever get your hands dirty, they've got you.* "You're disgusting," I said in a low voice. "You and whoever you work for."

Ronnie grinned. "I work for the US government. We make it a point to be good at what we do. You should be glad, Leah," he added. "We've discredited you so successfully that you're not a threat to us any more—as long as you hand over that diary."

"What diary?" I bluffed.

"The OPD found a page she had ripped out of her diary. Found it in James Ferguson's car the night she was murdered. We've been searching for it ever since. At first we thought she left it at your place. But we've searched your house."

I struggled to think ahead. Grace had written three notebooks. Ronnie seemed to think there was only one. Could I pass one of the other notebooks off on him?

"Bud told me Helene gave you Grace's diary. I searched your room a few times, but all I found was the autopsy report." Ronnie was still talking. "I knew Grace. She kept writing, even after Millie found her early diaries. Even after Millie beat her. We heard that professor calling you. We figure she must have given you something."

Ronnie knew a lot, but he didn't know everything.

"Yesterday you drove over to UC Berkeley," Ronnie continued. "You went into Maura Sayed's office. When you left, we lost you. You didn't go home after all. We found you later at Mike's place. We were planning to break

-in there and take the notebook. Then Mike showed up. A couple guys checked out Mike's place this morning, after you two left. Nothing there. It must be at Russell Street. So we're gonna drive over there and we'll pick the thing up."

"Yeah," I said. "You've figured out a lot." There were two diaries at Russell Street, and neither was the diary Ronnie wanted. That diary was in the trunk of Mike's car. Could I make Ronnie believe that one of the two diaries at Russell Street was the one he was looking for?

"We knew you were seeing Mike," Ronnie was saying. "Then he found the bugs in his apartment and destroyed them. So we couldn't hear what you two talked about last night. But it must have been about me—because you headed over here to talk to me today. You were full of information, and you tried to get more." Ronnie did not know what was in that diary. He did not know how much I knew. This was the point at which Mike had told me to bluff. Make a deal with Ronnie if I could.

"In case you still don't understand, Leah," Ronnie drawled, "let me clarify. Your friend Mike is down in room 1228. He's having a frank talk with one of my agents about what he's doing—snooping into matters which are out of his territory. If we don't come back with that diary in, let's say in two hours, I'm afraid those guys will lose patience. Mike could have an accident. Nobody will ever know it wasn't an accident. And with what we've got on you, no one will believe a thing you say."

"They'll kill Mike?" Was Ronnie bluffing? With Grace and Karella both murdered, I wouldn't risk Mike's life to find out.

"Direct killing's not our style," said Ronnie. He lounged on the couch, staring up at me with those inscrutable green eyes. "We get others to do it. The police. The Panthers. Local thugs. Maybe you heard about Fred Hampton, killed December 1969? That was the Chicago police. But it was our informant, Willie O'Neal, who gave them the floor plan."

I had seen Fred Hampton on the news a few days before he was killed. He had been young, vital, charismatic, shouting at a rally: *You can kill a revolutionary, but you can't kill the revolution!* "The man was asleep. It was a predawn raid. Cold-blooded murder."

"Not the first time," drawled Ronnie. "We fight fire with fire. The Panthers are a vicious group."

270

"Killing a man while he's sleeping in bed? I heard he'd been so drugged his friends couldn't wake him up when the shooting started."

"That was our agent slipped Hampton the drugs," said Ronnie. He looked proud. "We didn't want that spade too alert for what we hadda do."

"That's something you're proud of? And shooting his pregnant wife?" This is who I'm dealing with, I thought to myself. Remember this. Totally ruthless. But also cowards.

"Different times require different techniques," he said. It was as if he were teaching me. "The FBI old-timers just ruined reputations. Get the word out if someone was a member of the Communist Party. Get them black-listed. That's all it took. When we started dealing with the mob, it took stronger tactics. With the Panthers, stronger yet." Ronnie sounded sure he was on the right side.

"The Panthers build schools, Ronnie. They feed children." I was talking fast, buying myself time.

"That's not what they're about, Leah," Ronnie answered. "When King was assassinated in 1968, the Panthers tried to start a revolution. We had to go all out. Now we're developing other tactics. It's not hard to create factions. We've set it up so good, we've got Panthers at war with each other. We're past the point where we have to be that involved."

"Then why are you threatening Mike Fisher?"

"Once we pick up that notebook, I'll explain it all to you."

"It would look bad if anything happened to Mike or me. The newspapers are paying attention. Art Leopold knows where we are."

Ronnie smiled at me as if we were sharing a private joke. "Strange things happen in Panther cases," he said. "The public is getting used to it. When Fisher tried to call Leopold, one of our agents interrupted. Leopold doesn't know a damn thing. This has dragged on too long, Leah. We need to tie up the loose ends. I know you care too much about Mike Fisher to do anything to jeopardize his health." I could not mistake the menace in his words.

We drove back to Berkeley in Ronnie's pick-up truck. Ronnie's long fingers on the steering wheel moved restlessly, tapping with the wheel, touching the cigarette lighter.

We were headed to Russell Street, to my room, with its papers lying on the desk, with its messy closet. Grace had written three installments of her diaries. One was in the trunk of Mike's car. They had Mike, but they didn't have the diary Ronnie wanted. The other two diaries were stored away at Russell Street. Ronnie would not hurt me until he had the one he needed. My snubbie lay in the bottom of my purse. I struggled to devise a plan.

What would Joey tell me to do? "When you're in a bad situation, Leah, never let a motherfucker sense your fear. You know the guy's a nut, but act like he's normal. Distract him—and use that chance to save your life." Acting. Acting as if everything were normal—I was getting that message everywhere. Too bad for me, nothing was normal at this moment. Minutes were left to me. I had to reach Joey. Joey had been a link to the FBI and to Ronnie. He had also tried to warn me away from Ronnie. I had to trust that he would help me now. I sat up straight in the seat. "You were right about what happened," I said.

Ronnie raised an eyebrow. I knew I had his attention. "After I left Dwinelle Hall, I called Yoshi and gave him the diary. I told him to hide it. Let me call him to find out where he put it." We were driving in the center lane on the lower deck of Bay Bridge, drivers passing us on either side. The grey waters of the bay were choppy beneath us. Ronnie turned off at the Emeryville exit and pulled into a gas station. He turned to look at me. It was as if he was reading my mind. "I'll go in with you. I'll be listening."

I had hoped to call Joey, not Yoshi, but Ronnie was not going to let me dial the number myself. We walked into the convenience store with its vending machines and pay phones. Ronnie picked up the receiver, dialed a number, handed me the phone. "Hello?" I said. I prayed for Yoshi or Paul to pick up.

"Leah?" said Carol. "Where *are* you?"

"Is Yoshi there?"

"No."

"I need to talk to Yoshi, Carol. I'm on my way over with Ronnie."

"Ronnie? Why are you with Ronnie?"

"We ran into each other in the city," I said. "If Yoshi's not home, let me talk to Paul."

"This is all so strange, Leah," said Carol. "Always so melodramatic. So you're on your way over here?"

I wanted to scream at her, but forced my voice to assume a low, patient tone. "I'll explain when I get there, Carol. Please let me talk to Paul." I could see Ronnie at the coffee machine, holding a Styrofoam cup under the spigot. I was terrified he would turn around, yank the phone out of my hand, cut me off.

Through the handset, I could hear Carol's aggrieved tone. "Paul. It's Leah. Being mysterious again."

Then Paul's voice. "Leah? What's up?"

"I'm on my way over, with Ronnie. No news—good news—remember?" I said, keeping my eye on Ronnie. Ronnie turned, made a chopping motion with his hand. Cut it off. I dropped the receiver down hard in its cradle. Would Paul remember our old signal?

"I need to use the bathroom."

"If you're not out in sixty seconds, I'm coming in to get you."

I pushed open the swinging doors of the lady's room. There was no one there. I had only a few precious seconds. I pulled a paper towel from the holder, stuffed it in my pocket, walked into a cubicle. I couldn't find a pen, so I grabbed my brown eye pencil out of my purse. "Call Joey," I wrote, adding his home and work telephone numbers. The pencil smeared but the phone numbers were legible. I folded the paper towel into a compact square and stuffed it inside my bra. Then I flushed the toilet and opened the cubicle door. As the bathroom door swung open, I heard Ronnie's voice—"Leah!"

"Coming," I said. I caught a glimpse of myself in the mirror, white face, dark eyes, wild black hair. In the red leotard and black pants—despite my dishevelment—there was still something glamourous about my image. My new look had been part of a plan to be so alluring Ronnie would tell me everything. But Ronnie had been on to us all along. Ronnie stood outside the door, his arms crossed on his chest. I patted my lips with the tissue and smiled. "Sorry about that. Drinking alcohol so early always upsets my stomach."

Ronnie was sizing me up—the analytic look of a trained operative. He was no doubt asking himself what I had been up to in those sixty seconds that could cause him trouble. But his evaluation seemed to lead to a reprieve. I was lucky. Ronnie didn't give me much credit. He saw me as naïve and harmless. I had to use that to my advantage.

"Leah, there's nothing to worry about." He took my arm, steering me past the vending machines toward the entrance. "We need this diary to close this case. Once we have it, we won't need you anymore. You'll be able to finish up at Cal." The phrase—"we won't need you anymore"—reverberated through me. Was Ronnie going to have me killed? Or do it himself. He may have already made the decision, or others may have made it for him. Yet the possibility seemed unattached to any emotion. It was only a question, hanging in the space of my mind, waiting for me to use it.

We headed up Hollis Street toward Berkeley. I forced myself to breathe. Who should I give the note to? I couldn't give it to Carol. And what would happen when I handed over the diary? Ronnie might get violent, when he realized the notebooks weren't the ones he needed. But I couldn't think about that now. I had to find a way to get a message to Joey. We were on Ashby Avenue now, approaching Telegraph, less than a minute away from Russell Street. To the rest of the world, Ronnie looked like an easy-going guy with tousled brown hair driving his girl around in his pick-up. Ronnie glanced over at me, then leaned toward me and encircled my wrist with his hand. "I heard what you were saying on the phone," he said. He was still smiling, like an affectionate boyfriend. "What was that no news is good news shit?"

"It means nothing is happening," I said, smiling brightly back at him. "It's an expression we use around the house."

His grip on my wrist tightened. "You think you're smart, Leah," he said, "but if I have to, I can put you out—like that." He let go of my wrist, but his right hand reached behind my neck. "Just remember, this is the US government you're playing with."

How easily men could snap wrists and fracture women's ribs. If Ronnie applied the very slightest pressure in the right place, I would become unconscious. I thought of Grace's words in her diary—"The things he's done in Vietnam." Right now, I reminded myself, act like he's normal. Don't show any fear. "You don't scare me, Ronnie," I said. "I know you're fond of me."

"Yeah, I'd hate for what happened to Grace to happen to you," Ronnie said. If Ronnie were in love with me, he might want to keep me alive. But he had expressed no remorse about Grace. We turned left on Telegraph, right on Russell Street. Could I get away from him after I had handed over the diary? "Ain't no use, Leah," Ronnie said. He had an uncanny way of guessing what I was thinking. "We've won this one. We got witnesses saw you making out with me in the elevator earlier. Nothing you say will mean a goddamn thing."

"I'm just trying to think where Yoshi may have put that diary. If he's not home to tell us himself." Ronnie parked the car and got out to accompany me into the house. I would not be able to use the telephone there.

Carol opened the front door. She had been waiting for us. Her eyes fastened on Ronnie. He laid a hand on her shoulder. "Hi, Carol," he said, easily pivoting her to one side to stand directly behind me. "Yoshi home?"

"Not yet. You could wait for him in the living room."

"No time, hon," said Ronnie, flashing his smile at her. "Leah and I have a little errand to take care of upstairs." Carol's face fell. "Look, I'll call you later and explain it all," said Ronnie.

The sliding door to the downstairs bedroom opened. Paul stepped out, staring first at me, then at Ronnie. "What's going on, Leah?"

"Ronnie and I are here to pick something up," I said. "Has there been any news?" I was trying to remind Paul of our code. I fixed my eyes on Paul's, willing him to understand. Call Joey, call Joey, call Joey, I tried to communicate. I had to give him the note tucked in my bra. Ronnie was pushing me ahead of him, so that I had to squeeze past Paul's boxer's belly. With Ronnie at my back, I managed to pull the note out of the V-neck of my leotard and drop it just inside Paul's room. My heart was pounding.

At the bottom of the stairs Carol stood staring at us. Ronnie pushed me forward. "Let's move it, Leah," he said. Carol's face was turned toward Ronnie. Ronnie pushed me up to the landing. I looked back, seeing Carol's pink moon face staring at us with a bewildered expression. I could feel Ronnie's breath behind me, following me step by step.

"The diary is in one of two places," I said, willing myself to speak slowly. "Yoshi most likely put it in my room. Let's look in there first."

Downstairs I heard Paul close the sliding doors of his room. Would he see the note inside the door? I made a show of checking books and notebooks on my desk, shouting back down the stairs toward Carol. "Did Yoshi say when he'd be back?" Ronnie shook his head at me, silently, but, as I had hoped, this was the opportunity Carol needed. I heard her steps on the stairs; then she was at the door to my room.

"What are you two up to, anyway?" She walked right into my room. "Can I help?"

"Leave us alone, Carol," he said. The mischievous tone was gone. He was stymied. He took a deep breath. It was the diversion I needed. I stepped into my closet, pulled the snubbie out of the bottom of my purse, and shoved it in the pocket of my jacket. I could hear Ronnie. "We don't need any help, Carol." I heard her footsteps moving around the room. I stood up in the closet, pulled open the top drawer, rummaged through it as Ronnie peered in. "Any luck?" he said, casually, for Carol's benefit.

"No," I said. "Let's check his room." I half expected Ronnie to reach in my jacket pocket and grab the gun, as he had grabbed the tiny tape recorder earlier in the afternoon.

"I need to talk to you, Ronnie." There was a plaintive note in Carol's voice.

"Not now," he barked at her, all pretense of informality dropped. A bad sign. "I told you not to disturb us." After a moment I heard her footsteps descend the stairs. Ronnie, in his tie, white shirt, sharp black pants, looked totally out of place in my room with its orange Mexican rug, Gauguin prints, Indian bedspread. I brushed past him. "I'm going to check Yoshi's room."

He followed me, closing the door to Yoshi's room behind us. I opened Yoshi's closet. Sure enough, the manila envelope with Grace's teenage diary was on the floor, under a pile of dirty underwear and jeans. A strong green aroma filled the closet. Yoshi was hiding his stash of weed somewhere in there.

"Here it is," I said. Ronnie grabbed it from me. He was flipping through the pages. "I have to use the bathroom," I said. I locked the bathroom door, turned on the water in the sink. Then I attached the gun in its ankle belt to my foot. It was invisible under my black slacks. Now I had the gun. I flushed the toilet and re-emerged with a bright smile.

Ronnie stood in Yoshi's bedroom door, the diary open in his hands. He motioned with his head, angrily. "Don't you go anywhere, unless I say so," he hissed, shutting the door again. He leaned his lanky frame against the door. I moved as far away from him as I could. Yoshi's room was a small annex with a back door that led down an outside staircase to the garden. Should I run for it? Or pull the snubbie and shoot Ronnie? If I did that, would I be killing Mike? What would Joey recommend? *Distract him, Leah,* I could hear Joey's voice, advising me. *The more time you spend in Yoshi's bedroom, the more time Paul has to reach me.*

"Find anything?" I asked Ronnie, willing my voice to sound interested.

Ronnie looked up from the diary. His face had changed. He wiped his hand against his forehead, then sat down on Yoshi's bed. "What a shitload of memories," Ronnie said. It was as if the trained killer had dropped away to reveal another person. "Two crazy kids—made crazier by the times. Grace was right to leave me. I was nuts by the time my mom left my dad." His voice and expression were those of a lost teenager. I could grab my gun now, shoot him, make a run for it out the back door. But there was Mike. Did they really have him? I took a step forward.

He stood up immediately, grabbing my arm, yanking my wrist downward, hard. "No, you don't," he said. It was the other Ronnie now, eyes cold and alert. "I was crazy then, but it took Vietnam to make me a killer," he said. "This notebook is the notebook Helene gave you. Where's the one you got yesterday?"

I shrugged. "There's another one, here somewhere."

Ronnie opened the door with one hand, pushed me ahead of him, picked up the hall telephone and dialed a number. He kept his hand around my wrist. "Don't mess with me, Leah," he said. "I can interrogate you in ways you wouldn't like. Hey," he said, into the receiver. "Yeah, it's me. I have something, but it's not what we want. —What?" He was silent for a minute. His right hand gripped my wrist. I knew I would not withstand Ronnie's techniques of intimidation. What could I do next? Should I tell him where the third notebook was—the one he really wanted? which was in the trunk of Mike's Plymouth parked in the Union Square parking garage? "Right," Ronnie was saying into the phone. "I'll be right there." He hung up the phone and looked at me. "Mike told my people where the car was. We searched it. We've got the notebook."

My time had run out. "We won't need you anymore"—Ronnie's words rang in my ears. Ronnie had his hand on my shoulder. He was pushing me ahead of him down the stairs. "We're walking back to my truck, Leah. I'm right behind you, and I'm armed. No saying anything to your roommates as we leave—just leave the explaining to me. I'll hurt you, if I have to. We're going back to the St. Francis," Ronnie said. "I have to read that damn thing. If it's what I think it is, we'll let you go. But for now, just keep moving."

Carol stood at the bottom of the stairs. She seemed forlorn, her mouth half-open like a fish. "Did you find what you were looking for?" she asked.

"Yes," said Ronnie, briefly. He was prodding me from behind. "Where's Paul?"

"He went out," said Carol.

"Well, me and Leah gotta run," Ronnie said. "I'll call you later and explain everything." Carol watched us. Ronnie yanked me around to the driver's side of the truck, opened the door, shoved me roughly inside, pushing me over the gearshift. I sat in silence as we drove back to San Francisco, staring out the window. Cars passed by. The late September sun glared blindingly on their chrome bumpers. I glanced at the drivers passing us on the bridge. Could they not see my terror? See the driver was a psychopath, trained in torture and interrogation? Could I die on a day like today, a day that was nothing special?

Ronnie was chatting. What was he gearing himself up to do? Or to order someone else to do? What was he going on about? "You noticed I have a pull with Carol?" he was saying.

"I noticed," I said. I needed to keep playing my role, the girlfriend of the weird guy beside me. "I'm surprised she would get involved with you after everything she said to *me* about seeing any of Grace's boyfriends."

"It's different for her," said Ronnie. His long restless fingers guided the wheel expertly; we were almost at the Fifth Street exit. "She never knew Grace." He gave me a sidelong glance. "And she thinks she's smarter than you, Leah. And she's good in bed, too. She likes me." He sounded triumphant.

"She probably thought you were a good ole boy. Like her cousins."

"And I am, Leah! I am!" He seemed happy. "Carol told me what she knew, but she couldn't tell me where the diaries were. She helped me ransack your room one day—couldn't find anything. I slipped a bug in your room while I was at it. I heard a lot, but never enough. That's why I admired you. You're one of the few cases I couldn't crack."

"Does Carol know who you work for?"

"Of course she doesn't know. I told her to keep our thing a secret. She thought I'd chosen her over you, and your feelings might get hurt."

"You're kidding!"

"Well," he glanced at me. "Haven't you always had a soft spot in your heart for ole Ronnie boy?"

Good, this was what I wanted him to think. "Why did she think you wanted Grace's diary?"

"Curiosity. About my old girlfriend, Grace."

278

I remembered what Mike had said. They all want to tell someone their story. They need to confess. I would keep Ronnie talking. "So all this time you've been an informant," I said. "Paid to investigate me and my friends."

"I'm far above an informant," Ronnie said. "The informants work for me. You heard about Cointelpro? J. Edgar Hoover started Cointelpro in 1967, after Huey Newton and Bobby Seale founded the Panthers. Right after the summer of the Detroit riots—Hoover started the Ghetto Informant Program at the same time. Get into the community, find out what's happening. Those are your informants, Leah, a lot of nickel-and-dime junkies who would sell their own momma for a bag of heroin. You gotta know how to handle guys like that."

"How did you get into this line of work?" I asked. Keep him talking. I could almost hear Joey's voice, guiding me.

"Vietnam," said Ronnie. "The Phoenix program, remember? I had to flush out Commies over there. That job was for men with balls. Sometimes we threw them out of helicopters to see if they'd bounce. You might call it torture. We didn't. We called it, whatever it took. Once you're trained like that, the government wants to keep you. I'm very good at what I do."

Say anything, I reminded myself. He wants to tell his story. "How can you live with yourself, Ronnie?"

"It's not always easy," Ronnie answered. "But it's necessary. You remember me warning you that day we drove up to Chico? That it's a war over here? You want a bunch of thugs running the country?"

"A bunch of thugs *are* running the country," I said.

Ronnie laughed. "They're *our* thugs. We may have to lie low for a while. Watergate is tying our hands. A couple of years ago antiwar protesters broke into one of our field offices and leaked files to the press. Hoover had to stop the program then. Now Hoover's dead. We have to be a little more careful. But it doesn't matter. When it comes to the Panthers, the best are gone. We've got people in key positions, factions that kill each other, leaders strung out on drugs—they're egomaniacal and paranoid as hell. They're finished."

He could dismiss torture and murder and betrayal that easily. I was frightened, but I was also angry. "You've made a few mistakes," I said. "There are cops investigating this murder. There's the newspaper stories. Art Leopold has information."

"Oh, you threw us a few curves, Leah," said Ronnie. "But how hard do

279

you think this will be? Take your communal friends—everyone of them has a chain we can yank. Your friend Yoshi could be extradited back to Japan in a second. You think it's some fluke he's having problems with his visa?"

"Yoshi's been working with you?" I couldn't bear to think this of Yoshi. Was this why he had been gone today?

"Hell, yes. But he's been giving us bogus stuff—trying to fool us. We could pull his visa for that shit. Your friend Paul is tougher, but he has a bad habit of getting into fights with cops. We could easily set up another confrontation where he ends up in jail. Or dead. And your friend Carol would be a pushover. I would just use my relationship with her against her," Ronnie added. He wasn't mentioning me. Was that because he wasn't planning on my being in the picture at all? As if he read my mind, Ronnie smiled again. "Everybody figures Art Leopold's gonna speak for his client. As for your poetry professor, she's Lebanese. An A-rab. The A-rabs killed a dozen Israeli athletes two weeks ago. You think anybody in this Jew-infested town's gonna pay any attention to what an A-rab has to say?"

Ronnie pulled into the garage under the St. Francis. He jumped out and opened my door, walking beside me through the cavernous reaches of that dark place, my arm in his iron grip. In a far corner he reached in his pocket for a key which unlocked a service elevator, then pushed me inside. My mind was racing as we ascended in the elevator. This was my last chance. Should I bolt once the doors opened, run, start pounding on any hotel door?

The elevator doors opened onto the fourteenth floor. A black man in a blue housekeeping uniform was leaning over an ice machine, his back toward me, scooping ice into a plastic bucket. I stepped out quickly and turned toward him. "Help me," I whispered urgently. "Help me, please!"

He turned around. Ronnie was on me in seconds, his hand pressing something hard into my waist. "Come on, honey," he said in indulgent tones. He nudged what was probably the barrel of his automatic deeper into my waist. "My wife," he said to the housecleaner, apologetically. "She lost the baby. She's confused."

The man's eyes were fixed on mine. My eyes beseeched him to stop, to ask some questions, but he turned away. "Take it easy, lady," he said, without looking at me.

We reached Room 1441. Ronnie inserted his key into the door. Ronnie shut the door behind us and turned to me. "You remember, I told you Freddie saw Grace leave the track that Sunday morning with someone?" he said.

"I remember. Yes." I looked around the room. Where was Mike?

"They saw her leave with me," said a deep voice behind me. Startled, I spun around. Wilson Tyler padded into the room, slowly, like a big cat, prodding Mike in front of him at gun point. "I left with Grace. And I killed the bitch."

"Wilson Tyler," Ronnie said. "He's your man."

Wilson Tyler was here in Ronnie's hotel room. Not in Oakland, not with James. Wilson Tyler motioned Mike down on a chair. Then he sank down on the sofa, his black semi-automatic pointing at Mike. "Let's talk about this diary of Grace's—the one that told you all this shit you ain't supposed to know," Wilson Tyler said.

The first time I had seen Wilson Tyler at Vinnie's Inn, I thought he was one of Grace's friends. He had been at a back table. The second time I saw Wilson Tyler had also been in Vinnie's Inn, the day I'd been set up by an anonymous phone call. Wilson and Ollie had been James Ferguson's back-up guys. I had seen him a third time at the George Jackson Clinic, the day of the Lighthouse brawl. Now Wilson Tyler, James Ferguson's right-hand man, a trusted Black Panther, was here, with Ronnie.

"You were that high up in the Panthers," I said to Wilson Tyler. "And you turned on them."

"That's nothing," Ronnie said. "We got people higher up than Tyler, more trusted, too. We've had Black Panther chapters with more informers than members."

"You and James were like brothers," I said to Wilson.

"That's not something you'd understand, is it?" Wilson sneered. "Ten percent blacks in America. Thirty-three percent blacks in the American forces in Vietnam. Guess how many in the front lines in Vietnam? Sixty-six percent. Some brothers have gone through hell for this country. I hate folks who mess with it. It feels to me like they don't give a shit about me."

His animosity shook me. He looked different today. The way he was dressed: pleated grey slacks, blue shirt open at the neck, black leather wingtips. If it were not for the acne pits on his strong-featured face, he would be a good looking man.

281

"We've got the diary, and we'll get James on something else," added Wilson. The cold smile on his face was one of hatred.

I put it together now. "You killed Karella."

"She was talking too much. I couldn't trust her anymore."

"But she was implicating Ferguson, not you."

"She was implicating Ferguson because Tyler told her to," Ronnie broke in. "She was Tyler's woman. A lot of Panthers knew that. We were just waiting for you to find that out. Everything she told you was true—about Tyler, not Ferguson. She was crazy about Tyler, but those drugs in her got her talking too much. Tyler didn't have a choice." Ronnie smiled at me. That old sweet Ronnie smile. Then he reached into his pocket. I wondered if he was going to pull out his revolver and shoot me.

"Here, Leah," he said, "After all your snooping, read this. The last page of Grace's diary—we found it in the glove compartment of Ferguson's car." He handed a piece of paper to me, with a raggedy left edge as if pulled out of a spiral notebook. Grace's handwriting, the same neat little script I had read all night. I glanced at it. My heart was racing. The gun was tucked inside my ankle holder. Could I go for it? Mike was quiet, but I could sense he was looking at me. We had a chance. Just maybe, we still had a chance. I read the note aloud.

> I'm going to bet those tips that Freddie and Timmons gave me. I'll give the winnings to James. Maybe he'll want us to escape together. Maybe in Europe it would be different. I have to tell him that Ronnie has another informer in the Party. It's his friend. Wilson Tyler.

Tyler stood up and moved toward me, smiling. He kept his handgun aimed at Mike. I looked at Mike again, trying to meet his eyes, looking for a sign. "Stupid white cunt," Tyler was saying. He said it with a mixture of triumph and hatred. "Trying to mess us up. One of our people killed because of her. I might have been next. I can still see the way she strutted out to the car that day, all that money in her purse. She thought she was getting over."

I, too, could imagine the proud way Grace would have walked, ten thousand dollars in her purse, and a wild hope in her heart. I could see the jaunty bounce to her step, that bravado she maintained, day after day. And then, when she saw James' Buick in the parking lot—didn't that hope flare even higher? When she saw the tall dark man in the driver's seat, didn't she think James was back? To forgive her? And when Wilson Tyler turned his head—not James—but Wilson Tyler? Did it hit her then?

"I told her I'd been sent for her. By James," Wilson was chuckling. "I had been sent for her, all right, but not by James. I'd been sent by the US government to get rid of her white trash self." Wilson's eyes blazed.

Grace may have believed him—or was she by that time beyond caring? The night before James had been enraged enough to tighten his fingers around her neck. She may have realized then there was nothing left for them. She had given James information. James had ordered a man killed as a result. Billie Thomas, the black man who had been Joey's informant, was now dead because of her. Even giving the Panthers information had not saved her. When she looked into Wilson Tyler's eyes, did she know then?

"We figured she named me in the diary," Tyler continued. "Looks like she never got that specific until the end of it. Unfortunately for you, though," he said, looking at me, "you've seen and heard too much."

I was desperately stalling for time. "So who is Ruby Bailey?" I asked. "Was she in on it, too?"

"Ruby Bailey?" Wilson Tyler gave a deep, satisfied chuckle. "The sister works for me, girl. She's just *one* of my women. Waitin' for me in the lobby right now. She and Karella were sittin' with me in Vinnie's back in July when you came in there with Grace. I always wondered if you'd remember and put the pieces together. But, nah, you were never as smart as you thought you were." So the woman at Vinnie's, with the big Afro and huge silver earrings, had been Ruby Bailey.

"Tyler's tough. He pushed gooks out of copters in Nam, just like I did," Ronnie interrupted. Ronnie's smile of pride could not have been broader if Tyler had been his own special protégé. "He killed Grace with two shots to the head and beat her afterward with an iron pipe to fool the cops. Tyler gets the job done."

Grace had gotten into Ferguson's car and had let Wilson Tyler drive her to a spot overlooking the bay. When she looked away, he shot her. Two shots to the head. Killed her instantly. Mike had read this in the first autopsy report. Then Tyler had done his other grisly work to make it look like a crime of passion. He beat her bloody with a metal pipe. Then he went through her soft red

283

leather wallet and took out her winnings. Ten thousand dollars. Meant for James and the Party.

All through this case I had seen men take out their aggression on women, any woman, rather than on another man. What had Wilson Tyler been feeling as he bludgeoned a woman's dead body? Hatred for her betrayal of his colleague? Hatred for her betrayal of James and of Ronnie? Or hatred for a white woman, because Wilson Tyler hated the white people who had taught him to kill so efficiently?

Wilson Tyler had put her body in the trunk. He was supposed to turn the Buick over to James that afternoon. Then police would stop James and find Grace's body. But Clyde Turner had called James. The clinic had been broken into, and Clyde needed Security right away. James had left the DeFremery Park rally. At midnight, Tyler was worried. Ronnie told him what to do. Tyler drove to the empty parking lot near Golden Gate Fields and dropped the body in the water. They figured someone would find it at daybreak. James' gun was tossed in the bushes, its barrel removed, then destroyed, since it wouldn't match the bullets in Grace's body.   Wilson placed Grace's wallet in the glove compartment. James' fingerprints were in the car, on the gun. Grace's blood was all over the trunk of James' car. Karella found Grace's wallet in the glove box and filched it. She became a danger to Tyler.

OPD convinced the assistant coroner to expand the estimated time of death. Witnesses had seen Grace leave Eli's Mile High Club with James Saturday night. Grace had gone to the race track late the next morning, but, wearing a head scarf and dark glasses, there was a chance no one would have known it was her. Freddie Corster had recognized her, but he could be intimidated into saying he had seen Grace get into the car with James Ferguson.

Wilson Tyler had done what he had been trained to do. Follow orders, complete a task. Unfortunately, for Wilson Tyler, for Ronnie, for the OPD— there was also me. I was with Grace Saturday night. I was in possession of a betting slip for the next day at the track. I had talked to Karella.

And there was also Mike, who had found the body first, responding when he heard the call on his police radio. Mike had noticed discrepancies in the body's condition and the newspaper reports. Mike had pinpointed the time of death accurately.   When the two of us teamed up and shared what we knew, we became too dangerous.

"Ron, remember your scripture?" Tyler was asking. He was talking to Ronnie, but looking at me. "Ecclesiastes. And the talebearer shall be defiled and be hated by all. Grace was a talebearer. This one is too." Tyler fastened a silencer onto his handgun. "Let's get rid of the talebearers."

"Flip a coin, Ron," he said to Ronnie. "Which of us gets the white girl?"

"Leave her to me," Ronnie said.

"Okay," said Wilson Tyler, kicking Mike with his toe. "Then you and I will just have a little fun. Get up and walk your black ass into that bathroom." Mike rose, with Tyler's gun in the small of his back. "Just git your black ass moving."

"No!" I shouted. I reached down, fumbled with my ankle holster, withdrew my snubbie.

"No, you don't!" said Ronnie to me. He knocked the Colt out of my hands, and grabbed me by the shoulders, pushing me down on the sofa. He put his gun to my head. I could hear Mike shouting, from the bathroom, "I'm a police officer, Tyler! You can't kill a cop! You'll get the death penalty."

Tyler was kicking the bathroom door closed, but as it shut, I saw two lightning flashes, heard a thump as something heavy hit the floor. After a minute, Tyler emerged. "Your lover boy detective is history," he said.

"No!" I shouted again, as if my voice could stop what was happening.

"It's because of you, Leah," said Ronnie. His hand was on my neck, his gun pointed at my head. "Mike wouldn't have been here today, if it hadn't been for you." His face wore a strange look, as if I were a beloved child who had misbehaved. "As a result of your misdeeds, we have to get rid of you. If only you had let matters be," he said, sadly, "so that we could have just done our job the usual way."

"No!" It was as if my voice belonged to someone else, someone hysterical and panicked.

Tyler turned. "I'm outta here," he said, placing his gun in an inside jacket pocket. "You got this?" He nodded toward me.

"I'll take care of our friend here."

"Good," said Tyler. He moved toward the door. "I'll send over some clean-up people to take care of the bodies."

I was struggling to think. Joey said, *Never show fear*. Now that Tyler was gone, maybe I had a chance. "Come on, Ronnie," I said. "You and me have an understanding."

Ronnie looked at me tenderly. "We do have an understanding, Leah. You're a straight-shooter, unlike that two-timing Grace. But you see my problem," he said. "Tyler only did what he did to make Grace's death look like a crime of passion. What people like you never see, Leah, is that Grace and her Black Panther boyfriend are a threat to the internal security of this great nation of ours." Ronnie pulled out of his pocket what looked like a drug prescription bottle. He opened it and took out a tiny black tab.

"What's that?" I asked. *Show no fear*, Joey's voice reminded me.

"Cyanide. It will put you out in seconds, no trauma, no pain. You'll just drift into the blissful arms of death. Leah. Make it easy on yourself."

"You expect me to swallow that?"

"It's either swallow this, or get two bullets in the head, like your friend in the bathroom. Believe me, Leah, it's painless." Ronnie set the little vial and the tab on the side table. Yellow lamp light gleamed on the shiny black tab.

I stared into Ronnie's green eyes as I walked toward it. So this is how it would end for me. With Ronnie's eyes on me like the eyes of a lover, his hands holding a gun on me, the hands of a killer. I reached toward the deadly little pill. A light tapping came from the direction of the door. I looked up.

"Shhh!" Ronnie put his finger up to his lips. Ronnie moved swiftly and silently to the door and peered through the peephole. After a few seconds, he jolted backward and rushed back to me, grabbing me from behind, and putting his gun by my head. "Don't make a sound," he whispered. He was breathing heavily, his voice was husky and low. I realized Ronnie was afraid. I had thought he was incapable of fear. More taps, a little louder. A voice.

"Leah, are you in there?"

Ronnie tightened his grip, pulling up his arm to encircle my neck. The seconds ticked away, timed with my heart beat. Ten seconds. Twenty. Thirty. A minute. The window of time which could save my life was ebbing away. Just as Ronnie began to relax his hold on me, the tapping resumed. It was a loud knock knock knock. "Leah, are you in there? This is Joey!"

"Joey, he's got a gun!" I tried to pull away, but Ronnie slapped me on the left side of my head with the barrel of his gun. The blow sent me falling to the floor. A wave of blackness engulfed me. I fought my way back to consciousness, crawling away from Ronnie.

"Let her go, Ronnie! She has nothing to do with this!" Joey's voice bellowed from the other side of the door, as he began to use his 270-pound frame as a battering ram, slamming it repeatedly into the door. "Ronnie! Did you hear me? I know you're in there!" grunted Joey, as his weight hit the door again and again. The door shook and rattled with each thud. Ronnie raised his gun, aiming toward the door. Suddenly the door cracked open with one loud slam, and Joey was in the room.

Ronnie fired, grazing Joey's neck. He fired a second time, hitting him squarely in the ribcage, knocking my cousin on his back. I pushed myself up off the floor and lurched forward, grabbing Ronnie's arm, trying in vain to wrestle the gun from him. He was shaking me like a rag doll, but somehow I held on to his arm, scratching his neck, biting his hand. Ronnie slammed me against the wall so hard I fell to the floor. The blackness washed over me again, and again I struggled to remain conscious.

Ronnie stepped back, catching his breath, then raised his gun. He was going to shoot me in the head. A shot rang out, but not from Ronnie's gun. It came from the direction of the door. Joey, on the floor, had managed to fire his .38 revolver at Ronnie. Ronnie stumbled back, clutching his gut. Blood the color of tomato sauce oozed over his sharply creased grey pants. Joey sat with his back propped up against the broken door frame.

I saw the shock in Ronnie's face as he looked down at the blood staining the grey slacks. "Goddamn it! Fuck!" he cursed, raising his gun. But he was too late. Another one of Joey's .38s slammed into his chest. He stumbled back against the side table as Joey fired again. Ronnie was knocked backward, doubled over in pain. There was a burning sensation in my chest every time I took a breath; my mouth was dry. I was sweating, struggling to stay alert. As if frozen in time, I watched the little black cyanide capsule roll slowly off the table and land on the rug.

I managed to get over to Joey. He was holding a handkerchief against his chest, red with blood. "Get over to Ronnie," he gasped. "Get his gun." I stumbled back across the room and pulled at his shoulder. He took one last breath and was still, slumped on the rug.

Through the half-open door I saw a clutch of policemen with walkie-talkies jump out of the elevator and run toward us. A crowd was starting to gather in the hallway; faces peeked in the door.

"Somebody call an ambulance!" I shouted. The security guards milled around, muttering into walkie-talkies. Joey was sitting in a chair, pressing a pillow against his chest. "Call a fucking ambulance," I screamed.

"Get medics up to Room 1441," he barked into his transmitter.

The next moments were a confused blur. I sat next to Joey, holding his shoulder. Two medics arrived and were bending over him. "You're lucky, man," said one. "You're gonna get all fixed up. It's nasty, but you'll make it outta here, which is more than I can say for a couple of the others."

I saw them place a figure on a stretcher. It was Ronnie. "One two three—stand away," one medic shouted. They all jumped back.

At that moment I glanced up. Wilson Tyler stood framed in the open door, his eyes widening. He looked hard at Ronnie's lifeless body and then spotted me. Our eyes met for a long moment. Then Tyler disappeared into the crowd.

The medics lifted Joey into a stretcher and wheeled it into the elevator. Downstairs an ambulance was waiting at the hotel's back entrance. I rode to the hospital with Joey, holding his hand the entire way, while the medics held ice bags to my head, checking me out for a possible concussion. They told me that Joey had lost a lot of blood. The bullet was lodged between his ribs. In the emergency room, Joey was wheeled into surgery immediately to remove the bullet. The medics replaced the ice bag on my head, warned me not to fall asleep—what my body most wanted. But my mind insisted I stay awake to find out what was happening to Joey.

Images had been fast-forwarding in my mind all afternoon. Ronnie demonstrating how easily he could take me out, placing his long fingers against the pulse in my neck. The two flashes of light from the bathroom. It seemed to me that I fell in and out of consciousness. I was reclining on a fold-out chair in Joey's room, waiting for him to be wheeled back from Surgery. Then suddenly he was back, and a doctor told me he would be fine. Doctors, nurses, cops—people seemed to be coming in and out of the room. I kept dozing off. When I awoke, several hours later, it was just me and Joey in the room. He had an IV in his arm. He was looking out the window.

One question kept pounding at me—what was Joey's role in all this?

"For God's sake, Joey, tell me what happened?"

"Try to stay calm, Leah. Please. We'll talk later. You need to get some rest." I spent the night half-dozing in the chair, unable to sleep. The only media coverage of the shoot-out was a brief article buried in the local news section of the Oakland Tribune. It was written by Miss Ruby Bailey. On Tuesday, September 26, the bodies of two men were found shot to death in Room 1441 of the St. Francis Hotel. They were subsequently identified as Ronald Xavier Jones and Michael Fisher of the Oakland Police Department. Police were investigating, but they thought the incident may have been a drug transaction gone wrong. Why the Tribune had picked it up, and not the Chronicle nor the Examiner, I had no idea.

XXIX

On Wednesday afternoon Joey was discharged from the hospital. A familiar miasma of yellow-grey pollution hung over the East Bay. By the time we pulled into his driveway in Alameda, my head was pounding. Joey's front yard was covered with sparse yellow grass, and a twisted cypress softened the outlines of his sterile stucco bungalow. An unwatered dracaena drooped in a red clay pot on the front steps.

Joey settled me on his living room couch and set a plastic prescription container on the coffee table. "Take two of these, Leah," he said, arranging an old brown afghan around my shoulders. He went into the kitchen, returning with two glasses and a quart of Jim Beam. He poured us each a shot, and took a seat in his recliner, worn from years of weekend football games. Joey took a big slug of the whiskey. He pulled open his collar as if to breathe more easily, working his hands together as if he were washing them.

"Leah. I'm gonna run this case down for you. You gotta agree to what has to be done. Maybe I should have told you everything before this, but I swear to God I had no idea it would get this bad." I took a tiny sip from the glass he had put before me. The bourbon burned my mouth and throat with a warm glow as it went down. Joey was talking. "Beginning of August I heard rumors we were gonna get Ferguson. I didn't care—I knew Ferguson had ordered the killing of my informant, Billie Thomas. Grace had squealed on us. She told Ferguson who the guy was. I wanted to kill that black SOB."

"So you hated Grace, too," I said.

"I never woulda guessed you knew the stupid dame. I heard the Feds had something on Ferguson. Maybe he was planning to pop Grace. It wouldn't have surprised me. She'd two-timed him and us. She left Eli's Mile High Club with him, turned up dead the next day. Her blood was all over the trunk of his car. The gun used to shoot her had Ferguson's fingerprints on it." Joey paused to take a sip of his whiskey, wiped his mouth with the back of his hand. "There were a few discrepancies, sure," he continued. "The gun was missing its barrel, but I figured Ferguson tossed it after he shot her. Then this young woman, Karella Cousins, calls me and I learn she's found Grace Neville's wallet in the glove box of Ferguson's car."

"Karella gave you the wallet."

"Yeah. Then she gets popped, just like Grace. Things were getting peculiar, but it still looked like we could nail Ferguson." Joey took a deep breath. "But you were always turning up. You were with her that night. You knew the official time of death was not what we were reporting. You had a betting slip with a phone number and a couple names we'd rather you didn't have. One of our sources out at the track told us about Freddie Corster. We put the screws to him, and he allowed as how he mighta seen her at the track the following day. But he wasn't sure. It was getting more and more complicated." Joey looked at me. "To make matters worse," he continued, "you wanted to look into it and write a stupid article."

"I knew things didn't add up," I said.

"I had an idea. You had that betting slip. I pointed you in the direction of the track. I'd throw you Landis. Senior and Junior. One of them was screwy, and both of them were corrupt. They weren't too dangerous and I figured they'd keep you busy for a while. Then you'd lose interest and go back to your schoolwork."

"You knew Jay Landis's history. Didn't you know he *could* be dangerous?"

"No. I knew they were corrupt. I didn't know they were part of a larger scheme that Ronnie had going on. I thought Jay could be handled. And I taught you how to use the snubbie in case any of them gave you problems."

"Thanks, Joey. Always there in a pinch."

"Don't be a smart ass, Leah. So much is riding on this case. I'm up for a promotion if this gets handled right. And the future of those gangsters—we let those Panthers go any further, they'd be running for Oakland City Council. I wanted to get you away from the whole mess."

"Thanks again." My headache would not subside.

"I never coulda guessed all the trouble you'd make. Grace's step dad, Bud Kemp, calls, says you've been up there. Says his wife talked to you, maybe she's given you something of Grace's, too, but he wasn't sure what it was. If you had something the Feds wanted, it would be bad for you. I wanted to get it first."

I pulled the brown afghan closer around me. I spoke carefully. "Ronnie thought Grace had left a diary in my house the night before she was killed. They found a page she had ripped out of her notebook in Ferguson's glove compartment. She had been writing about them. They were afraid she had mentioned Ronnie and Wilson Tyler in other places in her diary. When Ronnie couldn't get information out of me, he started sleeping with my roommate, Carol. Together they searched my room. He planted a bug there."

"Yeah," said Joey. "I figured."

"But Ronnie didn't know Grace had written three journals. The one from high school, she gave that to her mother. Who gave it to me. The other two she left with Maura Sayid, the literature professor. Maura gave me the first one back in August, but she didn't give me the other one until the day before yesterday. That's when I learned all this."

Joey took another gulp of the Jim Beam, burped. He wiped his mouth. "Ronnie scared the crap out of me. I've known guys like him in Nam, crazed and on a power trip. I found out about Ronnie from an old Army buddy who now works at the State Department. Ronnie was what they called an interrogation specialist in Nam. You know what that means, Leah?"

"Yes." In the days when *interrogation specialist* was only a phrase I read about in books, I had heard Yoshi and Paul talking about interrogation specialists in the Phoenix program. People who tortured Vietnamese civilians. I thought of the times I had been alone with Ronnie. My headache felt worse.

"When Ronnie came back to the states, military intelligence contacted him to work as a field agent. He worked closely with the FBI unit assigned to neutralize the Black Panthers, their affiliates and their sympathizers. In his eyes, you were a sympathizer. You needed to be neutralized."

Those words. *Interrogation specialist* for torturer. *Neutralize* for murder.

"He almost succeeded," I answered. Memories were coming at me in short jabs—me and Ronnie at Charlie Brown's, watching the sunset, while he quoted his plagiarized poetry. Me and Ronnie in the cab of his pick-up, Ronnie singing along to Willie Nelson.

"I tried to warn you away from him. Keep you busy at the track. I didn't know Jay Landis was an informant for Ronnie. Of course, I hadn't counted on your goddamned stubbornness. Whenever I bumped into Ronnie, we just talked like two fellow Vietnam vets. I let him know I was looking out for you. Maybe he was more cautious with you than he would have been otherwise."

"He was cautious up until today," I replied.

"I heard that Ronnie liked to boast there wasn't a woman—or a man, for that matter—who wouldn't open up to him, if he used his charm on them. He has a certain appeal, though damned if I see it. He couldn't figure out why you wouldn't sleep with him. After all, you live in a commune."

"Right, it was all free love at Russell Street."

"You think this is funny? Ronnie had leeway to do what was necessary. I was so busy tracking you and Ronnie, I almost missed that date you cooked up with Jay Landis. Yoshi got scared and called me, told me where you were. I used my connections with the SFPD to find out the room number. I called the St. Francis, put their security people on alert to make sure you were safe."

"Did you know I was being taped?"

"Ronnie must have gotten Jay to help. Maybe they were planning to blackmail you. It wouldn't surprise me. The Feds are like us, they want the job done. Whatever it takes."

"By any means necessary," I said. I kept hearing this from men. One way or another, they found reasons to kill. "Can you find those tapes and destroy them? I'm surprised *I* wasn't arrested for the murder of Jay Landis. Who *did* kill Jay, Joey—was it Wilson Tyler?"

"Probably," said Joey.

"I feel bad about Ronnie." I surprised myself. Ronnie had terrified me. Wasn't I relieved he was gone? The image kept repeating, Ronnie staring down at the blood soaking through his grey slacks. "You killed him, Joey. Don't you have to turn yourself in?"

"For Christ's sake, Leah. The guy would have killed you if I hadn't broken down the door. I'm trying to lay it out for you. Yeah, eventually I'll have a little talk with the captain. I'm a police officer who may have shot a man in self-defense. If it even comes to that. You saw the article in the Tribune. Nobody's talking about Acting Lieutenant Joey DeMartino. It's just a drug deal gone wrong. Trust me, cousin, it's okay. Just trust me."

Years later I remembered Joey's words. *Trust me.* I had learned never to trust anyone who said, *Trust me.*

"You gotta listen to me. I'm doing my best to give you the facts. It's not over yet, Leah. There's some things we're gonna have to do, and I want to be sure you understand why."

293

"Look, Joey, do we have to talk about it now? I can barely keep my eyes open. I can't handle one more plan at the moment."

"Okay," he said. "I'll wake you up in a couple of hours."

I pulled the brown afghan around my shoulders. "You're staying here, aren't you, Joey?" I asked.

"Hell, yes, you think I'd go anywhere right now? With all the shit you're involved in, I'm not about to set you loose so you can stir up more."

It was sometime after this I must have fallen asleep, because when I opened my eyes, a street light cast slatted shadows through the living room blinds. From the kitchen came sounds of pans clinking, footsteps moving. The radio was airing an old Frank Sinatra tune—"I've got the world on a string, wrapped around my finger." I could smell the garlic and onions, sausage. I walked into the kitchen. Joey had a chef's apron tied around his big belly.

"Joey, how long did I sleep?

"Couple a hours. It's eight o'clock. You hungry?"

"Yeah," I said. "You know what I'd really like? Oatmeal. Cooked oatmeal. The way my mother used to make it, with brown sugar and walnuts."

"Oatmeal?" grumbled Joey. "At eight o'clock at night? Oatmeal, she wants. But, hey, you want it, I'll make it."

Joey found a box of oatmeal and put a pan of water on the stove. He was talking as if our afternoon conversation had never been interrupted. "Mike Fisher was one of those Oakland Black Police Officer Association types, saw prejudice everywhere. When he started talking that hate crime stuff, I figured he was getting paranoid. Then Ronnie came by, asked for police back-up for Panther surveillance. Knew Billie Thomas had been killed. Said Ferguson ordered the hit. Said the Panthers learned about the informant from someone in *my* department—young detective named Mike. I didn't believe him on that one—Fisher might be paranoid, but he was loyal to the force in his own way, and I knew Ronnie was a liar. But Ronnie told me he had a plan to take care of all of them."

"Was Ronnie planning to kill Mike all along?"

"Didn't think he'd go that far. Still, I decided to take Mike off the case. He was too exposed. Only problem was, Mike wouldn't *stay* off the case. Instead he accused *me* of being a racist. He wanted to be a vital part of cracking the case, thought it would get him a promotion."

294

"A promotion," I said, angrily. "Is it worth someone's life?"

Joey stirred half a cup of rolled oats into the boiling water. "When the two of you decided to confront Ronnie, I knew the shit could hit the fan. We had taps on your phone, on Puckett's, on Mike Fisher's—hell, we even had Mike's Plymouth bugged. I took care of it myself," he said, with modest satisfaction. "I had some idea when you drove over to the St. Francis, why you were going. But I lost track of you for a few hours while you were there."

I remembered Ronnie in Room 1441, his hands fastened into the sockets of my neck. "When did you pick me up again?"

"I heard you calling Russell Street, talking to your Commie roommate, saying no news is good news. I remembered that line. I followed you to Russell Street and then to SF."

"You were there all that time, Joey?"

"Yeah. I called SFPD to back me up. I knew it was a helluva risk. Here's a protected matter, and I'm calling the whole damn police force in. Goodbye to handling the mess the smooth way. Goodbye, promotion. But what could I do? Ronnie might snap. I knew he'd worked the Phoenix program in Nam." Joey turned from the stove. "Leah, there was nothing those Phoenix guys wouldn't do."

"He had different sides to him," I said. I thought again of Ronnie's fingers in the sockets of my neck. Then the image of the blood soaking his grey trousers, Ronnie slumped on the rug. Then memories of Ronnie singing Bye Bye Miss American Pie. "At first he seemed like a country boy. I didn't see the psychopath in him until today."

"He was a psychopath, all right. They're damn good actors. He'd talk about how you gotta act vulnerable with women, that's what gets them." Joey turned off the gas, set the little pan aside. "Hell, Mike Fisher might be a loudmouth, that didn't mean I wanted him hurt."

"You saved my life, Joey," I said.

"Don't you forget it. So eat your oatmeal," he said, shoving a bowl under my face.

"No brown sugar?" I asked.

"You've had enough brown sugar for a lifetime, girl," said Joey.

He sat across from me, with a plate of fried onions, fried potatoes, sausage, and a beer in front of him. "Look," Joey said, "I've got a buddy. We did time together in Nam. He married a Thai girl, lives there now. I've been thinking about taking a vacation. Go visit him. I'm gonna take you along."

"What makes you think I'm gonna go?"

"Don't you get it?" Joey leaned across the counter and grabbed my wrist.

"Get what?" I pulled my hand free. "You don't like it that I worked with one of the few black cops in the OPD? Maybe I heard things you wish I hadn't heard? You're gonna send me away for that, Joey? I'm not a kid anymore. Remember?"

Joey was almost whispering. "You know everything. You could testify that Wilson Tyler murdered Grace Neville. That guy must be a trained assassin. He's so protected they'll let him get away with killing two small-time broads nobody cares about anyway. As well as that snitch, Jay Landis. He's so protected he can get away with killing an officer of the Oakland Police Department. What does that tell you? They want Ferguson that bad." He was glaring at me. "You're so smart. What are you gonna do without my help, cuz?"

"Mike and I both heard Tyler confess. Mike taped him."

"That tape has been destroyed, cousin."

Of course, I thought. Of course.

"The only other person who heard what you heard is dead, Leah. You're dispensable, Leah. Like Grace was."

"But Ronnie is dead now."

"Ronnie's dead. But there's still Wilson Tyler. Out and about. And there will be other Ronnies, agents who can do what Ronnie was supposed to do. And, unlike Ronnie, they won't hold off because of your cousin who did time in Vietnam. You remember the cops were told a woman had been shot and killed in Kanji's apartment? Wilson Tyler had told James he was passing along an order. James was supposed to kill you. For informing. You got away that time—thanks to Ferguson. He refused to do it. Or maybe he sensed he was being set up. You got away yesterday—thanks to me." He took another breath. "You think you're a cat with nine lives? Your luck could run out, Leah."

My mind was a like an electrical grid with the wires all crossed and lighting up in crazy zigzags. Mike was dead—that strong body that had lain

296

next to me only the night before last. Mike would never speak to me again, nor to Lily, nor to his mother, waiting for him in East Oakland. Mike's death was the thought I had been pushing away all day.

"I want us to leave very soon," continued Joey. "This week, if I can arrange it. And I don't want you to mention what happened today to nobody."

"Wilson Tyler knows what I know," I said.

"They'll move Wilson immediately. Too many Oakland Panthers know him, now. He can't stay around here. They'll relocate him."

"Where to?"

Joey shrugged. "Once he's gone, it will be safe for you here, and you can come back."

"He's a killer, Joey."

"Not the first one we've had on payroll," said Joey.

EPILOGUE

Friday morning September 29th Joey and I were on a plane to Bangkok. I would not be registering for Fall Quarter. I didn't tell anyone where I was going. I didn't say goodbye to anyone. The fourteen-hour flight felt like a limbo period between the past two months and whatever life lay ahead for me.

In Thailand, I moved in a daze. I wandered into the turquoise ocean off Hua Hin, lay on the sand and smelled the lemon-scented flowers. I chatted with Joey and his old Vietnam buddy, Mark, and Mark's petite wife, Tan. Joey was only staying two weeks, but he had arranged for me to remain six months.

Two weeks later I watched the plane ascend out of the Bangkok airport, carrying Joey back to the States. All I had left had been Joey. Now there was nothing left of my old life.

Eventually I adjusted. I lived in the hot, wet air of the tropics, writing and trying to understand what had happened to me. I wrote to Joey, and to Yoshi and Paul. I asked them to find out what had happened to James. Sometimes they wrote back, but no one ever responded to those questions. I began teaching. I created a life. I met Americans in the Peace Corps and Vietnam vets who had settled in Thailand. I learned Thai. I swam in the ocean and rode my bike to the market for fried bananas and sticky rice. America, the nightmare I had lived through, began to recede. I stayed gone two years.

When I returned in 1974, I moved to New York City's Lower East Side with a Vietnam vet I had met in Thailand. It didn't work. I would think of Joey's comment: "Only masochists need apply." I headed back to the Bay Area and tried to look up the Russell Street gang. Yoshi had gone back to Japan. Paul was finishing up his PhD, soon to be Dr. Paul Cohen, with a job offer on the East Coast. Art Leopold never answered my letters. Joey was living with a divorced woman and her three children. He had applied for a leave from OPD and was working at Santa Rita. We met for dinner at a restaurant in Dublin. Joey had lost weight. He looked relaxed. "You're looking good," I said to him. "Trim and slim. Too bad I never get to see you anymore."

"Married life keeps me busy," he said. "But just be glad, cuz, that I had a little more weight on me at the St. Francis hotel that time. Otherwise I never woulda been able to bust that door down." He seemed full of self-satisfaction.

"How did anyone ever get a confirmed bachelor like you to settle down?"

"Big bazookas," Joey said, making circles with his hands.   I had missed Joey in Thailand. I'd let myself forget how stupid he could be.

"Were those—bazookas—the reason you left the OPD?"

"I hadn't even met her then. I asked for a transfer. Too many politics. The Panthers have just about self-destructed, Leah. You hear about Ferguson? Serving twenty to life for the death of that cop. Hey, babe," he said, catching my look. "You can't blame that one on us. He killed the guy."

"Did he?" I asked. "OPD was determined to get Ferguson one way or another. What proof did they have? "

"Wilson Tyler testified against him," he answered. "Among others."

I stared at him, horrified. "You got me out of the country so I couldn't testify who Wilson Tyler really was. An informant who worked for the OPD and the Feds!" Joey had done it again. He'd tricked me, and he'd screwed James Ferguson. And hadn't I known—really? In my heart, hadn't I known that there was another reason he had gotten me on that plane to Bangkok?

"Don't go all crazy on me, Leah," Joey said. He held up his hands, both palms toward me. "Slow down. You would have ended up dead if you testified against Wilson Tyler. They wanted Ferguson, they were gonna get him. If you were in the way, it would have been all over for you."

"But it was wrong, Joey," I said.

"It was wrong of Ferguson to kill the cop, Leah," he answered. "That's what was wrong. You got some twisted values if you think otherwise. Tyler may have been an informant, but there were other witnesses. Don't expect me to shed no tears for a cop killer."

All the experiences we had shared, yet a gulf between us remained as deep and impassable as that Monday in August 1972 when I called him about Grace. By now stories had come out—how J. Edgar Hoover had founded Cointelpro to destroy the left. The Panthers had been the first group on their list. Joey had been a part of all that and, even now, he believed he had been on the right side.

Six months later I was on my way to visit my lover in New York City. We were going to try again. On the way I stopped off in Kansas, rented a car,

300

and drove to Leavenworth prison. I had written James Ferguson several times. His answers were poorly written, heavily censored. Borrowing press credentials from a journalist friend, I arranged to visit James Ferguson on the pretext of a possible story. I waited an hour and a half in order to talk to James for thirty minutes.

James Ferguson walked into the visiting area. He was wearing a blue prison jump suit. His head was shaved, his eyes somber, but he was still muscular and compelling. James took a seat behind the metal grill.

"Still got that same springy hair," he said.

"When do you come up for parole?"

He shrugged. "I got an appeal pending. They'll never give me parole."

"That last time we were together—did you have orders to kill me?"

"I had orders to kill you if you were an informant. I decided you weren't."

"Who gave the order?"

"I only followed orders from the top."

"Did Wilson Tyler give you the message?"

"I don't want to talk about Wilson. You know we were infiltrated. Cointelpro was working on us. Putting people in positions of power, getting them to sell out. I don't want to say anything I can't prove about a comrade."

"What did happen between you and Grace that night at Eli's?"

"You know most of it. She said she had to talk to me. I met her at Eli's. She wanted to get back together. But she had betrayed me. Betrayed the Panthers. There was no way back outta that."

The harsh jail light glistened off James' broad brow. His well-shaped lips were large and soft, as I remembered them. He bit his lower lip, then, looking up at me: "Someone told an agent we were storing weapons in this house way down Telegraph. Panthers got busted. I got sent up. When I got out, she started playing both sides. She told me the name of an informant. A comrade I'd liked. Billie Thomas. I had to have him killed. Then I got to thinking, *who* was it told the police about where the weapons were. Coulda been her, I figured. I didn't want to think it. I said there was no way she would have known. But it planted a question for me. Then she comes pleading to get back with me."

"Is that when you grabbed her by the throat?"

301

"I coulda killed her," he said. "I stopped myself. She was weak. And I had cared for her once."

"Then when her body turned up?"

"For the longest time, I believed I had as good as killed her. I figured someone under me had heard or seen us and thought he should finish the job. Out of loyalty to me or the Party."

"Wilson Tyler told me he killed her," I said. "He was state's witness in your trial. He's protected by the Feds."

James spread his hands flat on the counter that separated us, staring at his knuckles. "Wilson did it? What reason did he give?"

"She had double crossed the Feds. She gave you the name of that informant. Tyler was sure Grace would give you his name next. Grace took a tip from Bucky Timmons. The race was rigged and it won her ten thousand dollars—but the Feds had set that up. She was going to give the money to you. She hoped maybe you'd take her back if she gave you all that cash. Tyler showed up at the track. Told her you had sent him to pick her up. He drove out to Point Richmond, drove under the railroad bridge, to that park overlooking the bay, and he shot her. Then he beat her so it would look like a crime of passion. He was going to return the car to you later that afternoon, but Clyde called you to the clinic because of the break-in. Wilson drove around with her body in the trunk of your car until midnight, and then he dropped it in the bay." James was studying his spread fingers as if all the answers in the world were there. He did not look up.

"You never suspected Wilson Tyler?" I asked, urgently.

James shook his head. "Wilson saved my life. Twice. That's how tight we were. All that Sunday morning I was in a meeting at Central. Four other members there—not one would come forward for me. The cops tried to say the car was mine. It was registered to me, but no one owned a car in the Party. I thought the cops planted Grace's blood in it. Tyler told me he had spent the rest of the day at the DeFremery Park rally. I had been at the rally, too, until Clyde called because there'd been a break-in at the clinic. Tyler picked me up later that evening. I never doubted him."

"I was out of the country for two years. I didn't know you'd gone to trial. I could impeach Tyler's testimony, let them know who he really was. We could reopen the case."

"No, you're forgetting something." James gave me a somber, level gaze. "I'm not in here for Grace's murder. I'm in here for a cop's murder. Murder of a cop isn't something they'll ever let go of."

"But Tyler was the main witness against you—in the cop murder case."

James shook his head. "It might have happened the way you've just said," he said, softly. "I've heard all kinds of rumors. I can't afford to let myself believe them. Tyler turned state's witness on me. But I know the pressure they bring. They threaten you—threaten to harm your family." James shook his head. "If this is true—if he really did this?—planned for months to betray me?" He let the thought go. "But then again," he said, "it could be one more rumor to get me to hate a brother. One more way to make me go after my own."

He took a breath. "I gave my life for the Party. I have to believe in it." Then he raised his head and looked me in the eyes. A long, level stare. "If you knew all this, why the hell weren't you there when I went to trial?"

"I tried to get information about you. No one would tell me."

James Ferguson just looked at me.

"Why the hell weren't you there when I went to trial?" I could never answer that question to my satisfaction. I had my justifications. I had been tricked by Joey. I had been protecting myself. I was safer in a country eight thousand miles from the Bay Area. And I hadn't been sure whether or not James had killed the cop in New York. He had never denied it. But only I could have told the truth about Wilson Tyler.

With a combination of luck and tough experience, I pushed my way forward in the years that followed. I found I could evaluate people quickly. I often thought of James' words: "I am rarely surprised by what people do." I became a successful journalist. I was different from Grace. I had survived. But had I also betrayed James Ferguson?

More years passed. Grey, flat, disconnected years. I was successful in my career, but there was an emptiness in my life. Carol married an engineer and moved to Pleasanton. Yoshi was teaching in Japan. Paul was married and was teaching at a university on the East Coast where he had made tenure. Even

Edna had married although it had not changed her life style visibly. She was still available for a Saturday night at the clubs. I learned Art Leopold had died unexpectedly of a heart attack the first year I lived in Bangkok. He had been fifty-eight. I was saddened at his loss. Art Leopold had been another person I had longed to talk to about what had happened.

Once more I flew east to visit the man I had become involved with in Thailand. He was on a self-destructive course of drugs and alcohol. There were no possibilities with him.

One night in Manhattan I left his walk-up for the last time. A flier taped to a lamp post caught my attention. "The Black Panthers: Where We Went Wrong." It was a panel discussion by former Panther members at a hip coffee house on East 4th Street. Nostalgic for a past I had never understood, I decided to attend.

I found myself in a small room, surrounded by students, intellectuals, African-Americans, Asians, bohemians. Many of the men wore black turtlenecks and round metal-rimmed spectacles. They reminded me of photos of my Italian grandfather, a Wobbly of the early 1900s. At a table by himself sat a black man in a white silk suit, staring at a bouquet of red carnations placed in a glass of water in front of him.

A group of educators and community leaders discussed the corruption and violence that had marred the Panthers' final years. A pretty black woman with dreadlocks said the violence the Panthers condoned toward one another was a legacy of slavery. A brother with a shaved head and a single earring blamed the demise of the Party on bad leadership. An older white man, the editor of a leftist newspaper, blamed the refusal of white liberals to acknowledge the excesses of the left, their failure to oppose Panther violence and depravity.

A black man in his late thirties, in a tweed sports coat and black slacks, stood up to speak. He spoke with eloquence and increasing intensity. "I was a witness to many acts of violence. I watched brothers beaten up by brothers. Under orders, in my loyalty, I would have murdered another comrade. This was a misplaced loyalty, brothers and sisters. This was a fervor gone awry."

His husky voice reminded me of James Ferguson. I looked at my flyer. The blurb stated he had lived and written in the Bay Area, Africa and France. He had published a book on the Panthers. He was a leader of the black community, a former Black Panther; a writer now based on the East Coast.

I watched and listened to him. He was compelling and articulate, a tall man, large-shouldered. Only his pitted skin marred his good looks. He looked better than he had eight years ago, but he was the same man. The murderer of Grace Neville, of Karella Cousins, of Mike Fisher, the witness against James Ferguson. Wilson Tyler now stood in front of audiences as the expert on why the Panthers had failed.

www.ingramcontent.com/pod-product-compliance
Lightning Source LLC
Chambersburg PA
CBHW031204020726
47499CB00002B/478